Mary Jayne Baker grew up in rural West Yorkshire, right in the heart of Brontë country... and is still there. After graduating from Durham in 2003 she dallied with living in cities including London, but eventually came back, with her own romantic hero in tow, to her beloved Dales. She lives with him in a little house with four little cats and a little rabbit, writing stories about girls with flaws and the men who love them. Mary Jayne goes to work every day as a graphic designer for a regional magazine, but secretly dreams of being a lighthouse keeper.

 @MaryJayneWrites
 @MaryJayneBaker
www.maryjaynebaker.co.uk

Also by Mary Jayne Baker

The Honey Trap
Meet Me at the Lighthouse

MARY JAYNE BAKER

Runaway Bride

A division of HarperCollins*Publishers*
www.harpercollins.co.uk

Harper*Impulse* an *imprint* of
HarperCollins*Publishers*
The News Building
1 London Bridge Street
London SE1 9GF

www.harpercollins.co.uk

This paperback edition 2018

First published in Great Britain in ebook format by
HarperCollins*Publishers* 2018

A catalogue record for this book
is available from the British Library

ISBN: 9780008258337

Set in Birka by Palimpsest Book Production Ltd, Falkirk
Stirlingshire

Printed and bound in Great Britain.

To the Leeds/Cumbrian branch of the Brahams –
my dad Angus, stepmum Debra and siblings
Joe and Lauren – without whom this book would never
have been written.

Chapter 1

By the time I reached the main road, my lungs were sand-paper-dry. My hair whipped painfully around my face, and the heel of my left foot was bleeding.

It was one hell of a start to married life.

I'd been married, ooh, around three hours. I'd been running for the best part of the last one. Running with no aim or direction, no one in pursuit, but running like my immortal soul depended on it. Desperate to get as far as possible from Ethan and all the rest of them.

One foot in front of the other, Kitty. Eyes on the horizon. No turning back, no giving in… not this time.

Not this time.

But no matter how I fixed my eyes on the horizon, where the dusky satsuma sun had just started to sink behind the intimidating ridge of the fells, the hacking in my chest was bound to defeat me eventually. At last I slowed my sprint to a jog, then to a walk, and, when I couldn't bear another second's agony, I stopped.

I gripped the drystone wall that ran alongside the road in bleached knuckles, struggling for oxygen. Short, panting breaths surged painfully up through my windpipe. With my free hand, I clutched my stomach. I could feel bile rising up my gullet, the threat of another vomiting episode as anger and grief battled for mouthfuls of my sanity, but I willed it back. I needed to keep calm. I needed to keep focused. And above all, I needed to keep moving.

I slumped down onto the tarmac and allowed myself the indulgence of another round of angry, puzzled tears. Bewildered motorists stared at me as they whizzed by, but they didn't stop. Well, why would they? They had their own affairs to see to.

There was a part of me that didn't want to keep moving. That part of me wanted to curl up and die, right there by the side of the road. The throbbing in my gut, the images whirling in my brain, were almost enough to paralyse me. But deep inside, underneath the layers of taffeta and rage, some sort of survival instinct was fighting to make itself heard. Push on, it said. Get away, far away, and then there'll be time to mourn.

I don't think I'd been there long. I could've been wrong, it could've been hours; my head was spinning so much that time didn't really seem to exist. But I think it was about ten minutes later when a sunshine-orange VW campervan, one of those cutesy-pie '60s numbers with the bug front, pulled up beside me.

'Are you all right there, lass?' the driver asked, leaning out of his window to examine me.

Hastily I wiped my eyes.

'Yeah. Sorry, I, um – my car got towed.'

The dark-haired man cocked an eyebrow. 'What, your car got towed and they just left you here?'

There was the lilt of an Irish accent nestling among the deep, gentle tones. It sounded reassuring. Made me think of my nan.

'Er, yeah,' I said, wincing at the obvious lie.

Great start, Kitty. Keep it up.

The man didn't look convinced, but he refrained from commenting. 'Well I can't just leave you here. You get a lot of boy racers down these side roads, you know. Where're you going?'

'Anywhere.' I grimaced. 'I mean, Wastwater. I'm going to Wastwater. To a... um... gala dinner.' I glanced down at my fetching wellies, colour-coordinated with the off-the-shoulder green taffeta ballgown I was wearing. 'For farmers.'

Gala dinner for farmers. Of course that's where I was going. I mean, why wouldn't I be? Oh, this just got better and better...

'Are you a farmer?' the man asked.

'No. Just, er, trying to fit in.'

'None of my business,' he said generously. 'Come on, hop in. I'm heading to the Lakes anyway, I'll drop you off.'

I hesitated. I'd never hitch-hiked before and I couldn't suppress a feeling of danger – stranger danger, that fear that's bred into you in your schooldays. Don't get into cars with strange men, Kitty. Don't let them give you sweets and just say no when they ask if you want to get into their van to see their puppies. This guy could be anyone, couldn't he? Offering me a lift – what was in it for him?

I could hear my mum's voice in the back of my mind. *Never trust a boy who offers you a favour, angel. Men always expect to get paid...*

But Mum wasn't here, and this man looked friendly enough to me. He was handsome in a scruffy sort of way, with jet-black hair that curled onto his neck, long stubble and dark brown eyes. I think in the end, though, it was the smile, a lopsided, open grin, that convinced me I could trust him. That, and the fact I was seriously out of options.

The instinct driving me now was to get as far from home as possible, and I was desperate enough to take some serious risks, even with my own self – at least, whatever of it I still had left to give a damn about. A large chunk of me was some miles away back in Elden, my home town in the Yorkshire Dales, lying in a blackened, smoking puddle at Ethan's feet. Getting into a car with a stranger didn't feel like nearly the scariest thing I'd had to deal with today.

'Thanks,' I mumbled, walking round to the passenger side and climbing in.

'Jack Duffy,' the man said, holding out his hand to me.

I wondered for a second whether to give a fake name, but decided against it. I might be on the run, but I wasn't exactly James Bond. Who, come to think of it, was a bit shit when it came to cover stories, giving out his real name so often he'd actually managed to make it a catchphrase.

'Clayton. Kitty Clayton,' I said in true Bond style, shaking Jack's hand.

'I like it. Very... alliterative.'

'Er, thanks.'

'Got a bit of a secret identity vibe,' he said. 'Not a superhero, are you?'

'Maybe. But if I tell you I'll have to kill you.'

Not the world's most original joke, but the best I could manage in my current state. Anyway, it got a laugh.

'So would that be short for anything?' he asked.

'No. It's usually for Catherine, but my mum just liked Kitty.'

I started when I heard a little bark. Glancing over my shoulder, I caught sight of a tubby yellow mongrel curled in a dog bed, eyeing me with suspicion.

'Oh, and this is Sandy,' Jack said. 'Don't mind dogs, do you?'

'No, I love them.' I squinted at the tubby dog. 'Er, he certainly looks well-fed.'

'She. And it wasn't the diet that caused the belly, it was the randy Jack Russell back in Settle.'

'What, you mean she's—'

'Yeah. Less than a month to go now, I'm reckoning. Looks about ready to pop, doesn't she?' He turned the ignition key and the engine phutted into life. 'Right, now we're all friends, let's get going.'

So he really had asked me back to his van to see his puppies... hmm. Still, in a way it was sort of comforting. A man who travelled with a pregnant dog couldn't be too dodgy, could he? Maybe that was the logic of desperation but all the same, I relaxed slightly.

I could see him eyeing me curiously in the rear-view mirror as he drove, taking in my streaky mascara, my ballgown, my big green wellies.

5

'You look like you don't want to talk about it,' he said at last.

'God, I really don't.'

'Okay so. Then I won't ask.'

I shot him a relieved smile. 'Thanks.'

'We'll have to have some small talk though,' he said. 'I'm afraid the charge for this particular taxi service is scintillating conversation.'

'Not sure I can pull off scintillating today. I can just about manage to form words, I think.'

'Want to tell me why you're going to Wastwater?' he asked. 'I mean, really? Hate to break it to you, but the dress codes for farmers' dinners don't tend to include wellies, whatever stereotypes might suggest.'

I examined Jack in the mirror. His expression was relaxed and careless, as if he'd be equally comfortable whether I chose to open up or not. He certainly had an easy face to trust.

There didn't seem any harm in sharing my immediate plan with him, I eventually decided. I was heading for someone I knew I could depend on; someone who'd put me up until I'd sorted out my unholy mess of a life.

'Okay, if you really want to know, I'm going to visit my aunty,' I said. 'She's got a cottage in Wasdale Head.'

He glanced at the ballgown. 'Must be a posh family.'

'Yeah. She's big on dressing for dinner.'

'Muddy too, is it?' he asked, eyeing my boots.

'Something like that.'

We were on dangerous ground again. I tried to push the

conversation back towards him. I just needed to kill a bit of time...

'So, er, what do you do?' I asked, the ultimate fallback conversation starter.

'Human trafficker. I scour the highways for lone women and sell them into sex slavery. You?'

I laughed – the first real, genuine laugh I'd managed all day.

'Serial killer,' I said, matching my deadpan tone to his. 'I lure men into laybys then hack them to bits. Although that's really more of a hobby.'

He nodded soberly. 'Always good to keep yourself busy. What do you do the rest of the time?'

'I'm a project editor for this publishing company my step-sister Laurel runs, Whitestone Press.'

At least, I had been until about an hour ago. I think I'd effectively handed in my resignation when I'd decided to do a runner. My current occupation, if I was asked to fill in a form, probably amounted to 'bum'.

'What type of thing?' Jack asked.

'Travel guides. You know, things to see, restaurant reviews, handy phrases, all that.'

'Sounds interesting. I suppose you get to travel quite a bit?'

I shook my head. 'Someone else does. Then they write it up for me to edit and do the photo research.'

'Still, must be fun. Bit of armchair travelling.'

I let out a little snort.

'What?' he said.

'You know what I dreamt last week?'

'Was it about a hunky Irishman with a devastating smile and abs you could grill a steak on?'

So we were doing a bit of social flirting now, were we? Okay...

'It was actually. I love Aidan Turner.'

'Funny,' he said, eyes fixed on the road. 'Turner can bite me.'

His reaction made me smile. If I'd tried that joke on Ethan, it would've been a three-day sulk at least.

'So what did you really dream?' Jack asked.

'I dreamt I was in Iceland – the country, I mean, not the supermarket.' My eyes clouded. 'God, Jack, it was so vivid. The geysers, the glaciers, the lakes so dark they're almost black. I could practically smell the herring.'

'So?'

'So, it just reminded me I've never been to Iceland. I read about all these beautiful places and I look at hundreds of pictures, but I never get to actually experience them. The most exotic trip I've ever been on was two weeks at a resort in Alicante three years ago.'

He looked puzzled. 'So go, there's nothing stopping you. Get off your backside and do it, girl.'

'How? The thing about publishing – it's interesting enough but it's not that well-paid. Two weeks in Alicante every once in a while is about my limit.'

And then there was Ethan, who'd never wanted to go anywhere but a sunny beach with bars that showed the footie and hotels where there was always a full English on the breakfast table. The chances of getting him on a backpacking holiday to somewhere like Iceland had been exactly nil.

I mentally slapped myself. Thinking about Ethan was going to have me in tears again. I needed to hold it together, at least until I got to Aunty Julia's.

'So do you live in the Lakes?' I asked Jack.

'Yeah, when I feel like it. I live everywhere.' He gestured round the van. 'This is it for me. Home.'

'You're kidding! You can't live in this tiny van all the time?'

'Yep, me and Sandy. That's the way we like it, life without fences.'

'Bloody hell. You're not part sardine, are you?'

He laughed. 'Away with you, it's not that small. Anyway, it's just somewhere to sleep. We like to be off exploring.'

'How did it happen? Is it a hippy thing?'

He didn't answer. Just looked sober for a moment.

'Sorry,' I said, staring sheepishly into my lap. It felt like I'd crossed a line, although I was puzzled about where it had been. 'None of my business.'

'That's okay.' Jack forced a smile. 'Tell you what. If I ever see you again, I'll tell you all about it.'

Chapter 2

As we drove, I glanced in the rear-view mirror to get a better look at the van. I couldn't help being curious about the man who'd rescued me, and the unusual way he lived.

It was small. Really small. But efficient, as far as use of space went.

There was a brown leather sofa in the back that I was guessing folded out into a bed when it wasn't busy being a sofa. To the left of it was the world's tiniest kitchenette: just a two-ring hob, worksurface and sink, with a bank of pine cupboards underneath. The floor was chequerboard-patterned, with a hole in the middle for slotting in a table. I couldn't imagine how anyone could call the little tin can on wheels a permanent home.

Still. Life without fences. Lucky bastard.

'So how do you make a living then?' I asked Jack. I was struggling to think of any job that could fit with the nomadic lifestyle he seemed to lead. Unless he hadn't been kidding about the human trafficking.

He jerked his head behind him. 'Take a look, I'm not

precious. My portfolio's inside the sofa. Lever on the side of the seat'll swing you round.'

He pulled over while I unfastened my seatbelt, and I turned the passenger seat to face the inside of the camper.

I picked my way around Sandy's bed to the sofa. When I lifted the cushion to get to the storage space, I found a large portfolio case on top of a puddle of awning canvas.

'Be gentle,' Jack said when he heard me rustle the sheets inside. 'I haven't had those scanned yet.'

I laid the papers on top of the sofa, touching them as delicately as if they were bone china.

There were reams of them: gorgeous hand-drawn illustrations of a little pair of marionettes, a girl and a boy. In each, they were in a different scrape – dangling upside down in a tree, stealing biscuits from a jar on the kitchen shelf. A little dog like a skinnier Sandy lurked at the edge of each adventure, a sort of signature. They seemed familiar somehow...

My eyes widened as realisation hit. It said a lot for the foggy state of my brain that I hadn't recognised them right away.

'Oh my God!'

'Tilly and Billy,' Jack said. 'You know them?'

'Course. My stepsister's little boys love Tilly and Billy. When I read them bedtime stories they always ask for...' I paused while it sank in. 'Bloody hell, you're *that* Jack Duffy?'

'Er, I am, yeah.' I could see the back of his neck pinkening. 'Didn't expect it to mean anything to you, to be honest. I'm only really a big name among the under-fives.'

'This is unbelievable,' I muttered. I wished I could ring

11

Laurel and tell her, but my mobile, along with my handbag and the shards of my hopes and dreams, was back at Butterfield Farm where I'd left it.

Jack laughed. 'It's sweet you're so starstruck. Most people over three foot just shrug.'

I went back to join him in the front and he started the engine again.

'I can give you a signed book for your nephews if you want,' he said. 'I mean, if you think they'll be bothered. Kids don't set as much store by that sort of thing as adults.'

That was one thing I'd been trying not to think about. God knew when I'd see Toby and Sam again. Or Laurel, or Nan.

'Thanks. That'd be nice,' I managed to mumble.

I couldn't hold back the tear that had forced its way to the front of my eyeball. It slid down my cheek, and I dashed it quickly away. But Jack had already spotted it.

'What is it you're running away from, Kitty?' he asked gently.

'What makes you think I'm running away?'

'I'm not thick. Taking lifts from strangers, inappropriate clothing, no bag. No money either, I'm guessing?'

I flushed. 'No. I didn't take anything when I—'

I bit my tongue.

'Sorry,' Jack said. 'I know you said you didn't want to talk about it. I'm worried about you, that's all.'

'You don't even know me.'

'I know you're distressed. That you're on your own, and without a penny to your name apparently. Whatever happened to you today, it must've been pretty traumatic.'

'Well. Weddings are always traumatic, aren't they?'

He blinked. 'Seriously?'

'Seriously.' I gave a bleak laugh. 'Today's my wedding day. This is my wedding dress. And my fetching wedding wellies. It was on a farm, we had this whole quirky hayride-themed thing.'

'Jesus, Kitty! That's... God.' He shook his head in shock. 'So, what, you're running away from home?'

'That's about the size of it, yeah.'

'But you'll have to go back eventually, won't you? You can't run forever.'

I glared darkly at a little Fiat bobbing along ahead of us. 'I'm never going back. Trust me on that.'

'What happened?'

'Please don't ask,' I said, my voice strangled. 'I mean, thank you. I am grateful for the lift and I know you're just trying to be nice and everything, but I really can't. Not now.'

'But you've come away with nothing. Have you got a bank card on you? Anything?'

'No. But I'll be fine. Just get me to my aunty's, please.'

'Can I do anything to help?'

He meant it too. I could hear it in his voice, see it in the concern etched into his face. It was funny – I mean, I'd only met him an hour ago – but I couldn't help trusting him.

And why not? Why not trust a stranger as well as anyone? He'd been kind to me. He'd sounded like he understood – and what's more, like he cared – when I'd told him what I was running from. He'd even managed to make me laugh a few times, on what was without competition the single most miserable day of my life. On the other hand, I'd known Ethan for ten years when he'd solemnly promised to love and cherish me till death, and he hadn't even been able to make it to the end of the reception without a metaphorical knee to the groin.

My world was so different, suddenly. I wouldn't be sleeping next to Ethan tonight, as I had done for the best part of a decade. Wouldn't be feeling his safe, treacherous arms around me. Wouldn't be going back to the house we'd shared. If I had my way, I'd never set eyes on either house or Ethan again. How was it possible my life could change so drastically in just a few short hours?

'That *bastard*,' I muttered to myself. Every time I thought about Ethan, the shock and disgust hit me afresh.

Jack blinked. 'Pardon?'

'Sorry,' I said, with an apologetic grimace. 'Just thinking out loud.'

'So can I help? Whatever I can do, Kitty.'

'Yeah.' I mustered a smile. 'You can talk about something completely different the rest of the way. Something fun. Something... not about me. Please.'

'That's what you need?'

'I need to keep my mind off it till I'm alone, or I might go insane. Just talk to me, Jack.'

'Here then. Something that'll make you smile.' He made a clicking noise and in the mirror I saw Sandy's ears prick up. 'You in the mood for a performance, girl?' he called out.

Sandy didn't answer – because dogs can't talk, obviously – but Jack seemed to take her silence as a yes. He fired up the CD player and skipped to the third track.

I raised one eyebrow. 'The *Neighbours* theme?'

'Yeah. She's a funny dog, this is one of the only songs she'll perform to. Right, Sand, after three.'

He counted her in and I laughed as the two of them performed an impromptu duet for me, Jack on vocals and Sandy on hound-dog backing.

Neighbours…

Hooooowl!

Everybody needs good neighbours…

Owooooool!

With a little understanding…

Owowohowoool!

You can find the perfect frieeeend…

When they'd finished, Jack grinned at me.

'So? Reckon we've got a shot at *Britain's Got Talent?*'

I smiled. 'Wouldn't hold your breath. Still, impressive. Can she sing anything else?'

'She quite likes Radiohead, but she only gets that on her birthday. I'm not a fan.'

We sat in silence a while, listening to the music. White Lace and Promises by The Carpenters came on next, which for my benefit Jack quickly skipped over, then some Tony Bennett. P!nk, Green Day, a bit of Paul Simon…

I nodded to the CD player. 'That's some eclectic music taste you've got going on.'

'Not mine really. Someone I once knew made me this mixtape – well, mix-CD.' He shot a curious glance my way. 'How old are you anyway?'

'Twenty-six. Why?'

'You know what a mixtape is?'

'Yeah. I saw one once in a museum, sandwiched between a dial-up modem and a copy of *The Breakfast Club* on Betamax.'

'Funny.'

'How old are you then?' I asked, looking him up and down. I'd guessed he was a few years older than me, but I was finding it hard to put my finger on just how many.

'Twenty-one.'

'That's a whopping fib.'

'Okay, twenty-one and a half.'

I flashed him a smile. 'You're an odd bloke. Have you always lived like this, just going from one place to the next?'

'No. But I live like this now.'

'Fun?'

He shrugged. 'Bit lonely, but it's how I like things. I can't stand to feel trapped.' He reached over to squeeze my elbow. 'Keep your eyes open. One of the most spectacular views on the planet coming up just around this bend.'

I'd seen it a hundred times, but it still had the power to punch the breath right out of me. We turned the camper round a corner, and it hit me. The most beautiful stretch of water in the Lakes.

On that cloudless early May evening, Wastwater looked like it had come straight from a kiddy's paintbox: cobalt blue and glistening. Beyond it rose the distinctive peaks of Great Gable and its brothers – Scafell and the other one I could never remember the name of, though my dad had told me enough times when I was little. They were still dusted on top with a sugaring of late snow.

'Incredible, isn't it?' I said to Jack in a hushed voice.

'I know.' He glanced at me. 'Makes all our petty human problems seem not so bad, eh?'

It did a bit. This was the worst day of my life, the day everything I'd worked for and invested in had come crashing down around me. But something about the awesome natural wonders looming ahead reminded me, deep in my belly, that life was still worth the living. Just as long as there could be this in it.

'Oh, can you wind your window down?' I asked Jack. There was something I needed to do.

'Um, okay,' he said, looking puzzled.

When he'd done as I asked, I slid the spanking new wedding ring Ethan had given me just hours earlier off my finger, along with my engagement ring, leaned over Jack and chucked them as hard as I could in the direction of the lake.

'Something shiny for the mermaids,' I said with a shaky smile.

I gave Jack Aunty Julia's address in Wasdale Head, and a quarter of an hour later we were at the door of her little whitewashed cottage. Just the sight of it filled me with relief. The feeling of being utterly alone in the world gradually subsided as I ran my gaze over the familiar climbing briers around the door.

'Are you sure you'll be okay, Kitty?' Jack asked.

'I'll be okay. Aunty Julia'll look after me.'

'Here.' He took out his wallet and passed me a note – £50.

I shook my head. 'I can't take that.'

'Please. Just in case you need it. You can pay me back when you're all sorted again.'

'How? You haven't even got an address.'

'The universe will sort it out. These things have ways of settling themselves.'

'I can't, Jack, really. You've done enough for me.'

'I insist. And I'm refusing to take it back, so... ner.' He poked his tongue out at me. I couldn't help smiling.

'Thank you,' I said, squeezing his hand. 'For everything.'

I got out, then stood following the campervan with my eyes until it was just a tangerine speck in the distance. Finally, it disappeared and I was alone again.

Chapter 3

Aunty Julia was my dad's sister, the closest relative I had outside Elden. Since I was a little girl, when Dad and I had visited regularly to fish in the lake, I'd thought of the little whitewashed cottage and my aunty's smiling presence as things that meant safety. It had always felt more like home than the stark, minimalist innards of my mum's house.

I still made the trip up whenever I could and Aunty Julia, who had no kids of her own, always welcomed me with child-like excitement. Whether she'd do the same today, I wasn't sure.

As I knocked at the door, a vivid picture of little me wading in the shallows of Wastwater with my jeans rolled to the knee, clutching a jam jar full of minnows while Dad did the grown-up fishing and Aunty Julia laid out a picnic on the bank, popped up in my mind. It made me smile in spite of everything. The fishing trips were my happiest memories, although since losing Dad they often came with a tear served on the side.

I waited impatiently for Aunty Julia to let me in. Even though I was a good hundred miles from Butterfield Farm where, if I was lucky, my family and friends were still enjoying a wedding reception they hadn't noticed was now Kittyless, I felt paranoid being out in the open air, ultra-conspicuous in my daft bloody ballgown.

'Hello, can I – oh my goodness!' Aunty Julia said when she answered my knock, her eyes widening. 'Kitty, look at you! What on earth are you doing here?'

'Hiya.' I bent over her wheelchair to give her a kiss.

'Is Ethan with you? I don't understand, Kitty. Why aren't you at the reception?'

'Can I come in before we get into all that?'

'Yes,' she said, blinking. 'Yes, of course, my love. Come through to the front room.'

I followed her in and took a seat on the sofa.

'How did you get here, dear? Where's Ethan? How will you get back?' She didn't seem to know which question to fire at me first.

'Ethan's at the reception. I got here in an orange campervan with an Irish children's author and his pregnant karaoke-singing dog. And I'm not going back.'

'What do you mean, you're not going back?'

My stomach gave a growl, its way of reminding me that even fugitives needed to eat. I hadn't had a bite since pre-wedding nerves had kicked in to hurl yesterday's lunch down the loo the evening before. I'd been feeling pretty sick all day, first with nerves and then the shock I'd got at the reception, and my energy levels were drained.

'Have you got any biscuits, Aunty J? Or a ham sandwich or something? I'm starved.'

'Yes.' She recovered herself slightly. 'Yes, yes, of course. I'll make us some tea and see what I have in.'

She wheeled herself to the specially adapted open-plan kitchen, coming back ten minutes later with a plate of chocolate digestives, some finger sandwiches and a steaming mug of tea each. I tucked in ravenously.

'Don't wolf it down like that, Kitty. You'll make yourself sick.'

'Sorry,' I said, gulping down a sandwich. 'Not eaten for twenty-four hours.'

She scanned my crumpled clothes and tangled hair with concern. 'No offence, dear, but you look like you've fallen out of a bird's nest. What on earth have you been doing with yourself?'

I felt a wave of nausea as I gagged on the last bite of sandwich, but I forced it down.

'I've been hitch-hiking,' I said. 'Bit of an experience. Still, one thing I can cross off my bucket list, eh?'

'Don't joke, Kitty. This is serious.'

'You've got no idea,' I said through a mouthful of digestive.

'What did you mean when you said you weren't going home?'

'What I said. I can't go back, Aunty.' The mental picture of what I'd seen at the reception rose up in my mind, and I choked on a sob. 'I'm never going back.'

'But why?'

'Something happened. At the wedding reception. Something... something really bad.'

'With Ethan?' Her eyes were round. 'Did he hurt you, Kitty? He didn't, did he? Surely not.'

In her free time, Aunty Julia volunteered at a women's refuge, and she had her own bit of history in that department too – dear departed Uncle Ken, widely known among the family as 'that bastard'. So it was no great surprise that violence was her first thought.

'Nothing like that.' I tried to push back my tears, but they wouldn't stop coming.

'Then what? Was there – you didn't find him with someone else?'

I turned my face away to gaze out of the window. 'I'd really rather not talk about it just yet. It's... kind of raw.'

She stared at me for a moment, mouth open, as if she was struggling to take it all in.

'But you can't just run away,' she said at last. 'What about your mother? She'll be worried sick.'

'She'll cope,' I muttered.

'Let me call her, dear. She can take you home, and if Ethan's done something—' Her brow lowered. 'Well, never you mind about that. He won't be able to hurt you, we'll see to it.'

'No,' I said sharply. 'No. I don't want you to call her. Please.'

'But she'll be so anxious when she finds you're gone. At least let me tell her you're safe. Then you can stay here for a few days until you're calmer and we can work out what to do when you get home.'

'I told you, I'm not going home.'

'Then where will you go?'

I flushed. 'Well, I was hoping I could stay here. Just for a little while, until I can make a new start somewhere.'

She shook her head, bewildered. 'A new start! Don't you

think that's a little extreme? I mean, your job. Your friends, your family, your house...'

'It's Ethan's house. And there's nothing in that life I want to go back for now.'

'You can't let him chase you away, Kitty. Elden's your home.'

'Not any more.' I finally surrendered and let the tears flow. 'I can give up or I can start again, Aunty J. And really, I just want to give up. But something won't let me.'

'Oh, Kitty...'

She wheeled herself closer and put her arm around me. She had that comforting smell she always had, a combination of some floral perfume and the spicy aniseed tang of the cream she used for muscle pain.

'Now, don't you worry about a thing,' she said gently. 'What can I do for you, my love? Tell me what you need from me.'

'Can I stay? Just for a bit.'

'Of course you can, for as long as you want to. But I wish you'd let me call your mother. You need to be with your family.'

'You're my family.'

She smiled. 'Yes, I suppose I am. Well, dear, how about you go upstairs and run yourself a bubble bath? Get out of that silly dress and into a nice fluffy bathrobe while I make us something yummy for tea? You need something a bit more substantial than ham sandwiches, I think. You're looking very peaky.'

I sniffed, wiping my eyes with the back of my hand. 'That sounds nice.' I pecked her cheek. 'Thanks, Aunty, I knew I could count on you. Love you.'

Upstairs in the bathroom, a huge corner bath gaped

welcomingly. I turned on the hot tap, and watched as the steaming jet started to fill the tub. There was some lavender-fragranced bubble bath next to the tap, so I threw a bit in.

God, it was nice to feel safe again. Grounded.

I pulled off my wellies, then glanced down at my dress, which was a bit worse for wear by now.

I remembered the day I'd got it; how excited I'd been at the colour, the cut, the fit. Nan had been with me. I could picture her zipping me into it and the quaint little blessing she'd muttered in the accent that even after fifty years in Yorkshire, still had a trace of County Kerry about it – 'health to wear it, strength to tear it, money to buy another'. Then she'd kissed me, told me I was beautiful. Told me how proud my dad would've been if he'd been around to see me.

I wished I could call her, just to hear her voice for five minutes.

I hunted around the bathroom for a towel, but there didn't seem to be any. Opening the door, I went to ask Aunty Julia where she kept them these days.

At the top of the stairs, I stopped. I could hear muttered speech. Who was she talking to? Glancing down, I saw her on the phone in the hallway.

'Yes, she's here, safe and sound,' she was saying in a low voice. 'No, she won't tell me. Ethan must really have done something terrible to get her into that state. Complete break-down, it looks like.'

She paused while the person on the other end of the line said something.

'No, you never trusted him, did you? I should've listened.

But Kitty was so besotted with him, and he seemed such a nice boy, I did think... ah well. I suppose my record's against me.' She sighed. 'Poor little girl. What can we do for her now?'

Another pause, then:

'Are you sure? She seems quite adamant she doesn't want to go home. Of course, she'll calm down after a few days, but maybe she's better off here until then?'

She paused again. 'Okay, if you're positive it's for the best, you'd better come and fetch her. I'll look after her till you get here. Bye, Petra.'

I stiffened, then dashed back into the bathroom to yank my wellies back on.

My stomach lurched painfully, and I threw myself over the toilet bowl as the sandwiches I'd just eaten came back up. When I'd retched out the entire contents of my gut, I flushed the loo and rinsed my mouth out over the sink, staring at the pale alien looking back at me from the mirror.

I couldn't believe it! She'd only gone and called Mum, after I'd specifically asked her not to! Aunty Julia, the one person I'd really believed would be on my side; the person I loved and trusted most out of everyone.

But there was no time to reflect on my second sickening betrayal of the day. From the sounds of it, my mum was already heading this way to take me home.

I had to get out.

Quietly I turned the bathroom lock to shut myself in. Then I opened the window and looked down.

Yep. It was happening. I was going to do something I'd only

ever seen in films, something that twenty-four hours ago I could never have imagined myself doing.

I was going to shin down a drainpipe. In my wedding dress and wellies, like some low-budget Yorkshire remake of *Kill Bill*.

I eyed the iron drainpipe with trepidation. I didn't have much time: if Mum set off right away she could be here in two hours, and I wanted to be as far away as possible by then. But I'd never climbed down a drainpipe before, and although I asked myself how hard it could really be, the ground seemed a long way off.

'Kitty! Do you need a towel?' Aunty Julia's voice sailed up.

'Er, no,' I called back. 'Managed to find one, thanks.'

Okay, that settled it. I needed to get out, before she cottoned on that something was up.

I turned off the taps. It might take Aunty Julia a while to work out I was gone, and I didn't want to end up flooding her house.

Clambering up onto the sink as quietly as possible, I leaned out of the window to grab the drainpipe with both hands, my enormous flared skirt billowing over the porcelain. With a huge effort and a barely suppressed squeal, I managed to manoeuvre myself out, supporting my weight as best I could.

Still, as I scrambled down the pipe, trying not to look at the ground, it was really less of a climb than a slide. When I got to the bottom, the skin of both hands was friction-burnt and painful, little pieces of black paint dotting the palms where they'd embedded themselves in my flesh. I'd managed to tear my dress too, but that was the least of my worries.

Health to wear it, strength to tear it, money to buy another…

Money. I patted my bosom, where the £50 Jack had lent me was stashed in my bra. Thank God I hadn't talked him into taking it back. It was all that was standing between me and complete destitution right now.

I started walking towards the road. Once I was out of sight of the house, I broke into a sprint. My plan was to get as far away as possible on foot, out of sight of Aunty Julia and any of her neighbours and friends who might recognise me, before I tried hitching another lift. Christ only knew where I'd end up spending the night. Hopefully there'd be a youth hostel or something that wouldn't dent my £50 too much. As for what would happen to me after that, I had no idea. All I knew was, I'd rather sleep rough than go back to the place that used to be my home.

Chapter 4

Once I was a good mile clear of the cottage, I had my second go at hitch-hiking. It took a lot longer to get a lift this time – I think I probably looked a bit scary, with make-up all down my face and a big rip in my dress. But eventually a kind elderly couple, who obviously thought I was some sort of eccentric debutante who'd fallen on hard times, picked me up. They were heading to Keswick in northern Lakeland, a reasonable distance away, and offered to drop me off.

'Where do you want to be, my dear?' the old lady asked gently when we were nearly there. She said everything gently, so as not to get the lunatic in the ballgown too excited.

'Um... is there a pub near here? One that does cheap meals?' After throwing up my sandwiches I was starving again, and I needed somewhere warm to hole up while I worked out where I was going to sleep. Hopefully the bar staff would know if there was a hostel nearby.

'The Shepherd's Rest,' her husband said promptly. 'Main meal and a pint for £8 on Thursdays. Great ale selection too.'

'Trust you to know that.' The woman rolled her eyes at me. 'No drunk like an old drunk, I always say.'

I forced a smile.

Ten minutes later, they dropped me off outside and I waved them goodbye.

The Shepherd's Rest was a sweet country pub, all whitewash and mock-Tudor. The sign over the half-timbered front showed a cloth-capped old gent slumbering near a flock of Herdwicks, and a chalkboard by the entrance declared 'Well Behaved Dog's & Badly Behaved Women Welcome!!!'

Through the door, I could see an unseasonal but welcoming log fire and a wealth of brass and mahogany. On the mantelpiece were the obligatory pair of china spaniels, beloved of nanas and country pub landlords the world over, with an old shotgun and a moth-eaten fox's head mounted overhead. A brass plaque above the doorframe said, 'Duck or grouse – mind your head!!', while a mock specials board on the wall announced, 'Soup of the Day: Beer!!!' The landlord was clearly a man who liked his gags old-school and heavy on the exclamation marks.

There's something about the pub after a day on the move, isn't there? The way it glows with warmth and welcome, the door propped open invitingly. I think it calls out to the traveller in all of us, the one who longs to lay down his pack and rest away from the elements a while.

I ventured in, too cold and hungry to care what impression my bedraggled appearance was likely to make on the other customers. To his credit though, the young barman didn't say a word when I approached him.

'What can I get you, love?' he asked politely.

'Just a tap water.' I didn't want to waste the only cash I

had in the world on alcohol, much as I could've murdered a glass of wine. 'And a menu, please.'

'Sorry. We stopped serving food half an hour ago.'

It was only a little thing. But it was the last little thing in a long day of pretty big things, and something inside me just broke.

I burst into tears.

'Er, hey,' the lad said, his eyes widening. Hysterical customers in ballgowns clearly hadn't been part of barman basic training. 'No need to take it so hard.' He grabbed a packet of dry-roasted peanuts from behind him and slapped them down on the bar. 'Here. On the house.'

'Sorry. I'm sorry. It's just... I've had a rough day.'

There was something cold and wet pressing against the sore palm dangling at my side. I wiped my eyes with the back of my hand and glanced down to find a chubby yellow mongrel with its nose against me, tail wagging like we were old friends.

I frowned. 'Whose dog is this?'

'Still mine,' a voice behind me said. 'And we really must stop meeting like this.'

The surge of relief at hearing Jack's voice was so strong I could've hugged him. Yes, I'd only met him a few hours ago, but in that whole long day of betrayals and heartbreak, it felt like he was the one person who'd been unequivocally on my side.

'Oh God, I'm glad to see you,' I said with a shaky smile.

'Me too. You owe me fifty quid.' He nodded to the barman. 'Another pint, Ryan, and whatever the lady's having.'

'I already ordered a tap water.'

'Well now I'm buying. What do you really want?'

'I'd commit mass murder for a glass of white wine,' I admitted.

'Then it's yours. Can't have you turning to crime.' He glanced at the packet of peanuts on the bar. 'That's not your dinner, is it?'

'It'll have to be. They've stopped serving food.'

'You can manage a little something, can't you, Ry?' Jack asked with a winning smile.

Ryan looked unsure. 'Dunno, Jack. Dad'll go spare if I start taking special orders after hours.'

'He won't, not if you tell him it's for me. Go on, I'll explain to your dad.'

'Well... okay. Just this once then.'

'Good lad. Cumberland sausage in a giant Yorkshire for Kitty then, please.' He nodded to me. 'If that's okay by you. Best thing on the menu, I swear.'

'Um, yeah,' I said, blinking dazedly. 'Anything.'

Jack tapped the lad's arm as he turned to go to the kitchen. 'And can you ask the chef to serve the gravy properly, not in one of those daft pipette things? She wants to eat, not perform animal husbandry.'

'All right, no need to be a diva about it,' Ryan muttered as he headed off to break the bad news to the chef.

'Gentrification. You can't get away from it,' Jack said with a smile when Ryan had gone. 'So you want to join me?'

'Are you alone?'

'Yep. Just me and Sandy.'

'Oh. Okay.'

I followed him to a little table, a newspaper spread over it, and took a seat opposite. Jack folded up the paper and pushed it to one side.

'Never thought I'd see you again,' I said. 'What're you doing here?'

'I could ask you the same question.' He nodded at young Ryan behind the bar. 'Ryan's dad Matty is an old friend. Another Irishman from my neck of the woods. I always stop by when I'm in the area.' He scanned me with a concerned gaze. 'You look a bit more dishevelled than the last time I saw you.'

'Mmm. Slid down a drainpipe. It wasn't nearly as cool as it looks in *Ghostbusters*.' I held up my hands to show him the red, tender skin, spots of blood standing out against it where the jagged old pipe had torn into the flesh.

'Shit! What happened?'

'My aunty, she... she bloody Landoed me, Jack. Called my mum to take me home when I'd told her I wouldn't go back.' I gave my head an angry shake. 'I can't believe she did that to me. Out of everyone, she was... God.' I held back a sob. 'I'm a total mess.'

Aunty Julia's betrayal probably would've stung a lot harder if it wasn't for everything else that'd happened that day. Still, it gnawed, with a dull but steady intensity. Since Dad had passed away, she'd been the one person I'd always believed I could rely on in a crisis.

'So you ran away again then.' Jack's tone was concerned, but it was calm too. No nonsense, it said. I liked it.

'Yeah. I'm getting pretty expert at it.'

'Quite the adventure you're having today.' He took my hands in his to examine the palms. 'These are really sore, Kitty. You should get something on them.'

'Haven't had time to think about that,' I said, gingerly lifting my wine glass to my lips with my fingertips. On an empty stomach, the alcohol was going straight to my head, making my brain fluffy. Good.

'They could use some antiseptic. You don't want the cuts to get infected.'

'Well, hopefully they'll have something at the youth hostel.'

'What youth hostel?'

'There's one near here, isn't there?'

'About ten miles away, but I doubt you'll get a bed if you haven't booked in. They fill up fast in the Lakes.'

'Of course they do,' I muttered to myself. 'Why wouldn't they? Perfect end to a perfect day.'

'So was that your plan? Youth hostelling?'

'Haven't really got a plan. I just wanted a bed for a couple of days, till I could get something sorted.'

'Such as?'

I sighed. 'God knows. There's a few old friends I could ring round. One of them must have a sofa I can kip on for a bit.'

'And then what will you do?'

'Start again.' I tried to focus on the open fire, which had gone a bit blurry. 'Suppose I'd need a job first. And then... well, one day at a time.'

'Hmm.'

He looked concerned, but before we could discuss it any further, Ryan came over with a steaming plate of food.

The Cumberland sausage smelled amazing, the rich fragrance of red wine gravy and roast onions taunting my poor growling tummy. The pain in my palms forced me to eat slowly this time, and I savoured every mouthful. By the time I'd half-demolished an enormous, fluffy Yorkshire and nearly finished my wine, my emotional state felt ever so slightly more stable. Or it would've done, if it wasn't for the nagging worry that in just a few hours I was going to officially join the ranks of Britain's rough sleepers.

'Thanks for this, Jack,' I said through a mouthful of Yorkshire pud. 'Don't know what I would've done without you today.'

'So where will you sleep?'

'No idea,' I admitted. 'Can't afford a B&B. Bus shelter, probably.'

'Now come on.' He glanced at my bare arms and shoulders. 'You'd be a popsicle by morning.'

It was unseasonably chilly for May. I shuffled my chair ever so slightly closer to the open fire.

'I'll live,' I muttered.

'And what about tomorrow night? And the one after that?'

'I'll... something'll turn up. Like I said, I've got a few friends I can try.' I didn't have a mobile, but there was bound to be a phone box somewhere in town.

'You're really positive you can't go home?' Jack asked.

'I'm never going home.' I glared at the Yorkshire pud, the symbol of my people, and ripped into it with my fork. 'I'd rather sleep rough.'

'I couldn't let you do that.'

I glanced up at him. Concern was etched all over his features. It was reassuring, feeling there was someone looking out for me. Instinctively I started eating more slowly, fearing the inevitable moment when our impromptu dinner date would be over and the kind stranger who'd twice come to my rescue now would disappear out of my life for good.

'Why're you being so nice to me, Jack?' I asked. 'You only met me a few hours ago.'

He shrugged. 'Always been a sucker for a damsel in distress.' He jerked his head towards Sandy, spread-eagled at his feet like a dogskin rug – the best she could probably manage with a tummy full of puppies. 'That's how I ended up with her ladyship here. Isn't it, eh, old girl?' He leaned down to tickle her between the ears.

'What, she was a damsel in distress?'

'In her little doggy way. I picked her up as a stray pup, living rough on the streets of Leeds. Been mistreated, I'd guess from the state of her. Abandoned, or run away from home.' He quirked an eyebrow. 'Sound familiar?'

'Heh. A bit.'

'That's more like it,' Jack said as I mopped up my remaining gravy with the last mouthful of Yorkshire pud. 'You look a bit more human now.'

'Yeah, I feel a lot better. Thanks, Jack.'

'Dessert?'

'Kitchen's closed, isn't it?'

'Ryan'll sort it, long as I ask nicely. Sticky toffee pudding? Local delicacy, you know.'

'I'm fine, honestly.'

'Ice cream on the side?'

'No, Jack. It's too naughty.'

'Right so.' He beckoned to Ryan. 'I'll just ask for my usual two portions then, at the risk of ruining my girlish figure. And if you change your mind, I'm sure I can spare one.'

He bloody did as well, he got two portions. Ten minutes later, he'd twisted my arm with no great effort and we were both tucking into a plateful of moist sponge bathed in caramel sauce.

'My mum'd go spare if she saw me eating this,' I told him, chasing a spoonful round my plate.

'Aren't you a bit big to have your mam telling you you're not allowed afters?'

'Mmm,' I said, fork hovering halfway to my mouth. 'She's obsessed with calorie-counting. Always watching her figure.'

'What, and yours?'

'Yeah. She's... well, you'd really have to meet her to get it.' I swallowed a mouthful of pudding with a liberating feeling of defiance. 'But let's not talk about her.'

'Okay, you pick a conversation topic.'

'Tell me about you then, dark and mysterious man,' I said, smiling. 'Are you allowed to just drive around the country drawing? Thought you had to have a visa or something.'

'Not for Ireland. Anyway, I've got British and Irish passports.'

'Really? How come?'

'My mam's English.' He glanced warily around the pub. 'Although I like to keep it quiet, obviously.'

'Cheekiness. Where's she from?'

'Hackney. She moved to Ireland when she was tiny though. Lives up in Scotland now.'

'Ha!'

'What do you mean, ha?'

'You're a cockney.'

He drew himself up. 'How dare you. I am as full-blooded an Irishman as you'll meet today.'

'I knew it was all an act. I knew I'd seen you earlier at the bar.'

'Seen me what?'

'Doing the Lambeth walk.'

'I don't even know what the Lambeth walk is.'

'I bet soon as you're back in the camper, you'll be guzzling jellied eels and having a knees-up round the old Joanna.'

'The old what?'

'And I spotted those Chas and Dave albums hidden in the sofa earlier, by the way.'

Jack grinned. 'Okay, you've got me there. I do love Chas and Dave.'

'Who doesn't?'

'See, I knew sticky toffee would do the trick,' he said, laughing. 'If you're teasing me about East End folk duos, you must be feeling better.'

'I am.' I smiled at him. 'You're good at this, aren't you? Cheering people up. After the day I've had, I never thought I'd be able to laugh again.'

'When the stormclouds gather, pudding. Ancient Irish proverb.'

'Ancient cockney proverb.'

'Oi. Less of the backchat, my girl, or I might rethink my offer of a sleepover.'

I frowned. 'Sleepover?'

'Well, yeah. I'm not going to let you walk the streets, am I? You might get eaten by a feral Herdwick. Vicious feckers, the sheep round here.'

I hesitated. When he said sleepover, did he mean *sleep*over or did he mean, you know... sleep*over*? I mean, I did trust him, but... well, he was still a stranger. And a man.

He smiled, reading my expression. 'No ulterior motive, I promise. I'll put a camp bed up in the awning for me. And if you want to stay a few days while you make a plan, you can. I'll look after you.'

'Why though?'

'Because you've got no money and nowhere to go and I'm not a complete bastard.' He glanced at my sore palms. 'And not to be personal, but I'm not sure your mental state's any too stable right now either. I don't want to leave you alone.'

'I'm not your problem.'

'I'm making you my problem. Just until you get back on your feet.'

The sense of relief that there was someone in my corner, someone who wanted to help, was palpable. The feeling that it wasn't just me against the world any more surged through me like warm caramel.

'Thank you,' I said in a small voice. 'I'll pay you back for all this. Just as soon as... as something happens. I don't know what, but something.'

'Nothing happens but what we make happen.' He pushed

his plate away and stood up. 'And tomorrow is the first day of making the rest of your life happen, superhero Kitty Clayton. Come on.'

Chapter 5

So this was my wedding night. Walking by the banks of a star-spangled lake with an almost complete stranger who'd just offered to save me from a life of vagrancy. It wasn't the one I'd dreamed of, but it was certainly interesting.

'Is it far?' I asked Jack.

'Just a half-mile from here.' He glanced down at my wellies. 'How far have you walked in those things today?'

'Dunno. Quite a way.' I could feel blood pooling in one of the toes, but that was nothing compared to the pain in my poor burnt hands.

'Can you make it?'

'I'll cope.'

But the series of physical and emotional shocks I'd suffered that day were starting to catch up with me. As was the glass of wine I'd had in the pub. I stumbled dizzily against a rock, and clutched at Jack for support.

'Here.' He put his arm around my shoulders, and I relaxed against it gratefully.

As we walked, Jack pulled my body towards him so our sides were touching. He smiled as we passed a pair of elderly walkers, and they smiled back with a simper that told me they thought we were what we must have appeared to everyone just at that moment: the picture of a happy young couple. Sandy bounded ahead of us, for all the world like a big fat puppy herself rather than the dignified matron you'd expect her to be at this stage in her pregnancy.

'You always this touchy-feely with girls you've just met?' I asked, glancing at the arm curled around my shoulders.

'Not since I got that restraining order one time.' He shrugged. 'You were looking a bit like you needed the support. I can stop if it makes you uncomfortable.'

'No, please don't.' I looked up at him. 'Is it funny that I trust you? Twenty-four hours ago I wouldn't have known you in the street.'

'And yet today you've run into me twice within a forty-mile radius,' he said. 'Guess I must be written into your stars, eh?'

I held a hand to my head. I'd been cold earlier, but now I was sweltering. It was obviously one of those springs where the thermostat just couldn't make up its mind. My brow was coated in beads of sweat.

'You don't really believe in all that stuff, do you?' I asked Jack. 'Stars and that? Sounds daft to me.'

He shrugged. 'Not exactly. Still, sometimes things seem to happen that were too important not to happen. Call it coincidence or fate or whatever you like, but I'm a big believer in grabbing what life throws at you and wringing it dry.'

'Interesting turn of phrase, wringing life dry. Kind of bleak for a *carpe diem*.'

'Yeah, I'm a poetic son of a bitch,' he said with a grin. 'You know, in another life I could've been Bono.'

I shuddered. 'Thank God we're in this one then. I'm having a bad enough day as it is.'

We walked in silence for a while. I snuck a look at Jack. His mouth was haunted by a little smile, staring dreamily at Sandy trotting ahead of us with her engorged tum nearly scraping the ground. He was leaning his weight on me slightly, as if having me at his side was the most natural thing in the world rather than a novelty just a few hours old.

'Okay, so if we're going to be roomies for a couple of days I think we'll need a few ground rules,' he said after a bit.

'Um, okay.' He didn't seem like a man to live by rules much, with that whole free spirit vibe he had going on, but if he was willing to spare me a kip in a bus shelter I'd agree to whatever he wanted.

Within reason, obviously.

'Rule one: no questions,' he said. 'If you don't want to tell me why you won't go home, I promise not to ask. And vice versa for me. All right?'

'Suits me.'

'Rule two: no feeling sorry for yourself. First step to sorting your new life out is drawing a line under the old one.'

'It's not that easy though, is it?'

'I know. But if you make yourself look forward and not back, it'll get easier every day. Trust me.'

I smiled. 'How'd you get so wise, Jack?'

'I'm part wizard,' he said. 'Okay, rule three: don't squeeze the toothpaste from the top of the tube.'

'Why?'

He shrugged. 'It's just annoying.'

'Toothpaste... I haven't got a brush,' I mumbled absently.

My head was throbbing, and the dizziness seemed to be getting worse too. I forced my eyes to focus on a fixed point, trying to keep steady, and leaned heavily against Jack for support. Surely we were nearly there by now.

'I've got a spare, still in the packet. It's all yours.'

'Is that it then?' I said. 'No more rules?'

'No.' Jack's voice was quieter now. 'Just one more. Rule four: no running away. Not without telling me where you're going.'

That seemed an odd one.

'Any reason?'

'Just want to know you're safe.' He flashed me what looked like a slightly forced smile. 'And like you said, you are getting pretty expert at it.' He nodded to a pair of stone gateposts. 'Here's the campsite.'

***

'Home sweet home,' Jack said when we reached his van. 'Told you it wasn't that small.'

It'd certainly expanded since the last time I'd seen it. The roof had popped up, accordion-like, to give it standing room, and a little green awning jutted out at the back like a Victorian bustle. Another awning against the side practically doubled the living space, adding a second room.

Jack unzipped the flap and I followed him in. There was a camping table and chair with a little LED lantern in the centre, and a Stephen King book he must've been in the middle of turned face down. When he opened the door of the camper, I noticed that what had earlier been a sofa had folded down into a bed, extending out into the back awning so it didn't encroach too much on the kitchen area. A pair of curtains could be drawn across to give a bit of privacy.

'Your room, Madame,' he said, nodding to it. 'Just let me sort out Sandy's dinner then I'll show you around the rest.'

Jack opened one of the kitchenette cupboards and took out a box of dog biscuits. He filled a double bowl with biscuits and cold water, then put it down for Sandy.

'She's got a good appetite, hasn't she?' I said, watching her wolf it down. 'Still, I suppose the pups are in there having their tea too.'

'Nah, she was always a pig.' He gestured around the little space. 'So, this is where the magic happens, as they say. There's storage in the overhead compartments and sofa, plus the big cupboard and a rack outside for cases.' He pointed up at the accordion roof. 'So's a big lad like me doesn't give himself a hunchback.' He knelt down to the bank of pine kitchenette cupboards. 'Half-sized fridge, gas bottle under the hob, storage cupboards for cans. And that's it really. Small but perfectly formed.'

'How old is it?'

'1967 T2 – classic of her era, this old lady.' He looked around with obvious pride. 'The shell's probably all that's left from the sixties now though. It wasn't a camper then.'

'Right.' I frowned. 'What was it, a giant roller skate?'

'People carrier. Microbuses, collectors call them. Then in

the '80s some bright spark decided to gut it and turn it into this.'

'Did you have to do much to it?'

'I had the sofa moved back so the bed extends into the tailgate awning, gives me a bit more space. Modernised the decor, redid the electrics. It was a nice little project, took my mind off – well, other stuff I had going on.'

'Why orange?'

'Wasn't my choice. Someone else picked the colour.'

He'd turned away and was frowning into the distance. It felt like it was time for Rule One to kick in, so I quickly changed the subject.

'So, um, where will you sleep?'

'Got a fold-up camp bed and a sleeping bag under the seats. I'll put it up in the side awning.'

'Won't you be cold?'

He shrugged. 'Couple of thick jumpers on and I'll live.'

'I'll sleep in the awning. You have your bed.'

'Won't hear of it. Irish tradition of hospitality. Anyway, you need a decent bed after the day you've had.'

'Thank you.' I was too tired to argue. 'So, er... bedtime?'

I felt suddenly bashful. My cheeks and forehead were on fire.

'First things first.' He rummaged in the tall cupboard until he found a little green first aid kit. 'Your hands. Let me take a look at them.'

I sank dizzily onto the edge of the bed. Jack knelt in front of me to examine my inflamed palms.

'The left isn't so bad but the right's looking nasty,' he said.

'Better get some antiseptic cream on them and bind them up.'

'I'll be okay,' I mumbled. The world seemed a bit spinny suddenly.

'Metal drainpipe, was it?'

'Think so.'

'Hmm. Have you had your tetanus jab?'

'Yeah. Probably.' A little giggle bubbled out of me. 'Funny word, tetanus. Tet-anne-uz. Sounds like a... centurion. Brush on his head and all that.'

He frowned. 'You okay, Kitty?'

'Tetanus,' I repeated. 'Tett-an-nuss.'

He held one hand against my forehead. 'Jesus, lass, you're burning up.'

''M'okay. Sleepy.'

Suddenly, everything was black.

***

When I came to, a man's silhouette was leaning over me, stroking my hair.

'Ethan?' I mumbled.

'Morning, sleepyhead.'

I blinked to get the fog out of my eyes. 'You...'

'That's right, me. Who am I then?'

'You're... Jack. Jack Duffy.'

I could see him clearly now, leaning over me as I lay in his bed in the camper. He smiled.

'So you remember me. That's a good sign.'

'Did I fall asleep?'

'Yeah. For two days.'

'Two days!'

'You passed out with a fever. You've been in out and of consciousness ever since, raging temperature. Don't you remember?'

'I remember... pub. And you. What happened?'

'Oh, we've been having bags of fun together,' he said. 'Had to get you to A&E to start with, just in case it was tetanus. You had me worried sick.'

'Was it tetanus?'

'No, just a nasty dose of the flu. Not surprised, after what you'd been through. Your poor body must've been weakened past the point it could fight any more.'

I tried to sit up, but my head throbbed so hard I sank back down with a groan.

I put a palm to my forehead. It felt all fuzzy. When I glanced at my hand, I saw it was wrapped in a thick bandage.

'That can come off soon,' Jack said. 'Your hands should be healed enough by now.'

'You've been looking after me?' I mumbled.

'I have, yeah.' He shook his head. 'Good thing I found you. If you'd really tried sleeping rough in that flimsy dress, you could've killed yourself.'

Sandy was sleeping in her bed on the floor nearby. I leaned over to tickle her ears, reflecting woozily on the surreal fact I seemed to share the same backstory as my rescuer's pet dog.

'Do you feel like you could eat?' Jack said, standing up.

The world was spinning so much, I knew I'd struggle to

keep anything down. But my throat felt like it'd been sand-blasted.

'Drink,' I managed. 'Some water. Please.'

While Jack filled a glass for me, I ran my hands over my body.

'What am I wearing?' I asked when he came to sit on the bed by me.

'Here.' He put his hand behind my back and supported me while I drank. I gulped the water down greedily. 'No, not too fast. It'll only come back up.'

'My dress. Where…'

'With my laundry. I thought you'd be more comfortable in pyjamas.'

I squinted at him. 'Did you see me with no clothes on?'

'Yep. Very nice.'

'Naughty,' I said weakly, but I managed to smile. 'Where'd you get ladies' pyjamas?'

'Just something I had lying around. Lucky they were your size.'

My brain was spinning, but I still remembered Rule One. The first rule of campervan is you do not talk about campervan.

''K,' I mumbled. 'What happens now?'

'You get well again. It'll take at least a few days till you're back to full strength, I'd guess.'

'You mean I can stay here?'

'Unless you'd rather go home? Your family must be worried about you by now.'

I shuddered. The days of fever and delirium hadn't weakened the image that'd been seared onto my brain the day of my wedding. That was as vivid as ever.

'No. I want to stay with you. I don't trust anyone else.'

He reached out to squeeze my hand. 'Then you'll stay. And when you're feeling better, we'll work out what comes next.'

***

It was nearly a week before I was feeling completely myself again. My body and my immune system really had taken quite a battering, and it took longer than it should have done to fight the infection.

Jack was great: cooking for me, sitting by me with his sketchbook while I dozed, reading to me, playing card games and chatting. It was just what I needed to stop me dwelling on Ethan and the wedding. I still couldn't fathom why exactly Jack had taken me under his wing, except that I was another stray who needed his help and he was following a natural instinct to protect.

But I was grateful: so, so grateful. The more time I spent in his company, the more I thanked whatever guardian pixie looked out for Kitty Clayton and had made sure she'd fallen in the way of someone kind.

It was all so different from my old life, with Ethan. Jack was so different. Every ten minutes he'd ask if I needed anything, or offer to walk into Keswick for some little bit of food I'd expressed a taste for. When I'd been ill at home, Ethan had always made it quite clear he saw the whole thing as something I was putting on deliberately to inconvenience him, grudgingly making me the odd Lemsip until I was desperate to go back to work, just to escape the heavy air of resentment.

Because Ethan never got ill himself. That was why he had no patience with it in others, I'd told myself. And I'd excused him as best I could. Just like I always did.

Chapter 6

A week after I'd come to, the throbbing in my temples had subsided to a dull ache and I was eating again, although I was still weak. One afternoon, I decided I was ready.

Jack was at the hob, cooking us pasta for lunch. He'd got me on meals heavy in carbs till my strength was up again. I could just imagine my mum's expression if she could see my calorific staple diet right now. The thought of it created a half-guilty, half-exciting fizz of rebellion.

'Jack, can I borrow your phone?' I asked.

'Why, who do you need to ring?'

'Couple of people at home.' I flinched. 'I mean, where I used to live.'

'Oh. Okay. Yeah, it's somewhere here...'

He started rooting through the overhead compartments, pulling out bits and pieces and throwing them down on the passenger seat as he hunted out his mobile.

I smiled. 'I'm thinking you don't make too many calls?'

'No, I keep it switched off mostly. The only people I ever need to ring are my agent, my parents and the odd friend. There's no one else I want to talk to.'

51

'Thanks.' I caught the little old-fashioned Nokia he chucked me with one hand. 'Um, could you... you know?'

'You want some privacy?'

'If that's okay.'

'No problem.' He turned off his pasta and whistled to Sandy. 'Come on, girl. Let's take you for a waddle and a widdle while Aunty Kitty makes her calls.'

When they'd gone, I tapped in the number for directory enquiries. I could just about remember Nan's landline, but without my own mobile, I had no access to anyone else's contact details.

'Hello?' Laurel said when she answered. 'If this is another sales call, then no, I haven't had an accident at work and you can sod off.'

'Hiya.'

'Jesus, Kitty, is it you?' she gasped. 'Oh my God, oh my... where the hell are you? I've been scared out of my wits about you!'

I trusted Laurel – she was the closest friend I had – but she was still family. Maybe I was being paranoid, but I didn't dare confide where I was to her. No matter how much she tried to keep it secret, there was no guarantee it wouldn't get back to my mum. Or to Ethan via her husband Andy, who was a mate of his.

'I can't say,' I told her. 'I'm safe though, promise.'

'But where have you been? Your mum and Ethan have been scouring the globe! Everyone's been worried sick you'd turn up on the news dead in a ditch or something.'

'Sorry, Laur. I would've rung sooner but I've been ill. I was barely conscious for a couple of days.'

'Shit! Have you been in hospital?'

'Briefly. I'm staying with someone now, a friend. He's looking after me.'

'He?' She sounded suspicious. 'Who is he? Someone I know?'

I didn't want to mention his name. Laurel's boys loved Jack's books, and once I told her who my mystery rescuer was, it'd be an easy way for them to track me down.

'No, someone I met hitch-hiking. He's been very kind to me.'

'You're kidding! You're staying with a stranger you met hitch-hiking?'

'I didn't have any choice. I had nowhere else to go.'

'Christ, Kitty! What the hell are you playing at, putting yourself in danger like that?' she exploded. 'He could be a sex offender for all you know.'

'He isn't. Just a nice lad who wants to help.'

'Yeah? And what's in it for him? Did he try it on with you?'

'Course not.'

'He will. No one does anything unless they expect to get a return somewhere down the line.' She sounded like my mum.

'Not this guy,' I said firmly. 'He isn't like that.'

'Why did you run off, Kit?'

'I couldn't stay, after... it's Ethan.' I steeled myself. I was going to have to say it sooner or later. 'He... he cheated on me, Laur. At the reception. Maybe not for the first time, I don't know.'

'No! He wouldn't do that,' she said, her voice all amazement. 'Not Ethan, surely. He loves you to pieces, everybody knows it.'

'He would because he bloody did. I saw him at it.' The image rose up again in my mind; even more vivid, more painful in my memory than it had been to watch. 'If I hadn't, I never would've believed it.'

'Shit, I mean... what, like a drunken snog or – you know, the full works?'

'What's the difference? He did it. After ten years, on our fucking wedding day, he...' I could barely hold back a sob. 'I never want to see that bastard again. Never.'

'When are you coming home?'

I took a deep breath. This was going to be the hard bit.

'I'm not. I haven't got a home there, not now.'

'Course you have,' she said, gentling her voice. 'You don't have to go back to Ethan. There's your mum. Or I can make space for you. Come home, Kit, to your family.'

'I can't. I just... can't. I'm not strong enough right now. Physically or emotionally.'

'Strong enough for what?'

'For any of it. Mum. Ethan. If I see him, he'll... I don't know how I'd react. It just feels like—' I could hear the panic lacing my voice. 'It's too much, Laur; too much. You can't make me go back.'

'But it's a breakdown, can't you see that?' She sounded scared. 'You're not acting rationally. Please. Tell me where you are and let me come get you. You don't have to face anyone, just come on home where I can take care of you.'

'Sorry, Laur. I love you, but... no. I'm staying here, just until

I find somewhere I can start again. You can advertise my job whenever you want.'

'Never mind your bloody job. You're not safe, Kitty. You need to get home.'

'I am safe, I swear. And if you care about me, you'll respect the fact this is where I need to be right now. Tell the boys I miss them, okay? I'll ring you when I can.'

'But—'

I hung up.

Nan was next. I made sure to withhold my number before I called.

'Hello?'

'Hiya Nana. It's Kitty.'

'Oh, hello, love,' she said, sounding pleased to hear from me but not at all surprised. In the early stages of Alzheimer's, she tended to get a little confused about anything too recent. My sudden disappearance might already have slipped from her memory.

'Are you okay?' I asked gently.

'Can't complain, can't complain. Just the old pain in my leg, but it's bearable. Oh, did I tell you I saw Rita yesterday? She was asking for you.'

'Who's Rita?'

She tutted. 'You know. Rita, her with the fancy man. She used to mind you sometimes when you were a baby, don't you remember?'

I couldn't help smiling. 'Oh. That Rita. Er, yeah, course.'

'When are you coming to see me, Kitty? I haven't seen you or your dad for ages.'

I winced. 'Dad's... not here, Nan. Remember? He died last year.'

'Oh. Yes,' she said vaguely. 'Yes, he did, didn't he? We had corned beef sandwiches at the wake...'

This had been happening more and more recently. And it hurt like hell, every time. Nan forgetting Dad was dead almost made me forget, and then the grief hit me all over again, fresh as the day I'd lost him.

God, I missed him. If he was here, there was no way I'd be forced to rely on the kindness of strangers in campervans. Ethan might've been the golden boy in most people's eyes, but Dad had never trusted him; never liked the possessive way he'd behaved around me.

'I just rang to tell you I'm on holiday,' I said to Nana, my voice choked. 'I'll be gone a little while. I'll call whenever I can, okay? Love you very much.'

'Love you too, my chicken. Don't forget to send us a postcard, will you?' Nan had a massive collection of postcards, everywhere from Bridlington to Brisbane, insisting on one from every friend or relative who'd been away in the last fifty years.

'I'll do my best. The post isn't very good here.'

'Where are you, love?'

'Um... Iceland,' I fabricated wildly.

The sound of her musical doorbell trilled in the background.

'Who's that then?' I heard her levering herself to her feet, and a minute later the front door opened with a click. 'Oh, Petra! Now guess who I've got here on the phone? She tells me she's in Iceland.'

56

Mum! Of all the times she could've called round. I hurriedly hit the End Call button.

My heart was still pounding when Jack arrived back from his walk with Sandy.

'Something wrong?' he asked, noticing my pale face.

'Just a bit of a scare. Nearly had to talk to my mum.'

He came to sit on the bed, stroking my hair to calm me, and I rested my forehead against his chest. 'Don't let it get you too upset, eh?' he said softly. 'You'll make yourself ill again.'

'I'll try.' I focused on my breathing, forcing myself calmer, and my heart rate started to slow. Jack's hand on my hair helped me feel safe.

'Kitty, can I ask you something personal? I know we said we wouldn't, but...'

'Depends what it is.'

'Why are you so scared your mam might find you? You're an adult. She can't make you go back if you don't want to.'

'You don't know her,' I muttered darkly.

'You're afraid of her. Aren't you?'

His eyes were so soft and understanding. It might be a relief to confide in someone.

'Not exactly afraid,' I said. 'It's just, Mum... all my life she's – well, she'd call it looking after me. My dad used to call it managing me. She managed him too, till he'd had enough and left her when I was eleven. After that I got a double helping.'

He frowned. 'Managed you in what way?'

'In every way, when I was a kid. Picking out my clothes – all my clothes, even when I was a teenager. I remember once I was allowed to go out shopping with my friends and came home with this dress I'd bought out of the pocket money Dad had given me. It wasn't revealing or anything: just a nice summer dress for the hot weather. But she made me take it right back. Not because there was anything wrong with it, but because I'd picked it without consulting her.'

'Sounds like a bully.'

I shook my head. 'It was more complicated than that. See, with the clothes, it wasn't that she didn't want me to pick them. It was that she wanted us to do it together. Be our mum-and-daughter thing. And she was like that with everything, even down to the food I ate. Long after I left home.'

He looked shocked. 'Seriously, she controlled your food?'

I tried to fight it but I couldn't help it. I felt embarrassed. Jack was obviously appalled by what I'd just told him, and I knew that really, I should be too. And yet I felt the same way I had all my life: this desperate urge to shrug off behaviour that I knew, deep down, was unacceptable. To make excuses for the very person who for years had made me miserable.

Because she loved me, I'd always told myself, echoing the words she so often said when I challenged her. Everything she did, she did because she loved me. Tough love, right? That was the only real love. To protect someone from pain, you had to hurt them. Over and over and over.

'Yeah,' I said to Jack, the affirmative dropping from me with a great effort of will. 'Whatever fad diet she was following,

I had to do it too. I've been a vegan, a fruitarian, a macrobiotic... she just had to share every little bit of my life.' It was a relief to finally let it all out. 'God, Jack, it was suffocating – I mean, literally, I felt like I couldn't breathe. A hundred times I wished I could've lived with my dad and Bernie. That was his second wife.' I gave a bleak laugh. 'But oh no, Mum couldn't let that happen. And like a coward I never fought it. Just rolled over and surrendered.'

'And your fiancé, what did he think of it?'

'Ethan?' My brow lowered. 'He was no better. The two of them scrapped like cat and dog over me: who was going to get me on my birthday or Christmas, stuff like that. They were like two spoilt kids trying to share a favourite toy. And then when it came to the wedding... it was hell, Jack. They both wanted complete control over the whole thing, bickering constantly, and there I was in the middle. By the time the wedding day came – I mean, I loved him. But all I really wanted was for it to be over.'

'Jesus. You do know that's abuse, right?'

'No, it...' I hesitated. 'I mean, I... I thought they acted like that because they loved me. It was stifling, yeah, but it was kind of flattering. To know you're wanted that much.'

'That's not love, Kitty. Love isn't obsessive. It heals, it doesn't break.'

A tear trickled out as I remembered what I'd seen at the wedding. Ethan, handsome, charming Ethan, who I'd loved since I was sixteen years old, who I'd convinced myself was so completely, undentably perfect...

'I know,' I whispered.

'Come here.' He drew me to him for a hug. 'It's behind you now, Kitty. There's a better future somewhere. As soon as you're up and about again, we'll find it.'

Chapter 7

I stayed with Jack for two weeks after I was better. Not because I really had any excuse to, but because the little van, with its friendly human and canine occupants, had started to feel like home. I was stagnant, but I was safe.

Rule One was turning out to be a bit of a bugger though. There was clearly some mystery about Jack, something he didn't want to share, and my curiosity was piqued. Because it wasn't just the pyjamas he'd lent me. He had a whole stash of women's clothes in the van.

'Help yourself,' he'd said when he'd given me a cardboard box filled with assorted tops, jeans, dresses and scarves. 'Been meaning to drop them off at the charity shop for ages. You might as well get some use out of them, since they're your size.'

I extracted a flowing top and a scarf and held them up in front of me. 'Bit floatier than my usual style. Whose are they?'

He shrugged. 'Yours, now.'

'But who did they belong to before?'

'Someone who's got no use for them. Just take what you

61

want and I'll drop the rest off at Oxfam.' He gazed absently out of the window at the shimmering mass of Derwentwater in the distance. 'Should've done it years ago really.'

All signs seemed to point to some ex who was out of his life, and who he was perhaps still pining for. Still, he respected my wish not to talk about my personal stuff, so the least I could do was mind my own business too.

Living without TV was an experience. I read a lot of books in those few weeks. I learned a lot about my temporary room-mate too – about his fatalism, his humour, his commitment to living one day at a time. And about how to care for a heavily pregnant dog.

I think board game night was my favourite new telly substitute. Jack liked Scrabble best, mainly because he always won. Embarrassing, given I was a professional editor. He was a terrible loser as well, and if you didn't watch him, an opportunistic cheat. I'd never expected to find such a strong competitive streak in someone as laid-back as he was.

'Come on, you, get on with it,' I said during our second game. Jack had been staring at his letters for nearly five minutes.

'Hmm.' He frowned at the tile rack. 'All right. Here then.'

I squinted at the random jumble of letters he'd assembled on the board.

'That's not a word. That's not even a sound.'

'It's a Gaelic word.'

'Yeah? What's it mean?'

'Old Irish blessing. I swear. Ask anyone from the old country.'

'Meaning?'

'Er... may the Force be with you?'

I pointed wordlessly at the tiles. He sighed and picked them up again.

'Anti-Irish prejudice, that's what it is.'

But he managed to find a second wind from somewhere. Four goes and a triple word score later, he'd only managed to bloody win. Again.

I folded my arms. 'Not fair. You should get points knocked off for attempted cheating. And I'm still not convinced the Irish spelling of liquorice has got an S in it.'

He tilted his nose up and sniffed the air. 'Mmm. What is that intoxicating aroma?'

'Stinky dog?' I said, glancing at Sandy. After a week absorbing the dirt and smells of the muddy campsite, she was badly in need of a bath.

'No, there's something else. I think it's—' He sniffed again. 'Yes, yes it is. The sweet smell of victory.'

'You're a funny man.'

'Mmmmm,' he said, sniffing again. 'Go on, grab yourself a lungful. Such stuff as winners are made of. Not that you'd know.'

'Sorry, all I can smell is testosterone.'

'What does testosterone smell like?'

'Almonds,' I said with a smile. 'Come on, you daft sod, deal the tiles. Best of three.'

It felt like I got to know him better during those few weeks than I'd known Ethan in the ten years we'd been a couple.

Eventually though, I felt like I'd trespassed on his Irish hospitality long enough. I knew I was hiding, and the time had come to work out what my next step needed to be.

'Okay, so I can't go home, that's a given,' I said to Jack as we sat round the camping table out in the awning one warm evening, making a plan.

'Couldn't you though? What about your nan?'

Rule One had gone out of the window to some extent since I'd opened up to him about my mum, and he was pretty knowledgeable about the people in my life now.

'She's in sheltered housing. I wouldn't be allowed to stay there. Anyway, I wouldn't want her worrying about me.'

'Laurel?'

'No. I don't want to be anywhere near Ethan. I want a completely new start.'

'So you need to rent somewhere.'

'And there we hit on problem one.' I scribbled it down on the notepad in front of me. 'I'm skint. Not a pot to do the proverbial in.'

'You know I'll give you money if you need it.'

'And you know I won't take it. I won't take a penny I can't pay back.'

'You can pay it back when you're working.'

I shook my head. 'Could take me ages to get a job. I can't take your money, Jack.'

'If I said please?'

'Not even if you begged.'

'You've got that independence thing going on. Okay, I can

respect that,' he said, smiling. 'Have you really got no money of your own though?'

'Yeah, I've got some. It's sitting in Ethan's bank account, where I can't get at it.'

'Why?'

I flushed. 'It was his idea. Years ago, when we first moved in together. I was only young and I didn't have a current account, so he said I could share his. Just till I was over eighteen and we could put it in both our names. Then we just... never got round to it, somehow.'

'So he kept your own money from you?'

Jack looked shocked, and I couldn't quite suppress a feeling of humiliation and shame. I stifled an urge to defend Ethan from something I knew was entirely indefensible.

'No, I had a bank card,' I said. 'In his name, obviously. I left it behind in my handbag when I ran off, along with other useful things like my mobile.'

'Could you get it?'

'What's the point? He'd only have it stopped. That's the first thing he'd do, try to force me home again.' I shuddered. 'And I can't see him. Not yet.'

'You can't hide forever, Kitty.'

'Please, Jack. I really can't.'

'Okay, if you're not ready I won't push,' he said gently. 'Have you really got nothing at all in your own name?'

'Not that I can access immediately. Some savings in an ISA, but I have to give six months' notice to withdraw. And I'd need my passport to prove my identity.'

'Which is...?'

'At home – I mean, at Ethan's. Everything that proves who I am is at Ethan's or Mum's. Currently I'm Jane Doe, of no fixed abode. As a legal person, I don't exist.'

'Well, let's park that for now. Next problem?'

'Nowhere to live,' I said, scribbling it down.

'Haven't you got any other close family?'

'Just my dad's sister, Aunty Julia.' I frowned. 'And she's not to be trusted.'

'Any friends who could put you up for a while?'

'Couple of old university pals I could try.'

'Okay, that's an option to explore. So, problem three: work.'

'Mmm. Not so many jobs in publishing, especially something as niche as travel guides.'

'Who says you have to do that though? This is a new start, remember.'

'So… what, career change?'

He shrugged. 'If you like. What do you enjoy? What're you good at?'

I paused to think about it. 'Well, I've always liked writing,' I said at last. 'I've written the odd feature for local mags, unpaid. Doubt I could make a living from it though. I'll have to take what I can get, at least until there's an opening to fit my experience.'

'Hmm. Perhaps.' He looked thoughtful for a moment.

I scanned down my list of problems. 'It's the first one that's the real kicker, isn't it? I've got nothing that can prove my identity. And until I have, I can't get my ISA money.'

Jack fell silent, staring down at his fingers spread on the table.

'When does Ethan go out?' he said at last.

I frowned. 'What?'

'Just wondered if you fancied a spot of light larceny this Thursday.'

***

'Jack, I don't think I can do this,' I muttered, casting an apprehensive look down the too-familiar cul-de-sac. We'd parked at the end – parking right outside the door, where anyone could get a good look at the van and report back on it to Ethan, felt too risky.

Jack had spent hours talking me into this, and being so close to home after the events of the month before was sending my heart rate into overdrive.

'What choice have you got?' he said. 'You need that passport.'

'But what if *he's* there?'

'What if he is? He can't hurt you. He'd have to go through me.'

'I can't see him, Jack.' The panic trembled in my voice. 'You promised I wouldn't have to see him.'

He took my hand and stroked it soothingly. 'It's okay, Kit. He'll be at work for hours yet, you said so yourself. It's a ten-minute job, then we'll be on the road again.'

'Far away?'

'As far as Timbuktu if that's what you want.'

I sucked in a deep breath, exhaled slowly, then pushed open the door of the camper. 'Right. Okay. Let's get it over with.'

The house looked the same as the last time I'd seen it, except that the chrysanthemums were coming into bloom and the lawn was fresh-mown. It seemed almost absurd, finding everything just as I'd left it.

Mrs Bartholomew, our elderly neighbour, was in her front garden deadheading roses.

'Oh! Kitty!' she said when she spotted me. 'Well, you're back early.'

'Hello, Mrs Bartholomew. Um, am I?'

'Is the course over already? Oh, or do they give you half-term like at school? We weren't expecting you back until next month.'

I blinked. 'Sorry – weren't expecting me back from where?'

'Well, from the editing course. Ethan said you'd be away at least two months. Such a shame, straight after your wedding, but I suppose it was too good an opportunity to pass up.' She shook her head. 'The world of work's certainly very different than it was in my day.'

'Sounds pretty different than it was in mine,' I muttered. 'Oh, er, this is Jack. He's my... cousin.'

'Hiya.' Jack smiled his charming smile for her. I was sure I saw Mrs Bartholomew blush under her huge-brimmed sun hat.

When they'd finished exchanging pleasantries, all the time with me struggling to keep my anxiety from spilling out, we went round the back and I rummaged under the azalea pot where Ethan always stashed the spare key.

Jack was smirking as he followed me in.

'He didn't really tell the neighbours you were on a two-month residential editing course?'

'Apparently.' I couldn't help smiling too. It was pretty funny, in a grim sort of way. 'I suppose telling everyone I'm off learning the art of the possessive apostrophe is a bit less humiliating than admitting your new wife walked out on you right after the wedding.'

'So where do we find this passport then?'

'Bureau in the study. Come on. I want to get out of here as quickly as possible.'

Jack tiptoed after me as I made my way through the living room and up the stairs. Even though Ethan wasn't there, it felt like our new hobby of house burglary should be conducted in stealth mode.

'This was your home?' Jack whispered.

'Yeah.'

'It's a bit bare, isn't it?'

I glanced around at the white walls, unsullied with anything as vulgar as a picture, and the naked boards of the floor.

'It's minimalist. Ethan likes that.'

'Seems pretty sterile to me.'

I pushed open the study door. 'It'll be in here. Bottom drawer.'

But when I knelt and opened the drawer where the passports were usually kept, there was nothing but a pile of old bank statements. I felt a stab of panic.

'It's not here, Jack!'

'What?'

'My passport. It always lives here. Oh God! He's not hidden

it, has he? Taken it to work? I bet he knew I'd be back for it and he... bastard!'

I started rifling frantically through the drawer, chucking the bank statements here, there and everywhere as I tried to find the passport. If I couldn't get my hands on it, the only other way I could prove my identity was with my birth certificate, and I had no idea where that was. At Mum's somewhere, probably, and I sure as hell wasn't going there for it. It'd taken my last shred of courage to risk coming here.

'Kitty...'

'It's not here, Jack! What the hell's he done with it? I can't go without it.'

'Kitty!'

I stopped rifling to look up at him. He was holding one of the bank statements, frowning at it.

'What?' I said. 'Why do you look like that?'

'Have you seen these? Did he ever let you see them?'

'Bank statements? Well, no.' I yanked open the drawer above the one I'd been searching and let out a sigh of relief when I spotted the little red passport nestling there. 'Oh, thank God, it's here. He's been reorganising, that's all.' I scooped it up like an old friend and tucked it into my jeans back pocket. 'Hey, wonder if we can find my bank card while we're here? If he hasn't already had it stopped, I might be able to make one big withdrawal before he gets wise and cancels it.'

'You won't be able to.'

I frowned. 'What?'

'Kit, these statements—'

He stopped, and my heart did too. Because there was a sound coming from downstairs. The sound of a key, turning in the lock. I jumped to my feet.

'I thought you said he was at work!' Jack hissed.

'He is – I mean, he should be! Oh *shit*! What do we do, Jack?'

'It's too late. You'll have to confront him.'

'I told you I can't!' A panicked sob bubbled out of me. 'We have to get out.'

'You can do it. I'll be here with you.' He reached for my hand. 'You're stronger than you think you are, Kitty.'

'No, please! You don't know what he can do to me. Maybe we can hide until he—'

But the deep voice that sailed up the stairs made it quite clear that wasn't an option.

'Kitty! Where are you? I know you're here.'

I felt like a cornered animal. My eyes darted around the little room, but there was no way out except the door. The door that any second now, if the footsteps on the stairs were anything to go by, would be filled by Ethan's lean frame.

'You don't have to be afraid of him any more,' Jack whispered, and he squeezed my shoulder.

A second later… there was Ethan. Instinctively, I took a step backwards.

'Kitty, darling! You're really here.'

I don't know what I'd expected. Anger. Blame. But Ethan actually laughed with delight as he threw himself at me for a hug. 'Mrs Bartholomew said you'd come home, but I wouldn't

71

believe it until I'd seen you,' he said. 'Oh my God, baby, I've missed you so much. So much. Don't ever, ever scare me like that again, you hear?'

I blinked helplessly at Jack as Ethan continued to embrace me.

'It's okay now,' he said in a soothing voice, obviously under the impression I needed a bit of soothing. 'Everything's okay now, Kitty. We can make it okay.'

'Ethan, please,' I whispered. 'Let me go.'

'Yes, sorry. Sorry. I just had to feel you, make sure you were real.' He released me from the hug, but he kept hold of my shoulders, regarding me with undisguised joy. 'You've really come back to me. Thank God.'

Jack, lounging against the wall observing it all, cleared his throat. Ethan turned to look at him, as if he was noticing him for the first time.

'Kitty, who the hell is this?'

'A friend,' Jack said.

Ethan's eyes narrowed. For the first time, I think it dawned on him that my being there might not mean what he thought it meant.

'I'm not staying,' I mumbled, staring at the floor. I couldn't bring myself to meet his eyes. 'I just came...'

But the words stopped in my throat. There was something about his presence that, even now, even after what he'd done, still cowed me. I felt like a naughty little girl. I felt guilty for the obvious hurt in his eyes. I felt... exactly the way he'd trained me to feel when I'd upset him.

'Of course you're staying,' he said firmly. 'Look, I don't know what happened to make you run off like that, Kitty. Nearly giving me a heart attack with worry—' He took a deep breath to calm himself. 'Well, never mind that, we can talk about it another time. For now, let's just concentrate on the fact you're home safe.'

He put his arms around me again. I didn't push him away. I didn't hug him. I just stood, stiff and silent, wondering if I was going to be sick, and hating myself for letting him affect me like this, still. Why did he have that power over me, even now I knew the kind of man he was? I was so used to pleasing him, putting all my wants and needs aside for his, that it was a real fight with myself to break the habit.

Jack was frowning at me. 'Tell him, Kit. Tell him you're coming with me.'

I opened my mouth, but the words struggled to form into sounds.

Ethan glared at Jack. 'Who asked you anything? Who the hell are you anyway?'

'I told you. A friend of Kitty's.'

Ethan held me back to look into my eyes, his lip curling in disgust. 'Jesus. Tell me you're not sleeping with this guy.'

All I could do was shake my head.

'Some might say that's none of your business,' Jack said. I noticed he was no longer lounging and had drawn himself up to his full height.

'None of my business? This is my wife, mate! What the fuck do you think you're playing at, messing about with married women? Get the hell out of my house, before I get the police involved.'

73

'It's Kitty's house too. And I'm not going anywhere without her say-so.'

'I'm not your wife,' I finally managed to gasp. 'Not in any real sense. I left you, Ethan. Me and you – there is no me and you. Not any more.' Jack gave me an approving nod.

'Why are you talking like this, Kitty? What did I do?'

'You know what you did. At the reception. At the... the trees. I saw.'

Ethan frowned. 'Saw what?'

'You. What you...' But I couldn't bring myself to say it.

He laughed. 'Oh, this is ridiculous. I don't know what you imagined you saw, but...' He softened his voice to a croon. 'You're not well, darling. You need a bit of TLC, that's all. And then we'll get everything sorted out, take a delayed honeymoon, whatever you want.'

'And how were you planning to pay for that, Ethan?' Jack asked brightly.

Ethan blinked at him. 'Sorry, what?'

He yanked the bank statement he'd been looking at earlier out of his pocket and held it out. 'Kitty, take a look at this.'

'Give me that.' Ethan tried to snatch it off him but Jack held it high above his head.

'You know there's a law against reading people's confidential documents?' Ethan demanded. 'I could have you in court, whoever you are.'

'Is there a law against Kitty reading it? Because from what I hear, a good chunk of what's in this account is hers, regardless of your name being on the front.' He barged Ethan out of the way and pushed the statement into my hand.

74

I stared at it in shock. 'Six grand overdrawn! What the hell is this, Ethan?'

His cheeks had flushed crimson now. 'That's my business.'

'Your business? It's my fucking money!' My fear of him was entirely swallowed up in a sudden, white-hot ball of anger. 'You told me we had thousands put away. Where is it?'

'I invested it. Stocks and shares.' He took my hand in his. 'For both our sakes, Kitty. You know you were always stupid with money.'

I snatched my hand away. 'How would you know? You never let me manage my own money.' I stared at the statement again. 'All our savings, and six grand besides! How could you lose all that?'

'Just a couple of duff investments,' he said, staring at the floor. 'I was still learning how it all worked then. Now I've got the hang of it, if we apply for the money in your ISA—'

I actually laughed. 'You think you're getting your hands on my dad's money? Oh, no. Not a chance.'

'You selfish—' He looked angry now. 'Of course. I should've known you'd find a way to make this all my fault, when for a year you've been bleeding me fucking dry, demanding the big white wedding from hell plus all the trimmings. How much was that dress, eh?'

'Me? You were the one who planned the whole thing!'

'Because I thought it was what you wanted. Isn't that every girl's dream? God, I've nearly bankrupted myself trying to make you happy,' he snapped. 'You can be an ungrateful bitch, you know that, Kitty?'

I shook my head. 'Christ. Did I really love you?'

It almost felt like a dream now, those feelings, that life. When it came to Ethan, my eyes had been well and truly opened.

'Right. That's enough.' Jack held out his hand to me. 'Come on, Kit.'

'Where the hell do you think you're going?' Ethan demanded as I took Jack's hand and turned to go.

'Anywhere that isn't here. Anywhere that doesn't have you in it,' I said. 'Bye, Ethan. Oh, and in case it wasn't clear the last time, I'm leaving you. Expect to hear from a lawyer at some point.'

'Kitty, please!' He made his eyes wide. 'What about me? What will I do about all this debt? We're six grand overdrawn here.'

'No, Ethan, *you're* six grand overdrawn.' I smiled brightly. 'See, I don't actually have a bank account.'

I let Jack lead me back down the stairs and out of the front door.

'Wait!' I heard Ethan shout. I glanced over my shoulder and saw him running after us. 'Kitty! Don't you *dare* walk away from me!'

'Come on.' Jack took my arm and we burst into a sprint. I think he could sense I was too drained for another confrontation, and Ethan sounded dangerous.

'You're my wife, Kitty!' he shouted after us, drawing a shocked stare from Mrs Bartholomew in her garden. 'You're my fucking wife! Hear me? Mine! Get back here, now.'

'Drive,' I said to Jack as soon as we were back in the camper. Ethan chased us down the road until we eventually sped out of sight, leaving him an angry speck in the distance.

'You okay?' Jack asked once we were back on the road. I was panting heavily, and I could see in the mirror that the blood had drained from my face.

'No. Not really.' I summoned a wobbly grin. 'But God, that felt good.'

Chapter 8

I rang through four old uni friends from out of town before I finally got hold of someone who was willing to give me sofa space for a little while.

When it was all arranged, I hung up Jack's mobile and beamed at him. 'Sorted. Surinder says I can stay with her.'

'Didn't sound like she was too happy about it.'

'Well, hopefully it won't be for long. I've got nowhere else I can go.'

'You know, you could stay if you want. Here, with me. I kind of like having you around.'

His keen eyes flickered over my face, and I felt my cheeks pinken.

'I can't live in this thing forever though, can I?'

'Why not? I'm going to.'

'But you're... you. And we can't all illustrate books for a living. I need to find some work.'

Plus there was the other thing. I'd been noticing it more lately: the lingering looks, the... the something. Not just on his side, from me too.

What with one thing and another, we'd been together in

the van nearly a month. And the natural result of our confined quarters was an intense closeness, both physically and, increasingly, emotionally. I could sense there was something building between me and Jack, something inevitable, and with my head still reeling from the fallout of my relationship with Ethan, I was worried I was in danger of... let's say, of making choices that might not be for the best right now.

'Okay,' Jack said, dropping my hands. He looked disappointed. 'If that's what you want. I'll miss you though, Kit.'

'We'll stay in touch, won't we?'

'Course we will.' He smiled. 'For you, I might even keep my phone switched on.'

***

We set off that afternoon. We'd been camping near Derby and Surinder and her husband lived down in London, so we had a long drive ahead.

'So how did you say you knew this girl?' Jack asked when we were almost halfway there. 'University, was it?'

'Jack...'

'Hmm?'

'Jack!' My voice was urgent. 'Can you pull over?'

'Not car-sick, are you?'

'It's the puppies. I think they might be coming.'

In the rear-view mirror I could see Sandy squirming, shifting her hindquarters constantly from one side of the van to the other. I'd noticed her at it for a good quarter of an hour, looking steadily more uncomfortable as the van rocked on its way. Her mouth hung open, and a whispered, wheezy moan was coming from the back of her throat. As I watched, a shudder ran across her tight, round belly.

Jack glanced over his shoulder and his eyes widened. 'Shit! You're right.'

'What do we do?' I said. 'Can we get her to a vet? Oh God, Jack!'

'Stay calm, lass, I've done this before. You sit with her while I get us to a campsite. There's one with pitches for campers half an hour away.' He looked at Sandy again. 'Cross your legs, old girl.'

When we reached the campsite, Jack grabbed Sandy's blanket from the back of the passenger seat and chucked it to me.

'Cover her. I don't think we really want to explain to the site owner why we've got a dog having puppies in the back.'

I draped the blanket over Sandy. She gave a pathetic whine, looking up at me with eyes that begged me to make the pain stop. God, I hoped it'd be quick for her.

Luckily she was quiet while we checked in. Jack drove us round to our pitch and parked up, then sorted out the power hookup so we could have a bit of light. When he'd done that he came to join me.

Sandy looked at her dad and opened her mouth, but no sound came out. Another shiver ran along her belly.

'Not too long.' He patted her. 'Doing well, Sand. You're very brave.'

She wagged her tail with a few limp thumps.

'Let's get her into her bed,' Jack said. 'Lift her head.'

I did as he asked, and with an effort we eased a lightly whimpering Sandy into the dog bed.

'For your own good, girl,' Jack said, looking guilty at the discomfort he was causing. 'I want you and the babies to be comfortable, that's all.'

'What do we do, Jack?' I asked in a whisper when Sandy was curled awkwardly in her little bed, panting. 'You sure we shouldn't take her to a vet?'

'It's fine. I grew up on a farm, I've done this hundreds of times.' He went over to the tall cupboard next to the kitchenette and took out a cardboard box. 'Just need my puppy delivery kit.'

'What's in it?' I asked when he'd knelt back down.

'Take a look.'

I peered into the box. Inside was a shoebox, pair of scissors, post-it note and a one-litre bottle of vodka.

I frowned. 'What's all this stuff? I thought we needed hot towels and lukewarm water or something.'

'That's for babies,' he said. 'I mean, human babies. Dogs tend to sort themselves out. We won't need to interfere unless there's complications.'

I took out the shoebox and shook it.

'It's empty.'

'Yeah. Hopefully it'll stay that way.'

'Oh. I see.' I put it back and looked at the post-it note stuck to the bottom of the box. There was a phone number scrawled on it. 'What's that?'

'Twenty-four-hour helpline if she gets into difficulties. They can talk us through it, or put us in touch with an out-of-hours

81

vet if it has to come to that. And sterilised scissors, in case we have to cut any out of their sacks.'

'And what's the vodka for? Antiseptic?'

'No.' He unscrewed the lid, took a drink and passed it to me. 'For us. It's going to be a long night.'

I shot the vodka bottle a wary glance. 'My friend's expecting me though.'

'Sorry. Act of God,' he said, looking at Sandy. 'You can stay one more night, can't you? Then we'll get you a taxi to the station tomorrow so you can go the rest of the way. I won't be able to move Sand for a fortnight or so after the babies come.'

I felt a wave of relief at having an excuse to stay another night. Much as I knew it needed to happen, I'd been feeling increasingly anxious about the impending separation all through our drive.

'Okay, I'll text Surinder. Couldn't leave you to bring the pups on your own.' I took a swig of vodka and passed it back. It felt like we were sealing a pact, somehow.

After he'd drunk some, he put down the bottle and curled his arm around me. 'Thanks, Kit. Feel like I need you tonight.'

I turned my attention to Sandy. Her face was full of resigned pain. When I placed my hand against her hot belly, it felt like the puppies were dancing the tarantella in there.

'Poor little girl,' I said. 'You'll have to get her sterilised, Jack. She can't keep having litters, it's not healthy.'

'Yeah, I know. Just bad luck this time. She was only a pup when I got her. I wanted to wait till she was a bit older before

82

I took her to the vet, then the first time a boy got near her...'
He shook his head. 'Too late.'

'What is it with you and rescuing things anyway?' I said,
smiling. 'If it's not mistreated dogs, it's destitute women.'

He smiled back. 'Suppose I am building a bit of a reputa-
tion in that area. Hey, you know where there's any aquariums
round here? Always wanted a pet turtle, maybe there's one'll
want rescuing.'

I laughed. 'No, sorry. So did you really live on a farm?'

'Just a little one. My parents had a few acres over in County
Wicklow, where I grew up. Then they moved to Scotland.'

'Do you still have family in Ireland?'

'Mikey, my big brother – he took the farm on after Mam
and Dad retired. Grandparents. Few aunts and uncles.'

'Go back much?'

'When I can,' he said. 'It's a beautiful place, not far from
the sea. You been to Ireland?'

'No. I worked on a city guide to Dublin once.'

He smiled. 'All right, where have you been? Anywhere other
than Alicante?'

'Blackpool?'

'Wow. Exotic.'

Sandy let out a long, low whine. A small black bag had
started to emerge behind her.

'There's the first one,' Jack said in a hushed tone. He took
another swig of vodka and passed it to me.

When Sandy had shaken herself free of the puppy, it lay
by her feet in a little wriggling sack. Its mum blinked at it,
looking puzzled.

'What do we do?' I asked Jack in a panicked whisper. 'Do we need the scissors?'

'Give it a second, let instinct kick in,' he whispered back.

After a couple more seconds, Sandy bit the bag open and her first tiny baby spilled out in a mess of goo and life. She chewed off the umbilical cord then gave the little chap a vigorous clean with her tongue, and we watched as he squirmed his way blindly to her flank, attached himself to one teat and suckled noisily. Sandy shivered again as another contraction rippled through her, but she didn't make a sound.

'It should get easier for her now,' Jack said.

I looked at the little puppy. He wasn't yellow like Sandy but black, with a piping of white running around his collar.

'What colour's the dad?' I asked Jack.

He laughed. 'Brown, or I thought he was. Starting to wonder if Sand's been putting it about.'

I tickled Sandy between the ears. 'Slutty girl.'

'Definitely Jack Russell stock though,' he said, examining the pup. 'That's good. If they've got the ratter gene, I should have a home for them.'

'How can you tell?' I asked. 'He looks a bit rat-like himself at the moment.'

'Shape of the muzzle. Long and thin.'

I squinted at the puppy, sucking against Sandy's belly as she regarded him with a comical mixture of pride, affection and surprise.

'He's very tiny, isn't he?' I said. 'I mean, even for a baby. They seemed bigger when I felt her tummy.'

'You're right. Think we're looking at the runt here.'

'Can I pet him?'

'One finger, very quick. Sandy won't be keen.'

I brushed the little pup with the tip of my finger. His skin felt warm and silken. As soon as I'd withdrawn my hand Sandy started washing him again, as if to get the stench of stinky human off his magnificent doginess.

'Aww. Lovely, isn't he?' I said, simpering. 'Clever old Sandy.'

Jack shot me a concerned glance. 'Listen, Kit. Try not to get too attached, okay?'

'Why?'

'It's a risky time, the first twenty-four hours. And I don't want to scare you, but the little ones – well, they don't always make it. I don't want to see you upset if it's bad news in the morning.'

'Oh.' I looked at the little pup, his tiny eyes glued closed and his pink mouth clamped around Sandy's teat. 'Okay, I'll... try not to.'

He gave my shoulder a squeeze. 'He'll probably be fine. Just wanted to warn you.'

'Yeah. Thanks.'

'Look, can you mind her a bit? I want to get the awnings up before the light gives out.'

I turned wide eyes on him. 'You're leaving me? What if another pup comes?'

'I'll just be outside. Anyway, Sandy knows what she's doing.' He gave the nursing dog a pat. 'She's a smart little thing. Just leave her to it and yell for me if she seems to be having trouble.'

But by the time Jack had finished getting the awnings up,

there was still no sign of another puppy. Sandy was panting contentedly while she fed her single baby, although I'd noticed the shivers across her tummy getting more pronounced.

'Next one's on its way,' Jack said when he came back in, glancing at his dog's rippling flank. 'Textbook so far. Looks like we'll be all right.'

'Fingers crossed.' I passed him the vodka as he sat down next to me and he took a glug.

My eyes were drawn to Sandy, whimpering with quiet pathos. The next puppy had started to emerge.

'It's coming,' I said in an awed whisper.

'So it is.' Jack kissed the top of my head. It felt like the right thing, just then.

For this birth, Sandy got to her feet. Her firstborn sucked blindly at the air as he wondered where his meal had gone.

When the furry jellybean was free of his mum's little doggy body, there was no hesitation. She bit him out of his bag and cleaned him up, and minutes later the newbie was suckling happily next to his brother – or sister, the sexing would have to come later. Somehow it felt like all dogs were male by default, just as all cats were female.

The new boy was a solid chocolate, and nearly a third as big again as his older sibling. He didn't have the long, thin muzzle Jack had pointed out as the hallmark of a Jack Russell, instead bearing the rounder snout of his mother.

'Brown.' Jack gave Sandy a rub between the ears. 'Sorry I slandered you, girl. Looks like it was Ben's old mutt who did the deed after all.'

Sandy was whimpering again, and her contractions seemed

to be closer together. Sure enough, ten minutes later the next pup's head was visible, and she stood to finish the birth.

'That was quick,' I said, taking the vodka from Jack and swallowing about a quarter-shot's worth. Puppy midwifery was a stressful business.

'Yeah, there's not really any rhyme or reason to these things. Sometimes it's minutes between births, sometimes hours.' Jack looked at me as I rubbed a fist in my eye. 'No need for you to stay up though. I can see to Sandy.'

'And leave you on your own? Not a chance.' I squeezed his hand. 'You said you needed me and here I am.'

He flung me a grateful smile. 'Thanks, Kit.'

I looked at the newest pup. Sandy had freed it of its sack and was giving it a good wash, but the tiny thing just lay there. It didn't wiggle, and it didn't join its siblings at the all-you-can-drink milk bar. It just... lay there.

'Why doesn't it move, Jack?' I asked quietly.

He was looking at it with concern. 'Sorry, girl,' he said to Sandy. 'You won't like this but it has to be done.'

Jack scooped up the little dog. Sandy gave a faint warning growl, but she didn't try to stop him. Its tiny body looked limp and lifeless in his hand.

He lifted it to his ear. 'Not breathing.'

'Dead?' I whispered.

'No. Heart's beating.' Jack held the puppy between his two hands and rubbed it vigorously. 'Do me a favour, Kit. There's cotton buds in the big cupboard, can you grab one?'

'Okay.' I got them from the cupboard and handed one to Jack.

Very carefully, he cleaned the puppy's nose and mouth, then started rubbing it between his hands again. Sandy watched him nervously. After a minute, the puppy made a noise like it was choking on a fly, and I saw it squirm.

'Thank God,' Jack said with a low whistle of relief.

He laid the puppy gently down by its mum, who shot him a glare of displeasure – fine thanks for saving her baby's life, but that's dogs for you – before giving the little pup a violent wash until he smelled right. Then she dragged him by the scruff to her flank. After a couple of seconds, he managed to clamp himself to a teat and suckle.

'Airway got blocked up on the way out,' Jack said. 'A bit of milk'll soon get his strength up.'

I fixed him with an impressed gaze. 'How did you know what to do?'

He smiled. 'Like I said. Not my first time.'

He stretched his arm round me again, and I tried to work out what I was feeling as I settled into it. I think it was… pride. Yes, that was it. I was proud of Jack, and the kind of man he was. And I was proud that I was the one snuggled into his arm right now; that in some sense, he'd chosen me.

So many times when I'd been with Ethan, he'd managed to make me feel worthless. There'd be some offhand comment or insult that would hit home, and if I'd shown him just how much it hurt he'd tell me it was only 'banter', that I was being oversensitive as usual, until I really started to believe I was the unreasonable one.

Jack never make me feel like that. He made me feel like I was somebody who mattered. Somebody he needed.

As we waited for the next puppy, a warm contentment filled me. There was something so pure, so simple and honest and real, about life in the camper. The nights spent playing games, or reading together in quiet serenity. Delivering the puppies, side by side, like a team: like equals. It was so different to my life with Ethan; the dinner parties with his dull work colleagues, the corporate functions, all that grown-up stuff. Now I'd experienced life with Jack, that whole existence just seemed so shallow and artificial. And the feelings I'd once believed I had for Ethan seemed the most shallow of all.

Chapter 9

'Kitty.'

I grunted and wiggled my head deeper into the pillow. It felt lumpy, and I headbutted it a couple of times to smooth it out.

'Okay, ow. Kitty, wake up.'

Blinking my eyes open, I discovered my pillow was actually Jack's shoulder. I was nestled into the arm he had around me, and it was pitch dark outside.

'Oh. Sorry,' I said, hastily wiping away a bit of drool that had escaped from the side of my mouth. 'How long was I asleep?'

'Over an hour. It's after ten.'

I glanced at Sandy, now with five little puppies suckling against her. Her tummy was still shivering.

'How many more, do you think?'

'One, maybe two.' Jack turned to me. 'Look, let me sort the bed out and you can get some proper sleep. I can take it from here.'

'No, I'm okay, I want to...' I broke off to yawn. '... Stay up. You need me.'

He laughed. 'Not as much as you need a good night's rest. Go on, zombie Kitty. Bedtime.'

'You can't tell me what to do,' I said, folding my arms. 'I'm a big girl. I'm allowed to stay up late as I like.'

'My van, my rules, young lady. Go on, go do your girl stuff in the toilet block. I'll get the bed up.'

I was too knackered to argue. I hunted out the washbag we'd been sharing and went to get ready for bed.

When I got back, the bed was made, Jack's fat feather duvet spread across it invitingly.

'Sure you'll be okay on your own?' I asked.

'I'll be fine. I'll wake you up if you're needed, promise.'

'Well... okay, if you promise.' A deep yawn escaped me. 'Night, Jack.'

He smiled as I climbed into bed. 'Hey, remember I once told you some things seemed too important not to happen?'

'Yeah, why?'

'This is the second time now something outside our control's occurred to keep you here. You should think about that.'

***

I did think about it. It whirled around my brain as I fell asleep. I'd never believed in fate, but... first flu, now puppies. It did feel like some external force was acting to keep me with Jack.

Oh, it was silly. It was just coincidence. And my subconscious, maybe, trying to trick me into staying. I didn't want to leave the camper so my brain was looking for excuses to stay.

Pull yourself together, Kitty. Magical thinking won't fix anything. It's time to stand on your own two feet.

For the first time in your life, it's time to…

My inner monologue faded to black.

I woke in pitch darkness, feeling anxious without quite knowing why. But my brain quickly updated itself.

The puppies…

When I yanked the curtain across, I could just make out Jack's slumbering form in the swivelled passenger seat by Sandy's dog bed.

'You asleep, love?' I said softly.

His head jerked up. 'Hmm? No. Resting my eyes.'

'God, I bet you're freezing. Here, get yourself under the covers.'

He came over to sit on the edge of the bed and snuggled gratefully under a corner of duvet.

'How's Sandy?' I asked.

'Fine.' He flicked on a light so I could take a look. 'She's a natural at the mothering business. Aren't you, eh, brave girl?'

Sandy wagged her tail tiredly for him.

I squinted at the little nest. The new mum was lying on her side, looking spent, while six tiny babies suckled noisily against her. It looked like either Jack or Sandy herself had cleaned up the whelping area, which was now free of blood, goop and other icky but necessary accompaniments to new life.

Jack nodded to the lidded shoebox by the passenger seat. 'Not all good news though. Sorry, Kitty.'

'Oh God, not the tiny one?'

'No, he's doing grand, having a slap-up feed under his brother there,' Jack said, pointing out the runt of the litter for me. 'This is one that never had a chance. Stillborn, poor little fecker. I tried to save him but he must've been dead before she got him out.'

'You should've got me up,' I said gently. 'Must've been horrible bringing him on your own.'

'Sandy did it, not me. Old girl seemed to think she could lick him to life. Broke my heart to take him off her.' He sighed. 'Well, not the first time.'

'You've seen this before?'

'Yeah, stillbirths were common enough on the farm. Lambs, calves, dogs... you'd think you'd get used to it, but, well, you don't.' He turned wet eyes to me. 'How d'you feel about hugging me then? I could feel pretty good about it.'

He looked so vulnerable, just then; so badly in need of comfort. I folded him up in an embrace and he wrapped his arms around my waist, sighing.

'It's been nice having you here, you know,' he murmured by my ear. 'I've been alone a long time. Forgot it could be like this.'

So there had been a time he hadn't been alone. I wondered, but I didn't ask.

'It's been nice being here,' was all I said, enjoying the security of his body against mine.

'This reminds me of the first time I saw a stillbirth,' Jack said when we'd hugged a while. 'That was a dog too – our border collie, Poppy, one of her litter. I was so excited when she went into labour that my parents said I could stay up to see her whelp, and then the last one out was this poor little mite, dead on delivery. I'd never known anything die before.'

'How old were you?'

'Four or five. I remember asking my mam why the tiny thing didn't move like the others. I mean, it had all the same parts. I couldn't get why it wouldn't crawl and breathe and feed the same as its brothers and sisters. It just slept, and we put it in the ground and said a prayer, and Mam, she had to tell me best as she could why it wouldn't be waking up.' He gave a bleak laugh. 'Ah well, silly to get upset: that's how it is in nature. Growing up on a farm, you get used to animals being two-a-penny.'

I held him back to see his face. His eyes were shining with tears.

'Jack...'

'Yeah?'

'Why did you look after me when you first found me?'

'Because you needed someone, I guess. And I happened to be the one who tripped over you.'

'Not because you needed someone?'

'Hm?'

I glanced down at what I was wearing. This so obviously wasn't about a puppy.

'Who did these pyjamas belong to, Jack?'

'Just... someone. Someone I knew.'

'Lost someone, didn't you, love?' I whispered.

He smiled sadly. 'How did you know?'

'I just did.'

'You too?' he asked.

'Yeah. Me too.'

'Who?'

'My dad, last year. Undiagnosed brain tumour. He wasn't very old. Only forty-eight.'

'Poor Kit. I'm sorry.'

'What about you?'

He snuffled against my shoulder. 'My wife. Sophie, my wife.'

'Your wife! How?'

I heard him choke on a sob, and I sucked in my lip.

'Sorry,' I said softly. 'Rule One, right?'

'No... no, I want to tell you.' He was silent a moment as he struggled to get his tears under control. 'There was an accident. We were shopping. She... I mean, I only turned away for a second, Kit.' His voice was laced with desperation: almost pleading, like I was in any position to make it right for him. 'Just a second. That was all it took.' He gave a grim laugh. 'Isn't that just fucking ridiculous? That that was all it took?'

Rule Four. Never run away, never get out of my sight...

'What happened?' I whispered.

'We were buying stuff for the van. We'd just got it, for holidays or whatever, and Soph was all excited, you know? Spotted something in a shop across the road. I was looking in some window. Bookshop, I remember. Load of Ian Rankins, pretty cheap, thought they'd while away the nights.' He laughed again. It was the most depressing sound I'd ever heard. 'Funny what you remember, right? There was this weird muffled thump, totally insignificant. And when I turned around, there she was, lying in the road. I mean, not her, not really. But the outside. No fanfare, no screams. Just... no Sophie.'

'Jesus, Jack, you poor lamb. Oh God, you poor lamb! Come here to me.' I held him tight against me. 'When?' I whispered into his hair.

'Two years ago. Never read an Ian Rankin again, I can tell you that.' He laughed again, then broke off in sobs.

'You know it wasn't your fault, don't you?'

'I know. Doesn't stop me running through over and over again what might've happened if I'd turned just a split-second sooner.'

'You couldn't have done anything.'

'I'll never know, will I? Because I didn't turn. God, some days I don't know who I'm angrier at: Soph or myself. Or whatever bastard higher power's responsible for such an unfair fucking thing. The last one mainly, I think.'

I shushed him softly, waiting for all the tears of anger and frustration and grief to spend themselves in my shoulder.

'That's when—' he paused to gulp back a sob '—when I started travelling. Couldn't bear to stay in the house. The smell of it, the colours, the walls...' I felt him shudder. 'Christ, it made me nauseous. So I took the van and ran away.' He laughed through his tears. 'See, you're not the only expert round here.'

I pressed a kiss to the top of his head, cradled in the crook of my shoulder.

'Why are you telling me this, Jack?'

'Well, because you asked.'

'You know what I mean. I can tell it's hurting you, talking about it.'

'It helps though. Been a long time since I had someone to talk to who came on two legs instead of four.' He wiped his eyes and cast a glance at his watch. 'Sorry, Kit. Didn't mean to unload on you. Too much vodka, I think. Look, it's past one, you should get back to sleep. I can grab some kip across the front seats, keep an eye on Sand and the kiddies.'

'No need for you to be uncomfortable,' I said, flushing slightly. 'You can stay here. Share with me.'

He leaned back to look into my face.

'Are you sure?'

'Yeah. I know it wouldn't... well, we're friends, aren't we?'

'Okay. If you really don't mind.'

He flicked off the light and clambered in next to me fully clothed.

Once he was under the duvet, he kept himself at a little distance, as if wondering what the etiquette of platonic bed-sharing was.

'Will I hold you now?' he asked quietly.

In answer, I snuggled up against his warm body. I felt him exhale as he wrapped his arms around me.

'This is nice,' he whispered, pulling me close against him and burying his face in my hair. 'Been a while since I got a cuddle at bedtime.'

'Yeah.' I let out a contented sigh. 'It is nice.'

'Here. Look at me.' He put one finger under my chin to tilt my face up and sought my eyes in the almost-darkness, a sliver of moonlight through the clouds our only illumination. He brushed a few strands of hair gently from my cheeks. 'I'll miss you, Kit.'

'Will you call me?'

'Whenever I can get a signal. You sure you won't stay?'

'I can't, Jack. I've scrounged off you too long. Time I made my own way.'

'Sofa-surfing, you mean?'

'Till I can afford my own place, yeah.'

He was silent a moment.

'Suppose I offered you a job?' he said at last.

I frowned. 'What?'

'I'm serious. I've needed someone for a while to help me out with the book stuff. Set up signings, send out review copies, deal with fan mail...'

'You get fan mail?'

'Yeah, quite a bit. I could really do with a PA-type person. Someone canny, good at writing, publishing background. Someone like you.'

I squinted one eye at him. 'Hmm.'

'I'd pay you a fair salary, month in advance,' he said, sensing my doubts. 'Enough to keep you going till your savings come through. Room and board included, of course.'

'You can't really need someone. You're just trying to help me out, aren't you?'

'I do, honestly! My agent's been nagging me for ages to hire someone to update my website, deal with press, that kind of thing. I hate all that. I just want to draw.'

'You really mean it?'

'On my word as a good Catholic boy.'

I cocked an eyebrow and he grinned. 'Okay, okay. On my word as a gentleman then. I'll show you the emails if you don't believe me.'

'But I've got no experience.'

'You're smart. You can write. You're good with people, and you know the industry.' He paused. 'You know me pretty well too, that's a skill in itself. What else do you need?'

'You promise this isn't just... you know, because you're lonely?'

He shrugged. 'We're both people who life has shoved through the mangle a bit, aren't we? I trust you, Kitty: more than anyone I've known in a long time. And if you were up for throwing your lot in with me – well, I think I'd like that.' He caught my look. 'Just good friends, if that's what you want.'

I thought about what had been building between us lately. The long looks, the unspoken... something. I thought about where we were now, cuddling in bed together. About the intensity of the tiny living quarters we'd have to share. About Sophie. And Ethan.

But if he really needed someone, it was a great opportunity. I mean, Jack Duffy, much-loved children's author: that wasn't nothing. Plus a month's pay in advance, my independence guaranteed without having to borrow...

Any nagging feeling that I was just looking for an excuse to stay with the man who'd helped me, who made me feel safe, and in whose arms I currently lay, was quickly silenced.

'Only if you want to stay,' Jack said, reading my thoughts. 'I want you to stay because you want to.'

I did want to. I just wasn't sure I ought to.

'Let me sleep on it,' I said at last. 'It's a big decision.'

'Okay.' He pressed a soft kiss to my forehead. 'Night then, lass.'

I smiled at him in the pale moon glow. 'Night, Jack. See you in the morning.'

He soon fell asleep, his head nestled comfortably against my chest. It took me a few hours longer. I couldn't help noticing how Jack's hand, holding my wrist as he slept, twitched like a dog dreaming of the hunt.

Chapter 10

When I woke, Jack was gone, a slight depression in the mattress the only evidence of his presence next to me the night before. He'd been the perfect gentleman all through those long hours in each other's arms, never letting go of me except occasionally to go check on the puppies.

'Hiya, Kit,' he said when I emerged. He was at the hob, cooking. 'Sleep okay?'

'Hm... not bad,' I said, stifling a yawn. 'Aren't you supposed to wish me top o' the mornin'? Thought that's what your people did.'

'Mmmm. I love the smell of stereotypes in the morning.' He waggled his wooden spoon in my direction. 'Any more of that and I'll be cracking out the "ee bah gums". Don't think I won't do it.'

'Where're the pups?' I asked, scanning the bare floor.

'Sandy moved them out into the awning. Dogs'll do that sometimes. It's a survival instinct, not nesting too long in one place.' He poked at the lumpy yellow mess in his pan with the spoon. 'I'm making scrambled egg on toast, you want some?'

'Please.' I glanced at the scrambled egg. 'Looks a bit dry. How much milk did you put in?'

He frowned. 'Milk?'

'What, you didn't put any in?' I pointed to the pan. 'What's that then?'

'Well, egg. Isn't that what goes in scrambled egg?'

'Yeah, with the milk.' I shook my head. 'And I thought you had this *Good Life* bollocks sorted. Here, let me.'

I swung myself out of bed and took the spoon off him.

'Got butter?' I asked. 'No point adding milk now it's set.'

He handed me a block from the little square fridge under the worktop. I sliced off a chunk and chucked it in the pan.

'All right, you sort coffee while I finish this,' I said.

'Fair enough so.' He filled the kettle and put it on the other ring of the hob. 'You always this bossy when you're making breakfast?'

'Yep. Mugs.'

'Yes mistress.' He grabbed a couple of mugs from the draining board and spooned coffee granules into them. 'So?'

'So what?'

'You slept on it. Did you make a decision?'

'Oh.' I prodded the scrambled eggs. 'No, I... not yet. Still thinking.'

Actually, I'd been thinking all night, turning it over in my mind long after Jack had drifted into sleep. I just didn't know what to do for the best.

Okay, I certainly didn't want to sleep on Surinder's sofa, doing whatever minimum-wage bar work I could get while I waited for a decent job opening, but... but staying with Jack felt dangerous. Only last month, the organ in my chest that I used for blood circulation and romantic attachment had been damaged almost beyond repair. Throwing it in harm's way again so soon afterwards, with this man I now knew was dealing with his own pain and grief, didn't feel like the wisest idea.

And yet I wanted to stay. So much. Wrenching myself away felt like almost physical pain.

'What's the matter?' Jack asked softly, looking into my face.

'Nothing.'

'Liar.'

He brushed a saltwater droplet from the corner of my eye. He didn't move his hand, letting it rest against my cheek while his gaze darted over my features.

I knew what I must look like, with my first-thing-in-the-morning face on and my hair frizzy and tangled. I flushed, dipping my head.

'None of that.' He put one finger under my chin to guide my face up. 'You're beautiful.'

'Now who's a liar?' I said with a smile. 'You know I look like hell.'

'You're beautiful,' he said firmly. 'Even when you look like hell.'

'How does that work then, charmer?'

He shrugged. 'You'd always be beautiful, no matter how rough you looked.' He stroked his thumb tip over my cheek. 'It's the eyes, I think. You've got Audrey Hepburn eyes, Kit.'

My stomach was hopping now. His face was close to mine, and I could sense he wanted to kiss me.

This was wrong. Or at the very least, it was bloody bad timing. But in that brief moment it felt like all there was in the world was Jack Duffy, saying nice things about my eyes and moving his delicious parted lips slowly closer to mine.

Suddenly he released me and turned back to the kettle, which had started whistling.

'You going to grab a shower before breakfast?'

'What?'

'I'll keep it warm for when you're finished if you want to do that first.'

Shower? Why was he so interested in bloody showers all of a sudden, did I smell or something?

'Um, Jack...'

He shot me a sideways smile as he took up the wooden spoon again. 'It's your call, Kitty. If the time's ever right, that has to be for you to decide.'

'But...' I sighed, letting the spell evaporate. 'Yeah. Thanks.'

'Wanted to though, didn't you?'

'If you'd done it, I wouldn't have stopped you,' I admitted.

'I know it.' He nodded to the tall cupboard by the cooker. 'There's a fresh towel in there. Help yourself to clothes.'

I hesitated.

'What?' he said.

'It's just – well, they're Sophie's.'

'So? She's not going to use them, is she? You were fine in them before.'

'Yeah, but... dunno. Feels weird, now I know.'

'They're clothes, Kit. Just bits of fabric. I'm not sentimental about them, no need for you to be.'

'How come you kept them so long?'

He shrugged. 'Laziness really. Honestly, it's fine. Clothes are just clothes. They're not... Soph.'

Still. First thing I wanted to do when I got some cash of my own was sort out a decent wardrobe.

***

After a shower and breakfast, there was another sombre little job before I made a final decision on what I wanted to do next. Funeral.

There was a light drizzle misting the air when we stepped out of the awning, Jack carrying the shoebox-coffin and me armed with a dessert spoon – the best we could do in lieu of a shovel.

It'd been a bit awkward, working out where we could bury the little box. We couldn't do it on the campsite, but we didn't want to venture too far from the puppies. Eventually, Jack had gone on a recce and discovered an overgrown wildflower meadow over a wall behind the shower block. We could lay the poor stillborn puppy to rest there.

It took us a while to dig a deep enough hole with the spoon. Fortunately it was a weekday and the campsite was pretty much deserted, so we didn't have to deal with any curious passers-by. Jack kept watch for the strict-looking campsite owner while I dug, then we swapped and he finished off.

I stood soberly by as he lowered the box into the little hole and spooned the soil back on top.

Mary Jayne Baker

'Feels like we should say something,' I said quietly.

'Like what?'

'I don't know, just... something. Like what you'd say at a funeral.'

'Okay, um...' Jack paused to think. 'When we buried the pup I told you about, my mam read a simple poem. Wrote it herself. We didn't normally make a fuss when animals died on the farm, but that first time... I think she thought it'd help me understand about death.'

'Do you remember it?'

'Yeah. She wrote it out on a little card for me to keep.' He hesitated, pulling up the words in his mind. 'Okay, this was it. "This precious life is ended now, but don't think of it as gone. Think it instead a spirit free, now that it has passed on."'

'Aww. That's nice.' I took his hand, and for a moment we were silent, looking down at the mound of earth.

Eventually he sighed. 'We'd better get back to Sandy.' He gave my hand a squeeze. 'And then you've got a decision to make.'

***

I drew a tentative finger along the littlest puppy's back, then pulled it away with a guilty smile when Sandy's finely honed maternal instinct woke her up and she shot me a glare that clearly said 'I know we're mates, but let's not push it, eh?'

'What'll happen to them?' I asked Jack in a hushed voice.

106

'I've got a home lined up, once they're big enough. The farmer who owns their dad said he'd take them, see if he can make ratters of them.'

'When will they be big enough?'

'Two months.' He glanced at my little runt, suckling happily with the others. 'Ten weeks maybe.'

'Two months! That's a long time for them to be packed in the camper. They'll be boisterous puppies in a few weeks, you know.'

'I know. We'll stay here till it's safe to move them, then I'll probably head up to my mam and dad's. Plenty of space there for them to play.'

'In Scotland?'

'That's right, near Loch Rusky. Gorgeous place.'

'I've never been to Scotland,' I murmured, half to myself.

'Then let me take you,' he said, his eyes beguiling. 'I could show you the loch at sunrise. You won't see anything more beautiful this lifetime.'

'God, that sounds amazing.'

'With the mist on the water and the little painted rowing boats bobbing about...'

'Stop it, Jack.'

'Attack ships on fire off the shoulder of Orion...'

'Okay, that's from *Blade Runner*.'

'Well-spotted,' he said with a grin. 'It's a sight though. It'll kick the breath right out of you, I guarantee it.'

'No. No, I shouldn't...'

'It's a genuine job offer, I swear,' Jack said, sensing me weakening. 'Here, wait. Let me prove it to you.'

I stroked Sandy while I waited for him to dig out his laptop and connect it to the campsite wifi.

'See?' he said, turning the screen to me. 'From my agent.'

Jack Duffy, I swear, if you don't get someone to sort your website out you'll be picking my boot out of your backside. It looks like a twelve-year-old's MySpace page in 2006.

I laughed. 'Doesn't mince words, does she?'

He shrugged. 'Me and Di have been working together a long time. She knows I can take it.'

'Not sure I could do much about your website looking like a MySpace page.'

'But you could brief someone to build me a new one. A freelancer. Couldn't you?'

'Yeah, I guess,' I admitted. 'I used to look after the company website in my old job so I've got a few contacts.'

'See? You're perfect,' he said with an air of triumph. 'I wouldn't even know where to start.'

I smiled. 'You're like a grandpa or something. What's this laptop running, like Windows 95?'

'So? Will you take the job?'

I hesitated. 'Jack... what happened in the kitchen?'

'I said I was sorry about forgetting the milk. I'll know for next time.'

'Not the bloody scrambled egg,' I said. 'The other thing. The almost thing.'

'Yeah, I know.' He drew a gentle finger down my cheek. 'That's up to you, Kitty. I mean, I want to. But you're hurting, I get that.'

'So're you.'

'I've learnt to live with mine. Yours is fresh.'

'So if I stayed, it'd be just a job? I mean, you'd be my boss and my friend and... and that's it?'

'That's it. If that's what you want.'

It was hard to resist those sticky-treacle eyes of his, especially with Sandy backing it up with a couple of big browns of her own. I did want to stay. And a decent job, with travel, writing: all those things I'd dreamed of that Mum and Ethan had kept out of my reach for years. It was a more inviting prospect than Surinder's sofa, that was for sure.

I supposed what was really worrying me – again – was Ethan. Not the actual physical threat of Ethan, although I was still terrified of what might happen if he ever tracked me down. But the way he'd conditioned me to need guidance and control, to cling to the nearest proper grown-up because of the overwhelming feeling I wasn't fit to look after myself. That wasn't Jack's fault, and God knew he was nothing like Ethan, but... was I just replacing Ethan, and Mum too, with him? Finding myself a new protector instead of standing on my own two feet?

But then it was paid work. And it would be my money, wouldn't it? My own money, that I'd earned and I could put into my own bank account with my own name on it. Money meant independence. And a professional job meant professional skills, to shore up my CV against the future. If my new goal was a well-rounded, strong, adult Kitty Clayton who could face whatever the world threw at her, then surely staying with Jack, for a little while at least, was my best option?

Not just because I didn't want to leave him. It was simply

the best option, objectively. Any jury in the land would see that, if I had to put my case to them.

'Okay, Jack. You win.' I held out my hand for him to shake. 'Looking forward to working with you.'

Chapter 11

I jumped out of bed bright and early next morning and bounced into the awning to wake Jack.

'Rise and shine!' I yelled in his ear. 'Oh, sorry.' I whipped off a salute. 'Rise and shine, sir.'

'Hm? Z'it time to get up?'

'Yep. 7.30 a. m. All ready for my first day.'

'It's Sunday, Kit. You don't start till tomorrow. Go back to bed.'

I stuck my lip out. 'Aww. Go on, I'm excited.'

'Ugh. Fine. You can start by getting the breakfast on then.'

'That's not PA work. You make the breakfast. I want a proper job to do.'

'The phrase "buying a dog and barking yourself" springs to mind.' He pushed himself grumpily into a sitting position. 'Okay, you win. We'll both make breakfast. Then I'll get you started.'

He wasn't kidding. First thing after breakfast, he cleared the slot-in table and dumped a stack of paperwork in front of me.

'What's all this?' I said.

'Just a few bits you might find useful.' He riffed the pile with his fingertips. 'My bio and a press release template for interviews. List of bookshops round the country for setting up signings. Contact details for my publisher, agent, press and a few others you might need. And a load of other bumf. I'll email it to you too, once we get you sorted with a laptop and phone of your own.'

'Bloody hell. It'll take me ages to read through all this.'

'You don't need to do it all today.' He opened one of the overhead storage compartments above the kitchenette. 'Actually, you'd be better getting going on this. It's more urgent.'

'What is it?' I asked as he dumped a little mailbag down on top of the papers.

'Fan mail. Needs sorting through. I've been neglecting it lately in favour of my new hobby of bride rescuing.'

'God, there's loads,' I said, peeking into the bag. There must've been fifty envelopes in there.

'Yeah. I'm a star.'

I smiled. 'All right, your celebliness. How do you get it? Royal Mail don't deliver to campervans, do they?'

'I've got a PO Box address. Whenever I move on, I let Diana know – my agent – and she gets it forwarded to the nearest post office for me to collect.'

'Ah, right. Clever. So how do I sort it?'

'I usually go through and put it in three piles. Requires Response, Doesn't Require Response and Pervert.'

I quirked an eyebrow. 'Pervert?'

'Yeah, there's always a couple.'

'Can I hold my puppy first?'

'Suppose a job's got to have some perks. One minute, that's all, or Sand'll get anxious.'

He went out to the dog bed in the awning and scooped up one of the little jellybeans, the firstborn. Sandy eyed him warily, but she didn't object. Now she'd had a couple of days to get used to motherhood, she seemed less nervous about letting the humans play with her babies.

'Here you go,' Jack said, placing the little pup gently on my lap. It yawned and snuggled contentedly into me.

I couldn't help having a little simper. 'Aww. The love.'

'You ever had a dog of your own?'

'No. Mum wouldn't let me get a pet when I was a kid. Always wanted one though.' I ran soft fingers over the silken fur. 'Lovely, isn't he?'

'She, actually. I checked this morning while you were in the shower.'

'What about the others?'

'Two girls, four boys. So you're outnumbered now, ladies, sorry.'

'We should name them really, shouldn't we? Seems a bit mean just calling them all "Puppy" till they get rehomed.'

He nodded to the pup. 'Well, why don't you name this one? Since she's yours.'

'She's not really mine,' I said, running a gentle palm over the little dog's back. 'Not for long anyway.'

'Oh, I don't know. I think we could squeeze one more in.'

I glanced up to meet his eyes. 'Really? You're letting me have a pet?'

'If you like. You'll have to walk her every day, mind.'

'But I thought your friend wanted them.'

'He doesn't need six ratters. He's just doing it as a favour really: feels guilty about letting his lad get near Sandy. Anyway, I'd feel bad taking them all off the old girl.'

I beamed at him. 'Thanks, Jack. I'd love to keep her.'

'Well then? What's her name?' he said. 'Nothing too cutesy or I reserve the right of veto.'

'Dunno.' I looked at the little black puppy, who'd settled down for a doze. 'She kind of looks like a bear, doesn't she? What about Yogi?'

'Hmm, not sure. She might grow up to be a picnic basket thief.'

'Okay, how about... Deefer?'

'Deefer?'

'Yeah, you know, Deefer. Deefer Dog.'

He groaned. 'Get your Christmas crackers early this year?'

'All right, best of three. If you don't like this one, I give up.' I stopped to think, and the puppy picked that moment to let out a juddery little noise, somewhere between a sneeze and a cough. It sounded like she was snickering.

Jack looked at me. 'You thinking what I'm thinking?'

'Muttley?'

'Yeah.'

'It's a boy's name though,' I said.

'It's a dog's name.'

I smiled. 'Does kind of suit her. Okay, Muttley it is.'

Something cold nuzzled my leg, and I looked down to see Sandy eyeing me expectantly.

'Sorry, Sand,' I said, rubbing her neck. 'Here's your Muttley back.'

I placed the sleeping dog on the floor by her mum, and Sandy picked her gently up by the scruff before trotting off back to her bed.

'Muttley's really just her human name though,' Jack said. 'In Dog she's probably got something far cooler, like... you know, Wuffles the Terrible.'

'Poor Sandy,' I said as I watched her settle back in her bed again with a full set of babies. 'It's going to be hell for her when they go.'

'Going to be pretty rough on us too,' Jack said. 'But it has to be done. And farm life's the best life for a dog.'

I rummaged in the bag for one of the letters while Jack settled down with his sketchbook on the sofa.

'Hey, this is all right,' he said as he selected a pencil. 'I could get used to watching someone else do the real work for me.'

The first envelope I opened contained a badly spelt letter in crayon, which I hoped meant it wasn't a contender for the pervert pile.

'"Dear Mr Jack,"' I read. '"Your books are my very favouritest books and my favouritest is *Tilly and Billy Bake a Cake* and especially the bit where Tilly gets all flour on her and Billy thinks that she is a ghost and Mummy says if I write a letter you will send me please a signed book and please to also send a signed picture of you please thank you. Olivia Eden Milly Brecon age six and a half."'

Jack glanced up from his pad to grin at me. 'Breathe there, lass.'

'So what pile does that go in?'

'Put it in Requires Response and I'll sort her out a book. Not really supposed to send free copies out, my publisher's always telling me off about it. But I'm a soft old bastard.'

'Don't forget the signed photo.' I glanced up at his annoyingly handsome profile, bent over his pad while he sketched. 'That'll be for the mum.'

The next letter was clearly from an adult, typewritten and very formal in tone.

'"Dear Mr Duffy,"' I read. '"I observed you recently speaking at Scarborough Literature Festival and was most impressed. I enclose a photograph which I think you may find of interest. Please respond asap for further details."' I rummaged in the envelope for the Polaroid, and my eyes went wide. 'Jesus Christ! Pervert pile.'

Jack smirked. 'Go on, let's have a look.'

I passed it over.

'Oh,' he said, blinking.

'Yeah.'

'Nice idea putting his shoe down next to it. Gives that bit of perspective.'

'I can see why he's keen to show it off, to be fair.'

'Unless he's a size six.' Jack handed the photo back and I stuffed it hastily in the envelope. 'Stick it in the Requires Response pile. Given he's so polite, I'm sure I can manage a "thanks but no thanks".'

'And maybe a download link for Grindr.'

The next letter was puzzling. It was typewritten, but it read like it had come from a kid. I couldn't tell which pile it was supposed to go on.

'What's up?' Jack asked when he noticed my furrowed brow.

'It's this letter. Can't work it out.'

'Go on, read it to me.'

'"Hi Mr Duffy! It's me!"' I read. '"I hope you are well and Sandy is also well! I have been very busy crocheting and I am making her a new coat for the winter which I will send when it is finished! I loved *Tilly and Billy Go to Sea* and I think it is your best book yet and I have bought it for all my friends at church who agree! I cannot wait to see you at your next book signing so you can sign it for me!"'

'Sonia, right?'

'Um, yeah. Who is she?'

He laughed. 'My biggest fan.'

'How old is she? Is she a kid?'

'No, she's mid-forties I think. She's... well, she's a character. But she's very sweet. You'll see her at my next book signing, she comes to all of them.' He nodded to the middle pile of Response Required letters. 'Put it on there. I'll post her a photo of the pups, she'll like that.'

'Will she crochet jackets for them all?'

'Heh. Wouldn't be surprised. Go on, what's the next one?'

'"Dear Jack. I met you recently when you visited my son's school for World Book Day. I just wanted to let you know that my husband takes our little boy to football practice every Wednesday afternoon, so if you were interested you could come round and— "' I blinked. 'Okay, pervert pile again.'

'Offer any good?'

'Depends how you feel about leather catsuits.'

He shrugged. 'Meh. I can take them or leave them.'

'Probably not worth the petrol then,' I said, tossing it in the pervert pile. 'Do all children's authors get propositioned this much?'

'Just the sexy ones. I hear Judith Kerr keeps a scrapbook.'

Chapter 12

When I was done sorting fan mail, I started looking through the documents Jack had put together for me.

I knew he was a pretty big deal in the pre-school market. His books were everywhere: there were Tilly and Billy toys, colouring books, all sorts. But it didn't quite hit me until I started filtering through stuff like his bio that as his PA, I was suddenly someone quite important.

The bio read like a CV. Name: John Matthew Duffy. Born: Bray, County Wicklow, February 1987. Which, I quickly calculated, made him thirty-one: something he'd never told me. Graduated Dublin Institute of Technology with a First in architecture, married 2014, widowed 2016. Five children's bestsellers, winner of the Hans Christian Andersen Award for Illustration in 2015, honorary degree from the Royal College of Art... it went on for ages.

Jack was a big hitter, and it was clear I needed to do a bloody good job for him.

There wasn't much else I could get done that day: things like contacting bookshops and journalists would have to wait for the official working week to start. When I'd read through some of the documents, I borrowed Jack's laptop to draft a quick press release I could post out with review copies of his latest book, *Tilly and Billy Go to Sea*, then pushed it away.

'All right, think I'm spent for now,' I said to Jack, who'd long abandoned his drawing and was deep in a book.

'Productive day?'

'Think so. You?'

'Yeah, pretty good. Some preliminary sketches for the new one done.'

'Which is?'

'*Tilly and Billy in a Hot Air Balloon.*'

'Okay, that's got marketing potential.' I had a sudden brainwave. 'Ooh! We could do a book launch in a balloon. How awesome would that be? Bet I could get you a bucket of press.'

He smiled. 'Oh, Di is going to love you.' He patted the seat next to him. 'Okay, come here. Staff appraisal time.'

I went to join him on the sofa.

'So, how'd I do on my first day?'

'Not bad. Seven out of ten for enthusiasm—'

'Pfft, what? I was Miss bloody Enthusiasm!'

'Exactly. Right over the top of my Sunday lie-in. But nine out of ten for competence. Well done.'

I beamed. 'Thanks. How do I get a ten then?'

'Less humming while you read the post. Distracting. Also, the penis photos tend to take me out of my drawing a bit.'

'You asked to see that!'

'PA lesson one. Never let me have what I ask for. I'm a bad

influence on myself.' He stood and went to the fridge. 'All the same, I think you earned this.'

He took out a bottle of something alcoholic and poured us both a glass.

'So what's next?' I said.

Jack took his seat again, handed me my glass and stretched an arm around me as usual. 'I thought we'd head off next week. Up to Scotland.'

'To your parents' place?'

'That's right,' he said. 'The puppies'll be happy there till they're ready for rehoming. We'll pick you up a laptop and mobile on the way so you can really get stuck in. And you'd better sort out a bank account too so I can pay you.'

'Yeah. I really want to do that asap. It feels kind of symbolic.' I laughed. 'My first bank account, how grown up am I?'

'What will you need to get it set up?'

'Good question.' I grabbed Jack's laptop and Googled the bank's website to find out what I needed. 'Passport and proof of address. Shit! Address, didn't think of that.' I glanced up at him. 'How do you manage?'

'I use my parents' address, when I need to apply for anything, and they forward the post on. Sure they won't mind you doing the same.'

'Are you sure?'

'I'll ask my mam when we get up there, but yeah, can't see it being a problem. What about your ISA money, do you know what you need for that?'

'I'll need the current account first so they can transfer the cash. Just a sec.' I pulled up the building society's website.

'But – oh, typical. They want two proofs of identity, either driving licence or birth certificate as well as my passport. And I don't drive.'

'Where's your birth certificate again?'

'At Mum's, I'm assuming.' I shuddered. 'And I'm not going there for it.'

'Well, I'm sure you can get a copy. We'll sort it out tomorrow.' He took the laptop from me and stood to stash it back in the overhead compartment where it lived. 'How come you never got your driving licence then? Didn't take to it?'

'Never had a lesson. Ethan didn't see the need for us both to be drivers. Said it was a waste of money when he could drop me anywhere I needed to be.'

'Hmm. He did, did he?'

I frowned. 'That's not unusual, is it?'

'And he stopped you opening a bank account?'

'Well, no, he never actually stopped me. It's just, when me and Ethan moved in together I was only seventeen. He said I could use his until I was an adult, then we'd upgrade to a joint account.'

'But you never did.'

'No. Ethan said his credit rating was better than mine so it'd be best to leave it in his name. In case we needed to get a loan or anything.'

'That's not how it works, Kitty.'

'Isn't it?'

'No.'

He was staring at me. I felt my cheeks start to heat.

'What?' I said.

'So every penny you ever earned went into his account.'

'Yeah. But I could get it if I wanted to. I mean, I had a bank card. He just... he thought I wasn't good with money so he wanted to keep track of our outgoings.'

Jack nodded. 'Soph was like that. She was always more aware of what was going in and out than me, worried we were overspending. Know what we did?'

'What?'

'We had a conversation. Agreed to budget more carefully between us, make sure we were putting a bit away for a rainy day.' He came to sit by me on the sofa again. 'That's what couples do, Kitty. One doesn't just loftily inform the other she can't access her own money, then gamble it away on the stock market without telling her.'

'No...'

'What did your family think of the arrangement?'

'They didn't know,' I mumbled, feeling ashamed without quite knowing why. 'My dad suspected something was up, I think. That's why he put the ISA in just my name. But Laurel, my nan, Aunty Julia... Mum. I knew they'd be worried by it. And it wasn't a big deal, really. I could always get money, Ethan was very generous with it.'

'Generous. With your money. How fucking magnanimous of him.' He took my two hands in his. 'Kit, will you do something for me?'

He was looking into my face, his eyes intense. I wondered what was about to happen. He'd promised my staying would be strictly professional, but there was still that... something, always in the air between us.

'Um, yeah. If you like,' I said, dropping my gaze.

'Replay what we just said back in your head, will you?'

'Why?'

'Please. For me.'

I thought back on the conversation we'd just had, then shook my head, bewildered. 'What're you getting at, Jack?'

'Don't you hear yourself? Defending him?'

Defending him... had I just done that? All I could hear was *Ethan said... Ethan said*. God, when I heard myself trying to justify it all, it sounded pathetic.

'I promised not to ask what happened between you two at the wedding, but whatever it was must've been pretty horrific for you to end up here,' Jack said. 'And I've seen first-hand that he's a controlling son of a bitch, not above a bit of emotional blackmail if it'll help him get his way. You need to ask yourself why you're still sticking up for him.'

He stood to refill our glasses while I stared blankly ahead.

'Well?' he said when he'd resumed his seat.

'Yeah, maybe that is what it sounded like,' I said slowly. 'But it's not really about him, not now. I know what he is. It's...' I looked up at him. 'It's me, Jack, I guess. I'm ashamed of myself for being taken in by him for so long. I mean, God! Like a child I let him... it's pathetic. Isn't it? I'm pathetic.'

'You're not pathetic. And there's nothing for you to be ashamed of,' he said gently, taking my hand and stroking it with his fingertips. 'He's conditioned you to think that way. It's classic abusive behaviour.'

'Abuse?' It was the second time now he'd used that word,

and both times it had sent a sickening pain through my gut. I pulled my hand away. 'No.'

Ethan might've been a selfish, patronising bastard, now I tried my best to look at it objectively. He might've babied and cotton-wooled me until I felt like I could hardly breathe. Kept my money from me; spent it without consulting me. But abuse? Abuse was what Uncle Ken did. Abuse was 'Oh, this? No, I just walked into a door' or 'burnt my hand on the iron'. After what'd happened to Aunty Julia, abuse was the one thing I'd always promised myself would mean an instant end to any relationship.

'He cut you off,' Jack said. 'Isolated you, financially and emotionally. Didn't he?'

'Well, he... I guess he did kind of keep me to himself.'

'They always do. Possession. That's what it's all about to someone with that mindset, dressed up as some sort of benevolent paternalism.' I'd never seen such a black look on his face before. 'It's about ownership, in the end. The power trip of owning another human being. Pah! There's more to abuse than a closed fist, Kit.'

I stared at him. 'I've never known you to get angry like that.'

'Guys like Ethan make me that angry. I just don't know how people can treat other people that way and have the gall to call it love.' He squeezed my hand tightly, and when he spoke again his voice was soft. 'Sorry you had to go through that. You know, you're a tough cookie, Kitty Clayton.'

I shook my head. 'But it can't be right. I always promised myself I'd never be a victim of that. I... I'd have noticed.'

'You're not a victim, not any more. You're a survivor.'

I felt uncomfortable suddenly. Queasy. I wished I could be somewhere else, away from Jack and his words.

'I'm going to bed,' I mumbled. 'I'll sleep in the awning if you're staying up.'

'Running away?' he said gently.

'No. I just want a bit of space, that's all.'

'I'm sorry, Kit, I wasn't trying to make you uncomfortable. I just think it's important you face up to this. You told him where to go in real life, but he's still there in your head. Isn't he?'

'He... maybe. A slice of him.'

He was still holding my hand. God, I needed to escape. I had to get away, from Jack, from what he was trying to make me face up to, from his hand around mine and his stupid kind understanding eyes.

And then, suddenly, I didn't. Away from Jack was the last place I wanted to be. I wanted to be as close to him as humanly possible. I wanted him to make Ethan go away for me, to push him right out of my head. I wanted him to... to...

'Jack, can I sleep with you tonight?' I blurted out.

He frowned. 'With me? Why?'

I flushed. 'I thought... I mean, a hug would be nice. Um.'

Jack blinked. 'Okay.' He wrapped his arms around me, looking bewildered at my sudden shift in mood.

'That's good,' I whispered, drooping against him. 'Jack?'

'Yeah?'

'Will you kiss me? Please.'

He hesitated.

126

'No,' he said at last. 'Not now.'

'But you said you wanted to.'

'Not like this.' He stroked my hair away from my face. 'Not while you're hurting. If I kiss you, I want it to be... well, I want you to be thinking about me.'

'I am thinking about you.'

'You know what I mean. I want it to have joy in it, Kitty. When you make that decision, I want it to be about us. Not about him.' He tilted my chin up and planted the smallest kiss on my forehead. 'Get him out of there. Then maybe there'll be room for me.'

Chapter 13

It was catching sight of the calendar on my shiny new PA phone on the following week that convinced me I couldn't put it off any longer. Now we were officially living together in the camper, there was a conversation Jack and I needed to have.

I finally plucked up the courage to broach the subject while he was washing up after breakfast.

'Jack...' I began hesitantly.

'Hmm?'

'Er, I wanted to talk to you about... well, there's this, um...'

Oh God, why couldn't I come right out and say it? I'd tried to open the conversation a dozen times already.

I tried again. 'It's just, um, I'm a girl and everything.'

He smiled. 'I had noticed.'

'So, er...'

Arghhh! Getting embarrassed talking about periods to boys at my age was just ridiculous. And Jack had been married, it's not like he wouldn't understand.

Was this bloody Ethan's fault again? He'd always been squeamish about what he called 'women's issues'. I could still picture his look of horror when I'd asked him to pick up some tampons from the shop one time, way back in the early days. I'd never dared ask again.

'And girls have... things...' I tried. 'Times, you know, when things aren't so great...'

He was still staring blankly at me.

I took a deep breath. 'I mean, times of the month where I'm not so fun. To be around. Where I might feel a bit crap, you know?'

'Oh. Oh!' he said, the penny dropping at last. 'I'm sorry, Kit, you should've said before. Do you need me to pop out for anything?'

I smiled at his attempts to be sweet. 'I didn't mean right now. I just thought we should have the conversation, that's all.'

'Okay. Um... so, what would you want me to do? Hot water bottles and things?'

'No, what I'm getting at is – I suppose I'm just worried about being cooped up in this tiny van in the middle of nowhere, feeling all tummy-hurty and grumpy. Wouldn't be much fun for you either. And it'd be nice if we could be somewhere with proper loos and everything, you know...'

My face was beetroot by now, but Jack didn't seem embarrassed. He just gave an understanding nod.

'Fair enough. If you let me know when, I'll make sure we're not on the road for as long as you need. And if you want a bit of space I understand. Just kick me out into the awning if you feel like I'm crowding you.'

I exhaled with relief. 'Thanks, Jack. That'd be great.'

***

Jack spent twenty minutes after lunch on his mobile outside the camper. When he came back, he chucked it on the passenger seat and threw himself down next to me on the sofa.

'Who was it?' I asked, looking up from the press release I was tapping out on my new laptop.

'Nobody.'

'Come on, it must've been somebody.'

'Okay, nobody important.' He turned to face me. 'Kit, would you be able to mind the pups this afternoon? I need to drive into town for something.'

'Er, yeah, I guess,' I said. 'What is it?'

He tapped his nose. 'That'd be telling.'

'You being mysterious?'

'Yep,' he said with a grin. 'Mystery is my middle name.'

'No it isn't, your middle name's Matthew.'

''Tis too, it's my Confirmation name. St Mystery of Vegas, well-known Catholic martyr. She got stoned to death with folded dollar bills for working as an exotic dancer to convert the heathens.'

I laughed. 'Go on then, I'll see to the doggies. How long will you be?'

'Couple of hours should do it.'

I'd got used to Jack's creative approach to timekeeping by then, so I wasn't surprised that it was actually closer to three hours when he finally drove back with the camper. Sandy and me were sprawled side by side on the grass in the blazing June sunshine, reading a book. Well, I was reading a book:

you could never get Sandy interested in literature, ignorant mongrel. The pups were in their bed at my feet, enjoying the warm weather.

I pushed myself into a sitting position to watch Jack park up in our pitch.

'What the hell is *that*?' I asked when he'd joined us.

Attached to the back of the van was a little orange – God, I didn't even know what to call it. It looked like a horse box for a knee-high Shetland pony.

'It's a present.' Jack sat down next to me. 'Hope you like it.'

'Er, thanks,' I said, shooting the thing a puzzled look. 'And they say diamonds are a girl's best friend.'

'That's a classic, I'll have you know. 1972 Eriba Puck caravan. Even managed to get one that matched the van.'

'What for though? Why do you need a teeny weeny caravan?' I turned wide eyes on him. 'Oh God. Tell me you're not getting another pet. What is it this time, a womble?'

'I told you, it's for you,' he said. 'There's a bed, bit of extra cupboard space – even a kitchenette. Home from home, if you like.'

'You got me my own room to sleep in?'

'Only when you want to. Or I will, once it gets cold. I prefer the awning in summer.'

'But why?'

'Just thought you might appreciate a sort of house extension, stop the van seeming quite so cramped when you're feeling rough,' he said. 'You know, what you said this morning about needing your own girly space sometimes.'

'Oh. Right. A little box of my own.' I patted his arm. 'Well, it was a nice thought. Hope you didn't spend too much on it.'

'Not really. It was only eight grand.'

'Bloody hell!' I looked at the tiny thing with new eyes. 'What's that, a grand per square inch of floor space?'

'That's a bargain, honestly. Told you, they're classics. Some collectors pay through the nose for that sort of thing.'

I shook my head. 'You shouldn't spend money like that on things for me.'

'Why not?' he said with a shrug. 'I've got feck all else to spend it on.'

'Seriously though. People'll think I'm some slutty retro-caravan-digger.'

He laughed. 'Well, call it an early Christmas bonus then. Here, come take a look inside.'

I followed Jack to the incy wincy caravan. He unlocked the door and ushered me in.

'See? Loads of space,' he said, joining me. 'Look, you can get two of us in no problem.'

'Er, yeah,' I said, smiling at Jack's bowed head and hunched shoulders.

I cast my eyes around the caravan. It looked like someone had attacked Jack's camper with a shrink ray. There was a kitchenette with a hob, fridge and sink, one tall cupboard and a couple of narrow sofas that could be slotted together to make a bed, a detachable table between them.

'I could buy you an awning for it too,' Jack said, looking downcast that I wasn't whooping and jumping as I examined the place. To be fair, there wasn't really the space. 'It's just for when you feel like you need a break from me, I'm not moving you into the campervan equivalent of a granny flat or anything. And I thought you could use it as your PA office too, away from distractions.'

'Such as?'

'Oh, you know. My body. I know it must be a struggle keeping your eyes down.'

I smiled. 'It's perfect, Jack. Just what I need. Thank you.'

He gave my shoulders an affectionate press. 'So you want to come help me get the awning back up? I was thinking barbecue for dinner.'

'In a minute. Let me alone in my horse box a sec so I can start to feel at home.'

He patted my head. 'All right, My Little Pony. See you soon.'

When Jack was gone, I shut the door and sank onto one of the sofas.

Actually, now there was just me it didn't seem so very small. Smaller than the camper, of course, but then that had to accommodate the engine and driver's area, unlike my itsy bitsy bubble caravan, so there was a reasonable bit of floor-space.

It was a sweet thought. I'd said I needed space, he'd bought me a caravan just a few hours later – a highly collectible caravan apparently – with some of the Tilly and Billy money he didn't seem to know what to do with. But I could still recognise it for what it was. An attempt to make me fit his life, his borderless yet claustrophobic future – to keep me with him on his own terms.

I'd just escaped a relationship with a man who'd gone out of his way to remodel me as he needed me to be instead of how I wanted to be. Jack wasn't like that, of course he wasn't. But he was still a man damaged by loss. A lonely man. A man who needed someone who could fit.

And for now, I did fit. I just didn't know if I could live that sort of life forever. Jack never thought of the future much beyond tomorrow, I'd realised that pretty quickly after meeting him. But I couldn't help thinking about it, formless and shadowy though it was.

I felt a wave of sympathy for him, still trapped in his grief no matter how much freedom he tried to claw to himself. Taking a last look around my new den, I sighed and went to seek him out for a hug.

Chapter 14

Sitting cramped in the passenger seat during the six-hour journey up to Jack's parents' house in Scotland was no picnic, but I waved away his suggestion that we stop overnight at the halfway point. I was far too excited, bouncing like a kid on their way to the seaside. I'd dreamed of travel my whole life, and yes, maybe Scotland wasn't so very exotic, but it was still another country. I couldn't wait to see the lochs, the mountains: all those wonders I'd fantasised about in my old job editing travel guides but never got the chance to see.

Torturous it may have been, but it was still an incredible drive. The further north we got, the more the landscape bubbled with heather-dressed mountains and hills, Jack's little van and its matching caravan dipping then climbing then dipping again as every corner we turned brought something new. My old home in the Dales wasn't exactly flat, but the Highlands were something else.

'It reminds me of a guide we did to the Canadian Rockies,' I told Jack in a hushed tone. Something about the cathedral-like giants hemming us in on both sides left me feeling I needed to lower my voice.

He smiled at the sparkle in my eyes. 'There's beauty enough this side of the ocean if you seek it out. This country can match any wonder in the world.'

An awesome crag loomed into view ahead, bleak and beautiful, dwarfing our tiny camper. I'd seen hundreds of photos of the Scottish Highlands from the guides, but seeing them in real life, in 3D and glorious Technicolor, just took my breath away.

'I think you might be right,' I murmured.

Finally our van and its motherload of dogs meandered through a big iron gate and up a dirt track before pulling up outside Jack's parents' place.

My eyes saucered. 'You've got to be kidding me. This isn't where they live?'

'Yep.'

'I thought you said they were farmers.'

'They were. They're retired now.'

'On what, a diamond farm?'

He smiled. 'What's a diamond farm, Kit?'

'One where they breed diamonds, obviously. You know, when a mummy diamond and a daddy diamond love each other very much and make lots of little baby diamonds doing special diamond cuddles.'

'What, you mean the diamond stork doesn't bring them?' He shook his head. 'There's my innocence shattered.'

'Seriously though. This place is huge.'

'Come on, it's not that fancy.'

It bloody was. I wasn't sure where the definition of house ended and castle begun, but this thing was definitely borderline. I mean, it had turrets. Turrets! Round our way, we thought the neighbours were going it a bit if they had a dormer window installed.

I fixed on a nervous smile as Jack knocked on the huge oak door. A few seconds later it swung open and a pleasant, open-faced lady in her sixties, eyes dark and soulful like Jack's and with long, pure white hair, appeared in the doorway.

'Arghh!' she said as soon as she caught sight of him, throwing up her hands.

'Arghh you!' he said with a grin. He picked her up, swinging her round while he hugged her. 'Hiya, Mam.'

She grinned back. Then she caught sight of me, lurking bashfully just behind him, and her eyes shot wide open.

'Arghh!' she said again, and she threw herself at me for a bear-like hug. I patted her back in bewilderment.

'Oh, sweetheart, you don't know how glad we are to see you,' she said to me, her tone glowing with sincerity.

I blinked. I mean, Jack talked about the Irish tradition of hospitality, but this seemed to be really above and beyond.

'Michael!' she called out. 'Come quick! Our Jack has brought a girl home!'

'Arghh!' I heard from somewhere behind her. A crinkle-eyed man with Jack's jawline and a kind mouth came dashing out from one of the rooms, then slowed into a casually sedate walk when he spotted me.

'Ah, are we pleased to see you,' he said, pumping my hand exuberantly behind his wife's back while she continued to embrace me. 'Come in, girl, come in. We've wine waiting to get to know you, and a couple of old folk too.'

'Um, thank you,' I said breathlessly as his wife released me. 'It's lovely to meet you both.'

'Come on, fellers, you're scaring her,' Jack said, smiling.

'Didn't tell us you had a new girlfriend, did you, sly boots?' his mum said, nudging him. 'New pets we expected. Girls, no.'

'I'm not a girlfriend,' I said, feeling a little windswept from all the screeching and hugging. 'Just a friend.'

'And employee,' Jack said. 'Kitty's my new PA.'

'Ah. I see.' His mum looked disappointed.

'Oh, well, for now she's a PA,' Michael said, apparently undaunted by this new information. 'And you're living in the van, are you, dear?' he asked me.

'Er, yeah,' I said. 'At the moment.'

Michael patted his wife triumphantly on the back. 'You see, Chrissy? Lives with Jack.'

Jack shot me a sideways smile. 'Sorry,' he mouthed.

'Well, come in, come in,' Chrissy said, ushering us through the door. 'I've done lamb chops and mash for dinner.'

'Pudding?' Jack asked. Over the last six weeks, I'd learned he was a big fan of pudding.

'Jam roll and custard. Good solid food.'

'She always seems to think I can't possibly be eating properly in the camper,' Jack whispered to me as we followed his parents through a long wood-panelled hall, heavy on the stags' heads and paintings, to the dining room. 'It's stodge all the way when I come to visit.'

I noticed his accent had got broader the instant his parents had answered the door. Did mine do that, I wondered? I flinched as I reflected I'd probably never get the chance to find out, now.

It was a very cool dining room, a lot more rock and roll than I would've anticipated from the antlers-and-oak theme in the hallway. The walls were decorated with old LP sleeves, and a 1950s-style jukebox gave the place an Arnold's Diner in *Happy Days* look.

'Nice,' I said with an approving nod at the jukebox.

Michael grinned. 'Thanks. Chrissy calls it The Mid-life Crisis Machine.'

'Chrissy calls it the waste of bloody money,' Jack's mum muttered. But her lips were twitching with a smile.

Michael strolled over to it and fired up a bit of classic rock – Bruce Springsteen, I think it was – before dancing his way to the dining table. The jukebox's multi-coloured lights flashed merrily in time.

'Ignore that daft fecker and his dad dancing,' Chrissy said, flicking a dismissive hand towards her husband. 'Come sit down, tell me all the news.' She indicated one of the chairs around the dining table. 'Kitty, you sit here, next to me.'

'Thanks, Mrs Duffy,' I said, sitting down.

'Chrissy, please.' She raised her eyebrows at her husband. 'Drinks, Michael.'

'She's so bossy,' Michael said to me in an audible whisper. 'What would you like, Kitty? Wine, beer? Or we've got spirits in the liquor cabinet. You're welcome to some of my Bushmills if it takes your fancy.'

'We've got a liquor cabinet,' Jack told me with comic smugness.

'Oooh. Get you.'

Chrissy shot her husband a significant look that I didn't have to work too hard to interpret. There seemed to be some serious matchmaking going on and I wasn't quite sure what to make of it.

'Just a white wine, please,' I said to Michael.

'I'll drink your Bushmills, Dad,' Jack said.

'Yes, I thought you might.' He flicked Jack's ear as he left the room to sort out our drinks.

'I'd better get the awnings up and bring the dogs in before we start drinking,' Jack said, standing up.

I frowned. 'Awnings? We're not sleeping in the van, are we?'

'You're not,' Chrissy said. 'I'll make up one of the rooms for you. Take some time off roughing it in that old tin of his.'

'I'm sleeping out,' Jack said.

'But why?' I glanced at Chrissy. 'There's plenty of space, isn't there?'

'There is.' She smiled encouragingly at her son. 'Come on, Jack. Just try it this once, eh?'

'You know I can't,' he said quietly, turning away.

I blinked after him as he left the room.

'What was that all about?' I asked his mum.

'Oh, I knew it was no good asking really,' she said, staring down at her splayed fingers on the table. 'He never sleeps in the house.'

'Why?'

She smiled sadly. 'Your guess is as good as mine, sweetheart. Something that went wrong in his brain, I think, when he—' She stopped herself. 'Sorry. I'm speaking out of turn.'

'It's okay, I know what you mean. When Sophie died.'

'Ah, so he told you, did he?' That seemed to cheer her up a little. 'That's a good sign. He tends to keep his cards close with most people.'

Her husband came back in and handed me a generous glass of wine – seriously, it looked like half a bottle's worth – before taking a seat on the other side of his wife.

'He's sleeping in the van again,' Chrissy told him.

Michael looked sober. 'Hmm. I did wonder, this time…' He glanced at me. 'I mean, now he's got his friend here.'

'How long have you known him, Kitty?' Chrissy asked.

'About six weeks,' I said. 'Why?'

'What do you know about him?'

'Jack?' I thought of the bio I'd read the day I'd started work for him. 'I know he studied architecture. That he's won a few awards—'

'Not his job. About him.'

'Well, he's… kind. Funny. Laid-back, most of the time.' I paused to think. 'Sort of a fatalist. Doesn't like to be trapped. And he's got this whole philosophy – living one day at a time, doing what feels natural. Wringing life dry, he once described it to me.'

'And yet he never used to be any of those things,' Michael said, topping up his whisky from the bottle he'd brought in with him.

I frowned. 'Didn't he?'

'Well, no, he's always been kind,' Chrissy said, shooting a look at her husband. 'But this philosophy, or whatever you call it. That came about after Sophie died.'

'How did you meet?' Michael asked.

141

'I sort of fell in his way really, at a time in my life when I was in a desperate situation. I'd just left a bad relationship, and I had no money, no home. Jack looked after me when I was ill. I think he decided he liked having me around.'

'He gets lonely,' Chrissy said, absently scooping some foam off her beer with her little finger and sucking the end.

'I know. And I needed a job, somewhere to live, so… here we are.'

Michael shot a look at his wife. 'We thought it might be something like that.'

'Why did you?'

'Oh, every time he comes home there's something,' Chrissy said. 'Puppies this time. Last time it was an injured bird. Before that there was an orphaned hedgehog. And Sandy, of course. The boy's a compulsive rescuer. I don't know if it's some form of post-traumatic stress disorder or what it is, but ever since he lost Sophie he's lived a different life.'

'We think he saves things because he couldn't save her,' Michael said, sipping at his second double whisky morosely. 'He blames himself.'

'Why though?' I asked. 'He couldn't have prevented it.'

'Mmm. But it haunts him, all the same.'

I looked up to meet his eyes.

'You're worried about him.'

'Of course we are.' He jerked his head at Chrissy. 'His mother's quite attached to him, you know.'

She elbowed him affectionately in the belly.

'We just want him to have a normal life, one with a proper future.' She fixed her gaze on me. 'Meet a nice girl, perhaps.'

I flushed. 'Oh.'

'He hasn't brought anyone to see us since Sophie—' Michael began, but our conversation was cut short by Jack coming back in, Sandy at his ankles and the dog bed full of babies in his arms.

'Oh no, Jack. Not in my dining room, not while we're eating. I can't do with all those little eyes staring at me.' His mum gestured to the door. 'Put them in the front room, they'll be happy by the fire. I'll start serving up.'

When he'd settled the dogs in the room next door, Jack came back in and threw himself back in his chair.

'They're getting to the naughty age, Kit,' he told me. 'Honeybadger's started territory-marking the bed. Time to start housetraining soon, I think.'

On my second day as his PA and general marketing bod, I'd taken over Jack's rarely updated social media accounts. My first innovation had been to run a Facebook poll asking his fans to suggest names for the other puppies. Hence in addition to Muttley, we had, in order of age, Princess Sparkle, Honeybadger, Puppy McPuppyface, Dr Geoffrey Bracegirdle and Puptimus Prime. Luckily for them it was only temporary: they'd be getting renamed when they got to their new home, hopefully with something more suited to working farm dogs.

'Rolled-up newspaper to the nose,' Jack's dad said with a knowledgeable nod. 'Tough love. It's the only way.'

'Me and Kit decided we'd try the non-violent approach,' Jack said. 'Mind you, can't say the naughty step's making much of an impact. Honeybadger pissed on it.'

'Political correctness gone mad, all this softly-softly parenting nonsense,' Michael said, shaking his head. 'Your gran beat me regularly as a child, and as I often tell my dominatrix during our Saturday appointments, it never did me any harm.'

'Matter of opinion.' Jack helped himself to a generous measure of his dad's whisky. 'Still, I'm sort of fond of you.'

'If you're really fond of me, you can go a bit easier on that whisky,' Michael said, rescuing the bottle so he could top himself up.

The Duffys certainly knew how to look after us. They were lovely, open-hearted people, warm and welcoming to me and affectionate to their son. Chrissy and Michael were just as keen to influence Jack's life as my mum had always been to influence mine, but it was all done so gently, with such obvious love and concern for his wellbeing, it couldn't help but make me think with bitterness about my own parent.

Every time Jack and I exchanged a smile or a joke, every time we touched, there were the significant looks between them. It was easy to see where they felt Jack's best hope of getting over Sophie lay.

'Right, that's me done,' Michael said after a few hours of food, drink and conversation, pushing himself up unsteadily. 'I'm an old man. Can't handle my spirits like I could as a lad.'

'I'll turn in too I think, once I've checked on Sandy and the kids,' Jack said. He stood and planted a kiss on his mum's head. 'Night, Mam.' He hesitated a second before dropping another on top of my dark hair. 'Night, Kit. See you in the morning.'

Michael beamed at his wife, giving her arm a squeeze as he passed us to leave the room.

'Another glass of wine?' Chrissy asked when the menfolk had left us alone. 'Then you and me can have a chat, just the girls. I want to hear all about you.'

'I probably shouldn't, but... go on, a small one. Thank you.'

'So where do your family live?' she asked when she'd refilled our glasses.

'North Yorkshire. I was born there.'

'And what do they make of this new job? I don't know what Jack's told you but a live-in PA isn't exactly the usual thing. I can't say I wouldn't be worried, if I was your mother.'

I flushed. 'They don't exactly know.'

'Really?' she said, frowning. 'Why not?'

I looked at her, wondering how much I wanted to share. Her brown-black eyes, so like Jack's, were full of interest.

'Sounds ridiculously dramatic but I'm kind of on the run,' I confessed at last. 'That's how I met Jack. He picked me up hitch-hiking when I was running away from home.'

'On the run!'

'Yes. It was my wedding day. Caught my husband with someone else, and... I just had to get away.'

'Bloody hell!'

'I know.' I smiled. 'Probably thinking twice about whether you want your son employing an assistant who's managed to screw her own life up so royally, right?'

'I am not. I'm thinking the bastard deserves a good kick in the you-know-wheres.' She shook her head. 'Your wedding day, Jesus! Do your parents know where you are?'

'There's just Mum. My dad died last year. And no. I've worked hard to keep it secret, if I'm honest.'

'Why, sweetheart? She must be worried to death about you.'

'She's... she's not like you.' I met the glass-eyed gaze of a stuffed raven peeping down at me from one of the Duffys' huge bookshelves. It felt like it was judging me, somehow. 'See, if I told her where I was, she'd come get me.'

'But she can't take you anywhere you don't want to go, can she?'

I snorted. 'That's the problem. She'd convince me I did want to go.'

'I don't understand, Kitty.'

'No. I don't either, really.'

She stared at me for a moment in silence.

'Sounds like it's not just our Jack who's got his demons,' she said at last.

'Yeah,' I said. 'You know, when he first asked me to stay with him I thought he was just being kind. But in the end I think it was that we were two lost, broken people. He needed me as much as I needed him.' I pulled my gaze away from the creepy raven to look at her. 'Still want us to get together?'

She smiled. 'Picked up on that, did you?'

I smiled back. 'Just a bit. No offence, but you and Michael are the least subtle matchmakers ever.'

'So are we barking up the wrong tree then?' she asked, fixing me with a keen gaze that was even worse than the raven's. 'Isn't there anything like that between you?'

'Not right now. No.'

'But you'd like there to be?'

'I... don't know,' I admitted. 'I mean, yes. If the situation was different. But I just left my husband, under pretty traumatic circumstances. And Sophie...' I swilled my wine absently. 'What was she like, Chrissy?'

'Oh, she was a lovely girl,' Chrissy said. 'Good for him. Organised. Good-natured. Same sense of humour as him, they were always laughing together.' She still had her keen gaze fixed on me. 'A bit like the two of you.'

'Do you think he'll ever get over her?'

'No. You never get over a lost love. Especially when it's so sudden like that.'

I blinked. 'Oh.'

Hearing her come right out with it like that, so stark... it hurt a lot more than I'd anticipated.

She reached out to squeeze my hand. 'But just because she's got a little piece of his heart doesn't mean there isn't room in there for someone new. And in that sense, I think he's been over her a good while.'

'Do you?'

'It's that awful, violent way she died that he can't deal with, that makes him the way he is now. But emotionally... yes. I'd say he's ready to let someone else in.'

'And you think it should be me?'

'If you can make him happy. That's all we ever wanted for him.' She pressed my hand again. 'And from what I've seen tonight, I think you can. Come on, sweetheart, let's go find your room. It's after midnight.'

Chapter 15

It felt like I'd only been asleep a few hours when someone shook me awake again.

'Kitty. Wake up.'

'Jack?' I mumbled. I opened my eyes to find him standing by my four-poster bed in the en-suite room Chrissy had got ready for me. 'Why aren't you in the van?'

'Came to show you something.'

'Show me something?' I blinked sleepily. 'What time's it?'

'4 a.m.'

'4 a.m.!' I jerked fully awake and sat up. 'Why the hell are you waking me up at four in the morning?'

'Shhh. You'll wake my parents,' he whispered. 'And I told you. Something I need to show you.' He handed me a thick fleece. 'Get that on and come with me. You'll have plenty of time to sleep after.'

'So come on, what is it?' I muttered, grumpily pulling on the fleece over my pyjamas. Christmas Day aside, I really wasn't a morning person. Or at least, not a four-in-the-morning person.

'It's a surprise. Something worth interrupting your beauty sleep for, I promise.'

'Not that I—'

'Not that you need any.' He grinned. 'Way ahead of you.'

Curiosity eating through my drowsiness, I shoved my feet into a pair of crocs and, as quietly as possible, followed Jack down the stairs.

'I feel like a teenager sneaking out when I've been grounded,' I whispered.

'Good,' he whispered back. 'You've spent all your life trying to be a good girl, Kitty Clayton. Now I'm making it my mission to teach you a bit of rebellion.'

'Where are we going then? Drug-fuelled rave? Orgy?'

'Nah, much better than that.' He unlocked the front door and slid out. 'Follow me.'

I tiptoed over the huge lawn after him, past the camper towards a dense cluster of trees that marked the far end of his parents' land. Jack took my hand and led me into the dark patch of wood.

Thick foliage quickly eclipsed the watery dawn light and I had to pick my steps carefully to avoid tripping. There was no sound but the crunch of twigs under our feet and the trees, whispering their secrets together in Tree Scottish. Which I imagined was something like 'Oooh, have you seen that oak at number three? She's only gone and got herself some lah-di-dah new ivy. And just turned 412 last Tuesday. Would you look at her, all climbing plants and no knickers?'

I giggled.

'What?' Jack said.

'Nothing. Just laughing at tree gossip.'

He shook his head. 'You're some weird girl, you know that?'

'What if I step on a badger, Jack?' I whispered, tiptoeing carefully after him.

'You won't step on a badger.'

'You don't know. I might do. I bet there's buckets of badgers in here.'

'All right, if you step on one it'll gnaw your leg off with its big, sharp badger teeth then drag the rest of you home to feed its flesh-starved badger babies.'

'Comforting. Ta.'

When we eventually emerged, blinking, into the open, I couldn't help gasping. I sucked my breath in sharply through my front teeth then let it out again in a low whistle of appreciation.

It was the loch. Loch Rusky, right there just half a mile from his parents' house. And it was every bit as beautiful as he'd described it to me when he'd triggered my dormant wanderlust, the day after we'd delivered the puppies.

There'd been an overnight fall of rain and delicate wisps like fish scales streaked the sky, lavender-tinted where the rising sun touched their tops. They were bright against deep blue, and the lake... God, it was incredible. Perfect glass, the fish-scale clouds within its still waters just as bright and clear as their twins above. A handful of colourful fishing boats dotted the surface, and a thin film of mist hovered over the water where it met the far shore. A playful early-morning dragonfly darted around us, his tail shimmering emerald.

'Jack...' I whispered. He'd been right. It had kicked the breath out of me.

He moved behind me so he could put his arms around my waist. 'So?' he murmured close to my ear. 'Better than it looks in any travel guide, am I right?'

'Much better.'

For a while we gazed at the mirror loch in silence. Jack's arms were still around my waist, and I could feel his hot breath on my neck.

It occurred to me that wasn't quite right for employer and employee. Laurel very rarely used to hug me on the banks of lochs at sunrise. Still, it felt wonderful.

'Worth waking up for?' Jack asked after a bit.

'Definitely.'

'And fighting off those herds of vicious Scottish badgers?'

I smiled. 'What, waving claymores and shouting "freedom"?'

'Ah, those'd be your sellout Hollywood badgers. The others don't truck with them.'

'It's gorgeous, Jack,' I murmured, my gaze fixed on the glittering water. 'Really.'

'I knew you'd think so,' he said, sounding pleased. 'If you don't see the loch at sunrise, it's a trip wasted.' He nodded towards the little boats. 'Plus the place'll be overrun with daytrippers and anglers in a few hours, which tends to take the shine off.'

'Lucky sods.' I thought back to sunny days with Dad, sitting on the bank of a lake or canal clutching our sandwiches while we waited for that all-important twitch on the line. 'There's nothing like the peace of a day's fishing.'

'What, you fish?' he said, sounding surprised.

'I used to, when my dad was alive. We'd pack the car and head up to Aunty Julia's, see what we could catch in the lake.' I sighed. 'They were the happiest times in my childhood, when it was just us three.'

'Your mam didn't go?'

'Never. She hated me fishing. It was the one thing I remember my dad standing up to her about, insisting he was taking me whether she liked it or not.' I smiled. 'She thought it was dreadfully unladylike. She was obsessed with teaching me to be more ladylike.'

'How did that go?'

I shrugged. 'Well I can open a Heineken bottle with my teeth.'

He laughed. 'So you and your Aunty Julia are pretty close then?'

'Yeah.' I blinked back a tear. 'At least, we were. Before.'

'You know, she was probably only doing what she thought was best for you,' Jack said gently. 'You were in a real state that day. She must've been worried.'

'I trusted her. I trusted her and she let me down.' I lost the battle, the little tear meandering down my cheek. 'Dad would've never done that.'

'Why don't you call her?'

'I can't. Not yet.'

'Okay,' he said, in the same gentle tone. 'But you're running out of family, Kit.'

That was certainly true. Dad, Mum, Aunty Julia... all out of my life, one way or another.

Dad had been dead a year now, and it still hurt every day when I woke up and remembered again that he was gone. Yes, Aunty Julia's betrayal was still sore, but Jack was right: she probably had believed she was acting in my best interests. Did I really want to cut Dad's only sister out of my life forever?

'I'll think it over,' I said at last.

'That's the spirit,' Jack said, giving me a squeeze. 'So do you want to do some fishing while we're here? I'm up for giving it a try, if you think you can be patient enough to teach me.'

I glanced over my shoulder to squint at him. 'Hang on. Isn't your next release *Tilly and Billy Go Fishing*?'

'Glad to see you've been doing your PA homework.'

'You wrote a book about it and you've never even tried it?'

'Nope. And don't spread it around, but I've also never pirated on the high seas, gone up in a hot air balloon, grown a sunflower or met Father Christmas. I use this little thing called imagination.'

'Fraud.'

'Says the former travel guide editor who's never been further than Blackpool,' he said, smiling. 'So how about it then, Kit? My dad'll know where we can hire equipment and get an angling permit, no problem.'

'No, I don't think so.'

'Why not?'

'It's just... these days I kind of feel bad for the fish,' I said, fiddling sheepishly with the zip of my fleece. 'Their little faces gaping at me.'

153

He laughed. 'And yet you'd eat bacon sandwiches from now till Doomsday if you could get away with it.'

'I know, I'm an enormous hypocrite. The bacon doesn't look at me accusingly, that's all.'

'Was thinking we'd throw them back anyway. That's okay, isn't it? They can have a long, happy fish life and tell all their friends about the angler that got away.' He held his hand up high above his head. 'This big, he was.'

'Well, it's not just that,' I said, flushing. 'I haven't fished since my dad died.'

I just couldn't imagine casting a line without that familiar, smiling figure next to me. It didn't seem right.

I wondered if Dad could see me, wherever he was. What he'd think of my life right now. Things could have been so different for me if Grant Clayton had still been a part of my world.

But he wasn't. One day with no warning, he'd gone; left me at the mercy of Mum and Ethan, in the midst of plans for a wedding I'd never been sure I wanted. It felt like half the fight had gone out of me, the day he died.

'Oh. Okay,' Jack said gently. 'Sorry, I didn't realise it was something special for the two of you.'

'That's all right. It was a nice idea, just... well, maybe another time. I'm not ready yet.'

'What was he like, your dad? Tell me about him.'

'He was a pain in the backside. A relentless tease, a terrible joke-teller. Forever embarrassing me in front of my friends, just because he thought it was funny.' I sighed. 'Best dad in the world.'

'Would he like me?'

I turned to face him. 'He'd probably tell you you need a haircut,' I said, smiling at the scruffy curls. 'You would've won him round though. You'd make him laugh.'

'Miss him, don't you?'

'Course I do.' I paused. 'Only...'

'Only what?'

'I worry, sometimes. That I don't miss him as much as I should.'

'How do you mean?'

'Well... okay, do you remember that band Atomic Kitten?'

'Er, yeah, vaguely,' Jack said, looking puzzled at the abrupt change in conversation topic. 'Why?'

I stared down at my crocs, drops of dew settling on the pink rubber and trickling through the holes to tickle my bare feet. 'I used to love them when I was a kid. Had all their albums, posters plastering my bedroom walls...'

'Lots of little girls did, didn't they?'

'Yeah, they were pretty massive back in primary. And then when I grew up... it's like I forgot they ever existed. Completely forgot this huge obsession I'd had. It was only when I was clearing some old stuff out and found the CDs that it all came flooding back.'

I glanced up. Jack was looking at me, his eyes soft.

'And you're worried that's what'll happen with your dad?'

'Sort of. It feels like every day, I forget something else about him. And when I've forgotten it, it's like it never existed. Like another little piece of him's disappeared.' I blinked back a tear. 'When Dad died, I didn't think there could be anything more painful than that. But it's the little, gradual death in my memories that's worse. The pain that's there every day.'

'Come here.'

Jack pulled me against his comforting chest and I relaxed in his arms. His arms were a great place to be. More and more lately, I'd been idly daydreaming about how it might feel to move into them permanently. Memories of my life with Ethan felt almost like a dream – one that, I constantly reminded myself, had no power now to hurt me.

'Do you ever feel like that?' I whispered.

'About Soph?' He hesitated. 'No,' he said at last. 'It's... I don't know, it's the opposite, somehow. Every trick of speech, the way she'd fiddle with her hair when she was nervous or walk on the insole of her shoe, her laugh, her scent... I remember it all, in excruciating detail.' He shuddered. 'It's horrible actually.'

'You wouldn't want to forget her, would you?'

'No, of course I wouldn't. But even now, I can be walking down the street and do a double take because someone's wearing the same perfume or got their hair up the same way. For a split-second, every time, I think it's her. It's her, she's here and everything's okay. And then it hurts like hell when it hits me all over again that I failed her. That's she's still gone, and I... that I couldn't stop that.'

'It isn't your fault, you know.'

'I know. Rationally, logically, I know. But that doesn't make it stop.'

'Survivor's guilt, they call that, don't they? My grief counsellor helped me through mine.'

'It's not the surviving. It's the fact I saw it happen and I couldn't save her life.' He winced in pain. 'Feel like my brain needs bleaching.'

Poor damaged Jack. I squeezed him tight, pressing my cheek to his chest. Chrissy had sounded so sure, the night before, that emotionally he was ready to move on, but I couldn't help suspecting that might be a mother's wishful thinking. Who knew if he'd ever get over the wife he lost enough to properly move on – to make space for someone else?

Or, not someone else. Me. If Jack fell in love a second time, I couldn't bear it to be with anyone but me.

'Thanks for being with me, Kit,' he mumbled into my hair.

Chapter 16

During our time in Scotland, we quickly settled into a routine.

At weekends, it was like being on holiday. In the almost unrealistically gorgeous surroundings of the Highlands there was plenty of walking and sightseeing to be done, and like me, all three Duffys were keen walkers. They seemed to love taking me round the local beauty spots, telling me the history of the place, as if having someone to show it all off to made it new in their eyes too.

On weekdays, though, we worked. If the weather was fine Jack would take his sketchbook down to the loch and work on the next Tilly and Billy, or else shut himself in the camper, while I stayed in the house and got to grips with my PA duties.

I'd set up a little corner of my en-suite room as an office area, with my brand-new phone and laptop looking very official perched on the dresser, and from nine to five every day I sat there: updating Jack's Facebook, Twitter and the new Instagram account I'd set up, arranging interviews, answering emails and letters, and getting his website – which really was horrifically amateurish, for as big a name as he was – redesigned. I even managed to sort out my first book signing.

Jack was a terrible influence on his own staff, constantly trying to get me to play hooky so I could go out walking with him – egged on by his ever-unsubtle matchmaking parents. But I was determined to be professional, and no matter how the sun shone, how beautiful the loch looked, I refused to leave my desk.

My one concession was that sometimes, little Muttley was allowed to sit with me. At five weeks old our pups were getting to be quite a handful, tearing around the house chasing each other, chewing anything in sight, rough-housing on the stairs until Chrissy finally complained she was going to trip and break her neck if Jack didn't keep them downstairs.

He spent a lot of time with them, housetraining mainly, and encouraging Sandy to start weaning them. In just three weeks, he said, they'd be ready for their new home. I was already dreading the parting.

And it wasn't just rehoming the pups that was disturbing my peace of mind. It was what was going to be happening right after.

Once a week I called the only two people I wanted to talk to at home, Laurel and Nan – always on a Wednesday, when I knew Mum would be off doing her weekly shop, and always being careful to withhold my number. And while I'd tried to ignore it at first, dismissing it as tiredness or the general symptoms of old age, eventually I couldn't lie to myself any more. My nan's memory was worse every time I spoke to her.

'Are you sure you'll be okay to go visit?' Jack asked as he

perched on the edge of my bed one Wednesday while Muttley ran laps around his legs. 'It won't get you upset?'

'Probably. But I have to see her.'

'Will she tell your mam?'

I sighed. 'Her memory's so bad now, she probably won't even remember I've been there by the time she sees Mum.'

'Aww, Kit...' He reached out to give my hand a squeeze.

'I'd better ring her now. It's my usual time to call.'

He stood to go. 'All right so, I'll leave you to it. Better take the Muttster back to the others for another lesson on why piddling in Nanny's new boots is not going to make us any friends round here.'

'Well, I did tell you not to.'

He laughed. 'See you for dinner then.'

'Wait.' I grabbed his arm to stop him leaving. 'Stay a bit. I'll put it on speakerphone. I'd like you to meet her.'

He looked pleased. 'Oh. Okay. Will she remember though?'

'No, but I will.'

I withheld my number – a habit that'd become almost automatic, now – and dialled my nan. When it started ringing, I pressed the speakerphone option on my mobile and put it down on the dresser.

'Hello?' a frail voice said after it'd rung for a good minute.

'Hello, Nana. It's Kitty.'

'Kitty...' She sounded puzzled for a moment.

'Grant's Kitty,' I said gently. 'Your granddaughter.'

'Oh, Kitty! Hello, love,' she said, sounding happy to hear from me. I smiled at Jack, who pressed my shoulder. 'And how's university? I hope they're feeding you properly.'

160

'I've finished university now,' I said. 'I've got a job. I'm working for an author as his PA – personal assistant, that stands for.'

'A secretary, you mean?'

'A bit like that,' I said, deciding it was best not to get into a detailed explanation of the differences between secretaries and PAs. 'Only not so much typing.'

'Oh, well. It sounds very important anyway. Is he a famous author?'

'Yes, very. He writes for children.'

'Ooh. I can't wait to tell the milkman.' No family news was considered truly legitimate till my nan had passed it on to her milkman.

'Nana, there's someone I want you to talk to,' I said, flushing slightly. I nodded to Jack to introduce himself.

'Hello, Mrs Clayton.'

'Hello, Ethan. I hope you're looking after her.'

'It's Jack, Nan,' I said. 'Ethan's... it didn't work out with Ethan.'

'Didn't it?'

'No.'

'Oh, what a shame,' she said absently. 'Still, marry in May, rue the day, you know. Bad luck. I did tell Petra...'

That was my nan, a superstition for every occasion. But it did show she remembered there'd been a wedding, and the month too. That was encouraging. Maybe her illness wasn't progressing as quickly as I'd started to fear.

'Jack's my boss,' I said, bringing her back to the now. 'He's been very kind to me.'

'No need to worry about her, Mrs Clayton,' Jack said with a jovial courtesy I knew she'd appreciate. 'I'm taking good care of her.'

'Is that an Irish accent, lad?'

'It is. Good solid Wicklow stock. You?'

'I'm a Kerry girl myself. Tralee.'

'Ah, so that's where Kitty gets her good looks,' he said. 'No roses bloom like the roses of Tralee, my grandad used to say.'

She practically giggled.

'Oh, I like this one, Kitty,' she said. 'You hang onto him, won't you?'

I flashed Jack a smile. 'I'll try.'

'Now, before you go again, I've got someone here who'll want to say hello. She's just in the kitchen, putting my shopping away.' She raised her voice. 'Petra love! It's your Kitty on the phone.'

Mum! I stared at Jack, horror-struck.

'Hang up! Quick!' he whispered.

'Yes. Yes.' I started fumbling in panic for the phone, clumsily knocking it across the dresser in my haste. But it was too late. Before I could hit End Call, a too-familiar voice came softly through the mic.

'Hello, Kitty.'

She sounded very calm. It was the 'not angry, just disappointed' voice I remembered so well from when I was a kid. And not infrequently, from when I was an adult.

'H... hello,' I faltered.

'Seriously, hang up!' Jack hissed.

But I couldn't. Not now she was there. Like Pavlov's dogs,

162

I'd been trained to obey, and although I could feel my brain willing my hand to pick up the phone, some built-in reflex blocked it.

'Where are you?' she asked, still in the same calm voice.

'I'm... not telling,' I whispered.

'Where are you, Kitty Louise?'

Jack shook his head as I stared at him in horror. I could actually feel the words, the whole bloody address complete with postcode, lining up in my brain. It was going to force me to tell her. Oh God! And then she'd come find me and...

I thought of the wedding. I thought of Ethan. I thought of all the years I'd done nothing but what him and Mum had told me to do, and I forced myself to stay strong, physically biting my tongue to prevent the words spilling out.

'Mm-mmm' was all I could manage, my lips pressed shut.

'You're a silly girl who'll tell your mother where you are at once,' Mum snapped, the calm breaking at last. 'Do you know what you've put me through all these months? How worried I've been?'

'Well maybe it's not about you.'

I flashed a grateful look in Jack's direction for coming to my rescue. I couldn't trust myself to speak. And yet... and yet I couldn't bring myself to hang up either. I just stared with ghoulish fascination at the glowing screen of my mobile, silently thankful I'd remembered to hide my number.

There was quiet for a moment.

'Kitty, who is that man?' Mum demanded at last.

'Jack,' I managed to gasp, then clamped my mouth shut again before I let anything else slip.

'Jack? Jack who?' She paused, then when there was no answer carried on. 'Now stop playing games, young lady. I'm on my last nerve. Tell me where you are right now.'

'Jesus, that's how she talks to you?' Jack said. I nodded, one hand still clamped over my mouth.

'Now, Kitty,' Mum said in her most dangerously gentle voice. 'I can see you've fallen into some bad company. I'm not going to be cross. Just come home and you and I will make everything all right again, the two of us. You know you don't have to talk to Ethan if you don't want to.'

Ethan's name finally managed to break through whatever spell had taken my speech.

'No,' I said with as much strength as I could muster, anger forcing its way through my panic at last. 'No. I'm staying where I am. You can't tell me what to do any more, Mum.'

'We don't say no to our mother, Kitty Louise.'

'I think she just did,' Jack said brightly. 'Are you offended by strong language, Petra? Because I'm about to use some.'

'I'm sorry?'

'I'm not. Fuck off.' He grabbed the mobile off the dresser and hit the End Call button with force. I'd never seen him look so angry.

As soon as it was over I crumpled in my chair, sobbing hysterically. Jack stood over me, stroking my hair and making soft, comforting noises, until I was calm again. Poor little Muttley just blinked up at me, puzzled about why Aunty Kitty had all that water coming out of her face.

When I'd cried myself out, Jack took my hand and pulled me up into a comforting hug.

'What happened to you, Kitty?' he asked gently. 'Why didn't you hang up? I could see you wanted to.'

'I... couldn't,' I whispered. 'She... her voice. It has that effect on me.'

'She's brainwashed you.'

'No. No, she... I just got used to doing as I was told. When I was a kid, I mean.'

'She's brainwashed you, Kitty. Listen to you, making excuses for her. Just like you did for Ethan.' He shook his head. 'Peas in a pod, those two, aren't they?'

My brow lowered. Now Mum was gone, the anger was starting to take over. Anger at Mum, but more than that, anger at myself. That I still let her have power over me, even now.

'You don't know the half of it,' I muttered.

'The way she talks to you like you're a naughty five-year-old,' Jack said. 'All that "a girl's best friend is her mother" crap. God, what is she, Norman Bates in drag?'

'Never heard you swear at anyone like that before.'

'Never felt like it before.'

'You understand now, don't you?' I asked. 'Why I can't go home?'

He held me back to look into my eyes. 'But this is exactly why you have to go home.'

I frowned. 'What?'

'Don't you get it? She's trained you up, like a bloody performing seal. Trained you so that when she says "jump", you say "how high?" Or "off which cliff?", by the sounds of it. God, between her and that fucking husband of yours, I'm surprised there's any of you left.'

'That's not—'

'You're not going to get over it by spending the rest of your life running away. You need to confront her, Kitty, or you'll always be afraid of her.'

I wriggled out of his hug. 'What do you know about it?'

'I know I just saw my smart, confident PA crumple like a little kid because her bullying mother gave her a dressing-down. And I know no one has the right to make another human being feel like that.'

'It's my life,' I said, glaring at him. 'You're not the boss of me.'

'Well, technically speaking I am.'

'Don't joke. I told you I don't want to go home. If you really cared about me, you'd respect that.'

'Well I'm sorry, because I can't,' he said firmly. 'Some day, you'll need to go back and face her. You can't hide forever.'

'What, you're giving me lectures now?' I demanded. 'You're just like the rest of them. Telling me what to do.'

'I'm not telling you what to do, Kitty, I'm trying to give you some advice. You need to tell your mam clearly and firmly that you're your own person. She needs to treat you like an adult, with respect. Otherwise how can you ever move on?'

'That's a bit rich coming from you.' I bent to scoop up little Muttley, who was letting out a low, anxious whine at seeing her humans arguing. 'She wants Sandy. I'm taking her down.'

'What do you mean, it's a bit rich coming from me?' Jack demanded, jogging after me down the stairs.

I went into the front room and plopped Muttley down with

her sister Princess, who greeted her immediately by diving on her and biting her ear.

'Well, it's not like you're so great at facing up to things, is it?' I said.

'Meaning what?'

'You know exactly what.'

His brow knit. 'Cheap shot, Kitty.'

'It wasn't any kind of shot,' I said. 'I mean, Jesus, Jack, you can't even sleep indoors. It's pretty clear you've got some serious issues because of Sophie's death and you're doing bugger all to fix them.'

'Yeah. Well I'm sorry if seeing my wife get knocked down by a car right in front of me left a bit of a scar,' he said darkly.

'Of course it left a scar. And something like that, it never will heal completely. But you can't live in a campervan all your life because of it.'

'Why can't I?'

'Because you'll never be properly fulfilled, will you? You'll never be able to have a normal life with – with the things in it that other people have. You need professional help, Jack.'

'I know what I need. Freedom's what I need. The van gives me that.'

'You're not free, not really,' I snapped. 'You've made that thing a prison for you and your grief.'

'I'm okay how I am.'

'And so am I.'

'I don't need a normal life.'

'I don't need to go home.'

'And I don't need advice from you.'

'Me either.'

'Fine.'

'Fine.'

We were quiet a moment, seething silently.

'You know, you can be a sanctimonious son of a bitch sometimes,' I said at last.

'And you can be a stubborn cow when you put your mind to it.'

'You know your problem, Jack? You just won't see the world as it is. Everything's fucking Sunshineville to you, isn't it? Because there is no tomorrow, right?'

'You know yours? You latch on to the nearest convenient person, because that's what you've been conditioned to do. Your mam, Ethan, me. Kitty Clayton's never enough for you, is she? That's your problem.'

There was silence. He glared at me. I glared right back at him. Perhaps what was making me angrier than anything was the fact that I knew he was bloody right.

And yet... no. I couldn't go home. And I wouldn't be told what to do, not by Jack or anyone else. Those days were gone.

The air was heavy with tension. The weight of things said that couldn't be taken back. Of things unsaid we were both too afraid to put into words.

'Right,' he said at last, his voice hoarse. 'Bloody well come here.'

But I was way ahead of him. I flung myself towards him at almost the same time as his arms went round my neck, and the next second we were kissing. And crying, both of us. And kissing.

'Kitty, I'm sorry, I'm so sorry,' he whispered, peppering my neck with kisses.

'No, I am. I shouldn't have said that. Any of it.' I grabbed his face to kiss him on the lips again.

'What happens now?'

'I don't know,' I whispered. 'Jack, you know I—'

There was the sound of a throat clearing, and we turned to see Jack's parents standing in the doorway, grinning at us.

'I hope we're not interrupting,' Michael said, quirking an eyebrow. 'As if I didn't know we were.'

'Just came to let you know dinner is served,' Chrissy said. She was beaming like she'd just found a winning lottery ticket.

'Oh. Thank you,' I said, flushing crimson. 'Um... thank you. We'll be right there.'

Jack just smiled.

Chapter 17

The heavy thing on my shoulder shook me again. I tried to ignore it, but it wouldn't go away.

'Kitty.'

'Hmm?' I mumbled.

'Come on, wake up.'

It was that voice again. I blinked my eyes open to focus on Jack, silhouetted in the moonlight that was streaming through the chink in my curtains.

I yawned. 'Okay, why're you sneaking into my room this time? Because much as I love a sunrise, I really wouldn't mind a full night's sleep every once in a while.'

'I'm courting,' he said in a formal tone. 'Come to claim a date off you.'

I blinked. 'A date?'

'It felt like the right time.'

I glanced at the glowing alarm clock on my bedside table. 'But it's midnight.'

'Yep.' He grabbed my hand and pulled me up. 'Get dressed, Kit. We're taking the van for a drive.'

***

'How long will it take to get to this place?' I asked. We'd been driving for half an hour, the landscape becoming increasingly rugged. I wasn't sure what sort of date Jack could have planned out in the middle of nowhere at nearly one in the morning, but I was intrigued.

'Nearly there.' He swung the camper down a bumpy track and parked up on a patch of gravel at the bottom.

I opened the door and got out, feeling equal parts curious and bewildered. Jack joined me a second later carrying a large holdall.

'What's in there?' I asked.

'You'll see.'

I laughed. 'Mysterious bugger tonight, aren't you?'

'Yep. Mysterious and sexy.'

'And modest.'

'That too.' He reached into his holdall for a little LED lantern and flicked it on. 'Come on.'

He led me towards the reflected gleam of what looked to be a pond in the distance. But as we cleared the last of a group of trees, I discovered it was actually a largish pool, midnight black, well illuminated by the full moon. It was sheltered by a high granite crag, curling round it in a semi-circle.

'It's so... sparkly,' I said in an awed whisper.

'Here, let's sit.'

'Okay.'

'Wait,' he said as I was about to lower myself onto the

171

stubbly grass. He yanked a blanket from his bag and spread it on the bank. 'You'll be more comfortable on that.'

We sat down together on the blanket. Jack pulled me against him and I nestled into the crook of his arm, looking out across the still water.

'Pretty,' I said, quietly so as not to disturb the night-time hush. 'Like liquid moonshine.'

He laughed. 'Very poetic. Only I'm forced to remind you liquid moonshine's that redneck homebrew they have in America.'

'Oh yeah.'

He drew a gentle finger down my cheek. 'Kit, about today... we've not really had a chance to talk, have we?'

I flushed. 'No.'

'But I've been thinking. And I thought, how about we just don't talk about it? How about we just go to some beautiful place and be together and don't talk?'

'Fine. I hate talking.'

'Me too.'

I snuggled against him. 'It's a lovely idea for a first date. Thanks for bringing me.'

'Ah, but this is only the first bit of the date,' he said, shuffling round to look at me.

'Are we having a picnic?'

He shook his head. 'Guess again.'

'Wine?'

'Maybe afterwards.'

'After what?'

He grinned. 'If I asked you to get your kit off now, what would you say?'

'I'd say "bloody hell, you don't waste any time, do you, you cheeky git?"'

Jack reached into his bag of tricks and pulled out a couple of large towels. 'In that case, get your kit off, Kit. We're having a swim.'

My eyes widened. 'Seriously?'

'Yep. Might be a bit chilly but trust me, it's worth it.'

'Are you having me on?' I nodded to the pool. 'You don't expect me to swim in there?'

'Why not? I promise there aren't any sharks. A few feral sticklebacks, maybe.'

'I might get cholera or something.'

'No you'll not. That's good clean water.' He nudged me. 'Come on, did you not tell me when we first met you dreamt about swimming in Icelandic pools?'

'Well I did, but...'

'So dark they were almost black. See, I remembered.' He gestured to the water. 'Not everything worth experiencing is across an ocean, Kitty.'

'I didn't bring a swimsuit.'

He grinned. 'Me neither.'

'But it's... I've never...'

'Ah go on. I double treble dare you.'

'Someone might come.'

'It's one in the morning. Who do you think's going to come, the Sandman?'

I rubbed the towel's soft cotton between my fingers. Skinny dipping by moonlight. It was a romantic idea for our first date, I had to give him that. And sweet that he remembered what I'd told him about my dreams all those months ago.

I mean, I wanted to. Naked in the cold, clean water, the freedom of it, just like I'd dreamed. It sounded incredible.

The question was, did I dare? Dream Kitty had more of a nerve than Real Life Kitty when it came to public nudity. In fact, I could count the number of men who'd seen me full-frontal naked on one hand: just Ethan, my dad when I was a kid and my uni friend Carl, who'd never been particularly interested in seeing girls in the buff whether they chose to take their clothes off or not.

Even with Ethan I'd always exercised damage limitation on those early-to-bed Saturday nights: made sure the lights were off and I was first under the covers. And now there was the lantern and the full moon, ready to show up every bump and flaw on my scrawny little body.

'Well?' Jack said. 'Will we risk a public indecency charge?'

'Can you look the other way till I'm in the water?'

'Nope. If you take your clothes off, I'll be looking at you.' He tapped the side of his head. 'Not stupid, lass.'

'You're a one, aren't you?' I said, shaking my head. 'Has there ever been a time you haven't done exactly what you wanted?'

'I do what feels right. That doesn't always mean what I want.' He leaned over and planted a quick kiss on my cheek. 'And this feels right. I want to see you as nature made you and I want to tell you you're beautiful, Kitty Clayton. Go on, be a rebel.'

'We'll get in trouble if anyone sees though.'

'Is that you or your mam talking?'

I smiled. 'Skinny dipping is pretty unladylike, isn't it?'

'Yep. Common as muck.' He nudged me. 'Come on, I dare you. Do something shocking.'

'I want to. I'm shy, that's all.' I ran my gaze over his broad frame. Oh yes, it was all very well for *him*.

He shrugged. 'Well, I'm going in. You can come join me if you change your mind.'

With an air of complete unconcern, he took off trainers and socks and started struggling out of his t-shirt.

I put a hand on his arm. 'What, you're going to strip off? Just like that?'

'Er, yeah. Why?'

'Aren't you even a bit self-conscious?'

'Why should I be? There's nothing wrong with being naked, is there?'

'Well, no, but... look, couldn't we keep our pants on?'

'You can if you want. I prefer skinny dipping the old-fashioned way.' He finished wriggling the t-shirt over his broad shoulders and stood to unfasten his jeans, sliding them off along with his underwear.

'Sure you won't join me?' he asked, kicking away the discarded denim and standing in front of me in the full, bare glory of his naked body.

I didn't say anything. I just stared.

'You know, for someone embarrassed about nudity you're not above getting an eyeful of it, are you?' he said with a grin.

'Huh...'

'I'm going to interpret that noise as "wow, what a man".'
He took my hand and pulled me to my feet.

'So will you?' he said when I was standing.

I don't know what colour my face was by this point but
from the temperature in my cheeks I suspected it was at least
fuschia, possibly verging on magenta. Maybe even puce. I felt
like a Dulux catalogue in Barbie's Dreamhouse.

'Okay,' I whispered.

'You sure?'

'I'm sure. Try not to laugh, that's all.'

He smiled. 'Here, come to me.'

Jack drew me gently into his arms. His big, bare arms, my
cheek resting against his equally bare and attractively rippling
chest. I fought against a sudden urge to touch him, to feel
every inch of that sleek flesh under my fingers.

Fought... and lost. There was something about Jack, the
way he just did whatever felt natural, that I couldn't help
finding infectious. I let my hands glide up his back, caressing
the ridges of his spine and the strong contours of his shoulder
blades; savouring the way his body felt against my palms.
Smooth, firm...

I suddenly found myself wondering how he'd taste.

'How do I feel then, Kit?' he asked softly.

I trailed my fingers down, letting them come to rest in the
small of his back. My heart thudded against my ribs like some
frantic caged thing, and I didn't know any more if this was
the prelude to a swim or something else.

'You feel... good. God, Jack...' I moved my hands over the
firm buttocks and sucked my breath in sharply.

'So?' he whispered.

'You do it for me.'

I felt his large hands slip under my clothing. He unhooked my bra, and I lifted my arms so he could peel off my top. Down went top and bra onto the blanket.

He held me away from him so he could scan my now naked upper body. I crushed my eyes closed while he drank me in.

'Open your eyes, Kit.'

'I can't. You might have a look on your face.'

'What look might I have on my face?'

'Oh, I don't know. Horror. Disgust. Barely suppressed laughter.'

'Open your eyes.'

I forced the lids up again. Jack was examining me, his gaze darting over my exposed breasts with nipples puckering to the light summer breeze.

'Now tell me what look I've got on my face,' he said.

'Is it... wait, are you drunk?'

He laughed. 'Nope.'

'Shock? Revulsion?'

'This is my impressed face.' He pointed to the curve at the corner of his mouth. 'See? You're beautiful, Kitty.' He reached out to draw one feather-soft fingertip over the swell of my breast, and I shivered with pleasure. 'My God... and you are that.'

'Hold me some more,' I whispered. 'I like feeling you there.'

He pulled me back into his arms, and I shuddered when I felt us flesh to flesh, the bare skin of his chest pressing against my breasts. His breathing quickened as he rubbed his hands down my back.

'You going to finish undressing me or what?' I whispered into his chest.

'You're the boss.' He put his hands on my hips and moved them back so he could unzip the front of my jeans. Hooking his thumbs under the waistband of my knickers, he slid down jeans and pants together, his palms caressing my buttocks and the backs of my thighs while he guided them down my body. I wriggled the jeans off and kicked them away, along with my shoes.

The breeze tickled against my bare skin; that odd sensation of having all the bits we know everyone's got but are usually tucked modestly away, exposed to the elements. It felt incredibly liberating; naughty, because that's what we're taught to think, yet at the same time so simple, so pure.

I flicked away the whispered voice in my head – the one that sounded like my mum – telling me this was wrong. Banishing it to the air, I pushed Jack closer against me and savoured the sweet, uncomplicated press of flesh on flesh.

'There's a naked girl in my arms,' Jack whispered.

'And there's a naked man in mine.'

'Can I see you?'

'Yes, love. Try not to laugh though, eh?'

He held me at arm's length so he could look at me again. He inhaled sharply, and this time the physical evidence of his appreciation was unmistakable. A group of muscles I was barely aware I had lurched towards my stomach in response.

'You gorgeous thing,' he murmured. 'Why would I ever laugh at you?'

'I don't look like you, do I?'

'Well, no. Good thing too.'

'You know what I mean.' I dragged my gaze over his toned legs and torso, well-defined muscles bursting out in all the right places. 'Honestly, look at you. Disgraceful.'

He laughed. 'Who's disgraceful?'

'You are. It should be illegal to be that pretty. Makes me sick.'

'Look, I didn't come here to be insulted in the most flattering way possible.' He gentled his voice. 'I mean it though, Kitty. You're gorgeous and you're sexy and you're... well, I can't think of another word but if I could you'd be that too.' His eyes lingered on my breasts. 'I could touch you forever.'

And his body told me he meant it. I flushed again, with pleasure rather than embarrassment. Little by little, his words and his arousal had eased my inhibitions away. For perhaps the first time ever I felt completely in control of my life, my body, myself, because I knew I was with someone who wanted me to feel that way.

'Here,' I whispered. 'Like this.'

Banishing the last shred of bashfulness, I took Jack's hand and guided it to my breasts, trailing his fingers over one erect nipple then along my tummy and around the little strawberry birthmark just above my belly button – the birthmark that had got me teased through five years of changing for PE and that until a little while ago I'd hated anyone to look at, let alone touch.

He followed the progress of his fingers with his eyes. 'What're you doing?' he asked huskily.

'Taking control. How do I feel?'

'Silky. Warm.' He shivered as I guided his hand over the bone of my hip. 'Unbelievably sexy. Mainly the last one.' He squeezed my hand. 'Come in the water with me. I want you to feel something before we take this any further.'

'Feel what?'

'You'll know when it hits you. Best sensation in the world, I promise.' His eyes skimmed my body again. 'Well, in the top three anyway.'

He led me to the water's edge and nodded to the satin-smooth blackness spread in front of us.

'Ladies first. Off you go.'

'But you'll see my bum.'

'I know. Lucky old me.' He patted one cheek with the flat of his hand.

'Stop it,' I said, giggling. 'The wobbles might cause a tidal wave.'

'Feels pretty wobble-free to me. Go on, let me have a look. Then if I drown I can die a happy man.'

'All right. But you promised not to laugh, remember.'

'Scout's honour,' he said with a solemn three-finger salute.

'Were you a Scout?'

'Yeah, I was a Sea Scout.'

I quirked an eyebrow. 'Not really?'

'Honest to God, back in Wicklow. Probably explains the abiding attraction to water.'

I smiled as I tried to picture a young Jack in a sailor suit and cap.

'Aww. Bet you were cute as a button.'

'I'm still cute as a button.' He gave my bum another encouraging pat. 'Off you trot then, my treasure.'

Screwing up my courage, I tiptoed to the lake. From the corner of my eye, I could see Jack tilting his head to get a better view of my backside.

What the hell. I gave it a little wiggle for him.

'Nice,' he said, shooting me a thumbs-up.

'You're a privileged lad.' I chucked him a grin over my shoulder. 'This girl doesn't shimmy for just anyone. In fact, you may be the first.'

'So proud.' He thumped his fist against his chest. 'Gets you right here.'

At the water's edge, I poked one toe in and shivered.

'Ugh. It's cold, Jack.'

'I'd rush it if I were you. Easiest way.'

'Rush it. Right.' I pressed my eyes closed and did that shoulder-throwing, huffy-breathing thing I'd seen Olympic divers do on telly. It didn't seem to help. 'Easiest way, you reckon?'

'Trust me, I've done this a million times.'

'Okay, here goes…' Throwing caution to the summer breeze, I ran forward and human-canonballed myself into the deepest part of the water.

'Arghhhhhhh!'

Jack grinned at me from the bank. 'Nothing like it, right?'

I spluttered water out of my mouth.

'You *bastard*!'

He laughed and waded out to join me.

'Well?' he said when he'd swum over to where I was treading water. 'How's it feel?'

'Cold as fuck.'

'And?'

'And cold as *fuck*. I hate you, Duffy.'

'Ah, you don't.' He sliced through the water and gathered me up in his arms. 'Come on, tell me you don't feel more alive right now than you've felt in your entire existence.'

'I feel like I might not be alive for long, what with the hypothermia.'

'Your body'll acclimatise. Wild swimming's something you should try at least once in your life.'

'It bloody well will be once, since I'm about to freeze to death,' I said through chattering teeth. 'What colour am I? Blue?'

'Whisht, Smurfette. You're a nice, healthy pink.' He smiled, reading my expression. 'Getting it now, aren't you?'

Grudgingly, I had to admit he was right. Now the shock of entering the water had worn off, my body had started to adjust to the chill. And with the inky pool embracing our naked selves on every side, the star-stubbled sky above and no sound except a wood pigeon calling to its mate in the distance, I did feel what he said – alive.

There was something else though. Freedom. The existence-affirming joy of a life like Jack's, a life without fences. Once you'd tasted it, it was like a drug.

Or an aphrodisiac.

Jack was still holding me, scanning my face for my reaction. 'Good?'

I nodded. 'Good.'

'In that case, how about another kiss?' he said softly. 'I've been thinking about the last one all night.'

I reached up to brush the wet hair away from his face. With his black curls dripping, his breath coming through in rough pants from the rush of entering the water and a moonlight glow shining from his eyes, he looked just about as sexy as I'd ever seen him.

Surrendering, I covered his mouth with mine.

In the few months I'd known him, I'd quickly learnt that Jack Duffy, impulsive as he could sometimes be, never did anything in a hurry. He didn't woo in a hurry, he didn't live in a hurry and, I was now discovering, he didn't kiss in a hurry. Instead he kissed with a passion and skill that just refused to be rushed.

He twined his fingers into my hair while he pressed warmth through his lips into mine.

Already tingling from the heady thrill of entering the water, my body sparked to life as Jack's languorous tongue opened my lips. He was taking his time with me, and my body responded in kind: with touchpaper desire, loitering and intense, kindling in each nerve and muscle. I put my arms around his neck, pushing our bodies closer below the water-line.

'Here,' he panted, pulling back. 'Wrap your legs around my waist. I'm strong enough to tread water for both of us.'

I did as he said – just then there wasn't much I wouldn't

have done for him – and he brought his mouth back to mine, bobbing me up and down as he kicked like a demon to keep us afloat.

I'd been thirteen when I'd had my first kiss. Sixteen when I'd lost my virginity. But I didn't feel like I'd really had my sexual awakening until that moment, with the life-giving water and Jack's tender fingertips teaming up to caress every bit of my naked body. Pressing myself against him, I felt a heat surging up from between my thighs that no amount of freezing lake could fight back.

'Ah!' was all I could manage when we eventually broke apart, breathless with cold and lust. Jack was panting too, and for a minute we didn't say a word.

'So will I make love to you tonight, Kitty?' he asked when we'd got our breath back.

'What, in here?'

He laughed. 'Not sure my treading water skills are that good.' He pushed damp hair away from my face. 'You'll stay with me, won't you, dear? In the camper?'

'Yes.'

'Nothing needs to happen if you're not ready. A kiss and a cuddle's good for me.' He looked down at the water jealously covering my nudity. 'Although if you want to keep your clothes off, I won't complain.'

'No, Jack, I'm ready. I want to spend the night with you. I mean, really spend the night with you.' I shot him a provocative smile. 'With my clothes off.'

His fingers carried on caressing my cheek and neck. 'I'll make you happy, Kit.'

I found myself blushing again, in spite of the cold. Unwrapping myself from his waist, I wriggled out of his arms before the effort of supporting us both became too much for him.

'Come swim,' I whispered. 'Then you're taking me to bed.'

Chapter 18

Half an hour later we were back at the camper, one hand gripping the towels we were enveloped in, the other clutching each other's fingers tightly.

'Still cold?' Jack said.

I wasn't really cold. I was trembling though.

'A little,' I fibbed.

'Then let me warm you up.' He chucked his towel down on the sofa and pulled me into his arms for a long kiss.

'Bed?' I whispered when he drew back.

'If you insist.'

'No, I mean we need one.'

'Oh. Right. So we do.'

He released me and plundered one of the overhead lockers for the bag of bits and pieces that made up the tailgate awning.

'Won't be a sec,' he said, flinging the door open.

'Really? You're going to put the awning up in your birthday suit?'

'Meh.' Shrugging, he turned his attractive backside towards me and stepped out.

'Don't get anything caught, will you?' I called after him.

I heard a clattering outside and the back door of the camper lowered, the room suddenly bigger. Five minutes later, he was back.

'That was fast,' I said.

'Amazing how quickly you can work when there's a naked woman waiting to make love to you.'

He turned his attention to the sofa, and soon the cosy little sleeping area was ready for us, illuminated by an overhead lamp. Jack clambered in and patted the duvet.

'You coming then, fellow skinny dipper?'

I laughed and climbed in after him.

He nodded at the towel wrapped round me. 'Tell me you're not still shy. You've already had your legs halfway up my back.'

'No...' I ridded myself of the towel and tossed it away. 'Not now.'

He pulled me down with him so we were lying facing each other.

'So can I hold you, Kitty?' he whispered, just as he had in bed all those months ago, the night the puppies were born.

'You'd bloody better.'

He nuzzled into my neck, the kisses he left there soft and slow, as if he was savouring my flavour. Then he moved his lips along my collarbone, one hand lazily tracing the shape of my body in a way that soon had me shivering again. With anticipation, but also anxiety.

'You cold?' Jack murmured from the arch of my shoulder.

'No,' I whispered. 'Not cold.'

My sex life with Ethan had always been... fine. Two minutes

top half, five minutes bottom half, a few energetic thrusts and a sleepy kiss, then that was that. In ten years, that had been the sum total of my sexual experience.

Jack was different. He approached foreplay like a man who had all the time in the world.

'Not nervous, are you?' he whispered as he ran leisurely fingers over my bare, trembling skin.

'No...'

Did I want to tell him that at the age of twenty-six, he'd be exactly my second all-the-way lover? I could feel my body tensing as his hands moved softly, sweetly, over my breasts and down towards my legs. What if I got it wrong? Oh God, what if it was terrible?

He stopped running the backs of his fingernails over my thigh when he felt me stiffen and brought his hand up to caress my face. 'We don't have to do this, Kitty.'

'No, I want to, honestly. I'm worried it won't be any good, that's all.'

He smiled. 'Well I've never had any complaints.'

'Not you. Me.' I sighed. 'Okay, confession time. I've never... I mean, apart from Ethan there's not been... I was a kid when we got together, you know? Sixteen.'

'Is that all it is?' His fingertips traced tender shapes on my cheek. 'There's no trick to making love, Kitty. There's just two people who want to be with each other, and who trust each other enough to drop defences.' His hand whispered over my body and he followed its progress with his eyes. 'God. Can't believe I get to touch something this beautiful.'

I smiled. 'You smooth-talking bastard.'

'Aren't I?' He rolled me onto my back and covered my body with his, burying his face in the hollow of my neck. 'I want you to enjoy this, Kit. But you need to relax with me first.'

'I'll try. Just... I want to get it right.'

'It's not a test. Do what comes naturally.'

'You show me how.'

Jack looked up from my neck to smile. 'Sure, it's easy. For example, right now I've a strong urge to kiss you, so I thought I might give that a go.' He brought his lips to mine for a deep, slow kiss, exploring my mouth with his tongue.

'And now?' I murmured breathlessly when he eventually broke away.

'Now I want to touch you, so unless you've any objection I'll be doing that.' I signalled I didn't with a shake of the head and he leaned to one side slightly so he could run a soft palm up my body, letting it come to rest on my breast. I let out a low hum of appreciation as he massaged my nipple with his thumb tip, feeling it harden under his touch.

'And now?'

'Now I want to kiss every inch of this gorgeous body until you're panting for me. Every little inch.'

My stomach tightened in pleasure.

'Will I?' he whispered.

'Anything you want, Jack. I trust you.'

He shuffled down so he could kiss at my nipple, and this time I let my whole body relax. I pushed my head back into the pillow, letting him take control, and allowed the moment to wash around me, just like the freshwater still beaded on my skin.

But my body was soon tensing again, not with nerves but with arousal, as in his own sweet time Jack moved over my flesh, licking and nuzzling at every bit of it, spending the most time where my skin was tenderest in a way that made it clear he knew exactly what he was doing.

I could hear his breathing, husky but measured, as he kept a tight rein on his own desire so he could focus entirely on mine. As he left unhurried kisses that were just the right amount of lips and tongue along my legs, his fingers trailing after his perfect mouth, I felt like I'd never understood that phrase 'generous lover' until I'd let Jack Duffy take me to bed.

'Ah... Jack,' I gasped as he moved the teasing lips across my knee to my inner thigh. 'There, please.'

'Good?' he murmured.

'Yes, yes, it's good...'

'A little more then.' He nipped tiny kisses up the sensitive skin of my leg, and I heard myself let out a needy moan as he grew closer to the hot, wet flesh at the top.

And then the cruel man moved away to kiss my other leg. 'No...'

'Every delicious inch,' he whispered, dark eyes flickering up to look at me. 'You said I could, Kitty.'

The soft lips he was torturing me with brushed gently, slowly, over my inner thigh, and every time he spoke it sent a breathy whisper skimming across my skin. I felt taut, pulsing; like I'd go insane if he didn't touch me where I needed to be touched.

I moaned again in lust and frustration, arching my back so my hips were pushed towards him, but still he wouldn't relent. When Jack Duffy says he's going to kiss every inch of you, turns out he's not bloody kidding.

'Please, Jack – ah! I can't take any more...'

'I think you can take a little more.'

Suddenly he moved up to plant a single, nuzzling kiss between my legs, then just as suddenly moved upwards again to kiss the little birthmark on my tummy. The pleasure and pain were so intense, when his mouth met my body I could almost have screamed.

'That's just... *mean*,' I gasped.

'You know you talk too much?'

And then he was there, between my legs, caressing me with slow, sweeping strokes of his tongue, and my body exploded almost instantly into a shuddering climax that was as intense and unhurried as Jack's mouth against my shaking flesh.

When the sensation subsided, I sank back against the mattress and he shuffled up the bed to join me. I shook my head, still panting heavily.

'Muh,' was the best I could manage.

He drew one finger over my cheekbone and along my throbbing neck. 'You're welcome.'

'Why...?' I gesticulated with one hand to indicate that one-syllable words were all I was good for just then.

'Because I wanted to see your face that way.' He traced my parted lips with his fingertip. 'I did that,' he whispered.

'And you're so proud,' I said, laughing. I rolled him onto his back and swung my leg over so I was sitting astride his stomach.

He smiled as I nuzzled into his neck. 'Whatever happened

to that shy little flower who didn't want to let me see her naked? She's gone all sexy for me.'

'You,' I whispered against his skin. 'You made me feel beautiful. No one's ever done that before.'

He reached up to caress my breast with his fingertips. 'Tell me how you see yourself.'

'I don't know. Sort of a pale, waif-like thing with no curves, I guess.'

'Will I tell you what I see?'

'What?'

He put his hands on my hips and shuffled up so he was in a sitting position under me.

'I see curves.' He leaned forward to leave a single, soft kiss over one breast. 'I see beauty.' He planted a row of kisses along my shoulder. 'And I see Kitty Clayton, the hottest little thing I've ever had the privilege of showing a good time. And if you don't believe me then I'm sorry, but there'll be no more orgasms for you.'

I laughed. 'You know, you kind of rub off. The way when you want to do something, you just chuck all the hang-ups and do it. I think it's catching.'

'And what do you want to do to me, Kit?' he asked with a wicked smile.

'Guess.' I pulled him into a kiss.

When I drew back from his lips, I moved to his neck, dropping scalding kisses in the hollow of his shoulder and on every bare inch I could reach. My fingers trailed over the well-defined muscles of his stomach and moved down to caress his perfect thighs. Self-consciousness, anxiety, were long gone now. All I wanted was to keep feeling him there, against me; to make it last as long as possible.

As I touched him, kissed him, taking my time just as he had with me, Jack's measured breathing quickened into a pant. Eventually I could tell from the instinctive movements of his body, clamped between my legs, that there'd be no more holding back. I drew my fingertips gently along the length of his erection, and he let out a soft moan of longing.

'Make love to me,' I whispered into the ear I was kissing. 'Sure?'

'Sure.' I flicked my tongue over his earlobe. 'I'm ready, Jack.'

'Protection...'

'Oh God, you have got some, haven't you?'

'Yes. In the cupboard.'

I cocked an eyebrow. 'Good little Catholic boy, right?'

He grinned. 'I'll dig out the rosary later.'

Jack guided me off him and reached over to rummage in the big cupboard. When he'd located a condom, he pulled me back over him and rolled it on. I caught my breath when I felt our bodies connect.

I'd always felt too self-conscious to be over-adventurous in the bedroom, and being on top was a new experience for me. I wasn't quite sure how it was supposed to work but I tried to take Jack's advice and do what came naturally, pushing my hips against him slowly, rhythmically, as instinct guided. Anyway, he seemed to like it, digging his fingers into my buttocks to bring our bodies closer with each thrust, so I must have been doing something right.

Every groan from him sent a thrill through me, to think

it was my body, my movements, giving him pleasure. And as he bucked beneath me, that glorious friction, his hot flesh sliding deep into mine, I was soon matching him in the noise stakes. My moans must've sent ripples across the pool outside.

'Don't close your eyes,' Jack whispered, his voice ragged. 'Look at me, Kitty.'

I opened my eyes and looked into his face. His expression of vulnerability and trust, his wet, parted lips, were all it took to push me over the edge.

I felt my body catch, a river of trembling nerves, the orgasm thumping through me even more intense than the last – but I didn't break his gaze. Those eyes... if he wanted to, I bet he could make me climax just with those beautiful, liquid eyes.

'Jack,' I gasped. 'Jack, oh God...'

Seconds later he joined me, holding me still against him as with his last breath he groaned my name. And as we collapsed, panting, into each other's arms I felt a shiver of exultation, because Jack Duffy, the most exciting thing that had ever happened to me, was finally mine.

Chapter 19

It was tipping with rain when we arrived at Yellow Pages, the bookshop where I'd organised a signing for Jack. That didn't seem to have deterred the crowds though. There was already a long line of kids and parents out front, waiting for the place to open.

'There's Diana,' Jack said as we approached the place. He waved to a woman by the door and she peeled away from the crowd to greet us. 'She said she'd try to make it up from London. Think she's keen to meet this uber-efficient new PA of mine.'

Diana's style screamed Great British Summertime: long floral dress, jewelled flip-flops and a blue Regatta raincoat. When she pulled down her hood, a handsome middle-aged woman with twinkling eyes and a no-nonsense mouth looked back at us.

'Hiya, Di,' Jack said, dipping down to kiss her cheek.

Diana crinkled her eyes as she submitted to the kiss. 'Hullo, young Duffy. How's my favourite client?'

'Dunno. I'm all right though.' He nodded to me. 'This is Kitty.'

Diana examined me while appearing not to examine me at all – a good trick if you can manage it. I saw her gaze flicker over Jack's arm, slung around my shoulders, and her pursed lips broke into a smile.

'Good to finally meet you,' she said, pumping my hand vigorously. 'I've been following your career with interest. Jack's keywords have gone through the roof since he's had you working for him.'

I frowned. 'His what, sorry?'

'Keywords. The number of results for things like his name, the books or characters in a search engine. The rejuvenated website and social media stuff are working wonders.'

I flushed. 'Oh. Thank you.'

'What time do we start, Kit?' Jack asked.

'Ten minutes till they open. We should get you inside.'

Diana smirked. 'Guess who's here again, Jack.'

I followed her gaze to a mass of pink braids and a pair of oversized spectacles attached to a scarfy middle-aged woman in the crowd.

'Who is it?' I asked.

Jack groaned. 'Sonia.'

'Jack's got a special vein in his temple for Sonia,' Diana told me with a laugh. 'No matter where he goes in the country, there she is at the front of the queue. Come on, we'll get him in the back way so he'll be safe from the adoring multitudes.'

We headed round the back of the old pink-sandstone building, taking a wide route to avoid the queue.

Inside I sought out the fawning elderly owner, whose sallow complexion and high domed forehead made him look like a cross between Bert from *Sesame Street* and a liquorice torpedo, and introduced Jack. The man sat him down behind a table piled high with copies of *Tilly and Billy Go to Sea* while Diana took my elbow and guided me to a sheltered corner that hid the large-print romances.

'We'll be safe here,' she whispered. 'Things are about to get manic.'

As soon as the doors opened, I saw what she meant. Noisy kids and parents flooded the room, the owner chappie having a hell of a time trying to corral them into any kind of orderly queue.

We watched the lady with the pink hair, Sonia, claim what she seemed to think was her rightful place at the front. The Bert-from-*Sesame-Street* owner flanking Jack opened his mouth to object, but something in Sonia's determined expression must've put him off. He caught her eye and hastily closed it again.

'Mr Duffy! It's me!' Sonia said, flashing Jack a delighted smile.

'It's not!'

Her brow furrowed. 'Yes it is, it's Sonia. Don't you remember me?'

'Couldn't forget you, could I?' Jack said, with his best attempt at gallantry. 'Just joking, Sonia. It's nice to see you again.'

Sonia's face couldn't have illuminated any more if he'd taken his top off and invited her to cover him in whipped cream.

'You really mean it, Mr Duffy?'

'Of course I do. And I told you before you could call me Jack.'

'Wow!' The sound escaped from her like an exploding steam engine.

A mother was behind her in the queue, her little boy gripping a copy of *Tilly and Billy Bake a Cake* against his chest. She tutted impatiently, but Sonia was oblivious.

'I got your new book as soon as it was released. I queued up outside the bookshop till it opened,' Sonia told Jack breathlessly. 'They said I was the very first one to buy a copy. The first, anywhere!'

'That's great, Sonia,' Jack said. 'Did you like it?'

'Oh, yes! I think it's your best one yet.'

He smiled. 'You say that every time though.'

Her face fell. 'Oh, but I didn't mean the others aren't good. They're all brilliant. Please don't be offended, Mr Duffy.'

'I'm not offended, I'm flattered. And please try to call me Jack. Mr Duffy's my mother's name.'

She blinked. 'Don't you mean your father?'

'No, my mother. We're an unusual family.'

Sonia's brow knit into a confused frown and Jack was forced to explain again that he was joking.

'How's Sandy?' she asked, casting a smug look over her shoulder like someone in on a special secret.

'Grand. Her babies are getting very grown up now. I'll send you a new photo if you like.'

'Oh goodness, would you really? Thank you!' Sonia's eyes were like dinner plates. 'Are they all going to live with you?'

'One is. The others are going to live on a farm.'

'What's your one going to be called? I can make him a jacket to match Sandy's and sew his name on.' Her eyes sparkled at the prospect.

'It's a little girl. Muttley.' He nodded over to me. 'My friend Kitty there named her. After the cartoon, you know?'

Sonia turned to look at me, and I saw her eyes narrow.

'I didn't know you had any friends who were ladies,' she said, sounding sulky.

He smiled. 'A couple. But none of them say the nice things about my books you do.'

'Oh God,' I whispered to Diana. 'Why do I get the feeling I'm about to have my eyes scratched out?'

She laughed. 'Sonia's harmless, just a big kid really. I think Jack's got sort of fond of her over the years.'

My eyes widened. '*Years?* Bloody hell, how long has she been at it?'

'Since he started, pretty much. The first time she turned up at one of his signings, Sophie was still with us. I remember her being distinctly unimpressed.'

I turned to face her, pulling my eyes away from Jack and Sonia. 'Seems like you've got to know him pretty well.'

'I have,' she said, casting an affectionate glance his way. 'I've got a lot of clients, but Jack's the only one I'd call a friend.'

'How come?'

'I suppose we got closer after his wife died. He's got that sort of lost boy quality, hasn't he?'

'Yeah. I know what you mean.'

'I'm glad he's got a couple of us now anyway. Until you came along, I think I was the best friend he had who wasn't covered in fur.' She rubbed her chin. 'For as long as the supply of Immac holds out, at least.'

I smiled. 'Don't go saying that kind of thing around Sonia. Next thing you know she'll be on your doorstep with a lifetime's supply of Ladyshaves.'

'Heh. Yeah, she's not big on irony.'

'How did he become a client?'

'The usual way. He sent in some of his work,' Di said. 'Well, I'd have been a mug to turn that down. I emailed within ten minutes of opening the envelope with an offer to rep him.' She shook her head. 'Couldn't believe it when I met him.'

'How do you mean?'

'Suppose I'd formed this idea from the Tilly and Billy cartoons of a little old grandpa in cord trousers and slippers. Then into my office strides this strapping lad in his twenties... thought for a minute someone had sent me a strippergram, until he told me who he was.'

I laughed. 'You should be so lucky.'

She patted my arm. 'Well, don't worry, we're just good friends. I'm old enough to be his...' She looked over at Sonia. '... Er, biggest fan.'

It was nearly two hours later when Jack finally finished. After the signing he did a live reading, then kept his seat while the throng of Tilly and Billy fans filtered out.

When most of the others had gone, a dad and little girl approached him. The child was clutching something against her chest, blushing furiously.

'Go on,' the father whispered. 'Show Mr Duffy what you brought.'

'Scared,' the girl whispered back. 'Don't wanna any more.'

Jack smiled. 'No need to be scared, sweetie. What's that you've got? Something to show me?'

''S,' the child faltered.

'Yes, Mr Duffy,' her father corrected.

''S Mr Duffy.'

Jack laughed. 'Well, it's just Jack. What's your name, kid?'

'Isla.'

'Can I see what you've brought, Isla?'

Isla looked at her dad, who nodded encouragingly. 'It's okay, princess. Let Mr Duffy have a look.'

After hesitating a moment, Isla made up her mind. She thrust the little booklet she was holding at Jack, her eyes scrunched closed.

'She made it herself,' Isla's dad said, his face shining with pride. 'Didn't you, princess?'

The little girl nodded so hard it looked like her head might bob off. 'I want to make books when I grow up too, like you, Mr Duffy.'

Jack flicked through the book with interest, spending a fair amount of time on each page.

'What's your story called, Isla?' he asked.

'*Molly and Polly Drive a Car*.'

Jack smiled at the casual plagiarism. 'I like that.' He held up the page he was looking at. 'Is this Molly and Polly here?'

''S. They're dollies.'

'And what're they driving?'

'Spiderman car.' She puffed up a little. 'That's like the one I'm gonna have. When I'm a rich lady.'

'Good choice,' he said. 'Is Spiderman your favourite super-hero?'

''S. Coz he's fast and he can climb stuff and he's got all this sticky stuff.'

'Web, right?'

'Yeh, web, coz he's half spider, 'cept he's not got lotsa legs like a real spider coz that'd be too gross. And the web stuff comes off his hands and he catches all the baddies with it and throws them into prison.' The little girl's eyes sparkled as she chattered, quite relaxed now Jack had put her at ease. 'And that's *sooooo* cool.'

'That is cool. Hey, can you guess my favourite superhero?'

She squinted one eye at him. 'Erm... Spiderman?' she asked hopefully.

'Nope.'

'Hulk?'

'Right! Wow, got it in two. No one ever guessed that fast before.'

Isla looked pleased with herself, and her father smiled at Jack.

'I'm guessing the in-depth superhero knowledge means you've got kids of your own?' he said.

'No,' Jack said, colouring. 'No, none of my own.'

He couldn't see me, but hidden among the shelves, I felt my cheeks pinkening in sympathy with his.

Kids weren't something me and Ethan had really discussed in depth. To be honest, he'd tended to deflect the issue, putting me off when I brought it up with excuses about his career and our finances. Exactly why had only really became clear when I'd finally seen the bank statements he'd been hiding from me.

Still, there'd always been an assumption, by me anyway, that a family would be part of my future, when the time was right. But now, with Jack...

Well, it was early to be thinking about anything like that. It was less than a week since our relationship had made the jump from friend-slash-employer to lover-slash-friend-slash-employer. But I couldn't help thinking about it, all the same. Would Jack, apparently unable to face the idea of a life indoors, ever be able to have a family? And if not, was I willing to give up on that dream to be with him?

I could see Di examining my blushes from the corner of one shrewd eye, but she had enough delicacy not to say anything.

Isla had fixed the book in Jack's hands with an anxious look. He smiled when he saw where her gaze was directed.

'Don't worry, I won't pinch it,' he said, handing it back to her. She took it from him and clasped it against her chest, breathing a sigh of relief at having her masterpiece back. 'It's a brilliant book, Isla. I bet your mummy and daddy are super proud of you, aren't they?'

The little girl flushed. 'Not Mummy. She's in heaven.'

Jack looked at Isla's dad, who responded with a sober nod.

'Then she's proud of you in heaven,' Jack said gently. 'Can I ask you to promise me something?'

''S.'

'Promise me you won't stop drawing. Because the more you draw, the better you'll be. And since you're already so good, in a few years you'll be one of the best drawers there is.'

Her eyes widened. 'Better'n you?'

'Easy peasy. But you have to keep practising, then you can buy all the Spiderman cars you want. Plus, ice cream. Everyone needs more ice cream.'

The little girl's face shone with determination. 'I will. I asked Santa for all new pencils this year. I'm going to practise and practise and practise till I'm better even than Summer Jessop.'

'That's a girl in her class,' her dad said to Jack with a laugh. 'There's a bit of rivalry. Thank you, Mr Duffy.'

'Just Jack. You're welcome.' He smiled at the man. 'Keep encouraging her, won't you?'

'I couldn't stop her if I tried,' the man said with a fond smile at his now beaming daughter.

'And you write to me if you want me to tell you anything,' Jack said to Isla. He nodded towards me and Diana. 'One of those ladies can give you a little card with my address to keep. Nice to meet you, Isla.' He held out his hand and Isla shook one finger solemnly.

'Good with the kids, isn't he?' I whispered to Diana while the little girl and her dad headed towards us.

'Because he never talks down to them,' Diana said. 'He'd have been a great dad. You know, him and Sophie were trying when she—' She broke off, fixing on a smile for Isla and her father as they joined her.

I was left to myself a moment to ponder the new information Diana had let slip. Instinctively, I rubbed my stomach.

While Di sorted out the little girl and her dad, I wandered over to Jack.

'Hulk?' I said, raising an eyebrow.

'Obviously. He's a big green lump of uncontrollable rage who smashes stuff, what's not to like?'

I shook my head. 'You've got layers, man.'

'Who would you have picked then?'

'Thor.'

He curled his lip. 'Seriously, Thor?'

'Yeah. He's got such glossy hair. I like a superhero who knows how to condition.'

'Sorry, Kit, just realised this isn't going to work. It's not me, it's you.'

I laughed and punched his arm.

'So what do you want to—' I broke off when I caught sight of a couple of kids in the thinning crowd. 'Oh my God!'

'What?' Jack said. 'What is it?'

'Get your things. We have to go.'

He frowned. 'What? Kitty, I can't just—'

'We have to *go*! Come on!'

But it was too late. I'd been spotted.

'Aunty Kitty, Aunty Kitty!' a little voice yelled. A small body barrelled into my leg, shortly followed by a second.

'Where've you been?' Toby demanded imperiously. 'Mummy said you were on holiday but you've been gone *ages*.'

'Um. Hi boys. Why're you... where's your mum?'

'Here.'

I looked up from them to see Laurel, shaking her head in shocked disbelief.

Chapter 20

'Okay, so here's a cute story,' Laurel said when she'd dropped the boys back with their stepdad and we were sitting behind a wine each in a nearby pub. 'There I am, on holiday with the family, when I see this sign announcing the kids' favourite author's in town. Lucky, right?'

'Laur, I—'

'So I take them along to get their books signed, and who do I find chatting away to the guy like an old friend?' She threw her hands up in mock surprise. 'Only my long-lost stepsister and erstwhile employee Kitty Clayton, who everyone in the family's been worried witless about for months.'

'Look—'

'And then I find out that not only does she know this author bloke, she's working for him. As his PA. Out of the back of a campervan, no less.'

'Actually we're staying with his parents at the moment. Just until the puppies are bigger.'

'And there's puppies,' she muttered to herself. 'Of course there are. I mean, why wouldn't there be?'

'It's fine, honestly. I know it sounds weird on paper, but...

well, okay, it's pretty weird not on paper too. But it's where I want to be.'

'Why though, Kit? What the hell happened that you ended up here?'

'I told you. Ethan. Honestly, Laur, if you'd been there – I mean, can you even imagine if Andy did that to you? On your fucking wedding day?'

'You know you could've come to me.' She reached across to take my hand, softening her voice. 'Why didn't you? Don't you trust me?'

'No, I do, course I do. I just… I had to get away. As far away as I could. Gut instinct.'

'You'd have run today. If I hadn't already seen you. Wouldn't you?'

I dropped my gaze. 'Yes.'

'Why, Kit? We've always been close, haven't we?'

The colour in my cheeks deepened. It was so hard to explain it, that fear of being pursued. No, not pursued – hunted. Even the people from my home life that I trusted most felt like part of that world. The one that seemed to be always on my tail, trying to drag me back.

'I'm sorry, Laur. It's hard to explain. But it's really not about you, I promise.' I gave the hand I was holding a squeeze. 'It's good to see you anyway. Missed you.'

'Yeah.' Laurel shook her head, as if to clear it. 'Yeah, you too.' She scanned me up and down. 'You look well enough, at least. Your mum'll be glad to hear you're keeping healthy.'

That was it. That was the reason. Because Laurel meant Mum, and Mum meant Ethan, and Ethan meant… possession.

I leaned over the table to look earnestly into her eyes. 'Laurel, please. You have to promise me you won't tell my mum you've seen me.'

'Eh? Why?'

'Please. If you love me, just promise.'

'But she's frantic, Kitty! Ethan too. He said he'd seen you, and you were... not in your right mind, he thought. That you'd hooked up with some dangerous tramp-looking—' She stopped. 'Oh. Duffy, right?'

'Well yeah. Who else?'

'Still, Ethan's half-mad with worry. He's been looking every-where for you.'

I just bet he had. God knew what state his bank account was in now, but without my earnings going in every month I couldn't imagine it was any too healthy.

'You have to promise, Laur!' I said, panic ringing through my voice. 'You have to promise not to tell. You just said I could trust you. Please, do this one thing for me so I know it's true.'

She looked puzzled. 'Well, okay, if it means that much to you.'

'Say it.'

'I, Laurel Taylor, promise not to tell your mum I've seen you.'

'Or Ethan.'

'Or Ethan.'

'Now cross your heart and hope to die.'

She crossed herself solemnly, still with the same bewildered expression.

'But I don't get it, Kitty. How did all this happen? How did you end up living in a campervan with my kids' favourite author? That's the bit I really don't understand.'

'Not 100% sure myself,' I admitted, finally letting myself relax a little – she had crossed her heart, after all – and taking a deep draft of my wine. 'Jack Duffy was the guy I told you about. The one who picked me up hitch-hiking, the day of the wedding. Nursed me when I got ill, gave me food and clothes and a roof over my head when I had nothing. Honestly, I don't know what I would've done without him.'

'And then he gave you a job.'

'That's right. Been doing it nearly a month now.'

'A job for which you've got no training or experience.'

'Well, no,' I admitted. 'But it's straightforward enough now I've got my head round it, plus I learnt a lot about the publishing industry when I was at Whitestone that's transferable. You just need to understand Jack, really.'

'And you understand him pretty well, do you?'

'I think so, yeah. Now.'

I examined her face. She looked tired, and a little older than the last time I'd seen her.

'How is work?' I asked. 'No offence, but you look like you've been burning both ends of the candle.'

She shrugged. 'Same old, same old. We've got a temp in at the moment, covering for you. Mhairi. She's not great but she's very keen to learn.'

'A temp? Why?'

She smiled sadly. 'Suppose I was cherishing a delusion my AWOL stepsister might come back to work one day. Just show up at her desk like nothing had happened, and everything could go back to how it was. I didn't realise she'd moved on to bigger things.'

I squeezed her hand. 'Oh, Laur, I'm sorry. I really am.'

'Me too,' she said with a sigh. 'So is this going to be your life now then? Just going from place to place with this guy?'

I hesitated. It was something I tried to avoid thinking about unless I had to. The future was an awkward subject with me and Jack for the place we were in right now.

'S'pose it is,' I said at last. 'It'll be good for me. You know how I always wanted to travel.'

'But you can't live like that long-term, can you?'

I shrugged. 'Why not? It's no different from those people who live in canal boats, is it? Or, you know, yurts or whatever? There's all sorts of alternative lifestyles.'

'Kit, can I ask you a question?' Laurel said.

'I guess.'

'Duffy… he's your boss, right?'

'And my friend.'

'So he offered you a job because he's your friend.'

'Well, it'd be nice to think he believed I'd be good at it.'

'Not for any other reason though?'

I felt my cheeks pinken.

'Such as what?' I asked.

'Okay, if you're not going to pick up on my subtle hints I'll just have to come right out with it. Are you sleeping together?'

I was silent.

She groaned. 'I thought so.'

'What difference does that make? We weren't when he offered me the job.'

'I'm worried about you, that's all. You're living cooped up in some tiny van with this man you've known for all of, what, three months? Working for him, shagging him... that's got to get a bit intense.' Her gaze took on that piercing quality she got from her mum, my dad's second wife Bernie. 'Are you in love with him?'

'None of your business.'

'Come on, Kit. It's me.'

'I... okay, I don't know,' I mumbled. 'It's early days to be thinking about that. Anyway, it's not important right now.'

'He's a widower, isn't he?'

'Yeah,' I said, frowning. 'How'd you know?'

She shrugged. 'Wikipedia. I looked him up before the signing for small talk purposes.'

Bloody Wikipedia. That was my fault. Updating his page had been one of the first things I'd done as his PA, significantly expanding the biographical details from the documents he'd supplied me with.

'Well, what of it?' I said, trying to sound nonchalant.

'I don't want to see you get hurt, that's all.'

'Why would I get hurt?'

'You can't compete with a dead wife, Kit. She'll always be the ideal and you'll always feel like you don't measure up. And the grief... it never really goes away, you know.'

I knew she was thinking about Jason, the boys' dad. A regular in the army, he'd been killed in action overseas when Laurel's littlest lad, Sam, had been just a baby. I think it had only been the fact she had two young kids that had kept Laurel from curling up in a ball and never uncurling herself.

'You fell in love again, eventually,' I said after a moment's sober silence.

'I know I did,' she said, flinching. 'But it was hard. I almost had to make myself. And the guilt that went with it... I mean, I love Andy to bits, but the pain of falling for him was almost as bad as when the grief was new. I'm not sure I would've coped, if it hasn't been for the bond he'd built up with the boys.'

'I know, it was hell for you.' I pressed her hand. 'But you did it, all the same. Maybe this could be what Jack needs to move on too.' I thought about Chrissy and Michael, how chuffed they'd been when they'd noticed me and Jack getting coupley – something, by the way, for which they took all the credit. 'That's what his parents think.'

She shook her head. 'Oh no. If you start trying to fix him you're doomed, love. He'll only resent you for it.'

'How do you know?' I said, a touch of annoyance creeping into my tone. 'You don't know him. Jack's not like that.'

She was silent a moment, watching my face.

'You are in love with him,' she said at last.

'I might be. I'm entitled to fall in love with people, aren't I?'

'Hmm. Don't forget you've still got a husband at home.'

My brow lowered. 'It's not my home. And he's not my husband. Not properly.'

'You know what I mean. You are still legally married to someone else. That's not nothing, is it?'

I glared into my wine, trying not to picture Ethan's stupid chiselled face. 'Only until I can file for divorce. Or annulment, given it was never consummated. Not really sure how that one works but I'll find out.'

Laurel looked sober.

'What?' I said.

She took a deep breath. 'Look. I don't want you to think I'm not on your side, okay? You know I am, totally.'

'But...?'

'It's just, Ethan,' she said with an apologetic grimace. 'It's like he's completely changed, since you've been gone. He really is distraught, Kit. Desperate, even.'

'Good. Serves him right.'

She shook her head. 'You wouldn't say that if you'd seen it. Andy's been taking him out to the pub a few nights a week, trying to get him out of himself, and he says he's never seen him like this before. He started crying in the Blue Pig the other week. Actually sobbing, in front of everyone.'

I snorted. 'What, Ethan? I don't believe it.'

'Seriously. Andy was totally stumped by it. He's really worried about what he might end up doing.'

'Yeah, well. Maybe he should've thought about that before he cheated on me,' I muttered darkly.

'Bit harsh, Kit. Honestly, I'm not exaggerating. The man's a mess.'

I glared into my wine. It seemed to me the infidelity alone should've been reason enough for Laurel to unequivocally take my part. I really didn't want to go into the money issues too, and the... I still found it hard to say. The control. The...

the abuse I now realised Ethan had subjected me to for years. Not the Uncle Ken kind, but the kind that dresses itself up as kindness. As love.

I couldn't bear to tell Laurel about it. For all Jack's reassurances I had nothing to be ashamed of, I still felt humiliated at the way I'd let Ethan control my finances all these years. To see the look of shock on the face of someone who'd been playing big sister to me since I was twelve years old... too much pain, for both of us. I knew there'd be tears; recriminations; blaming herself for not having seen it. It just didn't seem fair.

But the cheating – God, it was still so blood-raw. It continued to bite, long after the love I'd once had for Ethan had turned into disgust. Not hate, he wasn't worthy of any emotion that strong. Just a sickening ache in the bottom of my stomach to replace what had once been an almost holy adoration I realised, now, had never been healthy.

In the end, I was glad he'd spent my money. If seeing him with someone else hadn't been enough to cure me fully, then that was the second kick in the teeth I'd needed to finally start seeing him as he was instead of how I'd wanted him to be. Without that, maybe I'd still be there, trapped in that weird half-life.

'But is it really totally hopeless? What did you actually see that day?' Unable to read my thoughts, Laurel still seemed determined to fight Ethan's corner. 'If he snogged some drunk wedding guest – okay, that is really bad. But if it was just a one-off... you two were together ten years, Kit. Maybe you can work things out, if you just talk it through. He does really love you, you know, whatever stupid mistake he might've made in the heat of the moment.'

'Yeah, except this wasn't just some drunk wedding guest.'

'How do you know?'

'Because this wedding guest doesn't drink.' I gave a bleak laugh. 'Too worried about the calories.'

Laurel was silent for a good minute, just staring at me. I felt quite calm as I sipped my wine. It hadn't been hard at all, really, to tell someone. As easy as a stab in the back.

Finally she spoke.

'Fuck,' she said quietly.

***

'Congratulations, Kitty.' My stepmum Bernie bent to kiss me. 'I wish your dad was around to see you.'

'So do I,' I said. 'And Aunty Julia. I really wanted her to be here.'

'Couldn't she make it?'

'Mum thought it'd be too difficult to sort out wheelchair access to the farm. I told her I'd rather have it somewhere else if Aunty J couldn't come, but it turned out she couldn't make it anyway. Well, so she said. I think she was fibbing so as not to make a fuss, personally.'

'You look beautiful anyway. She'll burst with pride when she sees the photos.'

I laughed, waggling one of my rubber wellies. 'I know. I'm like the Yorkshire Cinderella.'

She smiled. 'Yes, where is the handsome prince? Haven't given him my congratulations yet.'

I glanced around the large barn, where guests were sitting around on hay bales enjoying champagne or artisan gin from the pop-up bar Ethan had arranged. 'He's somewhere around, meeting and greeting. I'd better go find him actually. The photographer wants us on the back of the hay wagon for a photoshoot.'

I left her and went to seek out Ethan. He wasn't in the barn, which meant he must be outside somewhere.

Lifting my dress so it wouldn't trail in the mud, I headed outdoors. I couldn't see anyone other than the photographer, fussing over the hay wagon while he got it ready for me and Ethan, but I could hear a faint buzz of voices somewhere far away. Angry voices.

There was a cluster of trees in the distance, decorated with fairy lights for the occasion. The voices seemed to be coming from over there. I made my way towards them.

As I got closer, the voices started to solidify.

Oh God. It was Mum and Ethan, rowing again. You'd think they could knock it on the head, just for the day. Still, at least they'd had the decency to get themselves out of earshot of the guests before they'd started tearing chunks out of each other.

'I can't believe you went for red drapes when you knew Kitty would be in green,' Mum was saying. 'She looks like head elf in Santa's grotto.'

'What do you care?' Ethan snapped back. 'You never wanted this wedding to go ahead in the first place.'

'I never said that, did I?'

'Come on, Petra, admit it. You might as well, now it's too late for you to do anything about it. You've never thought I was good enough for her, have you?'

216

'Of course you're not good enough for her.' I was close enough to see Mum stick her sculpted chin out at a haughty angle. 'She's my little girl.'

'And you'll never think anyone is, will you? Not for your precious Kitty. Whether I love her or not weighs nothing at all with you.'

I stayed hidden, lurking behind a tree. It was sweet to have Ethan saying nice things about me, and I wanted to hear what he was going to say next.

'Let's face it.' I saw the silhouette that was Ethan grab Mum's shoulders in both hands. 'You never wanted a daughter, did you? What you wanted was a miniature Petra. A human Barbie in your own image, to dress up and order around and live your life through when you were getting too old to Botox the years off any more.'

I blinked. Human Barbie… that wasn't fair. Okay, so maybe Mum did baby me a bit, but that was just her way of showing love. I was about to come out from my tree to defend her when Mum spoke up.

'How dare you,' she hissed. 'How… dare you! Since the day you turned up in our lives, you've come between Kitty and her real family. Taking her away from us when she wasn't much more than a child.'

'She was sixteen. A woman.'

'And how old were you? Twenty-four?' I could hear the sneer in her voice. 'I've always wondered why you couldn't manage to find a girlfriend your own age.'

'Because I loved Kitty.'

'What you loved was getting her away us. From me.' She

scoffed. 'What was it, a power thing? Men, you're all the same. Pathetic.'

'Maybe I did try to get her away from you,' Ethan snapped. 'She needs to get away from you. You're bad for her.' He lowered his voice. 'You're toxic, Petra. As a mother, you're toxic.'

'And you're so much better for her, are you?' Mum spat. 'She's barely had any friends her own age since she's been with you. You've done your damnedest to push away everyone she was close to. Laurel, me – even her father when he was alive. Just so you could keep her all to yourself.'

'So I could keep her to myself? Oh, that is rich. Oh yes, I like that one.' Ethan was still holding Mum's shoulders. 'Why do you hate me so much, Petra? I think me and you should have a little talk about that, don't you?'

'You know why.'

'Yes, I know why. Because I've got something you want. Something you want but can't have, and it's been eating you for years, hasn't it?' I watched him pull her closer until their faces were almost touching. 'Don't you think it's high time you told me what it is?' he breathed.

'Kitty.' Mum's voice was so quiet it was almost a whisper.

'Not Kitty. We both know this was never really about Kitty.'

'Don't hold me like that, Ethan.'

'Why? Worried you might start to like it?'

My ability to move had long fled. I just stood behind my tree, transfixed by the horror show unfolding before me. In my heart, I knew what was about to happen. Something I'd rather lose my eyes than see. And yet I couldn't tear my gaze away. Even then, with Ethan's face inches from my mum's, I just couldn't believe what he was about to do.

'Let me go,' Mum whispered. 'Let me go or I'll scream. I swear I will.'

'Go right ahead. I'm dying to make you scream.'

'I mean it. I'll scream, I'll—'

She stopped suddenly, the last word oddly muffled. And even with the glaring sun in my eyes, there was no mistaking why. Those two silhouettes, merged now into a single entity. Oh yes, I could see clearly, too clearly, what had stopped my mum's speech.

Lips. Ethan's lips. My husband's lips.

My stomach heaved, and I fought down a strong urge to vomit.

Ethan! Even while it happened right there in front of me, I couldn't believe it. And as for Mum… well, there was no screaming. No pushing him away, no slap in the face. She was kissing him passionately back. As I watched, Ethan's arms twined around her, pushing her body closer into his.

Forcing my senses up through the shock paralysis, I backed away, just as quietly as I'd come. I had to stay calm. At least for now, I had to act like nothing at all was wrong. I had to not throw up.

Outside the barn, Laurel was smoking a sly cigarette away from the judgemental eyes of her mum and husband.

'You coming in, Kit?' she asked. 'Party's really getting started now. The band are just warming up for another set.'

'Yeah.' I smiled with forced brightness, willing my voice steady. 'Yeah, I'll be in in a minute. Thought I'd walk around the grounds

219

a while, get some air. It's all been a bit overwhelming.' I gave her hand a squeeze. 'Thanks for coming, Laur. I love you.'

'Um, yeah,' she said, surprised at the sudden show of affection. 'Love you too.'

She stared after me as I started walking.

I walked and I walked, out of the farm, along the little country lanes, stopping twice to vomit as my body finally rebelled against the shock it'd just received. When I was well out of sight, I broke into a run.

I didn't stop for a good couple of miles, until exhaustion eventually got the better of me. Finally I collapsed by the side of the road, where after a little while a nice man in an orange campervan pulled up to offer me a lift.

Chapter 21

It felt like a relief, finally to have told someone what happened that day. Laurel promised not to say a word to my mum, and there was no further talk of me going home. She did tell me when we said goodbye, though, that if I ever wanted to visit, she'd arrange it so there was no chance of me bumping into either Mum or Ethan.

Which was sweet, but I knew Jack was right. At some point – not now, God no, but sometime in the future when I felt mentally fortified – I needed to face my demons. Mum, that is. I had to truly break whatever hold she still had over me if there was any hope of moving on with my life in a healthy, grown-up way. It wouldn't be easy, but the more time I spent away from her, with Jack and his lovely, normal parents, the more I realised it was necessary.

'One step at a time,' Jack said when I confided this to him in bed in the camper one night. 'We're rehoming the puppies next week, then I'll take you to see your nan. That's step one. Once you've made yourself go back to that place the first time, it'll be easier to do it again.'

'What happens after we visit Nana, Jack?' I mumbled as I snuggled sleepily into his bare chest.

'I thought we could go to Wales for a bit, see what's to see. It's a beautiful country.'

'Where in Wales?'

'Snowdonia?'

'Ooh, yes. That sounds lovely.' I yawned. 'Will we just move around then?'

'Until you get sick of me.'

'Not going to happen,' I whispered as he nuzzled his face into my hair.

But it was there again. Our naked bodies were pressed close as we fell into sleep, but there was a distance, all the same, and its name was Future. Because after Wales... what then? A lifetime of just this: of me and Jack, living like nomads in the van?

In a way, that was everything I wanted. Freedom, after a lifetime of control. A world of horizons, mine for the taking. And Jack. Oh yes, and Jack. Freedom and horizons and Jack. Those were worth a few sacrifices.

So why did I feel more unsettled with each day that passed?

***

Jack's friend Ben lived on a little farm just outside Settle in the Yorkshire Dales. After saying an affectionate goodbye to Chrissy and Michael, who expressed an earnest wish to see us both again very soon, we packed all seven of our dogs into the van and set off. My stomach was in knots at being so close to home after all these months.

After a four-hour drive, including a few stops for the pups to have a run and a wee, Jack finally pulled up outside the steel gate that marked the entrance to Ben's farm.

He got out to nudge it open and juddered us along the cattle grid, parking outside an old sandstone farmhouse. A handmade sign in Yorkshire dialect announced 'MANURE FRESH FROM T'OSS – 'elp thisen!'. That made me smile. Family worries aside, I did sometimes feel homesick for the old place. There were a lot of beautiful places in the world, but none of them had a beauty or a character quite like home.

I was sitting in the back with the puppies. Two were snuggled into their mum's tummy in the dog bed, scared by the bumpy track down to the farm, while the other four engaged in boisterous rough-and-tumble. I'd seen Jack's gaze occasionally flicker back to them in the rear-view mirror while we'd been driving. For all that he'd found them the best possible home, I could tell parting with them was breaking his heart almost as much as it was going to break poor Sandy's.

Ben was waiting outside the farmhouse to meet us. He was a weatherbeaten old chap in wellies and shabby tweed, with an elderly-looking Jack Russell at his heel.

'Jack Duffy, you old bugger,' he said, slapping Jack's arm.

Jack nodded a greeting. 'Benjamin. You got that dirty old man of yours snipped yet?'

'Heh. Who knew the lad still had it in him?' Ben leaned down to tickle his dog between the ears. 'Nay, I couldn't do owt to him I wouldn't do to myself.'

'Lock up your wives, eh?' Jack said, grinning. He jerked his head in my direction. 'This is Kitty.'

Ben smiled at me. 'Nice to meet you, love. You're his young lady, are you?'

I wasn't sure if whatever I was to Jack constituted being his young lady or not. We hadn't really had that talk.

'Um, kind of,' I eventually managed to mumble.

'So where's these dogs of mine, young Duffy? I've sorted them out with sleeping quarters in one of the barns. Give 'em a few days to settle in then I'll set to training.'

'I'll fetch them,' Jack said. 'There's five in the end, is that okay? I'm keeping the other with her mam.'

'Two more than I need to be honest, but they'll have a happy home here. Always nice to have dogs around the place.'

Jack beckoned to me and we headed to the camper.

Two of the playing puppies had joined their mum and there were four now snuggled into Sandy, looking the picture of warmth, contentment and motherly love while their siblings raced energetically around the van. Jack's eyes were damp, and I gave his arm a squeeze.

'Has to be done, love,' I said gently.

'I know. Doesn't make it any easier though.'

He reached down to pick up Honeybadger, the little boy who'd nearly died when his airways had blocked during delivery. He gave a tiny yawn, snuggling against Jack's chest just as happily as he had against his mother. Sandy blinked at Jack sleepily, her gaze full of placid trust.

'Oh God,' Jack whispered brokenly. 'Poor little girl. It's going to hurt her so much.'

'You want me to do it?'

'Both of us.' He shot me a weak smile. 'Thanks, Kit.'

I smiled back, but I couldn't say anything. Words seemed to be sticking in my throat.

I reached down to retrieve a puppy, tucked him under my arm and scooped up another, Jack catching the runners until only Muttley was left.

Sandy shot me a suspicious look. She clearly trusted her dad with her babies more than me. Not that either of us deserved it, the traitors we were.

Jack sent a last apologetic glance Sandy's way as we pushed open the door. 'I'm so sorry, girl. Hope you can forgive me.' He looked at me, eyes filled with hurt. 'Soon as we get going, I'll book her in for a spaying. I can't go through this again.'

Outside, Ben cast an appraising glance over the puppies in our arms, wiggling restlessly during this extended period off ground.

'Fine animals,' he said eventually with the approving nod of a connoisseur. 'Healthy and strong. They'll make good farm dogs.'

'You'll look after them, won't you?' I asked. 'Sorry, I mean, of course you will. But you'll... you'll love them?'

'This is a working farm, lass, not a petting zoo. We don't have time to get sentimental.' But his gruff face softened when he registered our anxious expressions. 'Well, don't worry. Tough old bastard I may be, but I've never had a dog didn't have a good life. Just look at Raggles here.' He nodded to the old Jack Russell, who was eyeing his new family with an air of curious suspicion. 'Nigh thirteen now. He's not had to work in two year, since his back legs started to give. Well, you get fond of 'em, in the end.'

'So they'll be pets?' I said.

'No, they'll be workers. But they'll be well cared for. And loved, if you want to put it like that.' He smiled, his eyes crinkling, and I knew he meant it.

Jack's Adam's apple was bobbing, and I could see he was fighting back tears. He handed his puppies to Ben, who tucked them under his arms with the air of someone who'd done this a hundred times. Then he nodded curtly and headed back to the camper without saying a word.

'He's a sentimental sod, letting it get to him like that,' Ben said, following him with his gaze. 'Here, love, let me get these lads inside and I'll come back for yours.'

He went into the farmhouse to stash the wriggling puppies somewhere, then came back for my two.

'Cheers, Ben,' I said, handing the tubby little furballs over. They wagged their tails in a puzzled manner, snuggling against him as if they could tell that here was someone who'd keep them safe. 'Sorry about Jack, he didn't mean to be rude.'

'That boy's lost too many things he loved,' Ben said, looking sober. 'We all have. But for him it was too soon; too soon and too young.' He looked me up and down. 'You seem a clean, hearty lass though. Bit on the skinny side, but good birthing hips. You'll do for him.'

I squirmed under his gaze, feeling like a prize cow on show. Ben obviously wasn't a man to hold back when he had an opinion.

'Er, thanks.' There didn't seem much else I could say to a compliment on my good birthing hips.

'I'll look after these lads and you pair look after each other,' Ben said, turning back to the farmhouse. 'Try not to let him lose you too.'

The words sent a shiver of fear through me, like it was some sort of jinx. Silly superstition, my nan's legacy. Still, I practically ran back to Jack and the van.

Chapter 22

'And you're sure you don't want me to come with you?' Jack asked as I struggled into my coat.

'No. Thanks for offering, but you were right,' I said. 'This is something I need to face up to myself. I'll text when I want a lift, then we can get straight off. I don't want to spend the night round here.'

'You're not likely to run into your mam, are you?'

'No, I timed it. She'll have her weekly toning tables session today. Just need to make sure I'm out of there by five.'

'And if you do?'

Ugh. Mum. Just the thought of seeing her filled me with horror.

'If I do... I do,' I said, trying to sound confident. 'I'm not running away. Not any more.' I shivered. 'But God, I hope I don't.'

'Go on, say it again.'

'I'm an adult, this is my life and no one controls it but me.' I went over to kiss him. 'Thanks for pushing me to do this, love.'

He held me tight for a moment. The warmth of his body flowed into me; gave me strength.

228

'Your taxi's waiting,' he said at last, brushing my hair back from my face. 'Be brave, Kit. Just ring if you need me.'

'I will.' I gave him a peck. 'See you in a few hours.'

***

I was ready. I could do this.

Those were the words I kept carouseling around my brain as I stepped out of the taxi and made my way up the stairs to Nana's flat, occasionally interspersed with the lyrics to I Have Confidence from *The Sound of Music*.

Except I wasn't ready, not at all. I wasn't ready to be at home, so close to the two people who'd committed the ultimate act of betrayal right in front of me. I certainly wasn't ready to confront my mum. But if I could just take this first step, I was on my way.

The stairwell was the same familiar stairwell, clean and sterile, with a faint hint of synthetic apple from the disinfectant the cleaning staff used. It seemed like a thousand years since I'd last been there, although in reality it was less than four months ago. Life had changed so completely since then.

The visit was going to be a complete surprise. I hadn't told my nan I was coming when I'd spoken to her last, about two weeks ago. I knew she probably wouldn't remember, plus there was every chance that if she did, she might let it drop to my mum.

Sending a firm order to the butterflies dancing rumba steps in my belly to give over, I tapped at the thick, swimming-pool-water glass of Nan's front door.

It sometimes took her a while to answer. After a minute, I knocked again.

Eventually, a figure appeared behind the glass. It was distorted and warped by the weird ripple pattern, but I knew in an instant it wasn't my nan.

This figure was youngish, tall and slim, well-dressed in a figure-hugging pink lace shift dress and matching jacket. Thick flaxen hair hung loose over her shoulders. There was no mistaking those kitten heels, that immaculate pink-and-peroxide style I knew so well.

Mum.

What the hell was she doing here? She was supposed to be far away, getting toned in exchange for some extortionate fee. Typical she'd pick today of all days to change her routine.

Despite what I'd told Jack before coming over, my first instinct was to run again. Leg it down the stairs before she could get the door open, find Jack and the dogs and get the camper as far away from this hell of bad memories as possible.

But a voice, one that for some reason had an Irish accent, kept whispering in my ear. 'Be brave. You can do this.' I wasn't ready, but I knew if I ran again, now, it was another failure. Another victory for Mum and Ethan as I let them control me, dictate who I saw and where I went. I was a whole new Kitty now, and new Kitty couldn't let that happen.

'I can do this,' I muttered out loud to myself. 'I'm here for my nan. I'm an adult and I've come to see my nan and no one can make me do anything I don't want to do.'

The door opened, and there... there was my mum. Another round of Botox had shaved a couple more years off her age since I'd been gone, but apart from that she looked the same as ever.

'Hello,' I said, trying to sound firm and confident and all those other things I didn't feel. 'I've come to see Nana.'

I don't know what I was expecting. Hysterics, at the very least. Tears, recriminations, white-hot fury. The usual passive-aggressive guilt-tripping and emotional blackmail as she pleaded with me to come home. I definitely didn't expect the quiet, sedate hug I suddenly found myself enfolded in. I just stood there, wide-eyed, while my mum's perfectly manicured arms wrapped around me.

'I'm glad you're here,' she said in her gentlest voice. 'Come inside, please.'

I followed her in, blinking in bewilderment.

'I haven't come home,' I said. 'Not forever. I just want to see Nana then I'll be getting straight off again.'

I steeled myself for an onslaught of blame. But Mum just smiled sadly, as well as she could through the evil stuff she insisted on paralysing her face with, and gestured to the sofa.

'Have a seat, angel. Would you like tea? I've got some of my green, or there's the other kind if you really must. But I do recommend the green. It whitens the teeth, you know.'

'Thank you,' I said automatically, sitting down. I shook my head. 'No, I mean no. I don't want tea. Where's Nana, is she asleep?'

'That's right.'

Mum parked herself next to me on the sofa, and I instinctively recoiled. Even her scent, the expensive perfume she practically bathed in, caused some sort of visceral nausea in me. I was still haunted by those silhouettes, the two people who claimed to love me most in the world, committing the ultimate act of betrayal.

'It's good to see you,' Mum said gently.

'I'm not staying.'

'Why not, Kitty?'

'I... can't,' I muttered. 'I just came to...'

I trailed off. Everything had started to feel sort of dream-like, Mum's familiar scent regressing me gently back to childhood. In the familiar surroundings of my nan's front room, even the silhouettes started to fade.

'I just came to see Nana,' I managed to whisper.

'I fixed your room up,' Mum said.

'My room?'

'Yes. New bedding for you, and I put all your favourite books in there. There's a little television set, and I got you some new clothes so you wouldn't be short of anything you needed.'

'Why?'

'So you can come home, of course. A fresh start for you.' She ran a soft hand over my hair. 'You know you don't have to go back to Ethan.'

'Ethan.' I jerked awake when I heard the name, and pushed her hand off my head. 'Don't you *dare* talk about Ethan to me!' I snapped, surprised by my own passion.

'Don't raise your voice, Kitty.'

'Don't raise my voice! Are you fucking kidding me?' I glared at her. 'Go on, Mother. Ask me why I ran away.'

'Oh, I think we all know that,' she said in an offhand tone.

'What?'

'Well, it's what you do, isn't it?' She laughed, that little trilling laugh that made her sound like a silly affected school-girl. 'When you're upset, you run away. Everyone knows that.'

I flushed with shame and embarrassment. It was a cheap shot. And the dismissive way she said it, as if the whole thing had been some foolish little kid's fancy rather than what it was. A total breakdown.

Okay, so there had been another time I'd run away from home without telling anyone where I was going. After my dad died eighteen months ago, my brain, rebelling against the never-before-experienced pain of grief and loss, had started taunting me with frequent tricks. Seeing Dad where I knew he couldn't be. Forgetting he'd died and trying to call him on the phone. I'd genuinely felt I might be losing my mind.

Mum and Ethan had practically pulled me apart as they'd tried to 'look after me'. There'd been this horrible aura of What To Do About Kitty all around me, all the time, until I could barely think. Struggling to cope with my bereavement and the feeling of being watched twenty-four hours a day, I'd taken off from Mum's, where I'd been staying. Taken off in the middle of the night, with only the shakiest grip on what was real and what wasn't.

I hadn't got far that time. My mental health was too shat-tered for anything as logical as hitch-hiking. I'd gone to the Whitestone Press offices and slept on the floor, under my desk, where Laurel found me shivering next morning.

After everything she'd been through losing Jason, she under-stood at once. Taken me home to stay with her, convinced me to see a doctor, who'd referred me to a grief counsellor. And yet still, all my mum remembered was the time her daughter 'ran away'. Ran away from home, even though I'd been twenty-four years old and entitled to go where I wanted. Ran away from her.

'This was different,' I mumbled.

'I'm assuming Ethan did something to ruin your big day.' She softened her voice to a persuasive croon. 'Tell your mum all about it, angel. We'll fix things together, like we always do.'

I gave a bleak laugh. 'Yes, Ethan did something. And it's no good pretending you don't know as well as I do what it was.'

She frowned, creasing her perfectly smooth, white brow. 'I'm sorry?'

'You shouldn't do that. You'll get frown lines.'

She lifted her brow at once. 'What is it I'm supposed to know, Kitty?'

I leaned forward. 'I saw you, Mother. With Ethan. My wedding day, by the trees – ring any bells?'

She blinked. 'The trees? What trees?'

'The ones at the farm, of course.'

Mum looked thoroughly confused now. 'There aren't any trees there, Kitty. It's just open farmland.'

'Oh please, I'm not a child. The days when I believed something just because you told me it was true are long gone,' I snapped. 'There was a little clump of trees with fairy lights, and I saw what you and Ethan were getting up to behind them.'

'I beg your pardon?'

I swallowed hard. This was the most difficult bit to say out loud. But I'd come this far...

'I saw you... I saw you kissing,' I said. It was actually a relief to get it out. 'I saw what you did, Mum. Kissing my fiancé – no, sorry, my husband. Your own daughter's husband.' I could feel nausea rising just thinking about it. 'That is seriously sick, you know that?'

To my surprise, Mum let out a peal of laughter.

'Oh, I'm sorry,' she said, forcing herself quiet again. 'I'm sorry, I know it's not funny. It's just so... impossible.' She took my hand in both of hers. 'Kitty, honey, you're really not well. I promise you, that never happened.'

'You think I'm that easy to manipulate, that you can just say that and make it go away? I saw you, Mum! Both of you!'

'I'm your mother, Kitty. I love you. Do you really believe I'm such a monster that I'd do that to you?' She actually had the gall to look hurt.

'Yes.' I shook my head in confusion. 'I mean, no, I didn't. Until I saw it.'

'And with Ethan!' There was no mistaking her facial expression, even through the Botox. She was genuinely appalled at the idea. 'Even if he wasn't your husband, even if there wasn't the ten-year age gap—' it was a fourteen-year age gap, but Mum's rounding down when it came to her age was always generous '—what makes you think I'd have any interest in Ethan? No offence, angel, but I can't abide the man. You know that.'

235

'But I saw it,' I said, almost in a whisper. 'By the trees, the day of the wedding.'

'I told you, Kitty. There weren't any trees.'

'You were having a row, and then he... I saw it. I know I saw it.'

She guided my head to her shoulder and I let it rest there, too dazed to resist.

'It's happening again, baby,' she said in her softest voice.

'What is?'

'Do you remember last year? You told me you'd just spoken to your dad on the phone and you were going to arrange a fishing trip for the first weekend in July. Gave me all the details, right down to what sandwich fillings you were planning to have. Two weeks after he died, my love.'

'Yes,' I muttered dreamily. 'That's right. I did talk to him.'

Mum looked worried. 'Kitty...'

'No, I mean I know I didn't,' I said. 'But it felt like I had. It was so real, Mum. I mean, even now, I can hear that conversation like it happened. I think it's how my brain tried to medicate me – to numb the grief.'

She took my hand and stroked it with her thumb, just like she used to do when I was little to comfort me.

'Marriage is a scary thing for the brain to cope with too, Kitty,' she said gently. 'Especially if we're not ready. Sometimes it's not until the vows that it hits us it's for life. That's how it was for me when I married your father.'

'Yes...'

'Ethan pushed you into it, didn't he? Before you really had time to consider if he was the right one.' She shook her head.

'I always worried about you being with someone so much older.'

'It did seem to happen fast,' I mumbled. 'I was still getting over losing Dad, and he just steamed ahead with the plans while I was trying to get myself better.' I snorted. 'Taking my mind off it, he said.'

'He's a selfish man. They all are.' She dipped her head to look into my face. 'So you see now what's happened?'

'I... don't know. It felt so real.'

'It's this old brain, playing games with you again,' she said, tapping my head. 'You know I wouldn't do that. Deep down, you know. Don't you?'

'I was coming down with the flu. When I saw it. When I thought I saw it.' I glanced up to meet her eyes. 'Can flu make you hallucinate, Mum?'

'I think it probably can, if there are other factors at play too,' she said. 'Your mind was trying to send you a message, Kitty. It knows Ethan was never the right man for you.'

I didn't know what to think any more. What I'd seen... it'd been so strong. So vivid. But then, the hallucinations about my dad had felt real too. And Mum had sounded so genuinely shocked at the suggestion there could be anything between her and Ethan.

It did sound completely implausible. They'd fought all the years they'd known each other. If I hadn't seen it with my own eyes – or thought I'd seen it – I never would've believed it.

Had I been running all these months from something that didn't exist? Could it have been cold feet, pure and simple, that had turned me into a homeless fugitive and nearly seen me sleeping on the streets?

But I was so certain I *had* seen it. The whole thing had played out in so much detail, it just had to have happened...

I badly needed to get back to the camper and have a talk and a cuddle with Jack till my brain felt right again. He understood what grief could do. He'd get it.

'I need to go,' I said to Mum, forcing my voice even so she wouldn't guess what was going through my head. 'Can you wake Nan up for me? I'll just say a quick hello then come back another time, I think.'

Mum looked serious. 'I can't do that, Kitty.'

'Please. I don't like to interrupt her nap, but I can't just go without seeing her.'

'No, I mean I can't. Your nana's asleep.' She took my hands in both hers and pressed them gently. 'The other kind of sleep. The kind... the kind you don't wake up from. They took her yesterday.'

Chapter 23

When I left, my head was reeling, spinning around like a fairground Waltzer to the extent that I found it hard to walk steadily. A couple of passers-by shot me disapproving looks, clearly marking me down as a daytime drunk.

As soon as I was back in open countryside, I took a rest against a drystone wall before I passed out. I sagged down, my bum implanting itself in the wet mud with no thought for the jeans that had been clean on that morning.

But I didn't allow myself to rest for long. I had an aim in mind, something I had to check before I could let myself deal with the blow I'd just received. That's why instead of the text he was expecting, the one asking to be picked up so we could set off down to Wales, Jack got this.

Meet me at Butterfield Farm. Elden BD24. IMPORTANT.

When he arrived, I was standing about a half-mile from the barn where we'd had the reception, scanning my surroundings with a wild eye.

'Kitty!' he hailed me when he got within earshot. 'How did it go? Are you okay?'

As soon as he reached me he took me in his arms for a hug, but I wriggled away. He was blocking my view.

He frowned. 'What's the matter? Didn't it go well?'

'Not really, no...'

'Wasn't your nana pleased to see you?'

'She was right about the trees,' I muttered to myself.

'Trees? Where's trees?'

'Here.'

Jack scanned the sheep-dappled fields. 'I don't see any trees.'

'Because there aren't any. No trees, no stumps where they could've been...'

'So we've come to see some trees that don't exist?' he said, sounding thoroughly confused. 'I thought we were getting straight off to Snowdonia. Plenty of trees there to fulfil all your wildest tree-based desires, I promise.'

'You don't understand.' I turned to face him. 'Jack, you remember when we first met?'

'Wouldn't forget that, would I?'

'What did I tell you that day? About where I'd come from?'

He looked perplexed. 'What's this all about, Kit?'

'Just answer.'

'Okay then. You told me you'd run away from your wedding. That something traumatic had happened to you and you never wanted to go back home.'

'But I never told you what the thing was, did I? Rule One, right?'

'You know you don't need to tell me anything that makes you uncomfortable. Rule One or not.'

'It does make me uncomfortable. It makes me feel physi-

240

cally sick, in fact. But I'm going to tell you now, all the same.'
I took a deep breath. 'So this is the farm I ran away from that
day. Because I saw... no, well, I thought I saw my new husband
cheating on me.'

'I guessed it must be something like that.'

'With my mum.'

'Fuck!'

'Yeah. That's what everyone says.'

He shook his head, his lip curling in disgust. 'God, that
woman's some piece of work. I knew she was manipulative,
but – Jesus Christ, her own son-in-law. That's another level
of shittery.'

I glanced away into the distance, towards the barn. 'I know.
But now... I was so sure there was a little patch of trees right
on this spot, Jack. That's where they were hiding.'

'But there aren't any trees.'

'No. There aren't any trees. There's just my vivid memory
of there being trees. And seeing the two people I loved most
betraying me by them.'

Jack looked concerned and confused in equal measure. 'I
don't think I'm following all this, Kit. What did happen?'

'I... honestly, I don't know any more.' My voice was shaking
with panic and fear. 'There was this other time, when I lost
my dad, I started having these really vivid daydreams. Well,
no, they were hallucinations really, because I truly thought
they were real. Seeing him, talking to him, forgetting he was
gone: like an anaesthetic my brain was administering to itself
when the pain of that loss got too strong.' I glanced up at
him. 'You know?'

241

'I know. I've had something similar, it's not uncommon.'

'Yeah, that's what Lindy said. My grief counsellor.'

He took me in his arms, and this time I didn't resist, resting my forehead against his chest.

'So you think this is the same?' he asked.

I stared blankly at the ground. The ground I was so sure had been slap bang in the middle of a little wood. I could practically see it now, and the two silhouettes, as vivid as the pain still gripping my heart. In a way, I *knew* I'd seen it. In my head, in my heart, it had 100% happened. And yet... *there were no trees.*

'It felt so real,' I mumbled. 'I can see it like it was as real as you and me, here, right now. Different than with my dad. That was like... an echo of life. This, I would've sworn with my last breath I'd seen – something.' I gulped a breath, feeling the panic rise. 'If I didn't, I must be losing my mind. No delusion could feel like this felt to me.'

'You're not losing your mind,' he said gently. 'We'll work it out, Kit. Just try to keep calm.'

'Yes.' I forced my shallow, rapid pants into measured breaths while Jack made comforting noises to me. 'Yes. I need to.'

'What made you come here?' he asked when the panic had subsided a little.

'I saw Mum. And she was so certain, Jack, that I'd made a mistake. Actually laughed at me. And she doesn't laugh much.' I snorted. 'Too worried about laughter lines.'

'You saw her?' He held me back to look into my face. 'God, no wonder you're upset.'

'I survived though. It was awful, but I got through it, barely.' I ran a finger down his cheek. 'Thanks to you, I think.'

'Did your nana hear all this?'

'She... wasn't there.' I finally surrendered to the other feeling fighting for dominance through the shock and confusion, throwing myself back against his chest as I burst into despairing, grief-breathless sobs. 'That bastard illness... we came too late, Jack. Too late. She's never going to be there again.'

***

All the anger I'd been saving for Mum and Ethan, the resentment, the bitterness, every emotion I'd been slowly learning to cope with until I'd started to doubt my own eyes, was redirected towards the shadowy, murderous figure of Alzheimer's, the disease that had killed my nan.

I wasn't an easy person to live with over the next few days, in floods of tears one minute, ranting and raving about how unfair it all was the next. But Jack coped. He was understanding when I needed him to be understanding, angry when I needed him to share my anger, calming when I was in danger of hurting myself with it. He'd been through it all, and he knew what I needed.

The other occupants of the camper weren't much fun to be around either, struggling through a little doggy grief of their own. Sandy had turned the van upside down, and dug up half the farmer's field we were camped on, looking for her stolen puppies. Muttley, sensing her parent's anxiety and missing her siblings, had started letting out a constant low-level whine. All in all, the campervan was not a very happy place to be on those hot late summer days, for Jack or for the rest of us.

We were still in Yorkshire. Nan's funeral was scheduled for the Thursday, a week away, and I didn't want to leave without saying a final goodbye to her.

Honestly, I didn't know what I did want. If I'd been confused before, that was nothing compared to how I felt now. Because no matter how much anger I still felt towards Mum and Ethan, no matter how much the too, too solid image of them together haunted me, that didn't change the single fact that *there were no trees*.

To give Jack a bit of a break from my miserable face, I left him to spend a quiet evening with his dogs and took a taxi over to Laurel's. A dose of normality felt like just what I needed, and I couldn't wait to see the boys again.

'Come here, you,' she said as soon as I showed up on her front step, enfolding me in a tight hug. 'How're you doing, love?'

'Not so great, to be honest.'

'Sure you can get through the funeral tomorrow?'

'Not got much choice, have I?'

She held me back to look into my face. 'Will he be coming?'

'If by "he" you mean Jack, then yeah. I want him to.' I stared at my toes. 'Need him to.'

'Did you know Ethan's been invited?'

I winced. 'Ugh, has he?'

'Yes. My mum asked him, I think. Sorry.'

God. The funeral was going to be painful enough without trying to filter my muddled emotions about the still-legal husband who may or may not have cheated on me and the friend-slash-boss of four months I was currently sleeping with.

'Well, come on in,' Laurel said. 'The boys have been asking for you.'

I managed a smile. 'Have they?'

'Yep. Perfect timing for a visit: Toby's got some major news to share. I mean, *major*. Brace yourself.'

I followed her along the hall to her permanently toy-strewn living room. It made me smile to see it pretty much as I'd left it months ago. It was kind of reassuring, that 'life goes on' vibe.

Apart from visits to my nan and Aunty Julia, this was the one part of my old life I'd genuinely missed: the part that was messy and warm and boisterous and filled with love. A normal, healthy family, in other words – the only share in one I'd ever really had.

'Aunty Kitty! You've come home!' Toby yelled, abandoning his Lego and chucking himself at me.

'Oof!' I said as his little body collided with my middle. 'Yes, I've come home. Hiya, Tobes.'

'Yay! I knew you would.' Four-year-old Sam bounced over so he could fling his arms round my legs as well. 'We missed you, Aunty Kitty.'

'I missed you too, boys,' I said, my voice choking slightly.

'Lots?'

'Lots and lots. My favourite little terrors.'

I couldn't help blinking back a tear as the pair of them hugged me tightly, holding on just a little bit longer than usual. It felt good to reclaim my place as an aunty, and to know the boys had missed me almost, if not quite, as much as I'd missed them. Laurel smiled at me while they clung on.

'Good to have you back, Aunty Kitty,' she said in a quiet voice.

'Guess what I saw today?' Toby demanded when he eventually let me go, getting straight down to business with The Big News.

'Dunno. Velociraptor?'

'Nope. A horse doing a wee!'

I slapped on my impressed face. 'Did you? Wowsers trousers!'

'And then, right. And then...' He looked up at me earnestly, eyes glittering. 'It *farted*. Super loud.'

'Sounds like you've had an exciting day.'

'Me too!' Sam yelled. 'I saw the horse too, Aunty Kitty!'

'No you didn't,' Toby said, casting a withering look at his little brother. 'He's pretending, Aunty Kitty. He's just a big pretender.'

'Really? Can he do Back on the Chain Gang?'

Laurel snorted.

'I'll just finish this washing up then I'll sort us out a drink,' she said. 'Think you can cope in the madhouse for ten minutes, Kit?'

'Been looking forward to it.'

When she'd headed into the kitchen, I sat down on the sofa and patted my knee. 'Come on then, boys. I want to hear all about this horse doing a wee.'

'It was a massive wee!' Toby said with glee as he crawled into my lap, his brother claiming a spot at my side. 'I bet it could fill up a whole swimming pool!'

'But you wouldn't want to swim in it though, would you?'

'Ewww! No,' Toby exclaimed, squirming delightedly. He grinned at his brother. 'Would you swim in a horse-wee swimming pool, Sam?'

'No way!'

'For a trillion pounds though?'

'Nuh-uh.'

'Okay, for two trillion pounds. And my Charizard.'

Sam hesitated. 'Pikachu too?'

'Well... all right.'

Sam paused, weighing up a swim in horse wee against the acquisition of his brother's two most coveted Pokémon. Finally he came to a decision.

''K. But you'd have to give them me first.'

'Ha!' Toby nudged me. 'Sam swims in wee,' he informed me in a conspiratorial whisper.

'I drew you a picture while you were on holiday, Aunty Kitty,' Sam told me. 'Wanna see?'

'Yes please, Sammy.'

Sam darted off the sofa to fetch it, happily using my boobs as leverage to push himself down. He grabbed a crumpled bit of paper from among the general debris and hurtled back like a tiny blonde thunderbolt.

'Guess what it is,' he said, thrusting it at me.

The picture was just a fuzz of green with a blue stripe across the top, but I didn't need any clues. Sam had been drawing nothing but the same four green things with their different-coloured stripes for the past year.

'Is it... ooh, I don't know. A Ninja Turtle?'

'Yeah! Know which?'

'Easy peasy. Leonardo.'

'Yup!' He beamed at me.

'Thank you for my picture, sweetie,' I said, giving him a kiss. 'Leo's my favourite.' There was another snort from Laurel in the kitchen.

'How do you know about the Turtles, Aunty Kitty?' Toby asked, looking suspicious.

'Believe it or not, Toby Taylor, the Turtles were around even when your aunty was little.'

'Wow!' His eyes saucered. 'Were they in black and white?'

'He'll be asking next what you did in the war,' Laurel called. 'I had that one last week.' She came in with a glass of wine each for us. 'Come on now, boys, give Aunty Kitty some peace. It's bedtime.'

'Awww,' Sam said, jutting his bottom lip. 'But she just got here. And she's been away *aaaaaages*.'

Toby folded his arms. 'We haven't even had a story. I like when Aunty Kitty does the voices.'

Sam put on his best puppy-dog face. 'You're pretty, Mummy.'

Laurel sighed. 'Is it pathetic that even though I know he's just trying to get round me, that still works?'

I smiled. 'You big softie.'

'So, Kit? Want to do storytime?'

The boys looked up at me with wide, pleading eyes.

'We-ell...' I said, pretending to hesitate.

'Please, Aunty Kitty!' Toby said.

'You're pretty, Aunty Kitty,' Sam said, obviously deciding a technique that had been so successful the first time round was worth another shot.

I laughed. 'You're right, it does work,' I said to Laurel. 'Go on then, boys.'

'Yay!' Sam squealed. 'Can we have *Tilly and Billy Bake a Cake?*'

His brother gave him a scathing look. 'Not that. You always want that, big baby. I want *Tilly and Billy Go to the Fair*.'

'I'm storyteller so I pick.' I fished in my bag for the book I'd brought them. 'And I pick this one.'

Sam took it from me and his eyes went round. 'Hey! Tobes, we haven't got this one!'

'Yep, it's new,' I said. 'You can't buy it in shops yet. My friend gave it to me.'

'Is it for me?' Sam said, holding the copy of *Tilly and Billy Go Fishing* reverently.

'It's for both of you.'

'And I'm the oldest so I should get to look first.' Toby snatched the book off his brother and curled his lip as he flicked to the title page. 'Eurgh! There's writing in it.'

'That's right,' I said. 'My friend Jack wrote his name in it. He's the man who draws all the pictures of Tilly and Billy and writes the words.'

'It's naughty to write in books.'

'It's not naughty if someone wrote the book, Tobermory,' Laurel said. 'Then we like them to write in it.'

'Hmm.' Toby didn't look convinced.

'Read it to us, Aunty Kitty,' Sam said.

The boys listened, rapt, as I read them the story, Toby on my knee and hyper little Sam scrambling up the arm of the sofa so he could sit on the back and look at the pictures over my shoulder. Storytime was the only time they were quiet, other than when they were asleep. Only once did Toby interrupt, to tell me Tilly's voice was wrong and I was forgetting to do her lisp. After months off story duty, I was a bit out of practice.

They were both yawning by the time I finished, and Laurel insisted it was time for little boys to go to sleep.

When I'd helped her get them into their PJs, brush their teeth and put them to bed – a task equivalent to wrestling two small but energetic grizzly bears – we headed back downstairs and topped up our wines.

'Knackered yet?' she asked when we'd chucked ourselves down on the sofa.

'God, yes.' I sipped gratefully at the wine. 'Do they never stop?'

'Nope.'

'Patience of a saint, love. I don't know how you cope.'

'Well, that's my punishment for having unprotected sex.' She cast her eyes around the bombsite of a living room. 'Ugh, look at the state of the place. I mean I love them, but it's bloody exhausting sometimes.'

'Where's Andy?'

She looked embarrassed. 'He went out for a pint with Ethan.'

I winced at the mention of his name. 'They're still mates then?'

'Well, yeah. I mean, you asked me not to tell anyone so I didn't.' She shuddered. 'I try not to have him round here if I can help it though. I can't look at him the same now.'

I flushed. 'Laur?'

'Yeah?'

'Remember when my dad died and I went mad for a bit?'

'You didn't go mad. You were grieving.' She shook her head. 'God, I was worried sick about you though. When I found you at work, you looked wild. I mean, *wild*. I was scared stiff you might, you know, hurt yourself or something.'

'There was so much... noise,' I muttered. I shook my head to push the memories away. 'But Lindy convinced me it was probably a one-off. That a first bereavement can do strange things to the brain.'

'And?'

I stared down into my wine. 'I'm terrified, Laur. That it's starting to happen again. I am literally scared out of my mind that it's happening again and this time I won't be able to claw myself back out of the hole.'

She looked pretty scared too. 'What, you've been hallucinating about your nan?'

'No. Before that. What I told you, about the wedding, what I'd seen... I...' I shook my head. 'When I saw Mum the other day, she was so adamant it never happened.'

'But she would be, wouldn't she? That doesn't prove anything.'

'Laurel, you remember the barn? Where we had the reception?'

'Er, yeah. Why?'

'Do you remember there being a clump of trees about a half-mile from it?'

'Well, no.' She blinked. 'I mean, there might've been. I'd been drinking, I don't remember.'

'I can tell you there isn't now. Mum says there never was. And yet... and yet I'm sure that's where I caught them. I hid behind a tree and they were arguing and then I saw them.'

'Clearly?'

'I heard them clearly. The sun was behind them so they were sort of shadowy.'

'And you're absolutely certain you saw them kiss?'

'I... yes. I mean, I was.' I shook my head. It felt like I was balancing an anvil on top of it. 'God, Laur, it still seems so real. But the trees – I honestly don't know what to think any more.' I stared down into my wine. 'It's almost less horrifying if I did see what I thought I saw.'

She blinked. '*Less* horrifying? Seeing your husband getting off with your mum?'

'Yeah. Because if I didn't, the only alternative is I'm actually going insane. I'd have to be for it to be as vivid as it was.'

'No you're not,' she said firmly, no-nonsense as always. 'That's olden days talk, all that men-in-white-coats and strait-jacket toss. The human brain doesn't work like that.'

'But it can be permanently damaged, if the trauma's strong enough. And this, Christ, if you'd seen it—' I stopped, scared by the tremble in my own voice, and forced a few deep breaths. 'I mean, if you could've seen it. If it was there to see.'

Laurel came over and put her arm around me, waiting patiently until I was calm. Her tenderness was so businesslike, it was just what I needed. Laurel never offered empty comfort. She was always focused on solutions.

'So what will you do if that wasn't what you saw?' she asked when I'd pushed back the panic. 'Do you think it's too late to work things out with Ethan?'

'Yes. It's far too late for that.'

'Not if he didn't cheat on you it isn't, is it?' Laurel said. 'You can't scuttle a ten-year relationship because of something you might've only imagined. It's not fair on either of you.'

I took a deep breath. Okay, this was it. It was time.

When I'd seen her last, I'd decided it was my cross to bear. My fault, my own idiot fault for letting Ethan walk all over me all those years and never saying a word to the people I was closest to. But with Jack's help, I'd finally come to realise it wasn't my fault; it never had been. It was no one's fault but Ethan's, and he'd trained me, him and Mum between them, to always place the blame firmly on myself. Laurel was my friend, my sister, and she needed to know what he'd done.

'Laur... don't hate me for this, please,' I said. 'But there's something I need to tell you.'

She listened, wide-eyed and, eventually, open-mouthed as I gave her a potted history of my life with Ethan; all the parts I'd kept hidden or made excuses for over the last decade. The way he'd controlled our money, and ultimately spent the lot without telling me. How he'd stopped me learning to drive so I was completely dependent on him to take me places. How I'd deliberately lied to her on occasion, faking illness or appointments when she'd invited me over for a girls' night because Ethan had gone into a sulk about me leaving him alone. How he'd stopped me taking up hobbies and joining clubs where I might make new friends, telling me that if I really loved him, his company would be enough for me.

'Oh my God,' she whispered when I was done. And though I knew, now, it wasn't my fault, I couldn't help a flush of shame heating my cheeks at the look of horror on her face.

'Pathetic, right?' I mumbled.

'Yeah. But me, not you.' She shook her head. 'Jesus, my own little sister, all this time, right in front of me. How could I not see it?'

'It's not your fault. I didn't let you,' I said, staring into my wine. 'I wanted you to like him, I guess, so I only ever painted him in positive colours. I just thought they were his quirks, you know? Dirty laundry not to be aired in public.'

'That's your mum talking.'

'Yes.' I sighed deeply. 'It is, isn't it?'

She threw her arms around me. 'I'm so sorry, Kit,' she whispered. 'God, what must I have sounded like, trying to get you to go back to him? I honestly thought he was one of the good guys.'

'That's what people said when it all came out about Uncle Ken.'

'Monsters, the pair of them.' Her brow darkened. 'He's never getting into this house again, I can promise you that. The boys don't need that sort of influence.'

I blinked back my tears and looked up at her. 'Laur, can I tell you something else? I mean, something you already know, but I want to be the one to tell you.'

She looked puzzled. 'Something I know?'

'Well, something you guessed. The day I saw you in Scotland. Something that's going to make the Ethan situation a hell of a lot more complicated now I'm being forced to face up to it.'

She frowned. 'What is it, Kit?'

'You were right. What you said before.' I swallowed the last of my wine. 'I've fallen in love with Jack Duffy.'

Chapter 24

It was the same church where we'd held my dad's funeral. I'd hated the sight of it that day; hated its huge, gaping mouth as it swallowed up mourners, hated its blackened, sky-stabbing shard of a spire, and hated, hated, hated the way it seemed to be taking my dad away from me. Today, as it prepared to take my nana too, it seemed even more monstrous.

'You can do this,' Jack whispered as we made our way to the door. The gentle pressure of his hand in mine gave me strength.

One person I was feeling especially nervous about seeing again was my Aunty Julia, who I'd already spotted in her wheelchair by the door, greeting mourners. With the perspective of time and distance, my anger towards her had long dissipated, and what I mainly felt now was guilt about the worry I must've caused the day I'd run away.

Another was my mum. I knew she'd be inside, on the watch for me.

But the encounter really giving me stomach cramps as I approached the church was Ethan. After what had happened last time I'd seen him, the anger and desperation in his voice as he'd commanded me to turn back, plus what Laurel had told me about his mental state, I was seriously worried about what he might do.

I'd been studying for my GCSEs when Ethan had first shown up in my life: twenty-four, drop-dead gorgeous, a more than welcome distraction from revision. We'd been the gossip of my year group – Kitty's fit older boyfriend, with his fancy car and his well-paid job. *He plays in a band, you know. He drives an Audi. He wears Bench.* Oh yes, on the surface he was every sixteen-year-old's dream man.

I'd loved the attention, back then; the feeling of specialness at having been chosen by someone who could easily have their pick. I'd loved Ethan too, for the best part of a decade – well, no, not love exactly. What I'd felt for Ethan had been more like... worship. I'd given him my virginity, my trust, my money; my life, when it came right down to it. Yet in just four months, every shred of that love had evaporated.

I knew now that my feelings for Jack, muddied as they were by his problems and mine and still mere months old, were ten times more real than anything I'd ever felt for Ethan. Yes, I'd loved him: blindly, and with a schoolgirl's unhealthy fascination, long after I'd stopped being a school-girl. But we'd never been friends. We'd hardly ever laughed together, or shared a hobby. The time I'd spent with Jack had opened my eyes to the fact relationships shouldn't be like that.

All this, I knew, needed to be said at some point. There'd be no picking up where we left off, no reconciliation, whether or not Ethan had been unfaithful. I'd said it the last time I'd seen him and it still held firm: I wanted a divorce. And I was planning to tell him that, along with a few other home truths.

But first things first. Aunty Julia. I had to make things up with Aunty Julia.

'Is that her?' Jack whispered as we approached the church.

'That's her,' I said. 'Be lovely, won't you? It's important to me that she likes you. Do that charm thing you do.'

'Right.' He looked bemused. 'Er, what charm thing is that?'

'You know, where you smile and flutter your eyelashes and talk all Irishy.'

'"All Irishy"? That's just my voice.'

'Yeah, it works though.' I stopped to straighten his tie for him before we reached the church. He poked out his chin awkwardly while I got it just right. 'There you go, handsome,' I said, patting his cheek. 'Now we're ready.'

I fixed on a nervous smile for Aunty Julia as we made our way up the ramp to the door. Jack hung back to let us talk.

'Kitty! My goodness, you nearly scared the life out of me!' she gasped when she registered who it was. Obviously Mum hadn't filled her in on the fact I'd come home. 'Is it really you?'

'It's really me. Hi, Aunty J. Um. Missed you.'

'Oh, my dear, you're a sight for sore eyes, you really are. Give me a hug this instant.'

I let myself relax, crouching to embrace her. I'd been so worried she'd be angry with me.

'I'm so glad you're safe,' she whispered. 'You don't know how often I've blamed myself for you disappearing like that. I'm sorry, Kitty, I truly, truly am.'

I felt a stab of guilt. Aunty Julia had just lost her mum,

fast following the death of her only brother last year, and here she was, apologising to the only blood relation she had left: the selfish errant niece who'd done a runner from her house and never got in touch. The niece who by rights should be on her knees begging for forgiveness.

'No, I'm sorry,' I said when she'd released me from the hug. 'It was my fault, I should never have gone off like that. But honestly, Aunty, if you knew what I—'

I stopped myself. *If you knew what I'd seen,* I'd been about to say. Except I still didn't know what exactly that was.

'I wasn't thinking straight,' I said at last. 'I never meant to frighten you. I just... I couldn't go home. Not then.'

'I should have respected what you said you needed, when you asked me not to call your mother. I was scared, that's all.' She shook her head. 'You looked so frantic. After what happened when Grant died, I really thought you were – you know, having another episode.'

'Not sure I wasn't,' I muttered, half to myself.

'Where did you go, Kitty? We've been searching high and low for you. No one seemed to know a thing about where you were.' She scanned me up and down. 'You look well anyway, dear. Who is it you've been staying with? A friend, I hope?'

I blushed, and beckoned Jack forward from where he was waiting a polite distance away.

'This is Jack,' I told Aunty Julia. 'He's, er, my... he's Jack.'

Aunty Julia blinked up at him. 'Oh.'

Jack dropped to his haunches to bring himself level and smiled. It was a good smile, one of his irresistible specials, but Aunty Julia was no soft touch when it came to men. She kept her expression fixed.

'Hello, Mrs Blake,' he said, voice dripping Irish charm as requested. 'Kitty's told me all about you.'

'Oh,' Aunty Julia said again. Between 'ohs', her lips pressed into a thin line.

'Jack gave me a job,' I told her. 'As his PA. He writes children's books.'

'Did he now?' She was scanning Jack suspiciously, but he didn't let the smile drop.

'That's right.' Jack shot me a fond glance. 'Kitty's a natural at organising my marketing, press, everything like that. I don't know how I managed before I had her.'

'Before you had her...'

It was obvious Aunty Julia didn't like the suggestion under those words. But there was no time to go into it further. A couple of mourners behind us, old friends from Nana's WI, were waiting to offer her their condolences.

'We'll talk later,' I said, kissing her and standing up again. 'I'm sorry, Aunty Julia.'

'I told you, Kitty, you don't have to apologise. I'm just glad you're safe.'

'No, I mean I'm sorry.' I blinked back a tear. 'About your mum.'

'I'm not,' she said in a low voice, casting her eyes down to the hands playing nervously in her lap.

'What?'

'I'm sad, of course I am,' she said. 'But honestly? I can't help feeling relieved too. Relieved that she still had most of her wits about her, rather than having to watch that evil disease take her away from me piece by piece. That it was peaceful right at the last.' She looked up at us, her eyes wet. 'It's an awful thing to lose your parent. But it's worse to watch them die. Is that a really terrible thing to say?'

Jack seemed to understand. He reached out to squeeze her shoulder.

'It's not terrible at all,' he said gently. 'Not at all.'

'Thank you... Jack.'

The two shared a bittersweet moment, and she smiled at him, a real smile, as we passed her to go into the church.

Inside, I scanned the pews. Mum was sitting near the front, in a sober but tasteful black twinset I knew she'd have bought specially. She looked round when we entered, and for a second I thought she was going to come over, but she restrained herself. She'd dread a public scene above all things, especially in church, that bastion of English country civility, and I could see from the look she shot him that she'd guessed who Jack was and hadn't forgotten him swearing at her over the phone.

Ethan was less restrained. He was swivelled round on his pew, his grey eyes trained on the door.

Laurel had warned me he'd changed, and I'd been prepared for a difference since the last time I'd seen him. I thought he might be a bit more sober; a bit more puppydog. Still, I'd been convinced in the back of my mind that she'd been exaggerating.

She hadn't been exaggerating. The change hit me like a stack of dynamite.

A covering of stubble that was fast becoming a full beard blanketed his jaw, and his face was white – not even pale but white, stark against red-rimmed eyes. He'd lost weight too. His best designer suit hung off him like next year's school uniform. I fought back a vicious hankering to pity the man.

'Don't let him get under your skin,' Jack muttered as Ethan jumped up from his pew and made a beeline for us. 'Don't let him make himself the victim here. You know he'll try.'

'He looks awful, Jack. I've never seen him—' I broke off as Ethan reached us.

'Kitty, oh my God! You're here, you're really...' Ethan grabbed my hands. He looked so ecstatic to see me, I actually felt guilty.

Mentally, I gave myself a slap. I'd spent months trying to cure myself of that type of learned response, I couldn't afford to let myself slip back into it now.

'I mean, I knew you'd come back one day,' Ethan said. 'But now it's happened... honestly, I can hardly believe it.' He squeezed my hands tight, like a man desperate to reassure himself I was flesh and not dream.

He looked so sincere, so full of genuine joy, I almost found myself softening. But then I remembered the last time I'd seen him. The money – all my money. The way he'd chased me down the street, screaming for me to come back.

I yanked my hands away.

'I haven't come back for good,' I said in a quiet voice. 'I've come to say goodbye to my nan, that's all. I'm not here for anyone but her.'

He was still staring at me, the expression in his red-rimmed eyes somewhere between ecstasy, desperation and fear. I honestly thought he might be about to burst into tears. Ethan, who in ten years I'd never seen cry.

'No. No, I know, it's just I thought I might never see you again,' he said, not dropping his gaze. 'I've been looking everywhere. Oh, Kitty, darling!' he burst out suddenly. 'I'm so glad you're safe. When you went off with him, I really thought you might be in danger.' He threw his arms around me, then instantly dropped them, looking confused. 'Sorry. I didn't mean... I've been worried about you, that's all.'

He seemed genuinely moved. But... oh yes, I remembered. The echo of his words as he'd chased me. *You're my fucking wife, Kitty! Mine, you hear me?*

Possession. Not love. Jack was right, that was all it had ever been about to him.

'This isn't the place for a conversation, Ethan,' I muttered, casting a nervous look at a gaggle of disapproving mourners who were glaring at us. 'We're in church. Let's talk after.'

'Whatever you want, Kitty. We can talk at the wake.' He shot a dirty look at Jack, waiting respectfully for us to finish our conversation but with an expression that said he was alert for trouble. 'Are you bringing him?'

'As long as he wants to come.'

Jack nodded. 'While she wants me with her, I go where Kitty goes.'

Ethan stared resentfully at him, then turned back to me. 'But Kitty, what's he—'

He broke off at the sound of a throat clearing, and we turned to find a very irritated vicar with his arms folded.

'Could you take your seats, please? We're about to start the service.' He shot a pointed look at Ethan. 'And if you could perhaps moderate your excitement while we're saying goodbye

263

to your loved one, sir, that would be greatly appreciated. Please remember this is a place of worship.'

Ethan stood glaring at Jack and for a second I thought it was about to go a bit Wrestlemania, right there over the hymn book table.

'Okay,' he said at last. 'But here, Kitty, take this before you go. A first instalment. And I will pay it all back, I swear. Every penny.' He pressed something into my hand. 'See you after.'

He gave me a quick nod, and without another word he stalked back to his seat.

I glanced down at what was crumpled in my hand and blinked in shock. It was a cheque. For £2000.

'Bloody hell,' I muttered to Jack. 'What's this for?'

Jack took my hand and led me to a pew at the back of the church.

'It's a trick,' he muttered as we took our seats. 'It has to be. Don't fall for it, Kit.'

'But... he can't really be paying me back?' I blinked at the cheque. 'This is genuine. Real money. Why would he do that? Last time I saw him he was flat broke.'

Jack almost snorted, but managed to restrain himself.

'Real money, all right. Real money that was always yours,' he whispered. 'Too little, too late, isn't it? Does he really think he can win you back by doling out petty cash from your own earnings?'

I stared at it. Three big, fat zeroes...

'Maybe he does genuinely feel bad,' I said. 'Now he's had time to think about it. He certainly looks like he's lost a bit of sleep.'

'Yeah, and maybe *A Christmas Carol* was a true story.' Jack shook his head. 'Men like him don't change, Kit. That mindset, that entitlement... it runs deep. You can smell it.'

'I'm not saying I'd ever forgive him. I'd certainly never go back to him. But if he really wants to make it up to me—'

'We'll talk about it after.' Jack nodded to the vicar, clearing his voice in the pulpit. 'Right now it's time to say goodbye.'

'Yes.' I took a deep breath. 'Yes. This is for Nana.'

Sunshine streamed through the stained glass, bathing the old church in luminescent seagulls of pink and green. The organ played Amazing Grace. And the box bearing the body that used to be my nan made its way slowly to the front of the church.

Chapter 25

The wake was at my mum's house, the traditional post-funeral buffet and booze that in no way softened the blow of losing someone.

'You don't have to go, you know,' Jack said as we climbed back into the camper after the service. 'Not if you don't feel up to it. You've had enough emotional drain for one day.'

'No, you're right: I can't run away forever. Me and Ethan have got things we need to say to one another.'

'Okay so.' He pressed my hand. 'Be brave, Kit. I'll be right where you need me.'

'Like you always are.' I leaned over to kiss him. 'Thanks, love.'

'You are staying, aren't you?' he said, shooting me a worried look in the rear-view mirror as he started the engine. 'With me?'

'Unless I get a better offer. Best job I've ever had.'

'Kit...'

I smiled. 'Come on, Jack, you know I'm joking. I'm not going anywhere.'

'Are you not tempted though? Now you've faced your

demons here? I know Laurel's always got open house for you.'
He glanced around the van and sighed. 'I hate that I can
never give you any more than this. That I have to be that
guy.'

'Not even a tiny bit tempted,' I told him firmly. 'This is my
home now. With you.'

He smiled. 'Hoped you'd say that.'

He parked a little way from the house and we walked there,
hand in hand.

Mum had a large open-plan living room, sparsely decorated,
just a huge mirror accenting the pastel-peach walls. When we
arrived, the place was packed with Nana's friends and relatives.
It was touching to see such a big turnout.

'Kitty, ohmygod! Hello, stranger!' Bernie said when I walked
in, beaming at me from under her big black fascinator.
'Welcome home. Sorry it had to be to bad news.'

'Um, hi,' I said, returning her hug absently. I was on auto-
pilot, my brain distracted with anxiety about the looming
conversation with Ethan. 'Thank you.'

'And who's this?'

'Jack. A friend.' I glanced up at him. 'My stepmum, Bernie.'

Jack smiled and nodded. 'Nice to meet you.'

'Hello.' Bernie shot him a curious look, but she didn't
comment.

'You gave us the fright of our lives, disappearing like that,'
she said to me.

'I know, sorry. It was... well, there were reasons.'

'It was a good hour before anyone realised you were gone.
Honestly, the photographer was spitting tacks. He'd spent ages

setting up some fancy backdrop for the photos, then what happens? The bride goes missing before he can use it.'

'He thinks he's got problems.' I was only half paying attention. 'I have to go, Bern. I need to talk to Ethan.'

I soon spotted him, whispering furiously with my mum in the kitchen area. Even at a wake, they couldn't seem to let up.

'Me?' I heard my mum spit as I made my way through the crowd towards them. 'You're the one who scared her off! Hugging her like that in front of everyone, causing a scene. What were you thinking?'

'I didn't know she'd be turning up with that bloody overgrown leprechaun fuck buddy of hers, did I? You should've told me she—'

He stopped when he spotted us.

'Hi,' I said quietly.

'Kitty.' Mum came forward to hug me. I stiffened, but I didn't push her away. 'I'm so sorry, my love. We'll all miss Nana.'

'Mum, can you leave us?' I said. 'I need to say something to Ethan.'

Mum frowned. 'What do you need to say to him?'

'That's not your business. I'm sorry, but it isn't,' I said, noticing her hurt expression.

'I'd better go too,' Jack said. 'Give you some privacy.'

Mum shot him a look. 'I should think you had. I don't remember inviting *you* into my home.'

'Your daughter invited me. Problem?'

I shook my head. 'Just go, please. Both of you.'

'You know where I am,' Jack said, squeezing my shoulder

as he turned to leave. Mum hesitated a moment longer, regarding me and Ethan warily, but eventually she strode off to mingle with her guests.

When they'd disappeared, Ethan seized both my hands, his eyes flaming with eagerness.

'Kitty, darling—'

'No darling. Not any more,' I said, drawing my hands away. I took the cheque from my pocket and held it up before him. 'What's this, Ethan?'

'What do you think? It's your money. Well, some of it.'

'But why now?'

'You think I haven't been thinking about it? What you said, last time I saw you?'

'What, about the money?'

'No, not about the money. Fuck the money, who cares about that? About you.' He stared at the floor. 'About how I'd driven you away. You were right, Kitty. It was wrong for me to monop-olise you the way I did. I see that now.' To my amazement, he gasped out a sob. 'I suppose it was the thought of losing you that made me behave that way. And then you seemed so vulnerable, so naive about life – I wanted to protect you from the bad things, you know? Maybe... maybe I went too far.'

'Ethan—'

'You're not a child, I know that. I am sorry, genuinely. And I'm sorry for how I behaved, last time I saw you. I never meant to scare you. I was worried you were in danger, that's all.'

'So what are you saying?'

'I'm saying I'll pay back every penny that should've been yours. No matter how long it takes. I've had some luck with the shares, some of them are paying out now – it's all yours. And anything you want from the house, anything of mine... whatever I can do to make it right. You don't have to come back to me. I just want to make it right.'

I blinked in surprise. 'But why? Why now?'

He flushed. 'I want – okay, don't laugh at me. But you've been gone a while, and I've been thinking all that time. I want to be a good man, Kitty. I don't want to be *that* man.'

A good man. I thought about our wedding day. Those silhouettes... and again, the rising nausea. The man who was capable of that could never be a good man.

The problem was, I didn't know any more if that was a memory to be trusted.

'What man?' I asked quietly.

'The man you ran away from. The man you looked at with fear in your eyes the day you came for your passport.' He shuddered. 'With hate.'

'I don't hate you.'

'No.' For the first time, the ghost of his old smile flitted over his lips. 'You couldn't, could you? You could never hate anyone. My baby girl.'

'Please don't call me that.'

'Sorry. Sorry. I'm just... I'm learning. I want to be the good guy, Kitty. I just need someone to help me, I think.' He lowered his voice to an appealing whisper. 'Will you?'

I stared into his eyes. They were so earnest. So full of pleading. He really sounded like he meant it.

'No,' I said at last.

'What?'

'No.' I shook my head to reinforce the point. 'I want to believe you, Ethan. I want to believe you're capable of being one of the good guys. But if you do, you have to do it for your own sake. I can't be part of it. I'm sorry.'

'Kitty? I don't understand.'

I held up the cheque he'd given me. 'This. How many instalments do you reckon you owe me?'

"God, I don't know…'

'So it's an instalment in an amount you haven't actually worked out?'

'Well, I thought you'd—'

'Okay, I'll work out an estimated figure when I've got my laptop and you can see if it sounds about right. Then once it's all paid off, we can call it quits.'

'Kitty, please!'

'Do you want to be a good man, Ethan? Or do you want to convince *me* you're a good man? Because those're two very different things.'

His face crumpled. 'When did you get like this? You're so hard.'

I softened slightly. 'Honestly, I'm not trying to hurt you. I just finally worked out what I need in life. And I'm sorry, Ethan, but it's not you. I told you last time I saw you and it still stands: I want a divorce.'

'Now come on, baby,' he said in his most wheedling tone. 'I'm your husband, in law. We were together ten years. Isn't that at least worth trying to save? I'll do things all your way this time, I promise.'

'Too little, too late,' I said, echoing Jack's words at the

271

funeral. 'You've had the last decade of my life to be a good man. Now, if you mean it... well, it has to be down to you.'

'Well I know that, don't I?' He let out a forced laugh. 'You know, this is so silly. So you.'

I blinked. 'Is it?'

'Can't get your own way so it has to be an ultimatum. You're such a child sometimes.' He leaned forward, and before I could object he'd planted a kiss on my lips. 'It's all right. I know what's behind it. You were desperate, you had nowhere to go. I won't hold it against you if me and you... you know.'

I shook my head, confused. It felt like I was having a completely different conversation to the one Ethan was apparently having.

'Sorry – won't hold what against me?'

'I know you must've felt like you had to earn your keep. Your mum told me you'd been living with him.'

'Earn my...'

'Slept with him, didn't you? You were all alone and you were vulnerable and that bastard took advantage.' He shot a scowl at Jack. 'You're home now, Kitty. No need to be afraid of him any more.'

'Afraid of him? I'm not afraid of him! I—' I broke off. 'He didn't take advantage of me, Ethan.'

'So you're not sleeping with him?'

I flushed. 'What I'm doing, I'm doing because I want to.'

He curled his lip. 'Oh God. Then you are.'

'Ethan, I want a divorce. Do you hear me?' I said it again, slowly so the words would hit home. 'I want. A. Divorce.'

His pale face sagged. He looked half broken, but I willed

myself strong. *Don't let him make himself the victim… don't let him get under your skin.*

'Why though? What did I do, Kitty?'

'You know what you did. You manipulated me and isolated me. Stopped me learning to drive, took my money, shut down my friendships. That's what you did, Ethan.'

'I told you I'll change. And I will pay the money back, all of it.'

I shook my head. 'It's not just the money. For ten years, you controlled every bit of my life, made me dependent on you to the extent I felt incapable of fending for myself, and it was only when I finally managed to get away from you that I realised how fucked up the whole thing was. Do you see that?'

'Baby, everything I did, I did because I loved you,' he said, desperation creeping into his voice. 'I didn't mean to take your money. It just seemed best if I took care of it for both of us.'

'You spent it, Ethan! You invested it without telling me and you lost the lot. How is that taking care of it?'

He flushed. 'Okay, it was a gamble. I was just trying to build a little nest egg for us. Secure our future.'

'That's not a decision you get to take alone! I was an adult and that money was mine.' I shook my head. 'See, this is exactly what I mean. You, always "doing what's best" for me where other couples have conversations.'

'Kitty, please.' He drew a deep breath. 'Look, we can discuss this. I'm sure we can work things out, go to marriage guidance or something. Maybe even… I mean, if you want to have that conversation again, we could talk about kids.'

'Kids?'

'If you still want them. Just please, Kitty, don't do this. You're my wife, for Christ's sake!' He seized my hands, pressing them hard – too hard. 'I love you, hear me?'

I yanked my hands away. 'I'm sorry, Ethan. I don't.'

'Oh God.' He looked frantic now. 'You don't love him, do you? You're not leaving me for some bloody gypsy who lives in his car?'

'No,' I said, perfectly calmly. 'I'm leaving you for me. I won't be owned, not any more. I won't be a toy. It's time I found out who Kitty Clayton is and what it is she wants.'

'You're such a brat, you know that?' he snapped, his voice switching to anger in an instant. 'Always have to have your own way, don't you? You were spoilt and petted from the day you were born, it's ruined you. Mummy's little fucking princess.'

I could feel myself starting to tremble, a learned response to his anger, but I forced myself to stay strong.

'Keep your voice down,' I muttered. 'You can call me whatever names you want, it'll still be over. And I want a divorce.'

'Well I won't grant one.' He folded his arms triumphantly. 'What do you say to that?'

'You can't make me stay with you.'

'But I can make life bloody difficult for you. What're you living on anyway?'

I flushed. 'None of your business.'

'You won't get a penny, you know. It's in my name, all of it. I'll get that cheque stopped long before you've had chance to cash it.'

Ah, there he was, the real Ethan. So much for wanting to be a good man.

274

'You've got no control over the money my dad left.'

That threw him. He'd obviously forgotten the ISA was in my name alone, my dad's final legacy to stop Ethan making me completely dependent on him.

'Shit,' he muttered.

'Why're you being like this?' I demanded. 'Just to hurt me?'

He softened his voice again. 'Because I need you, Kitty. I'm sorry I shouted: I was scared, that's all. Scared of losing you.'

I shook my head in disgust. They were so obvious now, the controlling tactics. First softness, then pleading, then anger, then repentance: the same cycle, over and over. How could I ever have let them get to me?

'God, will you just hear yourself? It's over, Ethan. And one way or another, I'm getting that divorce.' I was glad he'd got me mad. It made it so much easier. 'I don't care how long it takes: I want you out of my life.'

I marched away, winner of the field, leaving Ethan blinking after me.

'Well done,' Jack whispered when I'd sought him out by the buffet table.

'Oh God, could you hear from across the room?'

'No, but the body language was pretty hard to get wrong. I liked the turning on your heel with quiet dignity at the end there.'

'Thanks. Thought I was going to wee myself.'

'Okay, you've ruined it now.'

'Can we go, Jack? I need to get out of this place.'

He squeezed my hand. 'Course we can. Whenever you're ready.'

I exhaled with relief. 'Great. I'll just nip to the loo then I'll meet you outside. I want to slip out without my mum seeing, if I can. I'm all confrontationed out for today.'

I headed upstairs to the bathroom, a dreamlike sense of calm prevailing.

When I passed my old bedroom, I couldn't help myself. I poked my head round the door to have a look.

Mum hadn't been lying. She'd got the bed ready, a new duvet with a pretty Chinese pattern spread over. On the shelves were some of my favourite books, colour-blocked to keep it tasteful, and a little dresser bore a couple of framed photos. Everything was pristine and untouched. It looked like a shrine to someone who'd died.

I went in and stared at one of the photos. I must've been about seven when it was taken, dressed as a Martian, my brown hair dyed green and a pair of big buggy glasses over my eyes. I think I'd been on my way to a Halloween party. Mum had her arm round me, beaming. Her hair was its natural brunette then, but thanks to the facelifts and injections she'd become addicted to in recent years, she didn't look that much younger. Although it'd been a long time since she'd been able to smile that broadly.

The picture looked familiar, and yet... there was something wrong. I took it off the dresser and opened the back of the frame.

Part of the photo had been folded back so it wasn't visible. The part that showed my dad, standing proudly on the other side of me. Mum, reinventing the family to suit herself. It wasn't the first time.

'I got you some clothes too.'

I dropped the photo with a guilty start. Mum was at the door, watching me.

'I wasn't—'

'It's okay, angel. It's your room. Go in and explore, if you like.'

'I just... I'm not staying, Mum. I'm going with Jack.'

'Oh, never mind Jack,' she snapped. 'How can he be what's best for you? You barely know him.'

'I know he's on my side.'

'He's a user, Kitty. He wants you for one thing and one thing only. That's all men understand, they can't help themselves.'

'Not Jack.'

'I don't see what makes him so much nobler than the others.' She came over and took my hand; held it against her cheek for a second. 'I'm the one who's on your side. I'm your mother.' She softened her voice to its most dangerous croon. 'Come back home, darling, where I can look after you.'

She was trying hard to hide it, but I could feel the eagerness underpinning her words. Or no, not eagerness; something more than that. Hunger.

I blinked at her.

'I need the loo,' I said at last.

'I'll be right here,' she called after me.

In the bathroom, I splashed water on my face and patted my cheeks a few times to sharpen my dazed senses. Jack was waiting for me. I had to get to him. Mum was... it was too easy to let her persuade me to things I really didn't want.

I scanned my face in the mirror. It was pretty haggard: not surprising after the day I'd had. Pale as a Tussaud's waxwork, as my nan used to say. My mascara had smudged, probably during the confrontation with Ethan, and I was looking distinctly panda-like.

A packet of wet wipes sat on the ledge behind the sink. I went to reach for one, then stopped suddenly, frowning.

There was some aftershave next to the packet, a little black bottle with embossed gilt writing. The expensive stuff. Stuff that had no place in a single woman's bathroom.

I recognised the bottle. I recognised the brand. When I unscrewed the lid to give it a sniff, I recognised the rich, spicy smell. I recognised it because for ten years, an identical bottle had sat in my own bathroom, where Ethan had splashed it liberally on his cheeks before work every morning.

'Shit!' I whispered. 'They fucking did, didn't they? Those... *bastards*!'

'Everything okay, angel?' I heard Mum call.

'Um, yeah,' I yelled back, forcing my voice steady. 'I'll be out in a minute.'

The hell I would. I needed to get out of there. Suddenly, I knew that what I'd thought I'd seen was exactly what I *had* seen. I had to get away; I had to find Jack...

Right. Okay. I'd done it before, I could do it again. With a few injuries, yes, but pretty minor ones, all things considered. And Jack said they'd given me a tetanus jab in the hospital, so what was the worst that could happen?

I turned the taps in the sink on full blast to cover the noise of me opening the window. I wasn't going to bother turning them off. If Mum's house flooded, good. Serve her bloody well right.

I glanced down at the ground. It was a long way to the back garden, and the drainpipe didn't look quite so solid as the last one I'd climbed down. This one was plastic. Still, it seemed sturdy enough when I gave it a shake.

'Okay. Here we go,' I whispered to nobody in particular. I climbed up onto the ledge, pocketing Ethan's aftershave as an afterthought, and swung myself out.

'Bollocks!'

The plastic drainpipe was starting to detach itself from the wall. I could feel it coming away under my fingers.

'Kitty! What's the matter?' Mum battered against the bathroom door with her palms. 'Kitty!'

'Help! I need some help, quick!'

I don't know what happened then. The house seemed to fall away, there was a white flash of pain, and suddenly everything was dark.

Chapter 26

'Jack?' I whispered.

My head was killing. It felt like a migraine, the worst migraine I'd ever had. My mouth was dry and sore, as if it had been bleeding, and when I reached up to touch my skull, I could feel a dressing covering a tender area at the back.

'Just be quiet,' the figure leaning over me said in a soft voice. 'The doctor says you mustn't get excited.'

I pushed myself up, not without an effort, and batted away the hand he'd laid on my shoulder.

'Ethan. What're you doing here?'

'I am your husband, Kitty.'

'Not for long.' I blinked at my surroundings. My eyes were struggling to focus. 'Where is here? Is it hospital?'

'Yes. You've got a concussion.' He shook his head. 'Why the hell were you climbing out of a window, you silly thing?'

'Why the hell was your manky aftershave in my mum's bathroom? Ow!' I reached up to rub my temples. Raising my voice was making the throbs batter me harder.

He blinked. 'You what?'

'I saw it, Ethan! Don't go giving me that hallucination crap again, Mum already tried that one.'

'But why would I keep aftershave in your mum's bathroom?'

'You tell me.'

I glanced down at what I was wearing. It was a blue hospital gown, standard issue. Everything was spinny and blurred but I could just make out my clothes, the suit I'd worn to the funeral, laid out on a chair a little way from me. My white blouse was spattered with blood – mine, I was assuming. I must've hit my head pretty hard to make a mess like that.

'Pass me my trousers,' I said to Ethan. My voice felt fluffed, like I was talking through cotton wool.

'You're not checking yourself out? You're full of painkillers, Kitty. It's not safe.'

'Just pass them me.'

He handed over the trousers with a puzzled look and I rummaged in the pocket.

'It's gone,' I mumbled to myself.

'What's gone?'

'The bottle, it... where's Jack?'

'Oh, sod Jack,' Ethan said, scowling. 'Who cares where he is? I'm your husband. I'm the one with the right to be here.'

'I want to talk to Jack.' My voice was trembling. The bottle, the aftershave... I was sure I'd put it in my pocket. And now... but my brain was so groggy with the concussion and the meds, I could barely think. Could it have fallen out? 'Ethan, give me my mobile. Please!' I said when he didn't move. 'I need to call Jack, now.'

'I can't,' he said, not without the hint of a smug smile. 'It's in bits. You smashed it to atoms when you fell.'

'But I have to—'

The curtains of my little cubicle drew back, and a friendly-looking doctor came in.

'And how are we feeling?' she asked me with a bright smile.

'Like my head's made of dough.'

It was only then I noticed how thick and slugged my voice was. I sounded like I'd just downed twelve pints. Of absinthe.

'That's just the morphine,' she said. 'Trust me, you'd rather have a head made of dough right now than one made of brain.'

'She's not in any danger, is she?' Ethan asked in a worried voice.

The doctor shot him a glance. 'You're the next of kin?'

'I'm her husband.'

'Soon to be ex-husband,' I muttered.

The doctor blinked. 'Oh. I see.'

'Am I in danger, Doctor?' I asked.

'Call me Sarah, please. And no, not if you behave yourself and do everything I tell you.' She approached the bed and leaned over me. 'Can you tilt your head back for me, Mrs Chancellor?'

'Clayton. Ms Clayton. Or actually, just Kitty would be nice.'

I did as she asked, and she shone a little light in both my eyes to check how my pupils responded.

'All looking good,' she said at last. 'Or as good as I'd expect after the knock you took. You had us worried when the ambulance first brought you.'

'So I'll be okay?'

'You're not about to drop dead, if that's what you mean,' she said, smiling. 'But you're going to have a bugger of a headache for a while, I'm afraid. Now, how do we feel about another visitor? There's someone in the waiting room desperate to see you.'

I brightened. 'A man? Irish?'

'No, it's your mum. She's very worried about you. Shall I show her in?'

My brow gathered. 'Oh. No. I don't want to see her.' I nodded to Ethan. 'And if you could kick him out, I'd appreciate it.'

Sarah looked confused. 'I'm sorry, I'm not sure I quite understand all this.'

'I don't want him here. I want you to make him go away. Please.'

'She doesn't know what she's saying, Doctor,' Ethan said in a low voice. 'She's been struggling with her mental health lately, and she thinks… there's been some bizarre delusions. There is some history of it, you can see from her medical records.'

'Don't listen to him!' I said, my tone urgent. 'My mental health's fine, honestly. I'm not delusional. I just don't want him near me.'

'Kitty, darling, you just jumped out of a window,' Ethan said in his most patronising voice. 'I'm sorry, but you need help.'

'I know what I need. I need you to get out,' I snapped.

'Sarah, you're my doctor. Please, just make him leave. Ow! Fuck *me*, that hurts.' My head felt like an elephant was stamping on it.

'Perhaps you'd better go,' Sarah said quietly to Ethan.

'But she—'

'Please, Mr Chancellor. It's getting her agitated and that's not good for her recovery. She needs complete rest.'

He hesitated. 'Okay,' he said at last. 'If it's making her worse.' He squeezed my hand as he went by, but I jerked it away. 'Get better for me, baby. I'll be right in the waiting room.'

'Your husband seems worried about you,' Sarah said when he'd gone.

'Yeah. It's upsetting when your favourite toy gets broken.'

'Your admission papers say you were injured falling out of a window.'

'I wasn't falling out, I was climbing out.' I laughed woozily. 'They just don't make drainpipes the way they used to.'

She shot me a searching look. 'Anything you'd like to share with me about your home life?'

'Is that something you have to ask me or something you want to?'

'In this case, both.'

I hesitated. 'No,' I said at last. 'No. There's nothing I want to share right now.'

'Well, I'm right here if you change your mind,' she said gently. 'Here. Take these.' She counted out a couple of capsules from a little box and put them down on the table, next to my glass of water. 'They'll help you sleep. That's the best thing right now if we want to get this poor head all healed.'

'Okay.' I swallowed them down. 'And if a man called Jack Duffy comes, can you let him in? Nobody else. Just Jack.'

'Who is he?'

'He's... someone I know. Just someone I know.'

Chapter 27

It felt like I'd only been asleep for a few hours. But when I woke, I knew from the change in the light coming through the skylight it must have been a lot longer. The pain in my head felt even worse than when it had been fresh.

When I came to, I found Mum and Ethan sitting either side of my bed, glaring at each other.

'Who let you two in?' I mumbled.

'Now Kitty, don't be like that,' Mum said gently. 'How does your head feel, my love?'

'Like it's full of rocks.'

'The doctor lowered your painkiller dose while you were sleeping. She said it might hurt a little more, but not to worry. That just means you're healing.'

'Where's Jack? I want Jack.'

'You don't need Jack. You need your mum.'

'She needs her husband,' Ethan snapped.

'I think we'll let Kitty be the judge of that, don't you?'

'Seriously, can you just give it a rest? I'm in a fucking hospital bed here.' Despite the crushing pain, I felt oddly light-headed – maybe from the morphine. It was filling me with a liberating sense of couldn't-care-less. 'How the pair of you ever managed to shut the hell up long enough to have sex with each other I'll never know.'

Mum looked shocked. 'Kitty!'

I let out a little high-pitched giggle, closely followed by a sob.

'This isn't good,' Ethan said in a low voice to Mum. 'Maybe we should get the doctor.'

'Not sure there's any cure for whatever's wrong with you two,' I said. It was quite fun, saying just exactly what I was thinking.

I giggled again. Then I burst into tears.

'Oh God, I think she's hysterical.' Mum sounded frightened. 'I'll go for Sarah. You stay with her, make sure she doesn't hurt herself.' She cocked an eyebrow at him. 'Think you can manage that?'

'Just go, will you?'

Eventually, my crying fit settled into gasping sobs and I could speak again.

'How long – was I – asleep?' I managed to demand.

'Two days, nearly,' Ethan said.

'Two days! Have you been here two days?'

'Yes. Watching over you. Where else would I be when you're ill?' He ran a finger down my cheek. 'You know I love you, Kitty.'

'Get off. Don't you touch me.' I thrust the finger away. 'Has Jack been?'

Ethan scoffed. 'Of course he hasn't been. It's like I tried to tell you. If he can't get what he wants from you, you're no good to him.'

'He's not like that.'

'Yeah? Then where is he?'

'He probably just—' I broke off, listening to the sound of voices in the distance. 'What's that?'

'What's what?'

'That voice. It sounds like... is that an Irish accent?' I paused to listen. 'That's him! Oh my God, that's him!'

I could just about distinguish the hum of two voices I knew well among the other hospital sounds. It was Mum and Jack, somewhere nearby. And it sounded like they were arguing.

I stared at Ethan in disgust. 'You've been keeping him from me. Haven't you? Both of you! Jesus.'

'We... no. We just didn't want you to get upset, that's all. It's not good for your recovery.'

I threw the covers back and swung my legs over the side.

'Kitty, don't! You'll hurt yourself!'

But it was too late. I'd already pushed myself out of bed. I stumbled towards the curtains and flung them open, the various wires and machines I was connected to trailing after me. I could see my mum and Jack, arguing at the door of the ward.

'You're not welcome here,' Mum was saying in a low voice. 'Kitty's made it quite clear she doesn't want to see you. Just go, please.'

'I'm not leaving till I've spoken to Kitty. If she tells me she doesn't want to see me, then I'll go.'

'Absolutely not. You'll only get her worked up. She needs rest and quiet, not—'

'Jack!' I called out. 'I'm here. I'm...'

The world started to spin, and I gripped the metal frame of the cubicle to steady myself.

'Kitty!' Jack swept my mum to one side and came running towards me. 'Oh God, Kitty, sweetheart, I've been so scared,' he whispered, wrapping his arms around me. 'No running away, remember? You promised me. No running away.'

I laughed breathlessly as he showered me with kisses. 'I'm okay. I'm okay.'

'You're not okay. You're about to fall down.' He guided me back to the bed and helped me lay down. I kept tight hold of his hand, anxious in case he slipped away again.

'Why didn't you come before, Jack?' I mumbled.

'I did come. I followed the ambulance. They wouldn't let me in to you.'

'Because we knew you'd make her worse,' Ethan snapped. 'Just like you're doing now. Look at her, she's grey with the pain. Not that you give a shit, eh?'

I did feel awful. Standing up hadn't been a good idea. But as long as Jack was there, holding my hand, I felt strong.

Mum came back through the curtains. 'The doctor's on her way.' She glared at Jack. 'I've told her there's someone here causing trouble.'

'Please don't go,' I whispered to Jack. 'Don't let them send you away.'

'I'm going nowhere, Kitty. They'll have to carry me out.'

The curtains opened and in came Sarah, looking irritated.

'What's all the noise about in here?'

'It's him,' my mum said, nodding to Jack. 'He's upsetting my daughter.'

'He isn't,' I whispered, as loudly as I could through the searing pain in my temples. 'I want him here.'

Sarah glanced round at the three of them, clustered around my bed looking daggers at each other. 'I think you'd all better leave. Visiting hours are nearly over. Kitty needs to rest now.'

'No, please!' I gasped, pushing myself up. 'Let Jack stay. Please. I need to talk to him.'

'I'm sorry, but I really must insist.'

'Sarah, please! Just let him stay ten minutes.'

She hesitated a moment, scanning my face.

'Well... ten more minutes then, if it's going to distress you,' she said at last. 'But you mustn't get yourself worked up, Kitty.'

'I won't, I promise.' My knuckles, wrapped around Jack's hand, had turned white.

'What's the matter?' Jack asked in a low voice when Sarah had gone.

'It's them.' I nodded to Mum and Ethan. 'I was right, Jack. What I saw, I... I mean, I still don't know about the trees. But I found his aftershave in Mum's bathroom.'

Mum laughed. 'What, is it aftershave now? First trees, now aftershave. You've got a good imagination, angel.'

'I saw it,' I said, glaring at her. 'This time I know I really saw it.'

'And where is it?' Ethan asked.

'I... don't know. Smashed maybe, when I fell.'

'Yeah?' He grabbed my trousers from the chair and held them up in front of him. 'Then these should be soaked in the stuff, shouldn't they? But they're not. No glass, no scent. No aftershave.'

He passed them to me so I could conduct my own sniff test. He was right. They smelt of washing powder, and fresh earth from where I'd landed in the garden. They didn't smell of aftershave.

'Maybe the bottle fell out,' I mumbled weakly.

'It's the same old thing, my love,' Mum said. 'Seeing things. You lost your nana. That's got to disturb your poor brain.' She smiled fondly. 'You were always a sensitive little girl.'

'No, I… I did see it.' I cast a helpless gaze up at Jack. 'I did.'

'I know you did.'

'It does no good to humour her,' Mum said to him. 'You'll only make it worse. She has to start distinguishing between these visions or whatever they are and reality. It's the first step in getting better.'

'Not in fact true, Petra,' Jack said brightly. 'Because I'm not humouring her. If Kitty tells me she's seen a man's aftershave in your bathroom, you see, I'm inclined to believe her.'

Mum scoffed. 'Believe her? She doesn't even believe herself. Not really.' She patted my shoulder. 'It's okay, angel. We'll talk to the doctors here, see what they can do to help you. Once you come home this will all go away, I promise.'

Jack shook his head. 'Don't listen to her, Kit. She's playing games with you. Messing with your head.'

My head. My head felt like it had doubled in size and was currently being pounded with a huge rubber truncheon.

'Rubbish,' Mum said. 'I'm her mother. Whatever I do is for her own good.'

'Sleeping with her husband, was that for her own good?'

'That was fantasy. It never happened except in her mind.'

'Did it not?' Jack rummaged in the pocket of his jeans for a folded piece of paper. 'Because you see – Petra, Ethan – while you've been doing your best to stop me getting to Kitty, I've been making the most of my time elsewhere. Doing a little bit of investigation.'

Ethan scoffed. 'What, are you Poirot now?'

'It was Kitty's stepmum – Bernie, is it? – who gave me a hint when she mentioned the wedding photographer. Even a Luddite like me could manage a basic Google search.' Jack unfolded his piece of paper and passed it to me. 'Does this look familiar at all, Kit?'

I blinked a couple of times until I'd forced my eyes to focus. It was a web page, printed off. The title at the top was Divine Photography. I recognised it. It was the local photographer Ethan had hired for our wedding.

Underneath was a photo. A little clump of trees, all decked out in fairy lights... oh yes, they looked very familiar.

'They call it their Wedding Wonderland backdrop,' Jack said. 'Fully reusable miniature forest, for indoor or outdoor use. Nifty, eh?'

'You bastards,' I whispered to Mum and Ethan. 'You *bastards*!'

'What did you do with the aftershave, Ethan?' Jack asked. 'Take it out of her pocket while she was lying there? Or were you big-hearted enough to wait till the paramedics had seen her?'

'Wanted me to believe I was going insane...' I muttered,

still staring at the Wedding Wonderland that had provided such a handy cover for their betrayal.

Ethan looked panicked now, his eyes darting around like a hare backed into a corner.

'I don't know what you mean.'

'Yes you bloody do,' I said, looking up to meet his gaze. 'And you really tried to make me think... God, I thought I was losing my mind. You *wanted* me to think that. That is *sick*!'

Ethan hesitated, his gaze flitting from me to Jack, and then to Mum, while he decided whether there was any point continuing with the lie. Mum gave her head an almost imperceptible shake.

'Kitty, I swear, it was just one time!' he blurted out at last, his voice laced with desperation. 'I knew she wanted it, and I... I'm only human. It was a mistake. I promise you, baby, it was just one time.'

'You idiot!' Mum hissed. 'God, can't you be trusted to do anything right?'

'Don't believe him,' Jack said to me.

'I don't believe him,' I said. 'Aftershave in bathrooms doesn't belong to a one-off. Not that that makes any difference. Once is plenty.' I shook my head in disgust. 'God, my own mother! You're seriously disturbed, the pair of you.'

'Kitty, please!' Mum's eyes were shining with tears. She looked absolutely terrified. 'I'm sorry, darling. I'm truly sorry. I did it for you.'

I snorted. 'You went to bed with my husband for me? How the hell does that work?'

She shot a resentful glare at Ethan. 'Because he's not good enough for you. He's just a man, doing the only thing men know how to do. He never loved you. I had to prove that to you.'

'Right. So you knew I'd find out, did you?'

'Well, I—'

'And then you lied to me about it because, what? You wanted to prove it to me but at the same time cover it up by convincing me I was going mad?' I shook my head. 'Thing about a lie, Mum. It really needs thinking through.'

She stared at me for a moment. Finally she dropped her head onto her palms and let out a defeated sob.

'It was… too hard,' she whispered. 'I tried to say no, but it was too hard. Kitty, I'm so sorry. I never wanted to hurt you.'

'And yet here we are.' I nodded to the opening in the curtains. 'Get out.'

'Kitty, please—'

'I said, get *out*, both of you. Visiting hours are over. Permanently.'

'I do love you, Kitty, I swear,' Ethan managed to whisper. 'Whatever happened between me and her, it was always you.'

'You don't know what love is. Either of you. You never wanted to be with me, you just wanted to own me. While scratching an itch you couldn't control behind my back at every opportunity.' I sagged back against the bed, exhausted. 'Just go,' I whispered. 'We're done.'

'Wait,' Jack said. 'Kitty, there's something else.'

I frowned. 'You can't mean it gets worse?'

'No. Not exactly.' He hesitated, taking in my pale, drawn

face, the tears gemmed in my eyes. 'Think your head can handle another bombshell?'

'What is it, Jack? Tell me.'

He nodded to Mum. 'That woman's not your mother.'

Chapter 28

'**W**hat?'
         'I'm sorry, Kitty,' Jack said. 'It found its way into my Requires Response pile, somehow. I opened it without even looking at the envelope.'

I blinked. 'Sorry, what? What did you open?'

'This.' He fished out a folded envelope from his pocket and handed it to me.

'Jack, what is this?'

Mum seemed to recognise the postmark. Her eyes widened in fear.

'Kitty, don't open that. Please don't open that.'

Ignoring her, I unsealed the envelope and drew out the contents.

'I said don't open that, Kitty Louise!' Mum said in her most commanding tone. 'Put it back and give it to me. Now.'

The power of that voice over me, the use of my full name, was so strong I almost instinctively obeyed. Then I felt the reassuring pressure of Jack's hand on my shoulder, heard his whispered 'go on'. Fighting back the instinct to be a good little girl, to do as I was told, I unfolded the letter and laid it out in front of me.

'It's the copy of your birth certificate we sent off for,' Jack said. 'For your building society application. Look at it, Kit.'

'Kitty, just remember, whatever that says, I'm your mother.' Mum's voice was needy with panic now, even more than when she'd finally confessed to an affair with Ethan. 'I've always been your mother. I always will be. And I love you very much, angel. Whatever's there, you have to know that.'

'What the hell is this?' I whispered.

I'd never seen my original birth certificate. I knew Mum kept it safe somewhere in the house, and sent it off for me when I needed to prove who I was. That had never seemed particularly suspect, until today. She did lots of stuff for me, it was her thing.

But now I could see what it was she'd been so desperate to hide.

'Jesus, I'm *adopted*?'

Mum didn't seem to know what to say. She gaped at me for a second.

'Technically,' she finally managed to whisper. 'Only technically. But I'm your mum, Kitty.'

I sagged back into the pillows, my head wheeling. Adopted! How could she not have told me that?

Even after I'd met Ethan, my mum had been the dominant force in my life. I'd never doubted she loved me, but it was a stifling love, the kind that hurt more than straight-out hatred. The way she conditioned me to obey her, the guilt I felt when I displeased her, the overwhelming happiness when a good

297

school report or some other little achievement made her smile.

I'd never enjoyed her company. We'd never laughed together, never played games, had fun. Those things belonged to my dad and my Aunty Julia. But it was my mum's approval I'd lived for.

And now, just like that, the hold she'd always had over me, the feeling that I belonged to her, was shattered.

'You lied to me.' I said it very calmly. I wasn't going to cry. I wasn't.

'I didn't lie to you,' she protested feebly, her lip quivering. 'I just didn't tell you the whole truth. You... you didn't need to know.'

'You're not my mother.'

'I am. I am!' She looked ready to burst into tears. 'I'm the only mother you've ever had. I love you, Kitty.'

'You slept with my husband. You controlled me for years. Whoever the hell you are, you're not my mother.'

'Angel, please—'

'Mum, there's a little speech I practised for you while I was away.' I took a deep breath. 'I'm a strong, independent adult, this is my life and you don't get to control me. Now please take Ethan and... you know, fuck off.'

Jack gave me an approving nod.

Mum looked stunned. She opened her mouth a couple of times as if to speak, but the words wouldn't seem to come.

'I'll be so lonely without you,' she finally said in a small voice.

'That's not my problem.'

But I couldn't help relenting ever so slightly when I saw the way her face crumpled through its mask of Botox, even though she didn't deserve it.

'Why didn't you tell me?' I asked, my voice just a very little softer.

She hesitated a moment. I'd never seen her look so child-like; so utterly broken.

'I was afraid,' she whispered at last. 'I didn't want to lose you, Kitty.' She gave a bleak snort, which instantly disinte-grated into sobs. 'I never did anything good in my whole life except you. To imagine someone taking that away from me, taking my place...'

And suddenly, it all made sense. The years of manipulation; the fear on her face every time I'd gone for a visit to Aunty Julia with my dad; her hatred of Ethan and his place in my life. The almost frantic tears of anger and joy when she'd tracked me down to Laurel's the first time I'd run away from home. It wasn't about me, my wellbeing or my safety; it never had been. It was about her. That ever-present horror of losing me.

'You need to go,' I said quietly.

'Will I ever see you again?'

'I don't know. Maybe not.' I couldn't quite bring myself to squeeze her hand, but I managed a brief nod. 'Goodbye, Mum. And... look after yourself.'

After staring at me for a few seconds, her eyes brimming with hurt and loss, she finally turned to leave. A silent, broken Ethan trudged after her, refusing to meet my eye.

When they'd gone, Jack sat on the edge of the bed and

hugged me until the tears I couldn't hold back any more had subsided.

'Well done, Kit,' he said gently. 'Proud of you.'

'God, that was awful,' I sobbed.

'But it's over now. That part of your life's been exorcised. She'll never hold that same power over you again.'

I glanced down at the birth certificate. 'And now there's this. It can't be real, can it?'

'It has to be. It's right there in black and white.'

Because it was no random stranger's name in the box reserved for the mother's personal details. It was a name I knew well. Very well.

Julia Blake.

***

It was another four days before Sarah decided it was safe to discharge me. By then, the pain in my head had subsided to a dull throb.

Jack came every day at visiting time. Mum came once too, perhaps hoping to find me alone so she could try once more to talk me round, but I'd given strict instructions to the medical staff that I didn't want to see her. Ethan, it seemed, had given up, realising that no amount of honeyed words were going to make up for the fact he'd slept with his wife's mother. Laurel came to visit once with the boys, as soon as I was well enough to have those two bundles of energy bouncing around my cubicle. Aunty Julia was back in the Lakes but she sent some beautiful flowers and a get well card, asking me to call her as soon as I felt up to it. Perhaps if she knew what I knew, she wouldn't be quite so keen to hurry that conversation along.

We talked a lot about the birth certificate, me and Jack. I'd wanted to call Aunty Julia right away to demand a few answers, but Jack convinced me to wait until I was all healed. Another big confrontation could set my recovery back weeks.

It was just so tough to get my head around. My parents weren't my parents. My coddling, manipulative mum wasn't my mum at all. My playful, loving dad wasn't my dad. I mean he was, he always would be, but genetically speaking he was my uncle. That was a pretty big thing to deal with.

And my Aunty Julia, my favourite aunty, was my birth mum. So my biological dad – God, I didn't even want to think about that. Ken Blake, sadistic, abusive Uncle Ken, who'd made Aunty Julia's life miserable until the happy day he'd dropped down dead. That bastard was my dad. The thought of it made me queasy. Was he in me? Did I have any of that monster in my personality?

I had so many questions, but the biggest one was, why would they give me up? I'd never told Aunty J about my mum, quite how controlling she could be – I'd never told anyone, apologising for her and excusing her whenever I could just like I'd always done for Ethan – but I think my aunty suspected from our confidential girly chats that I was afraid of her. Aunty Julia had given me up to that. Why? Why hadn't she wanted me?

Finally, the day came when I was well enough to go home.

To the camper, I mean. That was my home now. Jack came to collect me from hospital in a taxi.

'Here.' He swaddled me in a big fleece he'd brought for me. 'You need to keep warm.'

I smiled. 'I'm not an invalid, you know.'

'It'll be a little while before you're fully healed though. And I like looking after you.' He opened the taxi door for me. 'My lady.'

When I got back to the camper and unzipped the awning, I gasped.

There was a string of golden lights hanging all around the little tent, twined with single roses. It looked like an enchanted bower. Jack darted ahead of me and lit a couple of candles he'd placed on the table.

'Jack, it's beautiful,' I breathed. 'Why did you do all this?'

'For you.' He took me in his arms. 'A welcome home present.'

'So that's why you didn't want to pick me up in the van.' I kissed the tip of his nose. 'Thank you.'

'Couple of friends who've been dying to see you too.' He let me go and went to open the door of the camper. Our two dogs burst out, yipping excitedly as they threw themselves at me.

I laughed, crouching down to let them lick my face. 'Aww. Missed you too, girls.'

Jack squatted by me and put his arms around my waist, kissing my cheek. 'It's good to have you home again, Kit.'

I looked around the awning, bathed in flickering candlelight and filled with the fresh, uncomplicated scent of roses. I looked at Jack, and the two happy dogs, their tails wagging vigorously.

My little family. Despite all the soap-opera drama of the last few days, the heartache, the loss, the betrayals, a feeling of contented warmth filled me. For the first time in a long time, I felt genuine, unalloyed happiness. I felt safe.

'It's good to be home,' I said.

Chapter 29

All talk of Snowdonia was put on hold. Jack knew exactly where our next destination needed to be. After stopping in to say a quick goodbye to Laurel, Andy and the kids, the following morning found us on the road again, heading for the picture-postcard beauty of Wastwater.

'Does she know you're coming?' Jack asked as we hurtled towards the Lakes.

'No. I don't want her to think something's up.'

'But something is up.'

'She'll find that out when I get there.' I frowned. 'Why're you slowing down?'

'Just something I want to get a look at.' He nodded to a nondescript field we were passing, lined with drystone wall. 'There. Look familiar?'

'Why, should it?'

He shook his head. 'No romance in your souls, you Yorkshire girls. That's where we first met. Remember? You were slumped against that bit of wall, sobbing your heart out?'

'Oh yeah.' I blinked at it. 'God. Life's changed a lot since then.'

'And for me.' He glanced at a road sign. 'Another two hours and we'll be there.'

Finally, we pulled up outside Aunty Julia's little white-washed cottage. I hadn't seen it since the day of my doomed marriage.

'I'll wait in the van,' Jack said. 'Let you and your aunty talk. Come get me if you need me.'

'Thanks.' I patted my pocket, where I'd stored the copy of my birth certificate, and drew a deep breath. 'Okay, here goes.'

He planted a kiss on my cheek. 'Good luck, Kit.'

I rapped smartly on the front door, then waited for Aunty Julia to answer. It seemed to take her longer than usual.

I knew as soon as she opened it that news had been spreading. She looked anxious, and that increased tenfold when she saw it was me. She'd been talking to Mum.

'Kitty. You're here.'

'Well-spotted,' I said, summoning a watery smile.

'How's your head, dear?'

'Much better, thanks. Can I come in?'

She hesitated, and for a minute I thought she was going to say no.

'Of course,' she said at last. 'I was just making some lunch.'

Inside, I took a seat on the comfy chair. Aunty Julia wheeled herself into the open-plan kitchen and started bustling away with her back to me, fretfully clearing up crockery in a jitter of nervous energy.

'Did I tell you about Robin down the road?' she asked, speaking very fast, then went on without waiting for an answer. 'He's finally marrying her, the live-in one – well, not before time. Oh, and Pat's back on the bottle, I heard – I mean, literally, straight from the bottle, Donald saw her. Carrie's expecting another, this'll be the fourth baby in five years, I think she's starting to feel it now—'

I held up a hand to halt the barrage of gossip. 'Okay, stop. I didn't drive over for the monthly newsletter of the Wasdale Curtain Twitchers' Society.' I beckoned her over. 'Come here, please.'

'Just a moment, dear.' She was still faffing with a pile of plates on the draining board.

'I need to talk to you.'

'Would you like some strawberries, Kitty? I just rinsed them for lunch.'

I gave in. 'Okay. If you need me to have strawberries before we can have a conversation, then yes, I'll have strawberries.'

I watched her as she took a couple of bowls and started dividing up a punnet of strawberries between them, counting them out with childlike precision. One for me, one for her. One for me, one for her. There were an odd number, so she sliced the last one precisely in half.

'You can have the big half,' she said, though to me the two halves looked identical.

'Are you done?'

She sighed. 'I suppose I am.'

She wheeled herself back to me and handed over my bowl of strawberries. 'Sweet and plump, just like me,' she said with a shy smile. 'They were your favourite, back when I used to make our picnics. Your dad's too.'

'Which dad's?'

306

She flushed. 'So it's true. You do know.'

I fished in my pocket for the birth certificate and handed it to her. She stared at it for a good minute. Eventually, I heard her let out a little sob.

'I wasn't a mum for very long,' she whispered. 'But when I see my name there, it's still powerful.'

I stretched an arm around her and rested my crown against hers.

'Why?' I said quietly.

'How could I keep you? I couldn't walk, Kitty.'

'That doesn't matter. Lots of people who can't walk are mums.'

'It mattered when *he* was alive,' she muttered darkly.

'Uncle Ken?'

She nodded slightly. 'I couldn't bring a baby into that. Couldn't bear the thought of him hurting you and me not being able to stop it. When I think of what he did to me...' Her voice broke in a sob. 'No, Kitty. No.'

'Did he know?'

'Of course he didn't. He never even knew I was pregnant. I went to stay with your nana until it was all over.' She let out a hard laugh. 'Oh, he didn't like that, letting me get away from him. It was the one time I stood up to him.'

'Nana knew?'

'Yes, dear. I did worry, when she got poorly, that she might let it slip one day. But whatever else she forgot, I think she always remembered what she'd promised me the day you were born.' She smiled sadly. 'You were a beautiful baby, Kitty. It broke my heart to give you up.'

I blinked back a tear.

'Where did Ken think you were?' I asked.

'I told him I'd been referred to a special treatment centre for a course of muscle therapy. I don't know if he ever believed me, but I wouldn't come home, and I wouldn't let him see me. Not until I'd handed you safely to Grant and Petra.'

'Dad never told me...' I muttered, half to myself.

'I made him promise, just like your nana. I couldn't bear for Ken to find out you were his.' Her brow lowered. 'No child should have to live with that sort of abuse.'

And yet I had lived with abuse, of a different kind. The emotional abuse I now recognised my mum had subjected me to for years. A handy training course to get me ready for Ethan to do exactly the same thing.

'I knew Grant would take care of you,' Aunty Julia said. 'Give you a good life. The kind of stable, loving home I wanted my baby to have.'

'But my mum...'

'Yes, dear?'

Her eyes were wet through. She'd taken my hand and was gripping it hard, her thumb brushing fervently over the fingers. Just like Mum used to do when I was upset – my other mum, I mean.

'Nothing,' I said at last. 'We've had a bit of a row, that's all.'

'She didn't say anything. Was it about me?'

'No. About Ethan.'

'Do you need me to talk to her?'

'You can talk to her if you like. I won't be. Not for a long time – ever, I think.'

She looked concerned. 'What was so bad, dear?'

'It doesn't matter. It's done with now.' I lifted her chin and kissed her forehead. 'Come on. Let's take our strawberries and go eat them by the lake. I'll get Jack and the dogs. I'd like you to get to know them better before we go again.'

'That sounds nice.' She put a hand on my arm to stop me standing. 'Who is Jack, Kitty?'

'He's my... friend. My friend that I live with.'

'Do you love him?'

'Yes,' I said simply. There didn't seem much point skirting around it. 'I love him very much.'

'And he loves you?'

'I don't know. He lost his wife, and now he... I'm not sure how he feels about me. He's fond of me, certainly. And he wants me with him.'

'Be careful, won't you?'

'I will.'

'You know you'll always have a home here, if you ever need one.' She flushed. 'With your mother. If you want to think of me that way.'

'Thank you. I do want to think of you that way.' I flung my arms around her. 'Maybe I always did.'

Chapter 30

Snowdonia was tempting, but I didn't want to go too far from Aunty Julia just yet. There was a sweetness to having a mum who genuinely loved me and wanted to spend time with me, not in a controlling way but as one adult to another. She seemed to feel it too: that things were different for us now. Better.

And I loved watching her get to know Jack. When I'd met Jack's parents in Scotland, I'd been at least a little envious of that easy affection, how they laughed together. Now, for the first time in my life, it felt like I had that too. He smiled at how smug I'd started to get, showing off my new mum to him.

We stayed a week in Wastwater, then drove to Buttermere, a couple of hours away, where we could still pop back for occasional visits to Aunty – to my mum.

The days passed quickly in the camper with Jack, and yet they seemed endless, like school holidays when you're a kid. Every day we spent in the Lakes we discovered new places together, and every night he stretched himself out next to me, naked and beautiful, and wrapped me up in his arms.

I'd never been to Buttermere before, but I discovered it was more than a match for Wastwater in the breathtaking beauty stakes. Jack sought us out a pitch in a farmer friend's back field, where the mighty shadows of Haystacks and Fleetwith Pike muted the camper's sunny glow. I soon got used to him waking me in the early morning when the sky was clear, so that together we could watch the dawn mists cascading like downy hair over the felltops and the pines.

After a recuperation period for my head to heal fully, I dived right back into my PA work. It was so varied, I rarely got bored. And Jack's fan mail was always fun.

'This is weird,' I said one morning out in the awning, blinking at a picture in sickly green felt tip. 'Looks like someone drew you a courgette.'

'Pass it here,' he said, putting down his sketchbook. I handed it over.

He laughed. 'It's not a courgette. Look.' He held it up and pointed to what looked like a lumpy green sausage. 'It's Hulk, see? That little girl Isla from the book signing did it for me, her name's on the back.'

I squinted at it. Now I examined it more closely, I did detect a hint of purple that could be Hulk's super-stretchy trousers.

'Aww,' I said, smiling. 'Sweet kid. You going to stick it on the fridge?'

'No, I'll send it to Di, she keeps them in a scrapbook for me. I like to look through it sometimes when I go down to her offices in London. Reminds me why I do it.'

He folded the little picture and placed it carefully back in its envelope, then started fanning himself with it.

I opened the next letter, which was in an official-looking envelope and addressed to me.

'What is it?' Jack asked in a low voice. We'd both come to regard anything in a pre-printed envelope as potentially scary.

I smiled. 'Something good. The paperwork to have my marriage to Ethan declared voidable.'

'Then you can have it annulled?'

'That's my understanding, yeah. And then legally speaking it's like the whole thing never happened. Like it never should've.'

'Will he contest it, do you think?'

'Not sure how he could. He can hardly claim it was consummated, given I took off the same day.'

I put the forms to one side to fill in later.

'Aww,' I said with a little simper when I opened the next one. 'Look, Jack. From Ben.'

I held up the photo of a little group of farm dogs, blinking in a puzzled way at the camera.

Jack smiled. 'All grown up. Look well, don't they?'

'And happy.' I turned it round to examine the puppies – well, dogs now, really. I recognised the artist formerly known as Honeybadger, now renamed Bruce according to the names scrawled on the back, sitting proudly upright at the head of his siblings. 'Looks like our naughtiest pup's grown up into a bit of a swot. Ben must've worked hard on their training.'

'Who's the bruiser in the middle?' Jack asked.

I turned the photo round to look at the names. 'Meg, it says. That must be Princess Sparkle.'

'Yeesh. I pity the rat who gets on the wrong side of her.'

The next letter in the pile wasn't a letter at all. It was a big, fat parcel.

'Um... wow,' I said when I'd opened it.

'Ouch,' Jack said, wincing. 'From Sonia?'

'Who else?'

I scanned the matching dog jackets in a granny-square patchwork of rainbow colours, the names 'Sandi' and 'Mutli' embroidered onto the sides:

'Her spelling's a bit off,' I said.

Jack smiled. 'Ah well, it's sweet of her. Although woolly coats are the last thing they need today.'

It was bloody hot for September. Reeking hot. Hotter than Beelzebub's boxers, as my ever-classy dad used to say. He had that touch of the poet about him. Sandy, curled by my feet with her tongue lolling, let out a throaty whine to let me know her views on the matter.

'It's like a furnace in here,' Jack said, still fanning himself with Isla's picture. 'I'm sweating like a pig in a sauna.'

'Sexy.'

'As always.' He got to his feet. 'Right, ladies both human and canine, we're off out. Some of us are on deadline and I'm refusing to write the day off, Indian summer or not. I can't work in this heat.'

'Off where?' I said. 'It won't be any better outside, it's twenty-four degrees in the shade. And there'll be midges everywhere.'

'It'll be cool enough on high ground. Grab your walking boots, Kit: we're going hiking.'

***

I stared up at the intimidating ridge of Fleetwith Pike. Blinked. Stared again.

Nope. It wasn't getting any smaller.

'And you said it was how high?' I asked Jack, mesmerised by the swimming patchwork of gold on the mountain's flank.

'Around 2000 feet. Just a baby compared to some of the fells round here. It's a good thousand feet shorter than Scafell Pike.'

'Jesus.' I ran my eyes up the steep sides to the summit. 'If that's a baby, I'd hate to see the parents.'

'Oh, it's not so bad.' He gave my bum a pat. 'Pair of sturdy northern legs on you, you'll be skipping up. Come on.'

I groaned as we followed the frisking dogs to the foot of the fell. I could already feel my calves aching in anticipation of the climb that lay ahead. Still, at least we'd be nice and cool at the top.

***

It wasn't worth it. It *so* wasn't worth it. After two hours' walking, I'd decided no heatwave could be worse than the pain burning through every muscle and joint. I felt like I'd been meat-tenderised with a mace.

'Best... date... ever,' I panted to Jack as we scrambled up jagged rock towards the summit.

'I know. The look on your little face,' Jack said, grinning at me over his shoulder.

'You are so not getting laid tonight.'

'Those shining eyes, full of joy and wonder...'

'They're shining because I'm crying inside. Also, outside.'

'Oh, whisht, moany. It'll be worth it when we get to the top.'

And he was right, as bloody usual. When I'd collapsed, exhausted, next to the cairn that marked the highest point, I had leisure to catch my breath and absorb the view we'd walked all the way up here for. In the distance, the twin pools of Buttermere and Crummock Water shimmered luscious watermelon-green under a heat haze. The fresh, grass-clad flank of the pike itself sloped lazily down to meet them, giving me a real sense of achievement when I reflected on how far and how high we'd walked.

And it was cool: so deliciously, blissfully, sexily cool. I gulped in a deep breath of mountain air and exhaled slowly.

'Told you,' Jack said.

'All right, don't get smug,' I said, smiling. 'So are you going to do some work now?'

'Not on the summit.' He skimmed his gaze over a gaggle of fellow walkers tucking into their packed lunches. 'Come on, English. We'll find somewhere further down where it's quiet.'

In a sheltered nook overlooking an old slate quarry, we each picked a spot that suited us. Jack selected a flat rock where he could work undisturbed and the dogs, tired after their walk, settled down by his feet.

That looked like a good idea. Taking my cue from them, I spread myself out next to Jack for a good old laze. The press release about *Tilly and Billy in a Hot Air Balloon* I'd been planning to write could wait until my muscles had recovered a bit.

There was a beetle between me and Jack on the rock, its sleek petroleum-puddle belly turned to the sky and its legs wiggling as it struggled to right itself. Absently, Jack flipped it over with his pencil and the little thing scuttled away. You could tell a lot about a man from the way he treated a beetle in distress, came a fleeting thought.

'How does it work?' I asked as he took his sketchpad from his rucksack. 'Do the ideas just come to you?'

'Never really thought about it.' He paused to consider. 'I guess it's like... there's this shadowy void, and I throw thoughts into it and see what comes back. At the beginning there's just white, and I start to fill it and add to it, layer on layer, until at some point it solidifies and there are Tilly and Billy, having an adventure as if that was how it was always supposed to happen.'

'Sounds like hard work.'

'It can be. I love it though.'

'Must be strange drawing for kids when you don't have any of your own.'

I grimaced when I saw him flinch. God, Sophie... Diana had told me they'd been trying for a baby. Foot, meet mouth; mouth, foot.

'Sorry, Jack. That was a thoughtless thing to say.'

'No, I know what you mean. It is strange.' He reached into his rucksack again and pulled out a packet of sandwiches. 'Here, better eat these. You'll need to get your energy up after a walk like that.'

Abrupt subject change noted, I thought as I tore into the clingfilm.

An hour later, I was lying on my back, basking. My lazy gaze followed the assortment of buzzing, fluttering things that owned the mountain, and occasionally I reached up to bat one away from my eyes.

There was no sound but the rush of a beck somewhere in the distance, the drowsy hum of the insects and the scratch-scratch of Jack's busy pencils. I toyed with the idea of doing some work, but moving just seemed like too much effort.

After a while Jack put down his sketchpad and lay down next to me. He reached over to twirl a strand of my hair around one finger.

'What you thinking, John O'Dreams?' he asked softly.

'John...' The word triggered a memory. I turned onto my side to look at him. 'You're called John.'

'So my mother claims.'

'Hey, can I call you Johnny?'

'No.'

'Can I call you Jacky?'

'If I can call you Puss.'

'Okay, point made,' I said, smiling. 'Want to show me what you've drawn?'

'All right. It's only rough though, remember.'

We sat up and he passed me his pad. I glanced over the sketchy lines of graphite that were the skeleton of Tilly and Billy's next adventure.

'This is new,' I said, pointing to the corner.

'Yeah, didn't want to leave her out,' he said, smiling at the little Muttley scribbled into the picture alongside her cartoon mum. 'Can't be after having any favouritism in the ranks.'

'And who's that?' I asked, indicating the figure of a strict-looking woman with her arms folded. She was glaring sternly at Tilly and Billy, who, for some reason probably made clear in an earlier sketch, were covered in jam.

'That's Flora, their nanny. She's been an invisible character till now, mentioned but never seen,' Jack told me. 'The fans are going to love it. Sonia might launch into orbit.'

I looked up to frown at him. 'Jack...'

'Hmmm?' he said, casting innocent eyes skywards.

'Why does she look like me?'

'Does she? I hadn't noticed.'

'Did you put me in a book looking grumpy?'

He laughed. 'Okay, when you glare at me like that I guess she does look like you.' He took the sketchpad off me and guided me between his knees so he could wrap his arms round my middle. 'I thought it'd be fun for you to show Toby and Sam, that's all. Was going to dedicate the book to you.'

I smiled. 'You're very sweet.'

'Glad you like it. And I promise not to always draw you grumpy.' He shuffled me round so I was facing him, then brought his hands up to my face and moulded my mouth into a grin. 'There, that's better. Now I can draw you like that.'

'Mmf?' I said, my mouth movement restricted by his grin-making hands.

'Yeah.' He brought his arms back round my waist. 'I've heard they need a new artist at DC. Batman vs The Joker, I'll be a natural.'

'You're insulting.'

'I'm sweet. You just said.'

'You're sweet and insulting.'

'And you're beautiful. Even when you do look like The Joker.' He pressed a soft kiss to my lips. 'Thanks for being yourself, Kit.'

'Well, I've always struggled to be anyone else,' I said, flashing him a proper smile. I glanced again at the jam-covered Tilly and Billy. 'Where did they come from anyway? The characters?'

'Oh, somewhere in here,' he said, tapping his head. 'Before I went pro, I used to draw them for Sophie's niece. She couldn't get enough of them.' He smiled, a little wistfully. 'She's ten now, but I always send her a book when I've got a new one out.'

'What made you decide to do it full-time?'

'I probably wouldn't have thought much about it, except Soph kept going on. Wouldn't stop nagging me until I'd sent them out to a few agents. She could be a bossy madam when she got a fixed idea.'

'She did right to push you,' I said with an approving nod. 'Laurel's boys would be permanently *Lord of the Flies* without Tilly and Billy.'

He put one finger under my chin to look into my eyes. 'Do you mind me talking about her?'

'Sophie? No, love.' I reached up to stroke his stubbled cheek. 'It's good for you, I think. When my dad died it felt like ages till I could talk about it, but once I did it all came out in a rush. It was only Laurel being so willing to listen that helped me deal with it properly, open up to the idea of seeing a counsellor. She lost her husband years back.'

'Yeah. It does help.'

I hesitated. There was something I'd been wanting to talk to him about for a while, but things had felt so happy and settled since I'd finally managed to move on from Mum, Ethan and everything back home, I hadn't wanted to rock the boat. Still, it'd been preying on my mind, ever since the big row we'd had in Scotland that had exploded into our first kiss.

'Jack?'

'Hmm?'

'You ever think you might need more help than just talking to me?'

He frowned. 'A doctor?'

'I was thinking of a counsellor. I was a mess after Dad died, until I had Lindy to talk me through it. You know, it can really make a difference.'

He gazed away into the distance. 'Maybe if someone had said that to me right after, but... no. It's been too long, Kit. I am the way I am, now.'

'But you're hurting so much, still, because of it.'

It cost me an effort to say that. Acknowledging Jack's hurt, the fact he hadn't fully moved on, sent a ripple of pain through me. And there was something else too, something I knew was unworthy of me. Jealousy.

I hated myself for being jealous of Sophie, and yet I was, every day; I couldn't help it. Because there was still that little piece of Jack that would always be hers, the piece that was taking his future from him. And mine from me, as long as the two were linked. It wasn't her fault, of course it wasn't, but I couldn't suppress the instinctive envy bubbling away somewhere in my spleen.

There was pain in Jack's face now, just from thinking about it. I instantly hated myself for bringing it up.

'I couldn't, Kit. I couldn't talk to a stranger about that.' He shook his head, almost angrily. 'It's mine. To unpack all that for someone I don't even know, someone who's being paid to listen – no. It's private and it's mine. It's not for sale.'

'It doesn't feel like that when you're there. Yeah, they get paid, but they're trained to help you. It's what they do.'

'But don't you understand?' he said, anger still simmering under his tone. It frightened me, even though I knew it wasn't aimed at me. Jack so rarely got angry. 'That pain's part of me now, Kitty. I won't sell it off to the highest bidder.' He glared at his feet. 'It'd be a betrayal.'

I stared at him. This wasn't the first time I'd tried to raise the issue of grief counselling, but usually he'd just changed the subject, or found an urgent reason he needed to be somewhere else. He'd never gone into just why he was so resistant to the idea.

Grief was such a complex thing, and Jack's grief... it felt like there was layer upon layer, each contradicting another, each trying to fight its way to the top of the pile. I wanted to help, but Christ almighty. I was seriously out of my depth.

'Tell me what I can do,' I said quietly. It was all I had.

Jack was silent a moment, lost in his thoughts. Eventually he lifted his frown and looked up to meet my eyes, anger gone and a penitent look in his eyes. 'Sorry, Kitty. Did I snap at you? I didn't mean to.'

'Not really at me, I think.' I took his hand. 'I'm not a stranger, am I? And I'm not getting paid for anything other than opening your post and writing press releases. Tell me about Sophie, if it helps you.'

His eyes searched my face. 'Isn't it strange for you, hearing me talk about her?'

'Maybe a little,' I answered truthfully. 'But you talk about her as much as you like. I do like to hear about her. It helps me understand you a bit better: how you used to be.' I pressed the backs of his fingers to my lips. 'What was she like?'

'Oh, she was... one of a kind. Pretty, sweet – hot-tempered, sometimes. And she was funny, like you, but with a filthier laugh.' He smiled at the memory. 'You remind me of her a bit.'

'She looked like me?'

He shook his head. 'Couldn't have looked more different. Actually, she wasn't much like you at all – not how she looked or her mannerisms or anything. But you remind me of her, all the same.'

'How do I?'

He smiled. 'Well, you both give me hell.'

'No more than you deserve. Anything else?'

'Your sense of humour. And how I feel around you. That feeling I don't have to try to be something I'm not.'

'When have you ever tried that in your life?' I asked.

'There was a time I wanted to please, same as anyone. But when Sophie died I didn't have the energy for pleasing any more. It was take me as I am or don't bother.'

'I'll take you.'

'I know you will,' he said gently. 'That's why I like being with you. There's no – no pretence about you, Kitty Clayton.'

'And that's why you can read me like a book?'

'Maybe I can,' he said, his eyes darting over my features. 'I can tell when you want me to kiss you.'

'How?'

'Because it's when I want to kiss you.'

'And when's that?'

'Always.'

He leaned forward to prove it with a long kiss.

Chapter 31

I think I must've drifted into a half-doze, lulled to sleep by the rhythmic scratch of pencil on paper. I was only half aware of the wind picking up, and reached up to bat an irritating strand of hair away from my nose.

'I'd set off down if I were you.'

I forced my eyes open and sat up to face the walker who'd stopped to speak to us.

'Sorry?'

'You pair had better get off the fells.' He jerked his head heavenwards. 'Storm's coming.'

I looked up to find thick purple clouds had taken over what just a few hours ago had been a clear summer sky. The sun was refracting – reflecting? refracting? – whatever the word is, off the underside of the clouds, glowing through the cracks, fragmenting the heavens in a web of light. After days of tropical temperatures, it looked like the time had come to pay the piper.

'Jack,' I said, nudging him. 'We need to go.'

'Hmm?' He was frowning at his pad, completely absorbed. But he jerked to attention quickly enough when a fat blob of rain landed bang in the middle of the sketch he was working on.

'Bastard!' He pulled out a tissue to blot it away. 'Where did that come from?' He glanced up at the rapidly blackening sky. 'Oh.'

Jack hastily stashed pad and pencils in his rucksack. We jumped up, grabbed a dog lead each and started making our way down.

But within half an hour, the chubby raindrop that had tried its damnedest to ruin Tilly and Billy's jam-based adventures had been joined by a whole throng of brothers and sisters. I could barely see my hand in front of my face, and the dogs were whining pitiably. Worse, what sounded like the distant rumble of thunder was vibrating the ground under my feet.

Jack kept reaching round to pat his rucksack, looking concerned.

'It'll be soaked through in another ten minutes of this,' he said, raising his voice so I could hear him over the hiss of rain.

'But it'll ruin your sketches.'

'I know. Walking conditions aren't too safe when the visibility's this poor either. We should hole up somewhere till it's over.'

I blinked, trying to focus through swimming eyes. 'Up here? There isn't anywhere.'

'There's an old quarryman's hut not far away.' He seized my hand. 'Come on.'

'Are we allowed in?' I asked when we reached the ramshackle

hut nestled among piles of slate. 'It's someone's property, isn't it?'

'We're allowed. It's a bothy.'

'It's a whatty?'

'Bothy. Shelter for walkers who get into difficulties.'

The door was unlocked and I followed Jack inside, out of reach of the pelting rain.

The bothy's uber-rustic interior was about as basic as you could get: bare brick walls, a stone ledge under a little window, a simple fireplace with a pile of logs and kindling next to it. But it was dry and warm.

'We'd better get out of our wet things,' Jack said. He nodded to an old wooden chest. 'There's usually blankets in there. You get them out and I'll get a fire going.'

When I'd stripped to my underwear and swaddled myself in a blanket, I took a seat on the rough stone ledge and glanced out of the window at the rain still hammering down. A flash of lightning chose that moment to make an appearance, followed closely by a peal of angry thunder. Little Muttley whimpered, darting over to hide behind my legs, and I reached down to give her a reassuring stroke. Thunderstorms weren't my favourite thing either.

'It's getting dark,' I said to Jack.

'Mmm. We might be here for the night, I think.'

'What, you can sleep in these things?'

'In an emergency, when the walking conditions aren't safe.'

I blinked at him in the adolescent flicker of the open fire. 'I mean, can *you* sleep in these things?'

He gave a little shudder. 'Doesn't look like I've got any choice, does it? If it was just me... but it's not safe to take you down in this.'

'It's only one night, maybe it'll help you. And I'll be here.'

'Yeah.' He looked up from stoking the fire to meet my eyes. 'Glad I've got you, Kit.'

***

Two hours later, it was still raining, although the thunder had stopped. It was pitch dark outside now, the room's only illumination the ruddy glow of the fire and a candle stuck in an old Jack Daniels bottle on the mantelpiece.

At some point I must've dozed off. When I blinked myself awake, the two dogs were stretched out comfortably in front of the blaze and Jack was sitting on a stool cooking something, stripped off and wrapped in a blanket. I hadn't realised how hungry I was till the appetising smell hit my nostrils.

'What's that?' I asked, stifling a yawn.

'I did a bit of a recce while you were sleeping. Found a couple of tins of baked beans with pork sausages someone left. And...' He reached under his stool and waggled a miniature at me. 'Some kindly whisky fan left us a nightcap. Luxury, eh? I'll split it with you.'

The beans made a simple but satisfying meal, eaten straight out of the tins: proper cowboy tea, with the Kendal Mint Cake we'd brought for pudding. Afterwards, Jack split the whisky between a couple of cracked cups.

'Just a sec,' he said when he saw me about to knock mine back. 'Throw me my jeans there.'

I did as he asked. He rummaged in his pocket, pulling out a couple of squashed white flowers.

'What is it?' I asked.

'Honeysuckle, last of the season. Spotted it growing down in the lowlands this morning. Best with cognac, but it'll add some flavour to your nightcap.' He shrugged when he saw me staring. 'What?'

'You forage cocktail ingredients?'

'Sometimes. You need to watch yourself though. They don't look kindly on you stealing vodka from Asda and calling it foraging.'

After we'd finished our drinks, we set to work creating a makeshift bed. We laid the thickest blanket, doubled up, across the uneven stone flags, with another folded into a pillow and the final two to spread over us. It wasn't the most comfortable of quarters, but with the fire blazing away it was at least snug and warm.

I snuggled into bed while Jack sorted the dogs out with accommodation in a little outhouse. They gave him a dirty look for evicting them from the fire, but there just wasn't the space for all four of us. A bowlful of the dog biscuits he'd had the foresight to bring soon got him back into their good books though.

When he came back in, he knelt at my feet to give the fire a poke then dragged a battered old fireguard in front of it. He leaned down to give the toe peeping out from under the blanket a kiss before he crawled into bed to join me.

'You're not one of these feet people, are you?' I said.

'Don't think so.' He glanced down. 'Mind you, they are very pretty feet. Maybe I could be converted. Become one of those fellers who drink champagne out of stilettos and get turned on at the mere sight of a supported in-step.'

I laughed. 'Well if my shoes start going missing, I'll know who to blame.'

'Yep. Still, I think I like what's at this end of you best.' He leaned forward to plant a soft kiss on my lips.

'This is sort of nice,' I said, burrowing into his arms. There was no sound except the crackling fire and the sleeping dogs' wheezy breathing, and, if I listened closely enough, the distant chatter of the beck. 'Are you sure you'll be okay sleeping inside?'

'It's not the sleeping so much as the living,' he said, and I felt him shudder. Not for the first time, I wondered what went on in that big handsome head of his. Why being indoors for any lengthy period of time scared him so much.

'Hey,' he whispered, nuzzling into my neck. 'We'll have the place to ourselves for the night now. What do you think?'

I shook my head. 'One whisky and you're anyone's, aren't you?'

'Only yours. Want to?'

'Is there not something about shagging in bothies in the etiquette guide?'

'I won't tell if you don't.'

I smiled as his hands slid up to unfasten my bra.

'Thanks for being with me,' he whispered into the ear he'd started kissing.

I held him back from me. 'Why do you keep saying that, Jack?'

He blinked. 'Do I?'

'Yes. You say it all the time. Or things like it.'

'Well, because… I want you to know, I guess.' He drew a tender finger down my cheek. 'It's better when you're here, Kit.'

'What's better?'

'Everything. Me.' In the fading fire glow, he scanned my face. 'You know you can stay in the van with me as long as it feels like home, don't you? Forever, if you want. I mean, I want you to.'

Forever. That was a big word. And Jack so rarely thought about or talked about a future beyond tomorrow, for him it was an even bigger word. I flushed as his exploring fingers started sliding sensuously over my hip.

'I'm not going anywhere,' was the last thing I said before he covered my lips with his, and like so many times previously I lost myself in him.

***

'Soph!'

Jack's yell was loud enough to echo round the fells. I woke with a jerk to find him sitting up on the blanket, gazing around wildly with eyes still milky from whatever nightmare had caused him to cry out.

He looked down at me in the thin dawn light streaming in through the little window. 'Oh God, you're okay,' he said, sounding relieved. 'You're here.'

Jesus. He thinks I'm her…

'No, love.' I put a hand on his arm. 'It's me. It's Kitty.'

'What…' He blinked himself fully awake, eyes unclouding as the dream fled. 'Kitty. What happened?'

'Just a dream, Jack. Just a bad dream.'

'Yeah. I was dreaming…' His eyes went wide. 'Oh Christ, what did I do?'

'Nothing bad,' I said, massaging his back in soothing circles. 'Just a bit of panic. Everything's okay now.'

'Did I hurt you? Sometimes I thrash about.'

'No. I'm okay.' I blinked back a tear. 'You thought I was Sophie. That's all.'

'Oh my God. I didn't.'

'It's all right. It's only natural.' I guided him back down and wrapped my arms around him. 'Does it happen a lot, my lamb?' I asked softly.

'Not that much. I can go months not having the dream, then just when I start to feel relieved that it might be gone for good… I'm sorry. You shouldn't have to see that.'

'Is it always the same dream?'

'Yes. The accident.' He flinched. 'In it, I'm – I'm the driver. I'm the one who does it, Kitty. And I can't stop the car, I can just… watch. Her face.'

'Jesus! Jack, that's… oh, you poor boy.' I held him tighter, trying to fathom the unbearable pain of a loved one's dying face haunting your dreams.

'Like turning out a light,' Jack whispered after a moment's silence. 'That's what she told me, the paramedic who took her away. She told me Soph was gone – because I wouldn't believe it, not at first – and it happened so fast she wouldn't have suffered. Wouldn't have had time to feel anything.'

I didn't know what to say to that. I just held him close and gently stroked his hair, waiting to see if he'd go on.

'And the nights I wake from the dream,' he said after he'd choked back a sob. 'Those are the nights I wonder if it was true, or if it's just something they say to make you feel better.'

'It's true. They wouldn't lie.'

He let out a bleak laugh. 'Why, because they're doctors?'

'Because... because it has to be true,' I said, struggling to keep desperation out of my voice. 'Needs to be.'

'That's what I tell myself.' He made an odd little noise in his throat. 'Before you were with me, I used to get up and just drive. Leave bad thoughts behind in the old place and start again somewhere new.'

I was starting to understand. Houses meant being trapped with his memories, his grief. On the road he could be free.

The thing was, where did that leave us? Ever since my conversation with Laurel up in Scotland, the words she'd said to me that day – *you can't compete with a dead wife, Kit* – had been echoing around my brain. I'd tried to ignore them. Time after time, I'd told myself it would all be fine. All Jack needed was time and love and a listening ear, and eventually he'd be able to move on properly, with me. I just needed to be patient, that was all.

But I had to face facts. Getting over Sophie, that pain he called a part of him, wasn't going to happen any time soon. Maybe it never would.

'Glad I've got you, Kit,' he said, cuddling into me. In the eerie morning silence, I pressed him tight against me while he drifted off. As for me, I couldn't sleep a wink.

Chapter 32

'You're very quiet today,' Jack said as I stared thoughtfully into my coffee one morning in the campervan.

'Hm?'

Jack waved a hand in front of my spaced-out eyes. 'Hello? Anyone home?'

'Jack, are we a couple?' I blurted out suddenly.

'A couple of what?'

'Don't be cute, you know what I mean. Are we in a relationship?'

He shrugged. 'Sure. Whatever you like.'

'I mean it. Are we girlfriend and boyfriend? Because I've never once heard you call me that.' I looked up from my coffee to glare at him. 'When I was talking to your mum up in Scotland, she said every time she saw you, you had a new pet. I'm starting to wonder if that's not what I am, when it comes right down to it.' I jerked my head in the direction of the little caravan hooked behind the camper. 'I've even got my own kennel.'

'Now you're being silly. You know you never fetch those sticks I throw you.'

I refused to let myself laugh. 'How do you feel about me? Really?'

'Well when you look at me like that, terrified.' He sighed and came to sit by me. 'You know how I feel about you, Kit. Different than I feel about anyone else.'

'And how's that?'

'I feel... simple. Know what I mean?'

'No, not really.'

'Being with you. It's simple. Easy. Like I don't need to be anywhere else.'

I allowed myself a smile. 'That's how I feel.'

'So what's the problem? We're happy, aren't we?'

'Well, yes, but—'

'You can label it if that'll make you feel better. Call me your boyfriend or whatever you like.' He reached out to stroke my cheek with his thumb. 'I'm just glad I've got you with me.'

I sighed. 'I suppose what I'm asking is where we go from here. What's the future? We have to talk about it some time.'

'Why do we, if we're happy now?'

'Because it's coming. There always is a tomorrow, no matter how much you try to ignore it. And I'd like to know what mine's going to have in it.'

'But none of us really know that, do we?' He sighed. 'I don't know what you're asking me to say here, Kit. You know I want to be with you, that's future enough for me.'

'But what'll happen?'

'I don't know, do I? That's the joy of it. We take each day as it comes and see where life throws us.'

335

I should've known that'd be the answer. When did Jack Duffy ever plan for anything?

And yet I knew he'd done the whole relationship thing before. Properly, like other people did. Lived with someone, loved her, married her, planned a family with her. But it was like his parents had told me. Whatever had happened to him the day he lost his wife seemed to have left him incapable of anything but short-term thinking.

'I care about you very much, you know.' He was still stroking my face. 'Maybe I don't say that often enough, but I do. There's no one quite like you, Kitty. It's been another life, having you here.'

'For me too.'

'Kiss me then,' he said gently. 'We don't want to be fighting, do we?'

'No.' I leaned forward to kiss him. 'You're right, I'm being daft.'

'It's not daft if it's upsetting you. Anyway, if you want us to be a couple, my treasure, then that's what we'll be.'

I smiled. 'It's funny when you call me that.'

'Why, what did I call you?'

'Treasure. My grandad used to call my nan that. I always thought it was an old folk thing.'

'Maybe it is.' His eyes were gazing into mine, trying to fathom what I was feeling. 'Did they make each other happy, your nan and grandad?'

'They did. Never a cross word in forty years, Nan used to say. I mean, it was a massive whopping porkie, but they loved each other to bits all the same.'

'Then I'll always call you it.' He gave me a kiss and stood up. 'Right, I'm kicking you out into the caravan once I've got the awnings down. I need to take the van into Keswick and pick up the post.' When he reached the doorway he turned back to look at me, his large frame silhouetted against the bright autumn sunshine. 'Hey. What do you say to moving on today?'

'What, away from Aunty – I mean, my mum?'

'Just for a few weeks, then we'll come back this way for a visit. There's so much to see.'

I glanced out of the window at the sparkling breadth of Buttermere. It was a beautiful place. I'd miss it, but Jack was right: there was a world of horizons out there for the taking.

'That sounds good,' I said. 'Where will we go? Snowdonia?'

'I might have a thought about that. We'll talk about it when I get back.'

***

I frowned when Jack arrived home a few hours later and sought me out in my little caravan. He was carrying a bag – not a plastic carrier, but from some sort of clothes shop. It was the fancy paper kind with string handles, a feminine-looking logo on one side.

'What's that, lingerie?' I asked.

'Now why didn't I think of that?' He dumped the bag on the floor. 'Sadly not. It is something for you though.' He pulled out something big and soft, wrapped up in silvery paper. 'It's your size. Hope I chose right.'

I unwrapped the little parcel curiously, then gasped as I shook out the contents.

It was a dress. Correction: it was *the* dress. The dress I'd probably fantasised about as a five-year-old who still had a lingering affection for Disney princesses. It was satin, a gorgeous cloud silver. Layers of tulle gave the skirt a fullness that'd make you want to skim the dancefloor with it till the early hours, pumpkin coaches be damned.

'It's... wow,' I whispered.

'Good wow or bad wow?' Jack said. 'Ladies' outfitting isn't really my area. It was a bit of a wild guess based on factors such as shininess and depth of neckline.'

'Good wow. It's stunning.' I shook my head. 'You really shouldn't buy me things.'

He took a seat next to me and slung one arm around my shoulders. 'Ah, but you'll need this for where we're going next.'

'Why, where're we going?'

'Dorset.'

I blinked at the dress. 'Dress well down there, do they?'

He laughed. 'They do at this place. I got us tickets to the theatre.' He shuffled round and took my cheek in his palm. 'I was listening, Kit,' he said softly. 'What you said this morning, about being a proper couple. I'm taking you out on a real, grown-up date. All arranged for the day after tomorrow.'

I blinked at him, touched. 'Really? You did that just because of what I said?'

He planted a little kiss on my forehead. 'Of course. That's what boyfriends do, isn't it?'

***

'Come on, girl, are you not done yet?' Jack called from the awning. He and the dogs had been evicted from the van while I got ready. 'The performance starts in an hour.'

'Just a minute.' I took a last look in my hand mirror to make sure my eyeliner hadn't smudged while I'd been struggling into the humongous gown, gave its satin sheen a brush with my palms to rid it of any dog hairs and went to join Jack.

'So? How do I look?' I asked, glancing up at him through lowered lashes.

'Woah,' he said, running his eyes over me. 'You're... huge.'

I laughed. 'Not quite the response I was hoping for.'

'Come here.' He wrapped me in his arms – as well as he could without treading on the mountain of dress – and kissed my hair. 'You look gorgeous. Like a fairytale.'

'Thanks,' I said, blushing. 'Aren't you getting changed?'

'Now you've finished doing all your lady things in the van. Won't take me long.'

I think I might actually have goggled when Jack emerged from the camper twenty minutes later, my eyes popping out on stalks with a cartoon *badadadoing*. If I looked like something out of a fairytale – or a pantomime, possibly – that was nothing compared to the transformation he'd undergone. In a dinner suit and black tie, clean-shaven and with his permanently unruly hair neatly gelled, he'd gone from rugged-backwoods-lumberjack sexy to James-Bond-on-the-pull sexy. The difference left me speechless for a second.

'Will I do then, Kit?' he asked, smiling bashfully.

'God, you look... where did you get that?'

'This old thing?' he said, glancing down at the jacket hanging from his broad shoulders. 'I've had it years. It lives in storage for when Di forces me to go to awards ceremonies.' He held out his crooked arm to me. 'Shall we then, milady?'

I smiled, slipping my arm through his. 'We shall, sir. What're we going to see anyway?'

'It's a surprise. You'll find out when we get there.' He glanced down at the flimsy flats he'd bought me to match the dress. 'Oh, and you might want to bring a change of shoes.'

***

With a handbag clutched in one hand and a carrier containing my walking boots in the other – ballgowns and boots were clearly my look – I stepped out of a taxi at our destination. As soon as I emerged, I realised exactly why this particular trip to the theatre might require a change of footwear.

It was really more like an amphitheatre: steep rows of stone seats cut into a coastal cliff. A simple grass circle that wouldn't have looked out of place playing host to a few gladiator-hungry lions seemed to be the focal point, although how anyone could concentrate on the stage with the crystal blue-green of the ocean as a backdrop I didn't know.

'This is where we're going?' I said to Jack in an awed whisper.

'Yup.' He reached into his pocket and handed me a ticket. 'I know it's your favourite.'

I squinted, sun-blind, at what was printed on it – and my hand flew to my mouth.

'Mmf-mmf?' I managed through my fingers.

Jack laughed. 'Yes, really. It's the touring production of *Les Mis*, special one-off performance. Sorry if you were expecting The Chippendales.'

Slowly I let my hand drop, still staring at the ticket. Never in a million years could I have afforded to see the show, let alone dreamt of watching it in a gorgeous open-air theatre on the Dorset coast.

'But where did you get these?'

'Di got them for me. She knows a guy who knows a guy who's sleeping with the guy playing Marius.'

'Are you a fan then?'

'Never seen it.' He grimaced. 'Can't say three hours of all-singing, all-dancing French revolutionaries sounds right up my street, if I'm honest, but if you like it... well, I can grin and bear it. Maybe I'll become a convert.'

'You will. I know you will.' I stood on tiptoes to plant a kiss on his nose. 'Thanks so much for this, Jack. It means a lot to me.'

'Oh, get away with you. Not sure I can carry off a blush in this suit.' He took my hand. 'Come on, let's find our seats.'

It was a fantastic show. The cast were brilliant, and I don't think it was more than ten minutes in before I was in tears. I let my head fall onto Jack's shoulder, where my wet cheek dampened his dinner jacket.

The sun started to sink into the horizon just as the musical moved into Act 3, Marius and friends retreating behind their barricade for a rousing chorus of Drink With Me as the floodlights flicked on. I was half aware of a faint plashing sound, some movement in the ocean, but my attention was entirely held by the music. It was only when Jack nudged me that I managed to drag my eyes away.

'What?' I whispered.

'Do you see them, Kit? In the water.'

I followed his gaze and squinted at what looked like a bunch of shiny black buoys floating on the waves. Then I gasped as one of them jumped, flipped, and disappeared under the water.

'Oh my God!'

'Shh,' Jack whispered.

'But they're dolphins, Jack!'

'Yep. You sometimes see them playing near the shore when the weather's warm. I always wonder if they're attracted by the music.'

I stifled a giggle. 'Are dolphins big on musical theatre?'

'Oh yeah, they love it.' He nodded back to the stage. 'Hush now. We're missing the story.'

I smiled. 'You're enjoying it.'

'Am not. Shut up. You're enjoying it.'

'Ha! I win.' I shot him a triumphant grin before turning my attention back to the performance.

As the sun sank into the ocean in an explosion of red and gold, I felt Jack's hand slip into mine. The English Channel whispered its own sweet music under the mournful notes of

Marius and his doomed friends, and I breathed a deep, happy sigh, even while the tears cascaded over my cheekbones.

The perfect day.

Chapter 33

'Go on, admit it,' I said when we arrived back at the camper late that evening, giving Jack a playful nudge in the ribs. 'You did enjoy that. You've been humming I Dreamed a Dream all the way back.'

'All right, I admit it. It was... okay.'

'Is that it?'

'Good. It was good.' He paused. 'Quite good.'

'Can't bear to admit I might've been right about something, can you? Go on, what was your favourite bit?'

'Well, the costumes were pretty cool.'

'That's it, the costumes?' I shook my head. 'Philistine.'

'Ah, go on. Don't pretend you wouldn't fancy me in one.'

I looked him up and down. 'Dunno. Not sure you could pull off the hat.'

'Could so. I'd make a great Frenchman.'

'Yeah? Prove it.'

'Mais oui, mademoiselle.' He pulled me into his arms. 'Zere eez something between urz, Kittee,' he drawled in an exaggerated French accent, deepening his voice.

'I had noticed,' I said, glancing down.

'Sometheeng biggah zan both of urz...'

'All right, Pepé le Peu, no need to brag.'

'Do not attempt to deny it, mon petit chou-fleur! You want me. Certainement, toujours. And other Frenchy French things.'

He flung out my arm and started planting exaggerated kisses along it with a 'Mwah! Mwah!' sound.

I giggled. 'Oh God, please stop. It's only a matter of time till you say hoh-hee-hoh-hee-hor, isn't it?'

'Hoh-hee-hoh-hee-hor.'

'Here we go...'

'I warnt you,' he said, still kissing my arm. 'I neeed you. I luuurve you, Kittee.'

My stomach lurched when I heard him say those words. I knew it was just play, that fun teasing I loved, but... but that's all it was, wasn't it? A game. Who knew if I'd ever hear him say that and mean it, when he was still so damaged by grief?

'You okay, Kit?' he asked in his normal voice when he felt me shudder.

'Course I am. You're tickling me, that's all.' I managed a smile, pushing sombre thoughts away. 'Come on, you daft sod, stop pissing about being French and take me to bed already.'

'Thought you'd never ask. I was starting to wonder how French a man had to be to get some action around here.'

'And thanks, Jack,' I said in a softer voice. 'This was just what I needed today. I know you went to a lot of effort to make me happy.'

He smiled. 'Well. Nothing's too much for my girl.'

345

His girl. I hugged myself as I watched him putting up the bed. It wasn't an 'I love you' but it was something.

***

'So what do you think of Dorset then?' Jack asked as we lay recovering after a particularly energetic bout of van-rocking action.

'God, it's incredible. Those dolphins... it was like being on the Med.'

'This is the one of the only places I've been where the sea's as blue as it is at home. Wish I could show Wicklow to you.' He ran a tender finger down my neck. 'One day, eh?'

'That'd be nice.' I leaned up on one elbow to look at him. 'Sure they'll let me in, a mudblood quarter-Irish like me?'

He shrugged. 'Well, it's not your fault. We'll try not to hold it against you.'

'Cheeky.' I slapped his wrist.

'Ah, you know I love you really, English.'

There it was again, that word – and it was still just a joke, a throwaway comment. I tried to ignore it.

He bent to kiss the top of my hair. 'I'm glad you had fun today,' he said in a softer voice. 'I wanted to do something for you. To show you how much you mean to me.'

'It was... perfect. Absolutely perfect. Thank you.'

'You're happy then, Kitty? Living this way with me?'

'Very happy.'

'No more running away?'

'Not from you.' I planted a kiss on his neck. 'I love you, Jack.'

And there it was. Not a joke, not a tease: the words themselves, hanging right there in the air over our two naked bodies. I bit my tongue hard when I realised what I'd let slip out.

I knew right away it was the wrong thing. I felt Jack tense in my arms.

'Jack, sorry, I didn't—'

'It's fine, Kitty. It's... I mean, thank you.' His voice sounded strange, like the words were catching in his throat.

'Oh God, now you're upset. Jack, I—'

'I said it was fine. Don't worry about it.' He rolled to face away from me. 'Night.'

***

No matter how we fell asleep, spooning, cuddling or however, we always seemed to wake in the same position. Me with one leg thrown over Jack's waist, fingers thrust into his hair, and him with one arm clamped around my belly, his head snuggled into my chest. The next morning, I woke leg akimbo, my hand where his head would be – but no Jack.

'Jack?' I called out. 'Where are you?'

'Out here.'

I let myself breathe again. It was ridiculous, but after what had happened the night before I felt uneasy, like he might somehow have disappeared in the night.

When I drew back the curtains he was at the sink with a Brillo pad, scrubbing viciously at a dirty pan.

'Are you okay?' I asked.

'Course. Why wouldn't I be?'

'Here,' I said, patting the bed. 'We should talk.'

'Not now. Too much to do. We're moving on today.'

I yawned. 'Already? We just got here. Was hoping to see some more of the Jurassic Coast, hunt myself a few fossils.'

'No time for that.'

I blinked, fully awake now. 'Jack, why are you acting like that?'

'Like what? I'm not acting like anything.'

'You know you are. It's like you've got a fever.'

He was still scrubbing at the pan as if he bore it a personal grudge.

'Here.' I stood and prised the thing out of his fingers. 'Leave off that and talk to me.'

'Nothing to talk about. We're fine. I have to walk the dogs.'

'No you don't, you have to calm down.' I guided him to the bed, pushed him into a sitting position on the edge and sat down by him. 'Talk to me. I can't live in a box with a man who's sulking.'

His brow lifted slightly. 'I'm not sulking.'

'Then what? Look, Jack, I'm sorry about last night. It's a bit soon to be saying things like that after... after everything, I know that.'

'No, it wasn't – don't feel bad. Shocked me a bit, that's all. There's power in those words.'

I flushed. 'I know. It'd just been such a lovely day, and you holding me, I felt so happy and safe. Couldn't help it.'

'Aww.' He squeezed my hand. 'I'm sorry, Kitty.'

'It's not your fault. I know it must be hard...' I took his

left hand in both mine, steeling myself. 'With Sophie and stuff.'

He flinched. 'Yeah. No one's said that to me since... well, you know.'

'Loved her a lot, didn't you?'

'I did.' He bit his lip. 'I did.'

'I'm sorry, Jack. I never should've said it, I wasn't thinking.'

'It wasn't that.' He let go of my hand so he could stroke hair away from my face with his fingertips. 'It wasn't the words that freaked me out, it was how I felt when you said them. It made me worry I was starting to forget her – like you said about your dad. Made me decide...' He swallowed hard, and his eyes darted across my features. 'I've been hiding something from you, Kitty. For ages.'

I frowned. 'Have you?'

'Yes. Something I should've told you, and I – God, I'm such a coward.' He swallowed again. 'I love you too.'

My heart jumped in my chest. 'Jack – you really mean it?'

'I've known for so long, but I felt... I never believed it could happen more than once.' He pushed his fingers up into his hair. 'Not that all-consuming love I'd had with Soph. Felt like it shouldn't happen – as if I'd be betraying her to have feelings that intense again.' He laughed involuntarily. He still seemed feverish, avoiding meeting my eyes. 'And now there's someone else I feel like I want to spend my life next to, and it doesn't feel like a betrayal, Kit, not one little bit. It feels like... like it's what she'd want for me.'

I stared for a second, gobsmacked, then flung my arms around him.

'Jack, sweetheart,' I whispered. 'You don't know much I've wanted to hear you say that.'

'I love you so much. I really do, Kitty. And I'm sorry.' He held me back from the hug to look into my face. 'But I have to take you home.'

Chapter 34

'I'm sorry?'

'Time to go home, Kitty. Time to end this.'

'But you just said... I thought, thought we...'

'I can't ask you to live like this forever, can I? I do love you. Enough to realise it's not fair. I was awake all night, forcing myself to think about the future, me and you, and I—' He flinched. 'Remember when I told you what felt right wasn't always what I wanted?'

'But this doesn't feel right – not to me!' In their bed, the two dogs pricked up their ears. 'This is my home now.'

'You've got a home with your mam I can take you to. I mean, your real mam.' He swallowed hard. 'One where you can start building a proper life.'

'But that's my choice! I want to stay with you, like you asked me to.'

'I never should've asked. It was wrong – it was selfish. I tried to convince myself that if you wanted it then it must be okay, but...' He stroked the back of my hair, an expression in his eyes that was equal parts anguish and tenderness. 'You're young, Kit. You've got a life to make. Travelling round, it's fun for a bit, but you'll not want to do it forever.' He pinched his eyes closed, and I saw him swallow another sob. 'Oh God, I wish I could keep you. I'll miss you so much.'

'You can – you can keep me! Why are you doing this, Jack?'

'Where do you want to be in a year? Five years? Ten? Don't you want a house, a family, all that stuff?'

'I... don't know. I want you, that's all.'

'You will. You'll want all those things, one day, and I can't give them to you.' He flinched, struggling with powerful emotions. 'Life's just beginning for you, now you're rid of your mother and Ethan. I helped you get free of them, and now... now I have to let you go, don't I? I can't drag you back down again because it's what suits me or I'd be just as bad as them.'

I stared at him. 'And this is different, is it? Making decisions for me, calling all the shots? It's my life, Jack. My choice.'

He shook his head. 'But you're not seeing things straight. You're in love – for the first time, in the real sense of the word. It's blinding you.'

'You patronising bastard,' I whispered. 'Who are you to tell me what I want? Do you think I'm a child, that I—' I broke off to gulp down a sob.

'Then tell me you never think about that stuff,' Jack demanded. 'Tell me you've never wondered about kids. Can you do that?'

'That's... far away.'

'So you've never thought about it.'

'No, I – it's not for now, is it? We only met six months ago. You don't just dive into the baby conversation.'

'We need to. Because I can't give you that, Kitty. I can't give you any of the things you want. Someone else can, but...' Another little sob.

'What is it with you?' I yelled, giving in to the anger bubbling up inside. I took his hand and pressed it impatiently. 'Those things you think I want. Don't you want them? I know you did once before, and you're young too, Jack. You can't think you'll still be living like this when you're seventy.'

'Stop it, Kit.'

'Running away won't make things right for you.' I sought his gaze. 'It won't bring her back.'

'I said stop it.'

'You think she'd want this? To see you going from place to place the rest of your life, lonely and unsettled, when there's a chance of happiness? Sophie's dead, Jack. You hear me?'

'Stop it! Please.'

'I won't stop it. She's dead, and you need to get over her and you need to move on. I'm sorry but it's true. And if she really gave you hell like I give you hell, then I know it's what she'd want.'

'Stop saying those things! You're killing me, Kitty.' He jerked his hand away. Standing, he turned from me and raked his fingers through his hair. 'I didn't expect you to fix me. You'll not be able so don't try.'

'Then fix yourself. God, you pretend you've stripped all the borders off your life, that you're so fucking *free*, but it's an act, isn't it? You're more trapped than anyone.' I stood too.

'If you want me to go home to Julia's, fine. But I want you to come with me.'

'Don't I wish I could?' He turned to me, and his eyes were full of tears. 'It's not that easy, Kit.'

'I know it isn't. But we can work at it, me and you together. You slept in the bothy, didn't you? And maybe with time, professional help...'

'It's no good. It's too late for me.'

'No it's *not*! You just won't try, that's all!'

'Try what? To drag you down with me, make you miserable, after all the shit you've been through already? How could I do that to someone I—' He broke off and reached down to pet Sandy, who'd sidled up to his calf. 'Poor little girl. We're scaring her.'

'We're scaring me.' I glanced at the little dog. 'Always rescuing things, aren't you, Jack? Everything but yourself.'

'Because I know that's the one thing I can't rescue.'

I tried to bring him into focus through the tears pooling in my eyes and dripping unchecked down my cheeks.

'You're not really going to do this thing, are you?' I whispered.

'Have to.' He blinked hard and turned away. 'Get packed up, Kit. It's a long drive.'

And that was it. Cajoling, pleading, begging him to talk about it, sleep on it, anything: he wouldn't be moved.

I was going home.

We didn't speak at all during the seven-hour journey up to Wastwater. Occasionally I heard Jack choke on a sob, and once, just once, I gave in to the instinctive need to comfort him and reached out to cover his hand. But the silence remained unbroken until we finally pulled up outside Aunty Julia's – and that happened all too soon.

He leaned over to kiss my cheek. 'Goodbye, superhero Kitty Clayton. I'll miss you. I love you.'

'Then don't do this.' I turned wet eyes on him. 'Please, Jack.'

'I have to. You deserve more than this. Than me.'

'You don't think that's up to me?'

'It's up to both of us. I have to choose what's right, Kit; I couldn't forgive myself if I didn't. Neither could you, you know – not deep down.'

I snorted through my tears. 'Yeah. You're a real fucking hero.'

'I know,' he said, shoulders drooping. 'But hating myself for hurting you is nothing compared to how much I'd hate myself for ruining your chance at a proper life.' He choked on a sob. 'I just... I'm too broken. I can't break you too.'

I couldn't answer. The tears were strangling me.

He glanced back into the camper, where Muttley was curled up with her mum. 'She's your baby. You want to take her?'

I stared at him in disbelief. 'You wouldn't split them up?'

'I don't want to,' he said, looking ashamed. 'I just don't like the thought of you alone.'

'No thanks. I'm not taking her off Sandy to silence your guilty conscience.' I wiped my hand across my eyes and opened the door. 'Not everyone has to be ripped from the things they love, Jack.'

Chapter 35

It's a funny thing, crying, isn't it? The way the human body says to itself 'Oh, my occupant's upset. I bet expelling a load of saltwater out of their eye sockets will make them feel better'. And it doesn't even work: you can spend hours crying, and when you're done all you've got to show for it are puffy eyes, streaky mascara and the same overwhelming feeling of misery you had when you started.

A few hours after Jack had dropped me off, I'd cried out every bit of moisture in my body and I still felt like my heart was in half.

'Oh, Kitty,' Aunty Julia said, one arm around me. 'I wish I knew what to do for you, sweetheart.'

I laughed half-heartedly, nodding to the enormous pile of sandwiches on the coffee table. 'You've done plenty, Aunty Mum.'

It was hard work, learning new titles at this point in our lives. At first I'd tried correcting myself when I got it wrong, and eventually, half-joking, we'd settled into 'Aunty Mum'. An odd title, but we were a pretty odd family.

Aunty Julia smiled. 'Sorry. I know break-ups call for tea

and sympathy, but I'm a bit new to the mumming lark. Still learning the ropes.'

'Chocolate's good,' I sniffed. 'And wine.'

'I heard talking about it was good.'

'Nah. That's just propaganda put about by the anti-wine lobby.'

'Okay, I can take a hint.' She wheeled herself to the fridge and poured us a glass of white wine each. 'The sun isn't quite over the yard arm, I think, but this seems like an emergency.'

She wheeled back and put the glass in my hand, then went back for her own. I knew better than to offer to help. After all that Uncle Ken had put her through, she was fierce when it came to guarding her independence.

'So it's really over?' she asked when she came back.

'Yes. Yes, he was quite clear about that.'

'What happened, my love?'

'He said... told me...' I shook my head. It felt thick and bloated from the tears. 'It was horrible, Aunty. Just like Laurel tried to warn me. Sophie, his problems... God, I should've listened.'

'So how did it end?' Aunty Julia asked gently.

'He asked me to stay with him. In the camper, forever.'

'And you told him no?' She patted my shoulder. 'Well, I know it can't have been easy, but I think you made the right choice. You can't live in a van your whole life, can you?'

'Are you kidding? For Jack I would've lived in a bloody garden shed.' I blew my nose into the hanky she passed me. 'That wasn't what caused all the trouble. I told him... told him I loved him. I didn't mean to, but it just slipped out, somehow. He totally freaked out. Said he wanted to do the unselfish thing and take me home so I could have a proper future.'

'Hmm. And that's the unselfish thing, is it?' She leaned over to give me a hug. 'Well, maybe it's me who's the selfish one but I'm glad you've come home, Kitty. I have missed you.'

'Missed you too... Mum.'

She smiled. 'I don't think I'll ever get tired of hearing you call me that.'

'And I'll never get tired of having someone who deserves the title.' I dragged a sleeve across my eyes. 'What will I do, Mum? It hurts so much.' I gulped down another sob. 'God, I love him so much.'

'Did he treat you right? While you were away?'

Jack and Aunty Julia had got on great during the time they'd spent together, but there was still that ever-present spectre of Uncle Ken – I mean, my father – plaguing her. He'd been a charmer too, whenever there'd been anyone looking. Behind closed doors, he'd been a monster.

'He was the perfect gentleman,' I reassured her. 'Making sure I had everything I needed while we were on the road.' I smiled as a memory came back to me. 'He even bought me a little caravan to go on the back of the camper. For if I was feeling a bit grotty – you know, that time of the month? I told him I'd appreciate a bit of space and that same afternoon, there it was.' I blinked back a salt droplet that had beaded in the corner of one eye. 'Waste of money in the end, I only slept in it a couple of nights after we started – once we became a couple. Couldn't do without a bedtime cuddle.'

'He always seemed like a nice boy.'

'He is. Just... broken.'

'We're all broken, Kitty. We're all the things life makes us.' She glanced down at her chair. 'But we fight, and we come out stronger. And happier, I think, in the end.'

'Jack won't accept that. He won't even *try*, Aunty. That's what makes it so hard. Even for me, even though he's so adamant he loves me, he won't even try.' I swallowed. 'He just... his wife, Sophie. He's never really got over it: that horrible, violent way she died. Whether it's the trauma of having to see it, or the fact he was too late to stop it, it haunts him.' I sighed. 'Poor Jack.'

'And poor Kitty. What will you do?'

'I thought I might cry for a bit. Cry and get drunk,' I said, swallowing down a large mouthful of wine. 'Want to join me?

'That's not really a plan, my love.'

'I just broke up with my boyfriend. This isn't the time for a plan. It's the time for crying and drinking. Then tomorrow's the time for a hangover. A plan comes sometime after that.'

***

I put it off for as long as I could, but there did eventually come a time when I needed to make a plan.

I was heartbroken. I was jobless. And it wouldn't be long before I was broke.

I had a bit of money put aside from my wages as Jack's PA, nestled in the current account I'd finally set up. But the money from my ISA was still out of my reach, for at least five more months. Ethan had cancelled the cheque he'd given me and was refusing to give me access to my share of our non-joint account, and I had nothing coming in.

I'd had an email from Diana the day after Jack had dropped me off, offering her brief commiserations – she did sound genuinely gutted to hear we weren't together any more – and letting me know that if I wanted to, Jack would like me to stay on as his PA, working remotely. I'd sent a curt reply back, asking her to tell Jack in no uncertain terms that working with him, now, would be too painful to even consider. Actually, I think the phrase I used was 'tell Jack he can shove it up his arse'.

But after a day's reflection, I was forced to swallow my pride and send Di a slightly longer response, asking for a month's grace to find myself something else. This, of course, Jack's guilty conscience generously granted, although he wouldn't contact me directly.

'You know you don't need to worry about any of that,' Aunty Julia said. 'I'll look after you.'

'No. Thank you. I'm already living here rent-free. I'm twenty-six and I need to pay my way.'

That seemed to please her. I had eventually given her a slightly pruned version of my history with Mum and Ethan, and that, along with her experiences of working with victims of domestic abuse, made her appreciate my commitment to financial independence.

'Well, there's no rush anyway,' she said. 'Just take your time to look around.'

'I will.'

'Oh, you will be able to help out at the fair, won't you, dear? We could use your camping skills again this year.'

Camping skills. One time I'd shown her and Dad how to put up a tent on a fishing trip, one bloody time – essentially, by following the instructions. And now I was Bear sodding Grylls, apparently.

When I'd been living in Yorkshire, I'd made the trip up every year to help at the autumn fair Aunty Julia was on the organising committee for – the Wasdale Wet One, as it was called, a tongue-in-cheek reference to the ever-predictable British rain – and apparently no amount of broken heart was going to get me out of it.

'Only I told the committee—' She flushed. 'I said my daughter was staying and I was sure she'd help. It might take your mind off things a little,' she added hopefully.

There was a certain pride in her voice, the novelty of being able to tell her friends about me and our newly-revealed relationship. That she was so keen to show me off made me smile.

'Of course I'll help, Mum. Whatever you need me to do.'

Chapter 36

I malleted a wooden peg savagely into the damp ground.
Helping the community might be rewarding, but it was a
bugger on your shoulders.

At the beginning there'd been five of us working on getting
the refreshments marquee up for the members of the Seascale
Amateur Operatic Society to serve cream teas at this year's
Wasdale Wet One – all so the scary headmistress-like chair-
woman could complain about it being slightly too close to
the barbecue or slightly too far from the brass band, just like
she did every year. But the other volunteers had dwindled
away, and now the only ones left were me and Tiffany Bradley,
a local girl of about my age who my aunty-slash-mum was
determined I needed to become best friends with, despite the
fact we had literally nothing in common. I suspected she'd
only stayed on to enjoy her new favourite hobby of rubbing
her oh-so-perfect life in my face.

'I hope you don't mind if I get off now, Kitty,' she said,
watching me hammer in the peg with no sign of giving me
a hand. 'Joe's on his way with Robbie. He screams the house
down if I'm away from him for too long.' She shot me a

patronising smile. 'Of course, it's different for you, all on your own. You can be footloose and fancy-free, you lucky thing.'

Ugh. What was it with some parents? That smug you-wouldn't-get-it attitude they just loved to beat you over the head with. I wished Laurel was there to offer up a healthy dose of reality. She hated that sort of thing.

'Something like that,' I said.

Her face lifted into a bright smile as a white BMW pulled up outside the portaloos. 'Oh, my boys have come to get me!'

'Mummy!' Her little son Robbie, four years old and with the calculating features of a miniature psychopath, came hurtling towards her and flung himself into her round, six-months-pregnant belly.

'Oof! You little monster,' she said, smiling fondly at him. 'How's Mummy's little man?'

'Hungry. Where's tea?' demanded Mummy's little man. He jabbed an accusing finger into her stomach. '*You* didn't come home to make my tea.'

'I'm coming home now. I had to help the ladies sort out the fair for tomorrow, so you can have a fun day with all your friends.' She nodded to me. 'Say hello to Kitty. You remember her, don't you?'

Robbie eyed me with deep suspicion. 'No,' he said brutally, corking his thumb in his mouth.

I smiled at him. 'Course you do, Robbie. I let you have a turn on the water pistol game last year for free when you hurt your knee, remember?'

'No.'

I tried another tack. 'What's that you've got?' I asked, nodding to the floppy thing under his arm. 'A dolly?'

The child's look of disgust could have cut through diamond. 'Eurghh, no. Dollies are for girls. S'Billy.' He held up the little marionette toy to show me.

Well, of course. Otherwise it'd just be too easy, wouldn't it? Everywhere I went, everywhere I tried to forget him, there had to be some piece of Jack Duffy. The love of my fucking life.

'They're from these books he likes,' Tiff said with a laugh. 'Tilly and Billy, you know them?'

'A little.'

'He can't get enough of them.' She glanced over her shoulder to where her husband Joe was locking the car, and lowered her voice. 'I took him once to have one signed by the guy who writes them. You should see him! Not at all what you'd expect. He looks like he should be modelling instead of writing kids' books.'

'Oh yeah?' I said, keeping my face fixed.

'Bit scruffy, but face of an angel. And the body!' She shot a guilty look back at Joe's prematurely balding head as he turned to walk towards us. 'Not as good-looking as my Joe, of course. But I bet he's got women throwing themselves at him 24-7.'

'Lucky Jack,' I mumbled, starting work on another peg that was just begging for a good hammering.

Tiff looked at me in surprise. 'How do you know that's his name?'

'Oh, er... my stepsister, Laurel. Her little boys love those books.'

'Ah. Right.' She turned to beam at her husband. 'Bunny rabbit! So sweet of you to collect me.' Then she launched herself at him for a full-on snog, clearly for my benefit. Briefly, Robbie and I shared a moment when he caught my eye and we both grimaced at the exact same time.

'Yuck!' said the kid as his parents separated, unable to stop himself vocalising his disgust.

Joe laughed. 'You won't always think kissing girls is yuck, my lad,' he said, ruffling the boy's hair. Robbie, however, didn't look convinced.

'Look, I'd better get on and finish the marquee,' I said. *Since no one was going to bloody help me…* 'You guys get off home, I'll be fine on my own.'

'Thanks, Kitty. I should get Robbie his tea, before he starts bouncing off the walls.' Tiffany gave my shoulder a last patronising pat. 'I'll see you tomorrow for a proper chat. I'm next to you, running the buzzwire game.'

Oh, brilliant. An afternoon of Tiffany recycling celeb gossip from *Heat* at me while sticky kids manhandled the water pistol game I was always assigned to. What larks.

'Great,' I said, summoning a smile that was just a little too wide. 'Looking forward to it.'

***

Propped on my elbows, I watched a combination of local families and tourists milling about the field enjoying the stalls and games that constituted the annual Wastwater Wet One. In a cocked snook to the card who'd come up with the name, it was actually blazing sunshine, and unseasonably warm. The year's Indian summer was showing no signs of letting up.

The fancy-dress theme for this year was Toyland and everywhere I looked there were tin soldiers, teddy bears and rosy-cheeked ragdolls. Not to mention a generous sprinkling of Tillies and Billies. I don't think I'd realised, until I'd got the job as Jack's PA, just how popular the little puppets were.

Fancy dress was mandatory for helpers too. I was supposed to be a robot, my face painted silver, dazzling everyone – although very much only in the literal sense – in the tinfoil hat I'd hastily knocked up the evening before. The whole ensemble made me look like the lovechild of a conspiracy nut and a cyberman (which, I pondered, must've been some date).

'How much?' a bald, burly man demanded.

'Hmm?' I said, my gaze fixed on a little pigtailed Tilly over by the bouncy castle. She was clutching a Buzz Lightyear helium balloon in one hand while trying to stuff a jam doughnut whole into her mouth with the other, and I'd made a bet with myself on whether she'd get it all in.

'Your game. How much?' the man repeated.

'Oh.' I shook myself out of the daze. '25p or five goes for a pound. If you can knock three ping pong balls off the golf tees with the water gun, you win a big Galaxy bar. If not, it's a lolly consolation prize.' I smiled at the little lad clasping his dad's hand. 'Think you can manage it, sweetie?'

The boy nodded shyly, and I handed him the gun. But he

was too tiny to get his aim straight, and he only managed a wobble from one ball.

'Never mind. You still win this for trying so hard,' I said, handing him his lolly. I lowered my voice. 'And don't worry. I can't do it either.'

'Let me have a go,' his dad said.

'Okay. But I warn you, it's tougher than it looks.'

'Rubbish. I've been champion of the darts team three years in a row. Buggered if I can't hammer a few ping pong balls.'

The man grabbed the water gun, reeking of sweat and machismo, but in the end he fared even worse than his son. He failed to move a single ball. It was all I could do not to laugh at the wounded pride in his eyes.

'Sorry,' I said, giving him a lolly. 'Better luck next time, eh?'

'Fix,' he mumbled.

'I'm sorry?'

'Fix. Those balls are glued on.'

I raised my eyebrows. Silently, I lifted each ball off its tee so he could see there was no foul play.

'Well there's something going on,' he muttered. He unpeeled his lolly and plugged it in his jaw. 'No daft kiddies' game gets the better of me,' he said, in a tone that might've been menacing if there hadn't been a Chupa Chups stick poking out of one corner of his mouth. 'I'll be back.'

And he was as true to his word as the Terminator. Half an hour later, he'd had six goes and still hadn't won a big Galaxy bar. He could've bought two Galaxies with the money he'd spent on the game, but I was sensing that wasn't the point.

Tiffany, dressed as a fairy princess doll in a meringue-like pink dress – God knew where she'd managed to find a maternity version of the costume, but she had – leaned over to whisper in my ear.

'Think you've got an admirer there.'

I snorted. 'What, that guy? Why, you think he's got a tinfoil fetish?'

'Seriously. Why do you think he keeps coming back?'

'To show off to the little lad, probably. No dad wants to admit to his son that he can't win at a simple pocket-money game.'

She shook her head. 'You've got to be kidding me. You don't even know who he is, do you?'

I frowned. 'Why, should I?'

'That's only the area's most eligible bachelor. Justin Coleman, Joe's boss at Coleman's Accountants.'

'That guy's an accountant?' I stared at him in disbelief. 'He looks like the lost Mitchell brother.'

'He's loaded though.' She nudged me. 'So? Are you going to go for it?'

'With him? Don't be daft. He's completely—' I broke off, catching a glimpse of her husband Joe's almost bald head blending in with the merchandise on the coconut shy he was running. 'Er, completely not my type,' I finished, flashing her a weak smile.

She shrugged. 'Suit yourself.'

By 4 p.m., the sun was the hottest it had been all afternoon. Sweat was pouring off me, despite it being early October.

'Are you okay?' Tiffany asked, examining me with concern. 'You've gone very pale.'

'I'm... fine,' I said, holding one hand to my forehead. 'Touch of the sun, I think. Can you mind my stall a sec while I pop to the loo?' I felt a sudden need to be alone for five minutes.

'No problem.' She shot me a suggestive smirk. 'What shall I say if Justin Coleman comes back? Shall I give him your number?'

'Don't you dare. Look, I won't be long. Just hold the fort.'

I came out from behind my trestle table and hurried off in the direction of the portaloos. Thankfully there was no queue. I dived into one and locked the door.

Whether from the hot sun or too long on my feet, I was feeling very dizzy all of a sudden. A wave of intense nausea gripped me and I sank to my knees over the toilet bowl, retching until whatever was causing the problem was out of my system. God, I hoped there was no one waiting outside to witness the aftermath of me vomming my guts out dressed as a 1950s B-movie extra. How bloody embarrassing.

I flushed away the evidence of my upset stomach before the sight of it made me feel sick again. Second time this week. Stress, probably. Or heartbreak; the two seemed to go hand in hand.

I wondered if Jack, wherever he was, was going through it too. Did he still have my little caravan? That'd be bound to remind him of me. Hopefully he'd have the good sense to sell it now he didn't need the extra space.

I rinsed my mouth out at the sink then dampened a paper towel and held it against my clammy brow, concentrating on bringing the swimming reflection in the mirror into focus. Words whirled in my brain, fragments of old conversations.

I couldn't help feeling I was failing to process something obvious.

The caravan... suddenly I remembered what I'd said to Aunty Julia the day I'd come home. *Waste of money in the end... I only slept in it a few nights.*

A few nights! That's right, I only slept in it... I fumbled for my phone in a panic and shot a glance at the calendar.

'*Shit*! Oh, shit!' I stared at my ridiculous robot face in the mirror, the silver facepaint patchy and smudged.

'Shit,' I whispered.

Chapter 37

When I answered the door the next day, Laurel was outside, looking anxious.

'What the hell's the matter, Kit? I drove up as soon as I got your voicemail.'

'Oh God, am I glad to see you,' I said, throwing myself at her for a hug.

'Is something up? You sounded terrified. Where's your aunty?'

'She's away in Yorkshire for the week, sorting out some legal stuff to do with Nan's flat. Are the boys with you?'

'No, they're at home with Andy. You sounded like you needed grown-up time. Come on, what's up?'

'Here, come in. Something to show you.'

'Are you poorly?' she asked as she followed me inside. 'No offence, but you've looked better.'

'Sort of, yeah.' I chucked myself down on the sofa, Laurel parking her bum next to me. 'I was throwing up most of the night.'

'What was it, dodgy curry or something?' She was smiling, but she looked nervous. It occurred to me that she might've sussed what I was about to tell her. 'Or... is this about Duffy? You haven't had a message from him?'

'You could say that.' Wordlessly I reached under the cushion and handed her the white stick with its telltale twin pink lines.

She stared at it.

'Shit,' she said quietly.

'That's what I said.'

'When did you—'

'Yesterday.'

She blinked again at the little stick, as if hoping to change the result with sheer strength of will.

'You know, these things aren't always right,' she said at last.

'I know. But the four I did before that probably are.'

'Oh God. Then it's really...' She shook her head, anger biting through the shock. 'For Christ's sake, Kitty! How did you let this happen?'

'I didn't let it happen. It just... happened.' I stared blankly straight ahead, struggling to feel.

'Weren't you using protection?'

'Course I was. Mini pill, I went on it as soon as we started... when it got physical.'

'And did you take it every day? You only need to skip one, you know.'

'I don't *know*!' I said, anguish hitting me at last. I buried my face in my hands. 'I don't know, Laur. I thought I did, but we were on the road, you lose track of the days. And I was in hospital a while...' I shook my head, disgusted with myself. 'Ugh. What does it matter? It's too late now.'

'How far gone are you?'

'God knows. We were at it pretty much constantly, could've been any time. It's nearly six weeks since my last period.'

Her eyes widened. 'What, and it took you this long to bloody notice?'

'Well I was upset, wasn't I? Wasn't paying attention to time passing. It was only yesterday, with the sickness...' I burst into tears. 'What do I do, Laur? Oh God, what do I do?'

'Take some time to let it sink in, to start off with.' She stretched an arm round my shoulders and squeezed me. 'Wish I knew how you manage to get yourself into these things, Kitty Louise.'

I shuddered. 'Please don't call me that. My mum calls me that – my other mum, I mean.' I paused. 'How's she doing?'

She grimaced. 'You really want to know?'

'Might as well.'

'She's put her house on the market and moved into your old place. With... I mean...'

'With Ethan.' It was funny, but I didn't feel anything.

'Yeah. The family's totally closed ranks on them since it all came out.'

'They won't care.' I let out a bleak laugh. 'They'll end up throttling one another if they're not careful. You don't think they've genuinely fallen for each other, do you?'

'I think they're lonely more than anything. It's so weird, Kit. Like they despise each other, and at the same time they can't stay away from other.' She shook her head. 'God, can you imagine? What a fucking life.'

'Well, the pair of them deserve each other.'

'Are you okay, love?' she asked quietly.

'No. I'm knocked up and I'm single and I don't have a job and my life's a dystopian nightmare.'

'But other than that?'

I looked at her. Suddenly, we both burst out laughing. It was so depressingly absurd, what else could you do?

'You know, you could come home,' she said after a minute, when we'd finally managed to get the hysterics under control. 'They can't hurt you now. And if a baby comes... it does, that's all. I'll be there for the two of you, and Andy, and my mum. And the boys ask for you nearly every day.'

'I think... maybe for a visit. But I want to stay with Aunty – with my mum.'

'Okay, I get that,' she said gently. 'So do you think you'll... you know, keep it?'

'To be honest, I hadn't thought that far ahead. I'm still trying to get my head round how I'm going to tell Aunty Julia.' A tear trickled out of one eye. 'I hope she's not too disappointed in me.'

'Don't forget Duffy.'

I frowned. 'Jack?'

'Well, yeah. You have to tell him, Kitty.'

'But he left me. This was exactly what he said he didn't want.' I swallowed a sob. 'How could he be a dad, the way he lives? He told me he couldn't change. That he wouldn't.'

'That was then. Things are different now.'

'He told me the day I met him that he hated to feel trapped above anything. If he changes, it has to be because he makes that choice. It won't be me doing the trapping.'

'Still. He's got a right to know. That's half of him growing in there, you know,' she said, casting a glance at my tummy.

That's right. It was, wasn't it? Half of me, half of him. A little piece of Kitty and Jack made into a completely new, unique human being, long after Kitty and Jack were over.

That was deep stuff.

'So? Will you ring him?' Laurel asked.

'I... probably. When I've decided what I'm going to do. Right now what I really need is time to think.'

***

Laurel managed to wangle it so she could stay a few days, which was all the time she could spare before she needed to be back for her business and her boys.

She tried to take me out of myself, dragging me round the shops in all the nearby towns as we looked for Christmas presents for Toby and Sam. Still, it felt like there were reminders of Jack everywhere we went. Tilly and Billy books were in every bookshop window as they put their most desirable wares on display for the Christmas-shopping season.

And there'd be a permanent reminder coming along soon enough. I rubbed my tummy as I stared at yet another Tilly and Billy display. Maybe it was my imagination, but it felt like it was already swelling.

'You need to talk to him, Kit,' Laurel said, watching the movement of my hand.

'Not yet. Look, he made his views on the impossibility of

a future with kids in it pretty clear the day he dropped me off. This doesn't change anything.'

'A baby always changes things.'

'I know. But it doesn't always fix things.' I stared at my tiny, possibly imaginary bump. 'It shouldn't be used to fix things.'

'Well, no matter what happens, you're not in it alone,' Laurel said, putting her arm around my waist. 'I'll always be there for you. And your Aunty Julia. She'll be pleased as anything she's going to be a nana, wait and see. Us mums need to stick together, eh?'

I flashed her a grateful smile. 'Thanks, Laur.'

But the word 'mum' sent a stab of panic through me. It sounded so grown-up, so real. Could I really do this, all on my own?

***

When Laurel had gone back home, I threw myself into work with a vengeance, desperate to think of anything but my pregnancy. I still had a couple more weeks of PA work before my notice period was up and I was free of Jack for good.

Well, not quite free, I thought, rubbing my tummy.

Aunty Julia was still away. I was desperate to talk to her, tell her the whole story, but first I knew I needed a plan. And I had no idea where I was supposed to find one of those.

The stuff Di sent me – always Di, never Jack – was heartache and sweetness in equal parts. A synopsis for his next book, so I could put a press pack together. Some images I could use as teasers on his social media pages.

I was reading an email from her and coping all right, I thought, until the very last image I opened. Flora, the nanny who looked like me, now in full colour. And it carried Jack's familiar signature – our two dogs, sketched into a corner. When I saw the little cartoon Muttley there with her mum, I buried my face in my hands and wept like a baby.

We'd been such a perfect family, for a while. So happy. I found myself angry at Jack, with his stupid problems and his stupid grief and his stupid... campervan. And then I felt angry at myself, for telling him I loved him and making him go away. God, if I'd only kept my mouth shut, I'd be there now: reading while Jack cooked, Sandy's head in my lap. Or taking an autumnal stroll in some pretty place, maybe...

But that was Ethan's training, making me blame myself as usual. This was on Jack, not me. He was the one who'd run away, like the coward he'd finally admitted he was. Given up on happiness, future, love, because he'd rather hide than face his problems. And now there was a baby coming.

And that made it so much fucking worse, because it was no good now. The baby meant an end to any dreams I might've still been cherishing about us getting back together.

I mean, supposing I told him, and he said he'd try to make it work? I'd always know it was for the sake of the baby; that he was willing to fix himself for our child and not for me. How could I not resent him for it, in the end? You couldn't build a healthy relationship on a start like that.

Ugh. Well, so much for distracting myself from my personal problems with work. Jack Duffy had intruded into my thoughts again, just like always.

I shut my laptop with a click.

It was getting late anyway. There was nothing in the fridge – I'd been doing a rubbish job of looking after myself since Aunty Julia had been away – and I needed to find food. I was eating for two now, I remembered with a grimace.

I wasn't quite sure how it happened. I rang for a taxi, intending to go somewhere local to eat. But somehow I ended up at the Shepherd's Rest, the pub in Keswick where I'd met Jack for the second time. The Shepherd's Rest, forty miles away. I don't know what I was thinking. It cost a small fortune, and I wasn't far off being jobless. With a kid to support.

They did do an excellent Cumberland sausage. That was obviously the reason I was there. And if I happened to hear some news of Jack at the same time, well, I couldn't help that.

The place hadn't changed much, even though I felt I was a whole other person than the last time I'd set foot in there. It was still full of old tat and badly spelt signs. Young Ryan was still serving behind the bar, this time accompanied by a portly middle-aged version of himself who I guessed was his dad, Jack's friend Matty.

'Hi,' I said to Ryan, claiming a stool at the bar. 'Remember me?'

'Yeah. Hiya, Ballgown,' he said with a grin. 'Looking a bit less scary than last time. What can I get you, another tap water?'

I shot a longing look at the wine fridge.

'Just an orange juice,' I said at last.

'Hey, Dad,' Ryan said as he poured, nudging the older man. 'This is the one I told you about. Jack's girlfriend.'

'Just a friend.' I ran a finger glumly around the rim of the glass Ryan had placed in front of me. 'At least, I was a friend.'

'Dumped you too, did he?' Matty said with a sympathetic smile. Even his Irish accent sent a pang of sadness through me.

'Something like that.' I glanced up at him. 'How do you mean, me too?'

'He's given us the brush-off as well. Not heard from him for ages.'

'Did you used to hear from him a lot?'

'We'd speak on the phone every once in a while. Can't seem to get hold of him for love nor money now though.'

'Do you think he's okay?'

'Oh, he goes through these spells,' Matty said, waving a hand dismissively. 'He's back at home, most likely.'

'In Scotland, you mean?'

'No, Wicklow. Helping his brother Mikey out on the farm. That's what he usually does when he gets down.'

'What, you think he's in Ireland?'

He shrugged. 'Just an old man's guess.'

A dull metal taste flooded my mouth. Oh God, he was out of the country! That meant a whole ocean between us. Would he come back when I told him what had happened? What if he decided to move back there for good?

It was horrible, thinking of him so far away. Even when he'd left me, it still felt like there'd been a bond, some invisible thread binding us. If he was across the sea, perhaps it had snapped. Permanently.

See, now I was starting to sound like him: all that nonsense about stars and the universe fixing things. I gave myself a mental slap for being so ridiculous.

Still. Thinking about him so far away, out of my reach, there was a sickness lurking in the hollow of my tummy that I suspected had nothing to do with my pregnancy.

Over the next few days, while I was waiting for my aunty to come home, I settled into a sort of routine. In the morning, I'd set myself a strict diet of not thinking about Jack while I sat on the banks of the lake I'd once sat on with Jack. After an hour of that, I set myself a strict diet of not thinking about Jack while I went through some of the publicity for Jack's books. Then I went to bed and cried because I was an emotional pregnant lady who missed Jack.

The future still felt like a formless shadowland, the baby an unreal thing, even as I felt it growing inside me every day. Whenever I tried to think about it, my brain did a double somersault in my skull. Every night I went to bed hoping the answers would have become clear by morning, and every morning they never had.

At least I was doing a good job not thinking about Jack, I lied to myself. My broken heart was a million times better. A million. Maybe even a zillion. I was so focused on putting Jack out of my mind completely, I got a bit of a shock when I answered the door one evening to find him on the step.

'Hi, Kit. I missed you.'

Chapter 38

'Jesus! How're you... you're here.' I stared at the seemingly solid figure that had risen up before me. He'd been on my mind so much lately... 'You are really here, aren't you?' I asked, narrowing one eye at the possibly spectral Jack.

'I'm here.'

And I could see the mellow orange of the camper behind him, still with my little caravan hooked to the back. So I knew it had to be true.

Unable to help it, I threw myself at him. He gave a muffled 'oof' as my body collided with his.

Jack wrapped me in his arms and held me tight against him. 'Oh Kit, I'm so sorry,' he whispered in a cracked voice. 'You were right. You were right about everything.'

He sounded so different. So drained. I held him back from me to take in his appearance.

He was pale, the stubble flecking his jaw longer than usual, and there were heavy purple bags under his eyes. He looked like a man who hadn't slept in weeks. I felt a twinge of pity for him, pickled in the van with just his grief for company.

Then I remembered how he'd knocked me up and buggered

off, and my hormone-addled emotions veered from sympathy to anger. On a sudden impulse, I swung back my arm and brought my palm crashing into his cheek.

'*Fuck*!' he said, rubbing the angry red mark on his face where I'd slapped him. 'Christ almighty, Kitty! That hurt.'

'You absolute bastard!' I yelled, paying no mind to a couple of walkers who'd stopped to stare at this cosy domestic scene playing out in front of the classically Lakeland cottage. Well it wasn't exactly At Home with the Wordsworths. 'Do you even know what it's been like, this past month?'

'I know. For me too.'

'Well good, since it was all your bloody fault! And then you turn up with that hangdog face on like I'm just supposed to fall into your arms. Is that it, Jack?'

'You did just fall into my arms.'

'That was reflex. Doesn't mean I'm not fucking furious.'

His shoulders drooped. 'So do you want me to go?'

'Don't you bloody dare. Get inside. I've got a few things to say to you.'

He hung back, looking nervous. 'You promise you won't slap me again?'

'I won't slap you.'

'Promise? Because for a little lass you pack quite a wallop.'

'You deserved quite a wallop. Come on, get in. I promise.'

'Let me get the dogs first. They've been cooped up for hours.'

He opened the door of the camper, and Sandy and Muttley jumped out.

My little puppy looked very grown up, as big as her mum now. But she wasn't too big to forget her old friend Kitty. She went ballistic when she saw me, bounding over and barraging me with a series of yaps that I suspected were Doggish for 'Oh my God oh my God oh my God I MISSED YOU SO MUCH!' Sandy tried to headbutt her errant child out of the way to get her share of my attention, wagging her tail so vigorously her bum was a blur.

It certainly lightened the mood. I couldn't help laughing at their excitement, and Jack laughed too.

'Let's go in,' I said. 'We've got a lot to say to each other.'

He went inside and I followed with the dogs, leaving the disappointed walkers to carry on to the pub.

As soon as they spotted the blazing logs in the living room fireplace, Sandy and Muttley darted over to it and stretched themselves out for a post-drive snooze.

'Where's your mam?' Jack asked.

'In Yorkshire. She's not back until Sunday.'

'Will I go first then, or will you?' he said when I'd taken a seat beside him on the sofa, leaving a little distance between us.

'You. Why're you here, Jack?'

'Needed to bring you something.' He reached into his pocket and handed me a little polythene bag. 'Yours.'

'What is it?'

'Hair grips mostly, and a few other bits and pieces. Kept finding them round the van.'

I blinked. 'You looked me up to return grooming accessories?'

'Call that the catalyst,' he said with a bloodless smile. He shook his head. 'God, I've been such an idiot. It was when I burst into tears over a bobble that I realised what a prat I was being.'

'Then you've come to—'

'Yeah.' Jack looked down at the fingers splayed on his thighs. 'I'm a selfish fecker when you get right down to it, Kitty, same as anyone. I tried to do the noble thing, but in the end I just missed you too much.' He turned the look on, the one I found so hard to resist: long-lashed eyes round and smouldering. 'Will you have me back?'

I stared at him. 'What, that's it? You found a bobble and now you want me back in your life?'

'More than that.' He blinked hard. 'You were right, Kitty. Everything you said, about Sophie, about me. I tried to hide from it – God, those images, it hurt so much to face them. But compared to losing you...' He drew a deep breath. 'Sophie used to say I could be an ornery, narrow-sighted son of a bitch when I set my mind to it.'

'Sophie said that?'

'She said a lot of things. Usually about me. And I know what she'd say now is "Stop using me as an excuse to be a prick and go be happy, you ridiculous bastard".'

'Bloody hell. She sounds terrifying.' I paused. 'I like her.'

'Do I get a hug then?'

'Yeah. You get a hug.' I threw my arms around him, tears dripping down my cheeks. 'I've been so scared, Jack. I thought you'd gone back to Ireland.'

'Kitty, sweetheart,' he whispered in a choked voice, his fingers burrowing up into my hair. 'God, I love you so much. I won't leave you again, promise.'

I snuggled deeper into his arms. 'I'm so glad Laurel told you,' I whispered.

'Laurel?'

I held him back. 'She got in touch with you, didn't she?'

'No. Why would she?'

I felt a jolt, churning the hollows of my body. It hadn't occurred to me, until I'd heard the surprise in his voice, that he didn't know about the baby. The hair grips were a sweet touch, but I'd assumed Laurel's congenital need to interfere was the real reason for him turning up out of the blue.

'Then why are you here?' I asked.

He looked puzzled. 'I just told you. To see if you... if we... well, isn't it obvious?'

I stared into space while I grappled with this new information. So it was me Jack had come back for. Not the baby, or me and the baby: just me. I felt a wave of happiness, because there was no feeling of duty or obligation influencing him. He loved me and he was ready to face his demons so he could be with me, it was as simple as that. But I was afraid too. Because I was about to give him some news that was going to change everything.

I dried my tears with the heel of my hand and took a deep breath. 'Jack... when you asked me to take you back, did you mean – do you want me to come live with you again? In the van?'

'Well, yeah.'

'Sorry, but I won't be able to.'

He frowned. 'Why not? You wanted to before, till I made a mess of things. I know you can't forgive me just like that, but—'

385

'I do forgive you. It's not that.' Gently I took his hand and placed it over my tummy. 'Something's coming, love. And this is one pet you won't be able to keep in a caravan.'

He looked puzzled for a moment. I watched his face as realisation finally dawned, and he let out a short, shocked laugh.

'You're not!'

'I am.'

'But... how?'

I smiled. 'Come on. I know we don't need to have that conversation.'

'I mean, not how, but – why? When?'

'About two months ago, probably. My contraception must've failed.'

'What is it?'

I laughed. 'Well it's not that turtle you wanted. Sorry.'

'No.' He shook his head dazedly. 'Sorry, I'm just – bloody hell.'

'I know, it's a lot to take in all at once. I was the same. Except I had to get my head round it while throwing up dressed as a robot.'

It said a lot for his gobsmacked state that that little nugget didn't even make a dent. I gave his knee a pat.

'Let me get the kettle on while you take a minute.'

I was half-afraid, by the time I came back with the drinks, that Jack might've taken the van and fled for the hills. But he was still sitting exactly where I'd left him, staring into the distance with his mouth slightly open.

'Why didn't you call me, Kitty?' he asked when I'd sat back down.

The glazed look was finally starting to clear. I wanted to

snuggle into him in the way that always felt so natural, but I was afraid to until we'd properly talked it out.

'I only worked it out myself a week ago. And you were so determined, last time I saw you...' I sighed. 'Jack?'

'Hmm?' he said, coffee steaming untouched on the table beside him.

'You and Sophie were trying for a baby. Weren't you?'

He looked at me with surprise. 'Who told you that?'

'Di. Oh, don't be mad at her,' I said, seeing his brow knit. 'She never meant to tell me, it just slipped out.' I twisted round to face him and took both his hands in mine. 'Does it hurt?' I asked gently. 'That it's me and not her?'

He hesitated. 'No,' he said at last. 'I mean, it's a shock. But it doesn't hurt. It feels... right.' His face finally lifted into a smile. 'Not perfect timing maybe, but – God, I'm going to be a dad.' He blinked. 'That's weird.'

'So you're pleased?'

'Are you kidding?' He shook his head to clear the last of the fog. 'I always wanted children but I wrote that dream off after losing Soph. Never thought I'd meet anyone else I'd want to have a family with. And the way I live – it just didn't seem possible.'

The way he lived... Jesus, he didn't think we were going to raise the baby in his bloody campervan, did he?

'Um, Jack?'

He smiled. 'Oh, don't worry, lass, I'm not going to buy another caravan. We'd look like a travelling circus.'

'Then what?'

'That's what I came to say. Before you distracted me with

this baby business.' He flushed. 'I did it, Kitty. It was hard, facing up to all those things. I mean, it wrenched, you know? But then I thought about you, and I had a long talk with my parents, and... well, I'm three weeks in now.'

'Three weeks into what?'

'Therapy. It's a special course for people affected by sudden, violent bereavement. People like me.'

'You did that for me?'

'No. For me.' He flinched. 'God, it hurts. I've been trying to hide from those memories for so long. But I'm finally starting to feel like... like I can accept it. That there was nothing I could have done, and I don't have to feel guilty about moving on. Accept and forgive, that's the mantra the course leader tells us to remember.'

I hugged him tight. 'I'm sorry, my love. Sorry it was so painful for you.'

He turned wet eyes up to me. 'So I wondered... I mean, this is what I wanted to ask. I thought after we'd done our bit of touring I could come home with you. You know, if you'd have me. We could find a little place together near your mam, just us.'

'You mean you'd live in a house?'

He smiled. 'Well, yeah. I'm not talking about parking up on the drive for the rest of our lives.'

'But you told me you couldn't.'

'I'm not saying it'll be easy,' he said. 'I've lived a long time the way I do. Just the thought of four walls closing me in... Christ, it terrifies me.' He ran his gaze apprehensively round the cottage. 'But you're worth it, Kitty. And if you're willing to be patient while I take baby steps towards fixing myself,

388

I'll do my best to give you everything you deserve in life.' He glanced down at my tummy. 'Both of you.'

'Because of the kid?'

'Because of you. Because if there's one thing I know, it's that I want to spend the rest of my life with you,' he said, pressing my fingers to his lips. 'Any kids we make together are a bonus.'

'God, Jack...' I threw myself into his arms. 'I do love you. And I'm sorry I slapped you. I think it's the hormones.'

'Well, in the interests of keeping the peace I'll agree I had it coming, just this once. Don't make a habit of it though.'

I smiled. 'Okay. I'll try to restrict my pregnancy cravings to the usual gherkins in jelly.'

'I love you very much, you know,' he whispered, pressing me to him with bearish intensity. 'Be patient with me, eh? It'll take time. I can't get better all at once.'

'Whatever you need from me. We'll take it one day at a time.' I extricated myself from the hug to look up at him. 'So how do you fancy going out to the camper for a snuggle?'

'No...' He cast another nervous look around the cottage. 'Let's stay in the house. First step has to happen before the rest, doesn't it?'

'Really? You'll sleep inside with me?'

'Yes, Kit. Wherever you are is home for me.' He planted a tender kiss on top of my hair. 'Come on then, my treasure. Let's go to bed.'

And later, as we cuddled tightly, Jack's head on my chest and one hand laid protectively over my belly, I knew. There'd be no more running away.

Acknowledgements

Once again, enormous thanks to the team at HarperImpulse, especially my lovely (not to mention award-winning) editor Charlotte Ledger, easily one of the hardest-working women in publishing, whose guidance really made this the book it was meant to be.

Big thank-yous too to marketing whizz-kid Sahina Bibi, my copy editor Dushi Horti and the super-talented team at Books Covered for another enticing cover design.

Huge thanks as always to my agent Laura Longrigg at MBA Literary Agents for helping get this book out into the world, and all her editorial guidance and support as it evolved into its final form.

Drinks are on me (up to two each or cash equivalent) for the three beta readers who gave up their time to help me make the book the best it could be: the man who knows quite a lot about campervans and everything about the Lake District, John Manning; my lovely writer friend Kate Beeden, who went above and beyond to read this in a single weekend when I was on deadline and, as always, my usually gorgeous and always supportive partner Mark Anslow.

Eternal gratitude, too, on behalf of myself and all my fellow authors to the dedicated community of book bloggers who give up so much of their time to read and review our books. We couldn't do it without you.

A big shout-out to virtual and real-life author friends for all their support: Yorkshire-dwelling pals Rachel Burton and Kate Beeden, the Authors on the Edge romance writers of Yorkshire and Lancashire, and my local tribe at the Airedale Writers' Circle. Thanks for your patience, sympathy and feedback, all those times writing and editing felt impossible.

My family have been wonderful as ever, Firths and Brahams, as have my Anslow in-laws down in Somerset. Sorry, everyone: I'll come out of my room now, I promise.

Huge thanks to all my friends, local and further afield, especially Lynette and Nigel Emsley, Bob Fletcher, Lee Scholtz and Amy Smith. Thanks for the pub nights, the listening ears, the plot suggestions, and for believing in me right from the start. And finally, thanks once again to all my colleagues at Country Publications for their unfailing support while I do this writing thing.